Heart of VERIDON

Heart of VERIDON

Tim Akers

First published 2009 by Solaris
an imprint of BL Publishing
Games Workshop Ltd
Willow Road
Nottingham
NG7 2WS
UK

www.solarisbooks.com

ISBN-13: 978 1 84416 758 6
ISBN-10: 1 84416 758 5

10 9 8 7 6 5 4 3 2 1

A CIP catalogue record for this book is available from the British Library.

Designed & typeset by BL Publishing

Printed and bound in the UK.

To Jennifer, for leaving me alone when I needed her to, and being there when I needed that instead.

Chapter One
Downfalls

I WAS ON the *Glory of Day* when she fell out of the sky. I rode the flames and shattered gears down into the cold, dark Reine, survived because I was only half-alive to begin with. Two times I've been dragged out of the wreckage of a zepliner, two times I've walked away. This time I was just a passenger. The first time I was captain, Pilot, and only survivor. The sky doesn't like me much.

I boarded in Havreach, paid for a day cabin one way and sat quietly until dinner. No luggage because I'd been in town on business, having a talk with one of Valentine's wayward contacts, a guy trying to do a little business behind our backs. It was supposed to be a day trip that had stretched into an overnight when the guy tried hiding clever and earned himself some extra attention and convincing. Make sure he didn't hide next time I came looking for him, make double-sure there's no next time. So it had been a long day and I was still in yesterday's clothes, my eyes were tired and my hands hurt. So I got sloppy, okay. So I wasn't paying attention like I should.

Dinner was an affair on a trip like this, especially the night before Veridon, the last night of the cruise. There were two kinds of travelers on the zep. First are the daytrippers, like me. Took some other ship downfalls just to see the water, or for a little adventure on the plains. Not that Havreach was really adventure-land, but the shopkeeps made a good business of it. Havreach was just new enough that you could feel the wild outside, the untamed spaces prowling the edges of the streetplan. There were parts of Veridon like that too, but different. Not that Veridon was old. Just the danger was different up there, more personal. Less marketable.

Other than the daytrippers, there were the long haul folks. People who boarded in Veridon and stayed on until there weren't any more stops, until the *Glory* was just drifting over pure wilderness, the towns getting smaller and smaller until they just disappeared into the winding river and forested banks, or the wild, wind-stitched grassplains of the Arbarra Rare. An expensive trip, and as dangerous as anything that came with a luxury suite and cloth napkins.

There's a third kind of passenger, I suppose. Those coming in. Tickets purchased one way, for the return voyage only, people getting on in Red Simmons or little BonnerWell. Them you could pick out at dinner. They looked uncomfortable with the cloth napkins, and hadn't exactly brought formal attire through the bush. It was one of them, caused our trouble. Guy I knew. Marcus Something. Couldn't remember his name, at the time.

I saw him circulating during the appetizers. The dining room was cleared and the glass doors that led to the observation deck had been folded back and tucked away. One whole wall of the room was open to the night sky. The air was cool, the stars bright white and clear. A quartet played quietly in one corner, just masking the busy kitchen. I took a glass of white wine from a passing waiter and walked out onto the deck. A right civilized night, the kind that reminded me of home and family. Easy to forget trouble on a night like this. I went to stand by the railing. The water below was a shattered field of light, the moon on tiny waves far under us.

Most of the folks, eating delicate little things and sipping wine and murmuring, were dressed to the nines. Top hats and vest coats, ladies in fur, waiters in white coats. Marcus stood out like a lump of mud on marble, standing nervously by the far door. He was barrel-wide and a full head taller than anyone else here, his beard brushing the careful hair-piles of the luxury suite ladies. His coat was brown and dirty, and there were two feet of empty space all around him, while the rest of the deck was shoulder to cuff.

I was about to go talk to him, try to figure out where I knew him from, if he was one of Valentine's boys or someone from one of the other interests, when one of the passengers stepped in front of me.

"We'll be there after dinner then?" he asked. He was a short man, round in the shoulders and hands. A trim crescent of mustache clasped his lip.

"Sorry, I'm not crew," I said, and tipped my glass at one of the gray-tunicked mates standing along the rail. "Not clean enough, probably."

The man blinked and then chuckled. "Oh, oh, sorry. Sorry, it's just your eyes. You know."

I knew. My eyes, the implants, part of what made me a Pilot back before I wasn't a Pilot anymore. Not many visual signs of who's had that particular operation. Just the eyes, the dull gray irises like pewter rubbed clean of its shine. I still had the eyes.

"Common mistake. Now, if you'll excuse me."

"Hm. So, uh." He plucked my sleeve. "You've made this trip before, though. Of course you have."

I turned away, put my elbows on the railing and leaned forward. We'd been over water all day, ever since we'd left Havreach, and the Cusp Sea stretched out below us as far as I could see. The Breaking Wall was a gentle roar, still out of sight on the other side of the zep. The *Glory* was approaching the falls at an angle, keeping it out of sight until the last moment. The captain liked a bit of the drama, it seemed.

"Yeah, sure. Is there something you're getting at?"

"Sorry, no. It's just... I noticed you when you got on, earlier. Not many people got on and I saw... well, your eyes made me think you were maybe a Pilot. And I haven't had a chance to talk to our own Pilot, haven't even seen him since we boarded in Veridon some months ago. I thought you might..." he trailed off, flushing.

"Have some stories?"

"Well. Yes. Some stories."

I sat quietly for a minute, smelled the air and let the breeze flow over my face. Flying wasn't like this, not from the inside. I shivered and drained my glass.

"Yes, mister. I've made this trip before." I flipped the wineglass out into the air, watched it sparkle as it fell far, far down. "But I've got no stories. Okay?"

He went away, eventually. People usually do, if you're quiet enough and don't look at them. I waited until I was sure, then turned back to look for Marcus. Nothing but pressed tuxedos and fur scarves, far as I could see. Marcus had moved on.

"Excuse me folks, pardon me," someone said over the mixed conversation and wine. "If I could, please, have your attention. A moment of your attention."

I turned. There was a tiny platform, clamped onto the side of the observation deck and slightly elevated. An OverMate stood there, holding up his hands like a maestro. He laughed as someone dropped a glass. People quietened, the chamber music stopped. He smiled.

"Thank you, thank you. Just a moment of your time before dinner." He kept smiling while the last of the conversation died. "The captain and I would like to thank you for joining us on this trip, especially those of you who have been on board since the start. Quite a trip." His voice changed, shifting into the deep bass of a storyteller. "We've seen the winter flower of Empress, the song trees of the Jangalla. The massive grassplains of the Guarana, their mad fires and the smoke that carries them into the next life. We've followed the Lower Reine from the foot of Veridon, winding through the heart of a wilderness few of you dared believe existed. Yes," he smiled at those nearest him, including them in his story. "Yes, quite a trip. Our road has been long, and now we return."

He produced a wine glass and held it up in a grand toast, sweeping his arm out to sea. The *Glory* tacked hard. Passengers murmured and shuffled to keep their feet. A woman giggled. He continued, his voice rising with every word until by the end he was booming, like a benediction, like a war cry. "With weary hearts and heads uplifted, we return, to hearth and home, to our families, our friends, we return to the Shining City above the world. We return to Veridon."

Glory of Day swept around, wooden spars groaning, and came broadside to the Breaking Wall. The waterfall was enormous, miles wide and just as tall. With the zepliner out of the way, the waterfall's crash roared over us in misty waves. And high atop, almost lost in the starry sky, the lights of Veridon.

It was a pretty show, and the Mate was beaming proudly at his delivery. The crowd applauded, toasts were lifted. Someone started to sing quietly. The captain must have had one of the deck voxorators open, to time the maneuver. I went inside.

The dining room was empty, save a couple stragglers, groups of men in whispered conversation. The quartet had started again, picking carefully through a piece from Teromi's Sun Cycle. Stripped down to fit in the quartet's range, and a lot was lost in the process. Marcus was nowhere to be seen.

I had it now. Between my departure from the Academy and my employment with Valentine, I had gone through a rough period. Violent. The kind of trouble I had never gotten into as a youth, the kind of things the son of a Councilor couldn't get away with. Marcus had been part of that social circle, someone who existed at the periphery of bar fights and brothels, a face and a name and not much more. What was he doing on a fine zep like *Glory*?

Our storyteller, the OverMate, squeezed out of the press of bodies on the observation deck, shaking hands and clapping backs, laughing as he went. Once clear of the crowd he shot his cuffs and got a drink from one of the waiters. He saw me looking at him and nodded.

"Pretty good, huh?" he asked. I nodded. "We do that every time. Business guys love it, all the glory of Veridon stuff." He drank some of his wine, still smiling. "Your first time downfalls?"

I shook my head. "I've been."

"Oh." He squinted, looking at my eyes. "Oh, sure. Maybe your next flight, give that a try. What's your zep?"

"No zep."

"Still in the Academy, eh? They let you boys out sometimes?"

I took a glass of wine, drank it all, put the empty glass back on the tray before the waiter had a chance to glide away.

"Good night," I said, and turned to go. Beneath my feet the floor bucked, and the zepliner began to rise. We had started our ascent to Veridon.

I was at the door to the passenger corridors when the voxorator clacked open. The captain's voice was a dead metallic croak, like the taste of blood in your mouth.

"All crew, report to lastrites stations. Alert to lastrites." The voice cut out, and the hood to the vox fluttered, like a fish gasping for breath. There was a silence, except for the quiet tinkle of glass from the observation deck. *Glory of Day* lurched, moaning under sudden unseen stress, then jumped up. The quartet scattered, their instruments clattering to the floor in an atonal cacophony. There were a couple of screams on the observation deck, some of them startled, some of them desperate. Glass broke in a long succession of pops. The rate of our ascent doubled, then doubled again. I heard gunfire.

The OverMate was white-faced, on one knee. The thin glass of wine in his hand snapped in his fingers, blood leaking from his knuckle. I went over and shook him.

"What's your name?" I asked.

"Higgins. OverMate Higgins, First Rank." His voice was a ghost, just automatic reflex on a tide of panic.

"Get your legs, Mate. You've been called to lastrites."

Higgins stood. The passengers were boiling back into the dining room, fleeing the danger of the open deck as we rose faster and faster. Some of them were cut up pretty bad. The ship was groaning under the strain of the sudden ascent.

"Why are we going up?" Higgins whispered, his voice not yet his own. "If we're going to lastrites... crashing... should we be..."

"Lost control, maybe," I snapped. I looked around at the crowd of passengers, at the couple of confused looking crewmen who had dropped their wine trays. The floor was rocking back and forth. I grabbed Higgins by both shoulders and looked into his eyes. "Listen. Gather what crew you can and get those doors secured. Then try to calm these folks down."

"Yes, yes. I can do that. I can..." the man seemed to settle, his eyes focusing tightly. There were more screams from the passenger cabins aft and the service corridors above. "What the hell is going on?"

"Security to the Primary Chamber. Get to manual control all sections, all hands to lastrites." The voxorator again, the captain's voice a dull echo in the pipes. While the captain could talk anywhere on the ship through the vox, Corps practice was to only speak in the presence of crew, away from the passengers. Most people found the dull groan of the voxed voice disturbing, like something out of nightmares. That the captain was doing a general broadcast was worrying.

"We're closest," I said. *Glory* was a Hestes-class zepliner, similar enough to the trainers I had flown. The Primary Chamber was above us three levels, perched by itself on top of the zepliner's main hull, deep in the anti-ballasts.

Access was from the service corridors, but there was also a direct ladderway from the passenger cabin that doubled as an emergency exit to the open decks. The dining room served as a muster point for the passengers, so the evacuation route started here. "If the captain's guard can't respond, then we're the closest." I grabbed Higgins's arm and hauled him forward. "Come on."

"But the passengers..."

"If the captain's in danger, if he's in mortal-about-to-die danger, it doesn't matter one holy hell what happens to these passengers. He dies, we all die. Now come on."

The evac ladderway was behind a concealed door, recessed into the woodwork of the dining room. There was a body at the ladder's base, a security ensign, his face and hands bloody. It looked like he'd fallen down the ladder.

"Oh my Gods," Higgins said. He bent over the body, checking for a pulse, "It's Tehr. He's been... he's dead!"

"Yeah," I said. I leaned over and looked up the ladderway. There was blood spattered on the rungs and the sides of the 'way, enough to see that the guy had been bleeding before he fell. I turned and closed the passageway to the dining hall.

"I'm going to move him," I said, looking around the tiny space at the base of the ladder. There was a readybox just inside the evac door, still locked. I pointed at it. "Open that."

"Why?"

"Because your crew wouldn't let me bring a pistol on board."

OverMate Higgins hesitated, his hand still on the dead ensign's chest. "I should take the weapon, sir. It's my responsibility to see to the captain."

"Sure," I said, motioning to the body at his feet. "And before that it was his responsibility. Think you're up for the job?"

He looked down at the dead man, at the ruin of his face. He closed his eyes and went to open the readybox. I took the ensign by the arms and dragged him clear of the rungs. His chest groaned like a bag of marbles as he slid across the floor. Higgins gave a startled sob, not turning around, his hands shaking as he tumbled the lock on the readybox. Soon as it was open he handed me the service revolver and the cardboard box of extra rounds, then leaned against the metal wall.

"Follow me up." I pocketed the ammo. "Gonna need someone to vouch for me, if I run into security."

"I don't think that's going to happen," he said.

"Yeah. Me neither."

He nodded once, still not looking at the dead man at his feet. I checked to make sure the revolver had been maintained, spun the cycle and sighted the barrel. It was spotless, the grip and cylinder engraved with the city's seal and the *Glory of Day* crest in shiny brass. Tucking the weapon into my belt, I hopped onto the ladder and began the long climb to the Primary Chamber. Behind me I heard Higgins slowly start the same climb.

The rungs were slick with blood, an awful lot of it. The walls were smeared, too. It was like crawling across the floor of a butcher's shop. Halfway up I stopped at a door. It was unlocked. The ladderway kept going up, I assumed to the Primary.

"This leads to the open deck?" I yelled down to Higgins.

"Yes. This is the main access, though there are other ways, obviously."

"It's open."

"Shouldn't be. Should be secured at all times, until we go to lastrites."

"We're at lastrites," I reminded him. "Maybe someone already opened it?"

He shrugged. "Maybe."

I looked up at the blood-stained walls of the ladderway. The platform for the Primary Chamber was close. Establish control of the ship, I thought, or find out why the door was open, what was beyond it. I couldn't do both. My decision was made for me. There was a vox at the top of the ladder. It clacked open and the captain spoke.

"Impact," he groaned.

There was a tearing scream, metal and wood pushed beyond their limit, and the whole ship tumbled in a slow roll noseward. I banged against the wall, then the ladder, grabbing tight as the ship began to corkscrew upwards. Below me Higgins screamed, his feet becoming entangled in the rungs as he pitched backwards. That was all that kept him from falling, his knees looped over a rung as he hung upside down, blood pouring from his mouth.

"We hit the falls!" he sputtered. "We hit the cogsdamn falls!"

"We did," I said. Above us wood continued to groan, spars popping as they exceeded their tolerances. The anti-ballasts would be crumpling, bleeding lift. No time for mysteries. Control had to be re-established or the whole zepliner was going down. I climbed up to the Primary Chamber.

The platform outside the cabin was wet with blood. There was another body, the other guard. His chest had been opened, the ribs grinning through. He was on his back, facing the door to the Chamber, like he had turned and died before drawing his weapon. The door to the Chamber was ajar. I could see blood beyond.

Higgins reached the platform, limping. Standing up was difficult for both of us, the *Glory* was rising in wide corkscrews, spinning and shuddering as control systems failed. It was like a carnival ride, only slick with blood. Higgins and I braced ourselves on the railing, surveying the scene.

"Where's fucking security?" Higgins whispered.

"We're it," I said. I motioned to the body on the floor. "Take his pistol and follow me."

I waited until Higgins had the revolver, holding it in both hands, his elbows stiff at his hips. I put my boot against the door and pushed it open, slowly. The room beyond was a slaughterhouse, a nightmare of gore and broken machines. I crept inside.

The Primary Chamber, when fully functional, is a room of grim efficiency and noise. The captain has no need for luxury or comfort when he's buttoned in, so the Chamber is stuffed with the machinery of the zepliner. Pipes and gears that serve as the control manifold for the zep covered the walls, choking out all other sound. Burners roared nearby, feeding the anti-ballasts, guiding the zep on its flight. The Chamber is the zepliner's bursting heart; loud, hot and clamoring with vigor.

The room was quiet. The gearwork stood silent, the burners guttering, the pipes sweating condensation and blood. Blood, everywhere there was blood and silence. Higgins gasped.

"The manifold is idle. Coghell, how are we... how is the captain keeping us up?"

I shook my head and crossed to the Interface. It was a steel cylinder in the middle of the floor, held in place by a network of pipes in the floor. I stepped over the idled machinery and cycled the Chamber.

The captain's body was a puzzlebox that had been undone and strewn about the capsule. He was still plugged in to the zepliner, the cables socketed into the pewter eyes, the heart mechanism sprouting from his origamitrick chest, gearwork meshing with the interface of the Chamber, pipes and tubes digging smoothly into his skin to plug into the conduits of his bones. To the untrained eye it looked horrible, like a dissection half done. I had seen this before, though. I had been this before.

But beyond the usual violence of the Chamber, a greater brutality had been done. His belly had been laid open, burst and hacked apart, revealing the hidden inner mechanisms of his chest. The oil slick blackness of his secondary blood trickled in with the red and white of his dying body. There was a lot of blood in this room, and most of it belonged to this man.

Higgins stumbled up next to me, took one look at the captain, and turned away from the Interface to vomit. There was a fireaxe wedged between the body and the Chamber's gears, probably taken from a nearby ready station.

"Report," The captain groaned from the room's vox. We both jumped to hear the voice of the dead man at our feet. "Can control be established?"

Higgins coughed and spat. He straightened up and looked at the ceiling. His eyes were glazed. "No, sir. I'm-I'm afraid to report, sir, that you are dead. You've been killed."

The room was silent. Whatever remained of this man was simply an echo, a splinter of consciousness, wandering the soul-manifold that gave the captain control of the ship. What must it be like: dead and still flying, dead and talking.

"No matter. Get the manifold going. We've risen too far to take it down in the Cusp. I'm going to try to get us over the falls, ditch it in the Reine. Veridon will save you."

"Sir, there's no way. Did you hear me, you're dead. Whatever control you have, whatever remains... you'll never be able to get us—"

"Start the manifold. Leave the rest to me."

I closed the Interface, the coffin, and turned to the manifold. The axe had been used here, as well, though inexpertly. Mostly smashed gauges and severed vents. I slipped the manual overrides and began winding the primary soul-cog.

"You're a Pilot," Higgins hissed. "You have the implants." He grabbed me by the shoulder, his eyes wild. "You can fly us. You can save us."

"I can't."

"Why not! Even if you haven't finished your training, for Cog's sake, you can keep us from... from dying."

"I can't."

"Why! Please, please, why?" he sputtered.

I shrugged him off and threw the cog into motion. The Chamber boomed to life, the burners engaging with hell-bent fury. *Glory of Day* stabilized, stopped its lazy corkscrew and started rising more rapidly, leveling off into a smooth ascent.

"Because I can't, because that part of me is dead," I said. I picked up the fireaxe and started to leave.

"It's bad," The captain said. Even through the metallic flatness of the vox, his despair was heavy. "Get the passengers to the glide-boats. Soon as we're clear of the falls and a little upriver, evacuate. Veridon will send ships."

Just as I reached the door there was a cycle of thumps, the zep shuddering a little with each report. I looked up, then at Higgins.

"Those were the glides," I said. "Too soon."

"I couldn't... I don't know. Someone released them." The captain's voice was getting faint. "I'm sorry."

"Just get us to the Reine, sir. We'll swim, or we'll die."

"We'll die," Higgins said. His face was slack, the revolver hanging limply in his hand, resting against his knee. I shrugged and left the Chamber.

Scrambling down the ladder, I took a second to think things through. There were other entrances to the Primary Chamber, mostly service corridors that led from the crew chambers or maintenance shafts. Whoever had done for the captain probably came in that way, then left this way, killing the guards as he went. Probably those gunshots I heard, just as the ship began to lose control. Either way, the killer hadn't come out into the dining hall. I stopped by the door to the open decks, still unlocked, and pulled my revolver.

Killed the guard, climbed down this ladder and gone through this door. I cleared my mind and opened the door.

The open decks were really little more than a railed walkway that circled the zepliner just under the anti-ballasts. Only used for maintenance and access to the glideboats in the event of an emergency. Only the glideboats were gone and the anti-ballast was damaged. Tatters of it fluttered in the tearing wind, trailing wooden spars. The only light was the dull red roar of the burners, buried deep in the anti-ballasts. It was a peaceful color, everything warm like candlelight. To the front of the zep was the waterfall, slate gray and churning.

I braced myself against the railing and crept forward. There was blood here, not as much, a wet trail leading towards the empty glide berths. Maybe our murderer had gotten away clean, though he'd have to be a clever hand with the controls to land a glide safely from this height without crashing into the falls.

Was the crew still preparing the ship for lastrites, even though the glides were gone? They had to know. I was about to give up, to go inside and wait for gravity to take over when I heard a quiet sob, a strangled gasp.

I saw a boot, a leg, sticking out into the walkway. I snuck up and swung around the corner with the pistol at shoulder height. It was Marcus.

He sat in a heap on the floor, wedged between two of the joists for the anti-ballasts above. He was holding a pistol weakly in one hand and his guts in place with the other. A wide tear in his belly was leaking out between his fingers. His face was white and his eyes were fever hot and fading.

"Won't die," he said, just loud enough to hear. "Won't fucking die."

I casually kicked the pistol out of his hand and put my gun in his face. "Yes, I think you might."

His eyes refocused, as if he hadn't seen me until that moment. He was far gone, shivering and sweating. He put his hand on the gun, touching it lightly like a child in a dream.

"I thought I was free. On the ship, but he followed. Saw him on the deck. Ran. In the passage, I laid him out. I laid him open."

"The captain, you mean? That's who you laid out, man. No one else."

Marcus chuckled and spit blood. "Later. That was later. But it wasn't enough. Kept getting up, so I ran. Killed the ship and tried to get off. He got to the glides before me though." He shuddered and sank into himself, his hand to his face. "Oh, well."

"Who did? The guy who killed the captain, did he get into one of the glideboats? Is that what happened?"

"No, man. Glides were empty. He just overrode them and released. I was going to do the same thing, make sure he didn't follow." He focused on me again, maybe finally seeing me as something other than a dream. "You're a Pilot? I know you."

"Yeah," I said. "You do."

He fumbled in his coat and I pressed the barrel into his forehead. He ignored the metal and produced something round and shiny. He pressed it into my free hand and smiled redly.

"Jacob, right? Take this. Take it to the city."

"Sure," I said, and glanced at it. It was the most complicated Cog I'd ever seen. Hard to make out any detail, but it was about the size of my palm and seemed to be slithering inside itself, orbits within orbits, gears sliding beautifully into gears and around. Marcus coughed and I looked up, putting the Cog into my inner vest pocket. "Soon as we land, I'll take it to the city. So, what happened? Did you kill our captain?"

Marcus closed his eyes and balled up his fists, then started to sob. He collapsed on himself like a mountain with a hollow core. "Everybody. I killed everybody."

"Okay. That's okay. I'll take care of it." Then I shot him, just above the eyes.

"Who was that?"

I swung the pistol around, then lowered it. Higgins was standing about ten feet behind me, his hands up. When he saw that I wasn't about to put a bullet in him, he nodded to Marcus. "Was it him? Did he do it?"

"Sure." I looked beyond Higgins. Passengers were boiling up out of the evacuation corridor, lurching down the walkway in their dainty clothes, staring emptily at where the glideboats should have been. "What are they doing?"

Higgins looked back, shrugged. "We thought out here, maybe they have a chance to swim clear of the wreckage. Maybe." He turned to me, walked past where I was kneeling next to the still form of Marcus, then went to stand by the rail. He nodded to the wide white wall of the waterfall, gnashing closer and closer.

"Do you think we're going to clear that?" he asked.

"No," I said, and then we did.

The waterfall became open air, the tumult sliding away to be replaced by the lights of Veridon. At night, the city looked like a titan's jeweled shawl casually discarded, spilling out from the river in ripples of street and cut-stone wall. It was built into broad terraces, each level rising higher above the river, friction-lamps along the streets reflecting off the canals and decorative waterfalls that crisscrossed Veridon. The city was stitched in canals and avenues, tiny lights and broad domes, black lines marking where the Ebd and Dunje rivers cut through the architecture, stepping down in occasional waterfalls and control locks to eventually empty into the enormous Reine. The roar of the falls faded, to be replaced by wind ripping by, and the grinding of the damaged spars in the anti-ballast above.

Glory of Day tipped forward, clearing the precipice and sliding over the river. Distant klaxons sounded, echoing down the slopes of the Torchlight and in the harbor below. The passengers behind me cheered, and then the anti-ballast collapsed and caught on fire. Cheers became cries of terror. I turned to them, to see if there was a way out of this.

They were mostly still in their formal attire, a couple in regular clothes. They stared down at the water below. Their screams echoed in my head, matching the terror in my dreams, my memories, the screams I felt through my ship as I struggled to keep aloft. I was lost again, falling down. The screams became more desperate, and I opened my eyes.

Several people had gone over, one old lady trailing a banner of white fur as she fell. A man was forcing his way to the front, shoving others out of his way, heedless of what became of them afterwards. He cleared the crowd and knelt over the ruined hulk of Marcus. Ran his hands over the dead man's chest, ignoring the blood, ignoring the guts that slithered under his fingers. Looking for something. Not finding it, he looked around the deck in a very inhuman manner, like an insect. He stood, paying us no mind, and began to run to the front of the zep. He glanced at me as he passed, our eyes meeting. His face was completely slack, not with fear or calm. Just empty. Eyes like bleached summer sky, blue almost white. He went by before I could stop him, got to the prow of the zep and vaulted over the edge like a swimmer. He was wearing a long cloak, and it fluttered like wings as he disappeared over the railing.

"That's all," the captain said, the closest voxorator barely fluttering open. "That's all."

The *Glory* burst, the burners screaming to claw one last bit of lift out of the sky, the anti-ballast blossoming and collapsing. The river Reine was before us, flat and black, rushing at us like an avalanche.

I closed my eyes and waited for the cold.

Chapter Two
The Summer Girl

I HOLD TO old gods. My family is faithful to the Celestes, though their worship has fallen out of favor among the city's elite. As a child I remember my father sneaking off to the holy dome of the Singer, or the Noble, to pay his respects before dawn, before the streets were crowded with common folk and their new, common God of the Algorithm. Now it was almost illegal to worship in the domes of the Celestes. The Church of the Algorithm had such power, such influence. Eventually, my parents hid their icons of the Celestes, stopped risking even early morning services. We took service at the Church of the Algorithm, like good Veridians. But at night, in closed rooms, in our secret hearts, we held to the old gods.

Not that I expect much of them, either in this world or the next. I get by with my own help, by my own hand. And when I die, I expect a long, empty blackness. The Celestes teach nothing of an afterlife. Not like the Algorithm, with its infinite pattern, its eternal calculations and the intricacies of their metronomic prophecies. Their lives are a soulless pattern, and their deaths are as well. The holy Wrights of the Algorithm teach of an afterlife of clockwork, the hidden engines of the world swept back to reveal the calculation at the middle, the equation that is God.

I hold to old gods. Imagine my disappointment, then, when the darkness that took me after the *Glory of Day* shattered against the cold water of the river Reine lingered only for a while. Light came, and noise. I opened my eyes to a world of pattern, of engine. The world of the Algorithm.

"Ah, fuck," I muttered. My voice was husky, like I'd been yelling. The ceiling above me was a twitching tableau of clockwork precision, cogs and escapements and coiling springs that slipped and ticked and groaned loudly. Metal crashed against metal. Not my idea of heaven. I tried to sit up and found myself weak and naked. I looked down and saw that I was bound to a bed, covered only by a thin sheet of white linen. I spat, and a wad of dried leaves scattered across my chest. The taste in my mouth was of dry earth.

Embalming herbs. They meant to bury me. I looked around. There were other bodies, lined up neatly on either side. Lots of bodies. About as many as you would expect to recover from an airship crashing into a river. I struggled free from my ceremonial bonds and stood up. Behind me, someone screamed.

There was a door, and a crowd of Wrights of the Algorithm clustered inside it. They shook under their grease-lined brown robes. I wrapped the linen around my waist.

"Can I have my clothes back?"

They were quick to oblige. I walked out of the Church of the Algorithm with most of my possessions. The pistol was gone, along with my boots. My shirt had been cut off me, but they had been careful with my pants. They were nice pants. Probably some eye-wise Wright saw some quality he could sell, later on. My jacket was intact, too. And, surprisingly, I still had the Cog Marcus had pressed into my hand moments before he died, tucked into the inner pocket of my jacket, the lining still cold and damp from the river. Thank the Celestes.

"He didn't seem like someone on his way to die," I said. I held the thing Marcus had given me in the palm of my hand. The slightest movement of my arm set off its internal machinations, spinning gears and flexing cogs in the central complex. I turned it slowly under the light on Emily's desk. "He just seemed like someone who was on his way somewhere. Like he knew where he was going."

She shrugged. She wasn't really paying attention to me yet, not at this stage of the conversation. This is how it was with us. She was bent over a ledger, marking deliveries and balancing columns. Her fingers were inky. She had her hair up in a bun, but strands had fallen out, and her face was framed in a wispy nimbus of gold, reflected light from the incandescent on her desk. She looked pretty.

"Maybe he did. Maybe he didn't want to stick around to get burned up like everyone else." She glanced up. "Maybe he just wanted a quick end. Maybe he was just anxious to join the Fehn."

I shuddered. The river folk, the Fehn, were little more than animated corpses, possessed by some sort of flat worm that haunted the deep currents of the Reine. They talked like the people they had been before they died, but they were something else completely.

"I heard the Fehn are helping out with the recovery," I said. "The Council's gathering the *Glory* up, going to use the parts to make some kind of memorial."

"Fitting," she said. "Something to remember it by, I suppose. You have to do that sort of thing, when an airship crashes and kills everyone on board."

"Not everyone," I said. She sighed.

"Everyone who hasn't had half their body replaced with foetal metal, everyone with flesh and blood hearts and eyes that don't look like dirty dishes." She set down her pen. "Regular people."

"You're just jealous," I said. "You wish you had eyes like mine. Anything's better than those mud bogs." I nodded toward her deep brown eyes, eyes that were wet and warm and sparkled in the light. She smiled and looked down.

"Jacob Burn, the most charming man to ever survive two zepliner crashes, one of which he caused. Why, you must have to drive the ladies away with a stick."

I smiled. "You know I carry a gun."

She snorted. "Jacob, Jacob. Why are you here again? Not to show me souvenirs, no." She closed her ledger and packed away the ink kit. She did things like that very precisely, very neatly. Her whole apartment was like that. The plaster walls were clean, the dark wooden floor never hinted at dust. Once her desk was clear, she opened a different drawer and set three things on the desk. Two of them were envelopes, and the third was an inlaid wooden box, about the size of a short book.

"We need you to meet a man."

"We?"

She nodded. "This one comes from Valentine. You're okay with that?"

"Sure. He knows I do good work, and he pays well." I try to balance my obligations in the underworld, but Valentine was my main employer. I owed him a lot.

"A Corpsman. Register Prescott, of the *City Rampant*. Give him this." She pushed the first envelope a little closer. It was cheap butcher's paper, hand-folded over something thick. I picked it up. Felt like river clay, dense and cold in my hand.

"It's cassiopia, right? Pure."

She shrugged. "It's an envelope. You give it to Prescott."

I nodded and put it into my coat pocket.

"The name's familiar, but I'll have to do a little research. Most of my contacts are Academy. Pilots and Mates, not the desk crew."

"Won't be necessary. There's a formal dinner being held, to honor the Corps. One of those political things. It's being thrown by the

Family Tomb at their estate on the Heights. Many Corpsmen will be there, including Prescott."

"It's not a good place to make a deal. Too many curious eyes at a party like that, too many officials. I can make contact there, but the deal will have to happen somewhere else."

"It will have to happen there. Prescott has insisted. Doesn't trust us, I suppose."

I shrugged.

"I'll need an invitation."

She pushed the second envelope towards me. "There will be a ceremony, in remembrance of the *Glory of Day*. Naturally, as the sole survivor, you're expected."

"Naturally." I took the envelope. "Anything else?"

She presented the wooden box, turning it so I could see the clasp that opened it and slid it in front of me. "The party is being hosted by the Councilor-in-Standing for the Family Tomb. You know her? Angela Tomb?"

"I know her."

"Her family has been making... let's call them overtures in force. I'd like you to deliver that. Discreetly."

She opened the box, and a quiet song tinkled out. A music box.

"Is this going to get me in trouble with the Lady Tomb?"

Emily smiled and shrugged. "I hear you carry a gun."

She put the box into a leather folder and handed it to me. It fit nicely in the outer pocket of my coat.

When I looked up, Emily was holding the cog-wheel. She was weighing it in her hands, shifting it slightly to watch the inner gears spin and cycle.

I hadn't thought much about the thing when Marcus handed it to me on the *Glory*. Other things on my mind at the time. I assumed it was some memento, something he wanted to get back to family in Veridon. Second looks made it clear that it was no sentimental bauble.

"Marcus had this?" she asked.

"Yeah. Wanted me to get it back to the city. Gave it to me, then went on about how he had killed the captain, wrecked the ship."

"It looks like a Church thing."

I shrugged. The Church of the Algorithm was a strange group. That being said, they were the dominant religious organization in the city. Veridon was blessed with many mysteries, but the most profitable mysteries were the strange vessels that floated down the river at regular intervals. No one knew where they came from, or who sent them. They contained random collections of cog, half-built machines and enigmatic autonomic artwork. The Church of the Algorithm was built on the belief that these vessels were messages from a hidden God far upriver. They lived their lives trying to reassemble the machines, to reveal the nature of their deity. They worshipped a hidden pattern. We owed them a lot, sadly. Their divinations led to many of the technological discoveries that kept Veridon the dominant power on this edge of the world.

"Maybe," I said. "I'd rather not go to them. They'll saint me."

"I doubt that. No one's going to mistake you for a holy prophet."

"Stranger things have happened. Besides, this came from downriver. Their god is upriver, right?"

"So maybe the devil sent this?"

"Then the devil can have it back. I just want to know why Marcus had it."

"He gave it to you and told you to take it to the city?"

"He did. Hell if I know why."

"Hm. I have to ask, Jacob. Why'd you shoot Marcus?"

I shrugged. The details weren't important, but I felt like I'd done him a favor. I had offered finality, a clear judgment on his actions and a clean end. Lots of my fellow passengers lingered on for days before they passed. My friendship with Marcus had bought him something easier, even if he was responsible for the disaster to begin with.

"I wonder," she said. She set the device on the table. "Why did he do that? Give it to you, for one thing, but everything before? Why he took an axe to the Captain, and killed all those people by proxy? It seems he got off a little easy, dying at your hand."

"Maybe. He seemed to think someone was following him, someone he couldn't kill. Something wrong with his head, maybe." I cleared my throat. "I think wrecking the ship was his way of escaping, ensuring that no one could follow him, wherever he was going. He meant to get off. He was making for the glideboats when someone jettisoned them."

"Well, he certainly made sure no one followed him." She held the Cog out to me, held it between her hands like a plate. "Everyone who could follow him on that ship died, sure as fire burns and water drowns."

"Yeah," I said. "I remember." I took the Cog from her, placed my palm under it and lifted. My thumb brushed the inside of her wrist, and I hesitated. Felt her pulse through my hand, the warmth of her skin on my callused knuckle. We stayed there a second longer than we should have.

"Cacher's on the way," she said. "He's coming by to pick up these ledgers. Valentine wants monthly reports, now."

"He'll be here," I said, "sooner or later."

"Sooner."

I took the Cog and held it up, blocking her face from my view. "Sure," I said. "Soon enough."

She shuffled papers, retrieved the ledger and started checking it again. I stood still for a moment, looking at her between the workings of the Cog.

"Look, if you'd like, I could hold on to that. Ask Cacher about it, or maybe Valentine, later on. They might know something."

I hesitated again. She was a good job-boss, good as any in the city. Like me, she was independent. Like me, she was in this for herself. Anything she did with the Cog would be in her best interest, not mine. But she had a wider base of contacts, and a better chance of getting Valentine's attention, through Cacher.

"Sure, thanks." I held out the Cog again, waiting for her to take it. She didn't look up, just nodded and motioned to the desk. I set it down and left.

TOMB HAD SET up a private zep shuttle from the city up to their estate on the heights. There was a road, but it left the city and traveled twenty miles up the Ebd before crossing at the port town of Toth and winding up into the Thalleon Heights that overlooked the city of Veridon. It was a half-day's journey in most cases, and the zep was simply quicker and more glamorous. Expensive, too.

The Tomb Estate was a grand place, perched on the side of the Heights that overlooked Veridon's gentle slopes like a crown on a stony forehead. There were many such estates on the Heights, though not all of them were as dramatically situated as the Tomb. Most of the founding Families had preferred a little more privacy, perhaps more of an escape from the city to their country homes. Elizor Tomb wanted a view of the delta he had helped found, the wide arms of the Ebd and Dunje, the flat plain of the Reine, and all the buildings in between. More buildings now than when he set the first stone in this estate.

Yes, a grand place, and probably one of the last old holdings still in the hands that had built it. The rest of us were just glad to hold onto our seats on the Council and the pared down manors of the city. Most of the old estates that dotted this ridge now belonged to factory bosses and Guild capitalists, along with a bare minority of the Councilorships. Old names weren't worth much in Veridon anymore, not in the new city, the brave city of cogs hatched by the Church a couple generations ago. The city of my father was passing, with its traditions and lineage, and a new city was breaking through. Old names got you nostalgia and the occasional invitation to parties, and maybe a certain amount of tolerance with the Council and its agencies. And that was the product I sold, to Valentine, to Emily, to anyone who needed it. Someone else's tolerance, and a name people would recognize, maybe respect.

The crown of the Tomb Estate glowed under us. Night had already fallen, the countryside deep in velvet blackness that hummed with wild insect life, but the estate was lit up like a torch. It was early spring, and the weather was still wildly variable in the city. It was usually cooler up here on the Heights, but tonight was firmly in the grip of a promised summer. Most of the estates were still closed up, but Tomb had brought in the Summer help early, to host tonight's party. There were stepped balconies that crept down the rock face, and I could see people gathered, musicians playing. We passed over the estate to the landing square. A loose ladder rolled down the zep, and Ensigns clambered across to secure us. A more permanent mooring gate was hauled up, and soon we were debarking.

On my zep there was a cluster of Corpsmen, young officers, Academy-fresh and anxious to mingle with the city's elite. They kept looking at me sidelong, trying to see my eyes without having to make eye contact. Tricky. Did they know who I was, exactly? Did the instructors still tell my story, or did they leave it out to keep the youngsters from getting too nervous?

An avenue laid in river stone led from the mooring gate to the main hall. The stone crunched under my dress boots. The lawns were green and smooth, spotted with natural rock gardens and alcoves of trees. The house seemed to emerge from the lawn, another rock formation fitted together, smoothed in place by time. Like the lane, the walls of the estate were river rock, as smooth and black as night. It looked like darkness bubbling up out of the earth, darkness riddled with laughter and light and wealth.

The guests had been arriving for a while. When I stepped inside there was already a crowd in the grand hall, though most of the voices were coming from the balcony beyond. A man slipped up to give my invitation a glance and then take my coat and travel hat. The remaining envelope fit comfortably in my jacket, along with the trim wooden box I was to give Angela. The man looked me in the eyes and smiled, nodded towards the hall, and disappeared. Apparently my best suit was good enough to appear on the grounds of the Tomb Estate, or maybe it was my eyes that were good enough. Either way, I was in.

The grand hall wasn't packed, just a few clusters of men, sometimes women, holding drinks and nodding to one another. There was a bar and a fireplace, both lively. The walls inside were different, though still beautiful. They were steel gloved in warm butterwood, the gloss at once brilliant and soothing. The hall smelled like warm bread and linen, with a tinge of wood smoke that hinted at the countryside around us.

The broad length of the hall was all latticework windows and doors, leading out to the terraced balcony. There was a lot of light out there, and music. I got a drink and went outside.

The night sky was crystal bright, thousands of stars and the silver moon bearing down on the darkness. The city was far below, just as beautiful as it had been on the *Glory of Day* in the moments after we cleared the falls. Veridon glittered across the sloping delta, laced in blackness by canals and rivers, lights hunched up in avenues and buildings, a warm haze of streetlights and the illuminated domes of the Holy Houses of the Celestes. They still looked bright, no matter how dead their religion, how empty their shrines. I could even pick out their successor, the massive Church of the Algorithm, crouched near the Reine, shimmering with the flames of its deep engines of God. The whole city was like a stone broken open to reveal a heart of precious fire, washed up on the riverbank.

Out here on the balconies there were a lot more people. Frictionlamps hummed softly on sturdy tables, offering a place to lean or set your drink while encouraging mingling among the guests. A lot of the faces were younger than I expected, and unfamiliar. A lot of them were in uniform, as well, testament to the feast's honor. I walked among the crowd, nodding and smiling as necessary. I paused at the railing, leaning against the cold stone and looking out at the Tomb grounds. Below me and to one side there was another terrace, and a third below it. There were others, I knew, smaller and more discreet, but they remained unlit tonight. It was on these terraces, visiting as a child and leaning dangerously far over the rail, that I first dreamed of flying. A child's dream.

Laughter interrupted me. The Lady Tomb, holding court on the terrace below me. Her dress was trimmed in black and grey, the colors of the Corps. I found the stairs and went down to present myself.

The orbit of people around here was tight, mostly young folks in nice suits and dresses. I couldn't tell if they were the sons and daughters of merchants, hoping to curry favor among the Council's Named Seats, or if these were the very capitalists who had leveraged away most of the old Families, bought up their named rights and property. Either way, it was unusual to see their kind at a party of the Tomb. Tomb's seat was bought out, too, but the debt hadn't yet come due. Old man Tomb still lived, though barely. The Lady held the seat in his absence, as had generations of Tombs. When he died, the seat would go with him. Maybe to one of these young bucks.

I couldn't force my way to the Lady directly, so I joined the slow social progression, drank and chatted, or listened to others go on about nothing. It took a while, but I was able to work my way in, slowly, circling, shaking hands and patting backs, then slipping forward a little more, a little closer. Eventually I found myself in the presence of the Lady Councilor-in-Standing Angela Tomb. I nodded at her.

"Councilor Tomb."

She looked at me between long lashes. Her eyes were dusty, the faintest gray, and her hair was pulled back into a golden rope that trailed over her shoulder and down her back. She had a pretty chin and lips, but the smile she dressed them in didn't make it to her eyes.

She raised a hand, almost offering it to me but not quite, as though she was prepared to receive a kiss or deflect a blow.

"Pilot Burn. The hero of *Glory*. Good of you to come."

"Always a pleasure to see the old estate, Councilor. But I wouldn't dare assume the name hero."

"No?" She raised a nearly empty glass to her mouth and let the ice clink against her teeth. She wasn't drinking wine, I noticed. "I understand that you're responsible for rescuing every soul that survived."

There was a brief, embarrassed wave of laughter around us. I clutched my glass.

"Yes, I suppose. As the only survivor."

"Ah. I misunderstood. Still, I'm sure you did what you could. As a Pilot, I mean."

I didn't like that. I wasn't sure what she knew about my reasons for being here, if she knew that I was standing as a representative of Valentine, or if she thought I was just here in my role as disgraced nobility and fallen Captain, an example to others. Whatever she knew or believed she knew, I didn't like this.

The uniform standing next to Tomb leaned forward, a little smile on his face. He was older, wearing the plating of a Commodore. I didn't recognize his face, but by his age and rank it was a fair bet I had reported to him at some point.

"Let's not throw that title around, my Lady. Pilots, as you know, can fly. Can you fly, Mr. Burn?"

I was silent, awkwardly aware of my eyes and the hum of the dead machine in my heart.

"You know I can't."

"Ah. Then we have misnamed you twice. Hero and Pilot. It's too bad so much blood has been wasted on you, Jacob Burn." The man seemed satisfied to have used my full name, as though the absence of titles was insult enough. I put my hand on his shoulder and dropped my glass to the stone floor. It popped, and the crowd became quiet.

"Can you, Commodore?" I flicked my eyes to the nearby railing and the empty space beyond. "Fly?"

No one moved. No one said anything, the tight suits and uniforms all around held their glasses and their tongues and just stared. The Lady was looking at me cautiously, but made no call for help. The Commodore was white. I could feel his heart hammering under his skin. I liked this better. I laughed.

"Nevermind. It's a good party, My Lady. We should have more like this." I patted the Commodore on the chest. "I like your friends."

I left, and conversation resumed. I took a drink from a passing waiter, found a smaller staircase that led to the third, and lowest, terrace and found a quiet spot. There was a garden here, a ledge that had been built up and landscaped, an unnaturally smooth bit of grass and tree dangling over the ridge's height. There was a zepliner drifting in from Veridon, perhaps the last of the night. Upriver, far up the Reine, an accumulation of storm clouds was piling up. Lightning flashed deep in its heart, pink flickering into white. A breeze lifted from the delta valley, bringing a smell of wetness and growth and hot metal. Storms rolling in.

I thought about my little encounter. If Lady Tomb knew my purpose, knew I was there on behalf of Valentine, she might have just been trying my steel. Testing the limits of Valentine's broken monster. Then again, if she was just being a bitch. Well. Maybe I should have thrown her friend off the balcony.

I finished my drink and went to get another. The sky was changing, clouds stealing away the stars, getting dark.

THE ZEPLINER BROUGHT the girl, riding hard against the gathering storm. They docked at the same mooring gate we had used and hurried her down the cobble walkway while the zep jerked and bobbed. She was beautiful in the non-specific way common to engram-singers.

She was wrapped tight in a black shawl and dress, surrounded by the blue tunics of the Artificer's Guild.

Tonight's performance was to be *The Summer Girl*. It was an old song, a favorite of the Corps. The original performance had been at the christening of the first zepliner, the awkwardly-named *Lady of the Summer Skies*. The later exploits of this vessel, near-myth in the Corps circles, had solidified the song's place as the unofficial anthem of the Corps. That it was also one of the oldest recorded engram-songs, performed at the earliest cusp of that still-shady technology, added to the mystique.

From the balcony I watched the zep flee the Heights. Most everyone else had already moved inside. The coming weather gave the air a heavy dampness tinged with electric fire. I went inside before the real rain started. I only had the one suit to my name, and didn't want it ruined. Behind me the zep dropped rapidly into the valley.

There was a crowd of Corpsmen at the bar. Their conversation was boisterous, full of laughter and stern opinions. A few of them eyed me, probably because of my earlier outburst with the Commodore. I eyed them back, peaceful-like. When I sat at the bar they made room but ignored me. I got my drink and looked around. Maybe I could find this Prescott guy, or have a word with the Lady that wasn't quite so full of confrontation. One of the young tight uniforms beside me set his glass carefully on the bar and, just as carefully, knocked it over with his elbow.

It was clumsy. A clumsy way to start a fight, like he was trying to be clever with his pals. The liquor slithered across the wood, towards me. He turned in mock surprise.

"What was that about?" I asked.

"Oh, oh. So sorry, sir." The boy feigned shock. Just a boy, his Ensign clasp very shiny. "I hope no offense..."

"Push someone else, kid." I stood up before the spill got to me, let it cascade onto the empty stool and picked up my glass. "You've messed up the Lady's furniture. Go get a mop and put that Academy training to some use."

I went somewhere else, across the room. Heavy walls of water were beating against the glass, the rain mixed with lightning and a hammering wind. I stood by the fireplace and warmed up. My lungs got cold in this kind of weather, I could feel the pistons creaking, the metal chill where it touched bone and skin. I flexed my hands, alternating as I switched the glass from one hand to the next, trying to burn off the anger. I had lost my temper with the Commodore, and that was stupid. I couldn't afford stupid out here, in this territory.

"Don't mind them," a voice said near me. I turned to find an officer, OverMate, leaning comfortably on the hearth near me. Gray dusted his temples, and his fingers were exceptionally bony. "The young. They're full of wine and blinded by the polish of their shoes."

I shrugged. "You shouldn't be talking to me."

"Pardon?" He became even more casual, almost sleepy.

I looked him over close. The careful ease of his stance, the remarkable nonchalance of his character.

"Register Prescott, right?" I asked. He seemed a little surprised, but covered it well. "You shouldn't be talking to me. Stupid chance."

"Like picking a fight with the Commodore. That kind of stupid?" He hissed, keeping his face perfectly neutral. "Stupid, like arranging the meet here?" He waved a hand at the hall of Corpsmen, as though talking about the weather or the crowds. "Half the people here are Corps. The other half are Councilors or the instruments of some. Is that," he smiled coldly, "the sort of stupid you mean?"

I looked at him squarely. "I didn't arrange this."

"What?"

"I didn't arrange this. It wasn't my idea." I took a drink, looked out over the uniforms and evening dresses. "I assumed it was your idea. My contact said you were more comfortable on such neutral ground."

"My idea?" He leaned forward, for a moment letting his cool mask slip. "My contact insisted it be here. Said it was the only place you could make the exchange."

I snorted. "Fascinating. You probably don't want to exchange contact names?" He shook his head sharply. "No, I didn't think so. Finish your drink, Register. Get another and don't talk to me again." I met his eyes for a breath. "I'll let you know when and where."

He straightened up, finished his drink and walked away. His face looked like he'd been drinking piss. Maybe that was an act, so he could ignore me the rest of the evening. Maybe he just didn't like the situation. I didn't like it, that's for sure.

Emily seemed plenty clear that this meet came from outside. Whether that meant from higher in Valentine's organization, or from someone on Prescott's side of the deal didn't matter. It was a bad meet, but it was the meet we had to make. But now I knew it wasn't the client. Prescott had been forced into this, not by his people but by Valentine's. And they had told me it was on Prescott's side. Meaning someone wasn't being honest, someone didn't trust. I was being put in a bad position, and I didn't like it.

I drank and I waited, either for the show to start or some other part of this increasingly strange deal to fall into place. The show came first. A butler with high, thin hair and immaculate cuffs gathered us up and led us through a stone archway in the hall to the estate's private theater.

The place wasn't big enough. Most estates had a theater, at least the good ones, but they were made for extended families getting together for drinks and a light opera. We were crowded in, the air was hot and even the quiet whisper of such a crowd was nearly a roar in the pure acoustics of the theater. The concert hall was a tight circle, concentric rings of velvet seats terraced around a polished wooden stage. They led her to the center, the frictionlamps bright on her white dress, then several of the attendants busied themselves with the equipment that had been set up next to the stage. There was a young man seated next to me, a child really, the son of some Admiral. He leaned against me, straining to see.

"What are they doing? Is that the Summer Girl?"

I looked down at the thin white girl, alone on stage. "No, but it will be. You'll see."

The boy's mother patted his arm. "His first social affair," she whispered. "He's very excited."

I nodded. "He understands, right? He won't be frightened?"

The boy looked at me with hot green eyes. He shook his head firmly. His mother smiled.

"Oh," said the boy, his attention on the stage below. It had gotten quiet around us. "Oh."

I turned to see. The Artificers approached the girl with a jar. I leaned forward. The jar was glass, and the dark contents seemed to squirm. The girl closed her eyes and opened her mouth. I could see the furtive coiling of her machine. She had beautiful lips, full and shiny like glass, and they were quivering. I wondered if she was afraid.

The Master Artificer was a tall man with arms that moved fluidly, like they were nothing but joints. He dipped his hands into the jar and brought out something shiny. The queen foetus. He placed it on the girl's tongue and then stepped back, along with the rest of the Guildsmen. The girl's hands fluttered to her throat and she opened her eyes, wide and white. A second later she made a coughing, gasping sound. The boy's mother tutted and turned her face. The rest of the audience shifted uncomfortably.

It happened suddenly. The Artificers set down the jar and tipped it over. The swarm spilled out like glittering, jeweled honey, their tiny legs clicking against the wood as they washed across the stage. They climbed the girl and began to nest with her, become her, entering the secret machines that made up the engram. They were seeking their queen and her pattern, the song stitched into her shell and her memory, awaiting birth and creation. The girl shivered, and she became.

She straightened up, looking out across the audience. I hadn't seen *The Summer Girl* performed in some time, since my Academy days, in fact. But there she was, unmistakable. She stood in front of the audience like she ruled it, like these people didn't exist when she wasn't on stage, and when she was on stage they existed only to appreciate her. The girl had that stance, her back and chin and shoulders laying claim to the Manor Tomb. The swarm fed on her, rebuilt her before our quiet eyes. Her skin leaked white, her cheekbones flattened and rose, the perfect lips became more, writhing as they changed. She stood taller, her hair shimmered and changed color, cascaded down her shoulders. She was older now, fuller, her hips and breasts those of a woman. The audience was silent, stunned.

The Summer Girl stood before us, more perfect than she had actually been on that long distant day. She raised an arm to us, nodded to the Lady Tomb in her seat of honor, and then she sang. Perfectly, beautifully, her voice was a warm hammer in my head. This tiny hall could not contain her, the very bones of the mountain around us thrummed with her song. I remember nothing of words or themes, as it always is with *The Summer Girl*. Just warm glory and peace remaking my heart, flowing through my bones, filling the cramped metal of my heart like slow lightning in my blood.

When it was over, there was silence. I imagine we would have clapped if she had left anything in us, if we hadn't been drained by the beauty of her voice. The Girl nodded, again, content with our awe. And then she fell apart, her hair and face crumbling and tumbling down the girl, bits and pieces clattering against the wooden stage. The girl collapsed, trailing thin lines of blood from her proxy body as the shell of the Summer Girl left her. The Guildsmen scurried forward, sweeping up the scraps of miracle, the slowly squirming remnants of the Maker Beetles, helping the girl to her feet. They escorted her off the stage, her hand to her head, her legs dragging between two strong Artificers. Only when she was gone, when the last bit of the Summer Girl had been swept away, could we bring ourselves to stand and applaud the empty stage.

In standing, my eyes slid across the stage and settled on the darkness, where they had led the girl. There was a man standing there, dressed in the deep blue of the Artificers, though he was paying no attention to the other Guildsmen busy in their art all around him. He had his arms crossed, and seemed to hover in the shadow of the bright lights. His head turned slowly, looking out at the audience. As his gaze passed me I felt a deep shiver of recognition. Cold eyes, the lightest blue, like snow over water. He looked beyond me, paused, then turned his face towards me again.

He looked right at me. His face was empty, completely slack. Without a word he disappeared from the stage.

Around me the crowd was still applauding. Just a moment earlier I had been sweating in the close heat of the theater. Now that sweat froze against my skin. I looked around for an exit.

Lady Tomb was waiting at the end of my row. She was looking directly at me. She nodded and disappeared among the unending ovation. I turned and left the hall.

Chapter Three
Words in Metal

A MAN WAS waiting for me, one of the servants. He introduced himself as Harold, personal attendant to the Lady Tomb. He had high white hair, thin on the sides. He nodded to me as I stepped out of the roaring applause and turned, walking down a hallway, deeper into the estate. I looked around, but no one else left the theater. There must be other exits, though, someplace for the performers to rest and retire without troubling the guests. Harold got ahead of me, so I hurried to catch up.

Though there were no windows this deep, I could tell it was still raining. The air smelled like water and lightning. The lightning might have been the frictionlamps that glowed along the tight, immaculate hallway, but who knows. The whole place smelled like bad weather. The polish of the dark wood flashed as I walked along it, shinier than silver.

High and White led me to a parlor, a room carpeted in deep blue with walls of dark wood and old metal fittings. The Lady was waiting, faced away from me. She was still in her black and gray, but in this empty room the get-up looked unnecessarily fancy. The room might have once been a library or shrine. There were walls of shelves and glass display cases on three sides, but they were all bare. Nothing but dust and the Lady. She held a glass of wine and gazed at a plaque on the wall. There was another glass on a shelf by the door, condensation beading on its side and running down the fragile stem. The servant nodded to Tomb and left, closing the door behind him. I took the wine and went to stand by her.

"Did you enjoy our show, Mr. Burn?" she asked. Her voice was soft, none of the mocking formality from earlier.

"I did. It was chosen well."

She nodded absently. "I thought Mr. Valentine might send someone, eventually. When I saw your name on the guest list, I thought it might be you." She took a drink of wine and turned to face me. "Is it?"

"I can't visit my childhood haunts? Have dinner with some of my old Corps mates? See a show? You offered me an invitation. I accepted."

She snorted and looked back to the plaque. It was old brass, set in a stone that had probably been hauled here from Veridon in secret. It was the Tomb Writ of Name. We had one too, somewhere. I hadn't seen it in years.

"It doesn't seem like much, does it? Just metal and words."

"Metal, words, and power, my Lady." I put my hand on her shoulder. "We do many things for that, Angela. We do what we must."

She turned her head to me. "So why are you here then, Jacob Burn? Here to visit old friends?"

For a moment I wished it was true, that my visit was just social, that my invitation had come from her, rather than Valentine. I gave her the music box. She opened it, glanced over at me as the music filled the room. She set her wine down.

"Well," she said, quietly. She placed the music box on the shelf by her head and stared at it absently. "Such a thing. Not what I was expecting. I suppose I see why they sent you."

"Pardon?"

"Oh... it's nothing. A bit of nostalgia. Someone is playing a bit of a trick on me." She closed the box almost sadly, then turned to me.

"It is good to see you again, Jacob. Even in these circumstances." She leaned casually against the plaque, her fingers brushing the ancient metal. "Even if you are on the job."

"Good to see you, too. How are things in the Council?"

"More interesting than they've any right to be. You should visit more often. The Families, I mean." She giggled quietly. "I can't imagine you wanting to visit the Council sessions."

"Not someplace I'd be welcomed, anyway." I smiled. Angela and I had never been that close, but it was nice to be remembered.

"Yes, your father. And those horrid factory people, buying out so many of the Families. But I'm glad the Burns have stayed with us."

"Well. None of my doing," I said. She shrugged.

"Perhaps. Will you be staying the night?"

"What, here? I hadn't known it was that sort of party."

She laughed again, and years fell away. She suddenly looked overdressed, like a noble daughter in her mother's finest, awkward.

"It's not, not yet. We'll see how things end."

"I can't stay. Business in the city. But perhaps some other time. It'd be good to spend some time in the country again."

"Hm. Yes, perhaps." She closed the music box and took up her glass of wine. "You'll forgive me, but I have a party to attend. Um." She paused as she crossed to the door. "Perhaps you should stay here for a bit. You know, for propriety."

"Of course." I drank from my glass of wine and nodded.

She left the room by the same door I had entered. I waited, listening to her tromp down the hallway. I looked again at the music box, shrugged, and drank my wine. When it sounded as though the Lady Tomb had left the immediate area, I nodded my respects to the lonely plaque, left my wine glass on a nearby shelf, and went into the hallway.

I walked quickly, anxious to make my exchange with Prescott. I was lost in thought, my mind on the strange man in the theater and trying to decide how to make the deal with Prescott discreetly so I could get the fuck off this mountain and back to Veridon, when Harold slipped silently from a side passage and began walking beside me. He was carrying something under his arm.

"Mr. Burn. Was your meeting satisfactory?"

"I suppose. I'll be needing transport down to the city at the earliest convenience." I wanted to get back to Emily, find out what else she might know about the deal with Prescott. "I need to be in Veridon within the hour."

"I'm afraid that will be impossible, sir. The storm has grounded the fleet. Not even our private ships are willing to brave it, sir."

"I'll take a cab. I trust the roads are still open."

"Perhaps. But other arrangements have been made, sir. The Manor Tomb has been opened for the evening. The party will be staying the night, to return to Veridon in the morning."

"Just arrange the cab." I turned to go, to find Prescott and make the drop. Harold put his hand on my elbow.

"I have just this moment spoken to Ms. Angela. She insisted that no one would be leaving tonight, sir. Assuming that I could get a hold of a cab at this hour, it would take most of the night for it to get here and return to the city. You will get home sooner if you stay the night and take a zepliner in the morning. With the rest of the guests, sir."

I sighed and settled my hands into my pockets. I didn't like it, but he was right. And it gave me more time to make the Prescott deal cleanly, without rushing. Maybe even look in on Mister Blue Eyes.

"Fair enough. Rooms are being provided?"

"Of course. As soon as the accommodations are ready, you will be shown your room. In the meantime, refreshments are being provided in the Grand Hall."

"Swell," I said. I tried to leave for a second time.

"One more thing, sir." He held up the package. It was about the size of a professor's book, wrapped in butcher's paper and tied with twine. The paper was soaked. "This came for you, on the same zep that brought the… entertainment. I would have had it to you sooner, of course, but things have been hectic."

I took the package. It was heavy and solid, wood or metal under the damp wrapping. My name was written in smooth ink across the front.

"Sure, no problem. You have some place I could open this with a little privacy?"

"Certainly, sir." His eyes twitched, delighted for a little intrigue. "This way, sir."

THE ROOM HE led me to was empty except for a dusty old table and a window without drapes. Lot of empty rooms in this place. He shut the door and I set the lock before putting the package on the table.

The paper was damp, had been much wetter at some point and had time to dry. The ink of my name was a little blotted. It fit with the story, that this had arrived on the last zep up.

I cut the twine with my pocket knife and unwrapped the paper. Inside was a well-kept wooden box, with a hinge and a clasp that was made for locking but was presently unsecured. There was no note. A small steel plaque in the middle of the lid was blank. I opened the box. The interior was velvet-lined and custom built to hold a pistol. It was a Corps service revolver, intricately decorated with brass engravings. There were a dozen shells, each held individually in velvet notches beside the weapon. I picked it up and examined the chamber. Five shells were loaded, one chamber was empty. I closed the chamber. The handle felt very cold and slightly wet, as though the mechanism had been over-oiled. Across the barrel was engraved the pistol's provenance. It read **FCL GLORY OF DAY**.

It was the pistol from the crash, the pistol I had used to shoot Marcus, retrieved from the river. I stared at it in dull shock, then loaded the empty chamber, pocketed the extra shells and closed the box.

Who had sent it? That guy, the one who had jumped at the last second? Was that really him, out there on the stage, dressed as an Artificer? Everyone else was dead, weren't they? Had he seen me shoot Marcus? And what the fuck did this mean, sending me a pistol in a box?

I crossed to the window, cranked it open and squinted into the storm. The sky was tremendously loud, hammering into the room with a demon's roar. I hurled the box and its wrapping out the window, down the cliff and away. Then I closed the window, unlocked the door and went out. I needed a towel, and a drink, and a deal. And while I was at it, I was going to have a little talk with shifty blue eyes. Maybe the pistol would come in handy after all.

I SAT AT the bar and thought about the gun, about what it might mean. Was there another survivor from the ship, part of the crew who had seen me shoot Marcus? If so, what would they care? He was responsible for the crash, he was dying from that belly wound... it didn't make sense. And if there were other survivors, where had they recuperated, and why were they revealing themselves now, and in this manner? And how had they gotten the gun? I had lost it in the crash, assumed that it had gone down with the *Glory* to the bottom of the Reine. I had trouble believing that guy had survived his jump. It had been a long way down, and the Reine was a cold, dark river.

But if it wasn't a survivor, then who? I had been out for days after they'd dredged me out of the Reine. I didn't remember that time, other than a few brief glimpses of white walls and machinery. I might have talked. I might have said anything while the fever in my blood burned through me, repairing me, consuming and re-creating me.

There were people who lived in the river, of course. People might not be the right word. The Fehn, we called them. Some of the folks who disappeared under the Reine's black surface came back later, breathing water and gurgling worms, talking like they had been gone a thousand years, had seen the foundation of the city, and were coming back. I had a friend down there, a Wright of the Church. Old friend of the family. Maybe I should ask him.

Who would have cause and opportunity? That's where to start. Not many people knew I was here. Lady Tomb, obviously. Prescott, and whatever connections he might have. Valentine and Emily.

My first thought was Tomb. The package had appeared shortly after our conversation. She could have given it to the butler to give to me. That would explain her sudden insistence on letting me stay, if she was going to plant some kind of evidence or accuse me of a crime. She might have arranged it in anticipation of the meeting going badly. But what did she know about the events on the *Glory*?

Valentine? This mission had come from him, originally, so he obviously knew I was here. And he was fond of cryptic messages. The man was a puzzle himself, and he liked putting his people in difficult situations, to test them. Made for a tight organization. But again, I could see no purpose behind it, nor how it would be tied to the *Glory*. I wasn't getting anywhere.

None of it made any sense. If it was a threat, either from some hidden survivor, or Tomb, or gods forbid Valentine, it was too obscure for me. If it was a clue, again, I wasn't even aware that there was a puzzle. Too many things about tonight's deal didn't line up, and the more pieces I stumbled across, the worse things got.

If I'd talked about shooting Marcus while I was recovering, anyone might know it. Maybe not the specifics, but enough to know that producing a service revolver from the dead ship would rattle me. But whichever way I thought about it, everything came back to the last flight of the *Glory of Day*.

Which meant it had something to do with that artifact Cog. Right? That made sense, more than anything else tonight. The Cog. I'd left it with Emily, down in Veridon, and now I was worried about her, concerned that I'd exposed her to some danger without realizing. I stood up from the bar, took my drink and walked around the hall without talking, without even seeing. I kept a hand on the pistol in my jacket pocket, running my finger over the cool metal of the engraving on the handle. Nothing I could do, right now, and I didn't like that. I preferred active solutions to passive responses. The fastest way down the mountain was to just sit here and wait for the weather to clear. Unless I stole a carriage from the Tomb livery. Surely they'd have a garage. I stood by the fire and thought about that one, hard, weighing the anger that would earn me from Angela and her family against the perceived danger to Emily.

I didn't really know there was anything actively dangerous going on, did I? Might just be a coincidence that guy looked like one of my dead fellow passengers. And whatever relationship was forming between the Family Tomb and Valentine's organization was fragile. Borrowing a carriage could tip that balance, which could put me in a world of trouble with Valentine, trouble I didn't need.

I discarded that idea, got another drink and found a quiet corner near the windows, thought about the peril Emily might be in.

Who knew that I had given the Cog to Emily? No one. Who even knew that I had it? Marcus? He was shot, burned up, crashed and drowned. But someone knew, the pistol in my pocket said that clearly enough. And if they knew that… it was no good. Sitting here, all I could do was worry and drink, and that wasn't solving anything. Best to not worry, then. Probably best to not drink, either. Still had a deal to do.

I found Prescott with a tangle of other officers near the fireplace. I found an appropriate room, one with doors that led to the Great Hall as well as the service corridors that ran down the spine of the house, then spoke to one of the hiregirls Tomb had brought in from the local village. When the girl brought Prescott in a few minutes later I showed her to the other door and gave her twenty crown.

"Anybody see you?" I asked once the girl had left.

"Of course they did. She was insistent and rude." He adjusted the cuffs of his coat. Looked like the girl had dragged him in. "You have the drugs?"

"I have no idea," I said, and handed him the envelope. He sniffed the paper and grimaced. He disappeared it, produced another envelope and handed it to me. Felt like paper, folded over and over again. I put it away, next to the pistol.

"You aren't going to check it?"

I shrugged. "People don't cheat Valentine. Smart people, at least."

"Well. I suppose not. We're done here?" He motioned to the door. I shook my head.

"You're with a whore. Give it a little time, unless you want everyone making fun of you."

He frowned, then sat on the bed, folding his hands across his knees. "You're new. Never worked with you before."

"No, I'm not. But you've never worked with me because this isn't my usual thing." I put my hands in my pockets and leaned against the wall opposite the bed.

"Drugs?"

"Talking to people." I grinned.

He shifted uncomfortably and looked away. We sat like that for a minute, long enough that he was on edge.

"What do you know about five bullets in a gun? Five bullets and an empty chamber?" He jumped, but not in the way I was hoping.

"Sorry, I don't understand. Is that some kind of threat?"

"Twice tonight, people have asked me that. Twice. All the years I've been doing this, you think people would know when I'm making a threat."

"So... so it's a threat."

I sighed and flipped my hand at the door. "Long enough. Get out of here, Register." He nodded sharply and got out. I locked the door behind him, in case some other affectionate couple thought about using the room immediately. Wanted a few minutes before I returned to the hall. I had just turned from the door when the knob rattled, very quietly. Someone trying to open the door without making a racket.

Drawing the pistol, I turned and backed to the other door, the one that led to the service corridors. I opened it as quietly as I could and stepped inside. This hallway was plain and warm, but the floor was thickly carpeted to allow butlers and maids to slip through the house without bothering their betters. There was no one around at the moment, so I pulled the door nearly closed and waited.

Whoever was trying to get in was insistent. When the door didn't immediately open they hesitated. A second later there was a scratching sound, and the knob began to hum. That was a keygear, tumbling the lock hard. These doors weren't made to withstand that kind of attention and it popped in no time.

The door slid open, just a little, just enough to reveal a sliver of face and an eye, cloud blue. His hand rested on the doorknob. The cuff was dark blue; an Artificer's cuff. He looked around the room, saw that it was empty, and disappeared. I stayed long enough to see an officer enter a minute later, each arm around a girl. I left them to it, pocketed the pistol and crept down the service corridor, eventually returning to the hall by way of the kitchens.

I made a slow circuit of the main hall, looking for my light-eyed admirer. Most folks were milling about, talking in tight clusters or roaring drunkenly at the bar. The Corpsmen were the worst off; the night was in honor of a dead zep, after all. They were nervous, and making up for it with drink and song. I understood. I had spent a fair amount of time lost in drink. Less song, but that was my merciful side showing.

He was nowhere to be seen. There was no one in an Artificer's uniform anywhere in the room. I thought he might have dumped the outfit, so I paid close attention to people's eyes. That almost started a couple fights. I still came up empty, and now the night was winding down, drunks wandering off to their rooms and servants scurrying about to clear the detritus.

"Councilor Burn, is it?" A voice behind me asked.

I turned. There was a man standing against the wall, a glass of whiskey in his hand. The ice in his drink had melted and separated, the thin amber of the liquor at the bottom, water at the top of the glass. The man's suit was impeccably tailored; all black, with velvet cuffs and links of silver polished white. It was civilian garb, but he held himself with military precision. His eyes were dark and his head was bald. When he smiled it was without emotion; it was like watching a puppet smile.

"I am not," I said. "Though my father holds that title. And you are?"

"Apologies, sir." He tipped his head and offered a hand. He was wearing thin leather gloves, soft as a lady's cheek. We shook. There was surprising power in his grip. "I am Malcolm Sloane. Your father may have spoken of me? No?" he said, without waiting for a reaction. "Perhaps not. But we are acquainted. You must be his son, then. Jacob. The interesting one."

I adjusted my coat, flashed a bit of the pistol, enough to let him know he was talking on unfriendly ground. His smile became genuine.

"My. Yes. Interesting one, indeed. I must say, Mr. Jacob, I'm surprised to see you here."

"I was invited."

"Of course. I mean, just," he waved his hand at all the people around us, most of them in uniform. "You're not a very popular man with the Corps. You don't worry about that?"

"I should worry?" I asked.

"Well, I mean. A lot of young recruits, all of them drinking. You aren't worried that one of them will drink a bit much. Talk too much, maybe dare too much? Try to start a fight."

I snorted. "Fights start sometimes. I can handle myself."

"Oh, I have no doubt. Still. It's something to think about." He smiled coldly and looked out at the crowd. "Maybe you're right. Maybe none of them have the balls." He said that word strangely, like a very proper man trying to swear to fit in with the rough crowd. "But maybe they do something cowardly, hm? In the dead of night. A gun." He turned back to me. "You are, after all, a very unpopular man."

"How did you say you knew my dad?"

"Acquaintances. Old acquaintances. So." He set down the glass of liquor and patted my arm. "Just be careful, Mr. Jacob Burn. There are some desperate people here, I think. Ah," his eyes narrowed as he looked across the room. "You'll pardon me."

I turned to see where he was looking. Angela Tomb was making her way through the partygoers, trying to wrap things up for the night. When I turned back the strange Mr. Sloane was gone.

I sighed and finished my drink, then found Harold and plucked at his sleeve.

"Sir?" he asked.

"Those Guildsmen, the Artificers. Did they already head home?"

"No, sir. They've been made comfortable."

"Where?"

"Sir?"

"Where are they staying? What room?"

"The, uh. The entertainment, sir, does not usually mingle with the guests."

"Just tell me what room, okay?" I slipped the only hard currency I had brought with me into his palm. "Let's just say I'm a curious guy."

"Of course, sir. They are housed in the servants' quarters, near the zepdock."

"Stairs down somewhere?"

"Near the kitchens, sir. Just this side of the theater."

"Thanks." I cuffed him on the shoulder, then headed to my room. Didn't want to look too anxious.

THE STORM KEPT going, maybe even got worse. Angela had given me a third floor room with a window. Not a benefit on a night like this. The room had been closed up all winter, only opened hours earlier by the servants. The air was stale, and the sheets smelled like dust and cobwebs. The heavy curtains gusted with the storm outside, evidence of drafts in the old walls.

I lay in bed, fully clothed, until I figured everyone else was asleep or passed out. I took the pistol out from where I'd hidden it, checked the load again, then snuck out into the hall.

The lights in the hallway were dimmed. The carpet swallowed my footsteps as I crept downstairs. I got down to the servants corridors without anyone seeing me. It was quiet down there too, and dark. No windows out, just cold stone floors and wood paneling. I crept along, quiet as a cat. There were a lot of doors down here. Perhaps I could have gotten a little more detail out of Harold for my money.

I didn't have to look long. They left the lights on, and their door open. It was around a corner from the main stairs, away from the rest of the servants. Not unusual... people got nervous around Artificers. All those bugs and their history of heresy. I came around the corner and smelled it, that heat-stink of fear and shit, like a slaughterhouse. I took out the pistol and thumbed the hammer up.

They were dead. It happened quietly, no mess, no fuss. They had been sleeping, the Guildsmen all in one room on tiny bunks. The master was in a different room off to one side. Each had a stab wound, straight into the heart. I didn't check them all. I got the idea, after the first couple. There was another room, opposite the master's bed, where the Summer Girl had slept, probably. She was gone. Signs of a struggle in here, piss on the floor, some blood on a broken bottle. She had swung at her attacker. Probably woke up while her keepers had been breathing their last. Tried to defend herself. Where was she now? And why kill all these folks? Not like it was self-defense.

I went back into the main room. It smelled in here, more than it should. I went back to the tidy bodies, checking each one. It was the fourth one. He'd been dead for a while, maybe two weeks. And he wasn't an Artificer.

His bloated chest strained against the buttons of his military jacket. Square cut, the cuffs braided in the traditional knots of the Air Corps. But he wasn't a Pilot. Patches were torn off his sleeve and chest, the threads dangling. His buttons were iron and stamped in the double fists of the Marines. Assault trooper. Heavily modded, his bones and organs sheathed in metal cuffs, iron plates welded just beneath the skin. A little engine so he could walk longer, march harder, fight until the bullets ran out. What was he doing here? And why had the Guildsmen been lugging around a two-week old dead body?

I stuck my hand into his jacket pocket, fished around. Bits and bobs, dirt, some pictures of a girlfriend or something. Finally, an ID card. Not the slickest murderer, whoever had done him. Took the time to strip his jacket of unit patches, but left his ID card in his pocket. Sergeant Wellons. The card was worn and dirty, the edges ragged like a favorite book. I didn't recognize the unit, and he listed no ship. Maybe a garrison assignment, somewhere? Still. I pocketed it and left.

I was getting a little worried about Harold. People were going to find these bodies; people were going to ask questions. Eventually Harold was going to say something about how I was asking where the Artificers were staying, and then maybe people would be coming to ask me questions. I would have to have a word with Harold. Clear things up, before they could get messy. But first, I had to find out where my friend was. Why he'd killed these nice people, and what he wanted with me.

Wasn't Prescott a Register? Yeah, he was in charge of unit assignments and personnel. He might know this Wellons guy. Might at least be able to find out where he was stationed. Seemed like a golden opportunity. I'd drop by Prescott's room, give him the ID card and a way to contact me, and I'd go and find Harold. Then I'd find my friend, and we'd straighten out our differences. Prescott was somewhere near the main hall, probably near my own room.

I found it, sure enough. Again, his was the open door. This time there was more blood. Plenty more. The window to his room was open, too, and the storm was gusting in. I went in and shut the door, then secured the window. His tablelamp was humming quietly, next to an upturned book of erotic poetry.

Prescott was sprawled across his bed, his fingers curled around a gun belt that still held the pistol, peace-locked in place. I pushed him over carefully. His ribs grinned up at me. I let him settle back onto the bed. There was blood all over the floor, thinned out by the rain that had blown in the window. Blotchy footprints circled the bed, but the wind and rain had disfigured them significantly. The mess was all over my feet.

I was seriously freaked. I didn't want to talk to Harold, didn't want to find my creepy friend. I wanted to get the fuck out of this house and down the mountain back to Veridon. Nobody heard anything? It happened fast. A lot of drunks in the rooms around us, but still. Whoever killed Prescott had done it quick, and quiet. I wiped my feet carefully on Prescott's bed sheets, turned off his light, and then snuck out into the hall. Back to my room, so I could collect my coat and the stuff Prescott had given to me to deliver to Valentine. I was going back to town, even if it meant walking.

I almost got to my room before I ran into the guards. I ducked into a draped windowsill, just deep enough to hide me if I held my breath and thought skinny thoughts. They were sneaking up to my room. Ten of them, maybe more, with rifles and truncheons. They were Tomb House Guards.

They settled around the door to my room, checked the loads on their guns, then nodded among themselves. One of them, a sergeant, stepped forward and pounded on my door.

"Master Burn! By the authority of the Council of Veridon, spoken for by the Lady Tomb, we have a warrant for your arrest and detention. Please open the door!"

He waited half a breath, then put his shoulder into the door. I hadn't locked it when I left, and it burst open. I got a good view of my empty room. They milled about in the entrance, poking their rifles at the bed and under the covers, talking loudly. I started to go. Something caught my eye.

There was a sudden hard scrabble against my window, like hail or teeth on a water glass. I watched the window burst. The storm disappeared, to be replaced by a complexity of darkness and metal. There was a man standing, or nearly a man. His clothes were sodden and torn, the skin beneath like a dead man's skin, ivory and shot through with black veins. He had one hand on the sill, jagged glass snagging the flesh, and one of his feet was already in the room. Behind him flat planes of oiled metal shifted and ruffled, shiny leaves flexing against the buffeting winds. Wings. He had wings of coiling metal.

He came into the room, clenching his wings to fit through the window. Wet hair hung in ringlets around his face, a jaw line like a storm front, lips and skin that were porcelain smooth. And his eyes, blue so light that it looked like the thinnest clouds over sky.

The guards panicked. They fell back before him, rifles raised, yelling. He ignored them. He looked out the door into the hallway. Right at me.

"You are Jacob Burn," he said. His voice was a trick, tiny pistons and valves pushing air through the long hissing whisper of organ pipes. I raised the pistol and fired over the heads of the guards. The report was enormous; it filled the hallway with sharp smoke. The shot went into his chest, and my second took him just below the throat. He winced, bent forward like he'd been punched. When he straightened again his face was smooth. He raised a hand and it flickered, skin and bone shuffling away in a lethal origami, replaced by smooth, sharp metal. His arm became a knife. There was already blood on it.

The guards looked at me. Some of them turned to make that arrest they were talking about earlier. The rest kept their eyes on the angel. The close ones crowded around me, trying to keep me boxed in.

"Gentlemen," I said tensely and dived into their ranks. "Pardon."

They reached for me, would have taken me but the Angel crashed through after me. Two of them fell, their bones cracking like fireworks as he tore through them. There was shouting and I ran.

I took the first stairway, even though it led up and every exit was down. Panic. The next floor was closed, but I popped the door. It was quiet here, smelled like mold and linen. Footsteps hammered on the floor below, crowds mustering to the disaster. There was gunfire and the dreadful sound of bodies snapping. I walked quietly to a bedroom and slipped inside.

The room was empty, just a heavily worn rug and a window. The storm continued. The sounds of fighting had slowed, though they may have been masked by the wind and rain at my back. I knelt and fumbled two new shells into the revolver. I stayed there, breathing hard. It was quiet now, just the rain pounding the glass. I shifted to be able to watch both the window and the door.

I looked down at the gun. Had he sent it? He was on the zep, he might have known about Marcus. But if he intended to attack me, why arm me? Then again, the shot didn't seem to hurt him. I checked the cylinder, to see if the rounds that had been loaded were tricks, some kind of stagecraft mummery. I emptied them into my palm, turned them over with my thumb as I examined them in the dim light from the window. The dull brass cylinders looked real enough.

There was a rattling in the hallway. I caught my breath, and started reloading the gun as quietly as I could, the bullets slippery in my sweaty fingers as I struggled to slot them home. Footsteps, and the dry-leaf scraping of his wings on the walls and ceiling. I looked up, saw that I had forgotten to lock the door and dropped a bullet. I scooped it up, dumped the whole handful of loose shells and the revolver into my jacket pocket and ran to the window. He was outside the door, and the window was storm bolted.

I threw my shoulder against it and the glass splintered, the lead panes bending like a net. Again and a couple panes snapped, slicing my coat and my skin. He opened the door smoothly and hurtled in. I hit the window, he hit me, and we both burst out into the storm.

Tumbling down the slate roof, I kicked out and made a lucky hit. We separated and I hooked my arm around a chimney. There was blood leaking out of me, damage from the window and whatever brief contact there had been with the angel's wicked arm. I scrambled, trying to find him, finding nothing but the roaring storm. Something was wrong with my shoulder, and I felt my grip going away. A flash of lightning and I saw wings, diving. I let go.

I slithered down the roof, just clearing the chimney as he hit it. There was a dull thud above me. Splinters of slate shot past and the roof shook. I dug fingers into the flooding shingles, slapped at chimneys as they flew past. A bump and I was over the edge. I was falling and screaming the shredded air from my lungs. As I fell into a crash my legs collapsing and then something popped and became a rain of glass and more blood and tearing and falling.

I ended up in the Great Hall. I was bleeding red and black, the oil of my deepest heart mingling with my common blood. High above I could see the fractured skylight and a thin column of rain coming through. There were wings crouching, flashing past. He started to come through, unfolding as he emerged.

I stood. There was a lot of business at the other end of the room, a lot of voices and movement. Most of the Corpsmen were there, standing by a hastily constructed barricade that cut off the wing that held my former room. They were variously dressed and armed, very drunk men in pajamas wielding hunting rifles and croquet mallets. When they saw me, several of them formed a firing line. They couldn't see what was above, what was coming down.

Just a flash, but I saw several Councilors standing nearby, their faces cold and terrified. Angela stood with them, still in her complicated dress, her knuckles white across the barrel of a shotgun. She looked at me and blanched. The Corpsmen were getting closer.

"What did you summon, Jacob Burn?" Lady Tomb yelled, her voice shrill. "What darkness followed you into my house?"

I shot a look at the Corpsmen and their rifles, then up at the angel. He was almost through, his wings unfolding to descend. I couldn't see his face or his body, just the swirling mass of wings. I jumped, hit the balcony door and rolled outside. My bones were screaming with pain. Maybe I was screaming too.

I kept my eyes up, but the rain was too much. I couldn't see anything, not even the roof. I stumbled across the deck until my hand brushed the rough stone of the railing. I crouched and started to follow it. For now I just wanted to get away from the main house. Whatever the thing hunting me might be, I'd rather face it alone than worry about getting shot in the back by some sloshed Corpsman.

I turned to look at the house. The glass windows looked like a fogged aquarium, little more than shapes moving across the bright field of the Manor Tomb. As I watched a form fell from the ceiling, spreading out as it descended into the Great Hall. The Angel. The storm swallowed any sound, but there was a staccato brightness, gunshots, and tiny cracks appeared in the window. I was up and running, found the stairs to a lower balcony. They were narrow, with a small gate separating them from the balcony. I vaulted and clattered down the steps. Maybe the Corps and their rifles could manage the angel. Maybe not, but at least they'd buy me some time.

The central window shattered outward, spilling glittering glass and light out onto the balcony. A dark figure scurried out, disappearing into shadows. A line of Corpsmen appeared, bristling with rifles. They began to drag furniture and torchieres into the Manor's newest entrance, shining light into the storm.

I kept moving. These stairs were rickety, clearly not meant for running down in the rain. The ground fell away below me, and I got the feeling I was moving between terraces. I lost sight of the Manor, though I could hear voices yelling out into the darkness. They hadn't finished the thing, that's for sure. It was still out here. I was shivering with damp and adrenaline.

The stairs led to a small ledge, with a shed and a steep set of stairs leading down. A maintenance area of some kind. I kicked open the shed door and went inside. It was a gardener's storage shed, all right. A tiny frictionlamp clicked on as I opened the door, the mainspring sparking up. The light glittered off a wall full of tools, blades and shovels and spikes. I doused the light and took a hammer, then went back outside. I had just started on a downward stair when the thing landed, impacting the ledge hard. I froze, the hammer in my hand. Without looking at me, he rushed the shed, tore it apart. In the noise I clambered down, falling as I went. I ended up in the broad garden I had visited earlier that night. I ran for the path that had brought me here the first time.

The lawn was very wet, a spongy green plain. Up the hill I could see broken light from the Manor, wondered if the Corps would venture out into the dark to hunt me or help me. Plenty of people in that room wouldn't mind seeing me dead, people who might take advantage of the current chaos to put me down. I looked up at the sky, found a trace of moon among the jagged clouds. The storm was breaking down the valley, though rain still fell hard on the Heights.

He was waiting at the broad stone path that snaked up to the balcony above. I had the pistol in my left hand, the hammer in my right. I thought about running, but his wings were clenching and unclenching above his shoulders, like a giant fist waiting to strike me down. He looked at the pistol and shrugged. I raised the hammer.

"You are Jacob Burn," he said.

"Yes." Water was streaming down my face. The flooded lawn was reaching muddy fingers between my toes. I felt ridiculous and cold, and I was too tired for a game of question and answer. "And you?"

"They are looking, Jacob Burn. They are waiting for you."

"Who is?" I gestured with the pistol. "Is that what this is? Some kind of warning?"

He shook his head, slowly, once. He reached across the space between us, stepping forward until his open hand was near my heart.

"Give it to me, and this will end. I thought the man Marcus was the end of the chain, but it has come to you."

I listened to the rain hammering against my shoulders, watched it form a puddle in the shallow cup of his palm. The artifact, the Cog, sitting on Emily's desk.

"I don't have it."

"Who does?"

I smirked and shrugged. "Beats me."

"Yes," he said, gathering my collar in his fist. "It does."

I swung the hammer in a short, tight arc, keeping my elbow bent. The metal head buried into his temple. His hand fell from my coat, and he staggered backwards. I raised the pistol and got two shots off, pounding slugs into his right shoulder, before he lunged at me. We rolled across the lawn, hydroplaning on the grass, ending up side by side. I lost the pistol.

He screamed and came to his knees. It was an inhuman sound, a boiler bursting, metal torquing. His face was shattered in pain. He raised an arm and hidden mechanisms whirred, the hand folding and collapsing. I didn't give him the chance. I brought the hammer around, swinging wide, smashing at his wrist and knuckles again and again. Metal popped and bent, gears and pistons tearing apart as axles came out of alignment and tore the machine apart. Then something else broke, meat cracking under the hammer and his hand hung limply at an awkward angle. His scream changed, pitching through agony and frustration into animal terror. He put his other hand on me, but I elbowed it aside then drove the hammer's claw into his cheek. There was blood and bone, his skin came off in lumps that hit the wet ground and scurried away.

Shocked, I backed away. Half its face had crumbled, but there was something else behind it, pale white and bleeding. He threw himself at me, clubbing me with the ruined stump of his arm, the iron fingers of his other hand around my throat. I fell backwards. Twisting, I was able to get the hammer hooked against his chest. There was resistance, then blood, and I flung him over me. I struggled to my knees, gasping for air. When I looked up, he was throwing himself at me again, the wings beating and flailing, falling apart as he rushed me. I met him with the hammer, again and again, stumbling backwards as I struck, just staying out of reach of his hand, the whirring bloody machine of his stump, the hammer arcing back and forth, head then claw, head then claw, each blow hard and wet with gore.

The end was sudden, like a light being switched off. He fell to his knees, then his hands. His whole body seemed to pour off him. A glittering tide plunked into the water of the drowned lawn and swept out, tiny smooth shells like a ripple in a pond. When they had scurried away, they left behind a body, a girl. I turned her over with the hammer's claw, red blood smearing across her white dress. It was the Summer Girl, the performer, her mouth open. The delicate machines of her mouth were clenching in the rain.

I fished out my pistol and headed back to the Manor. The lights were still on, the Corpsmen running around shouting and pointing rifles. I snuck along the side and went to the carriage house. I stole one of the

Tomb's cogdriven carriages and crashed the gate, rumbling down the road, the long way to Veridon.

Chapter Four
Survive or You Don't

I TOOK THE carriage to Toth and left it in a stable under the Tomb family name. It was still raining when I got to the Soldier's Gate and my clothes were soaked through. The blood and oil had stopped leaking from my chest, but my heart had developed an awkward grind that I could feel in my teeth. Dawn was still an hour away, though the city's earliest and latest denizens were already on the streets.

I finally pried the hammer out of my cold-stiff fingers and left it in a gutter by the Bellingrow, then caught a ride on the pneumatic rail that circled the city's core. I ignored the stares of the factory boys and businessmen, took a seat on the pneumatic and rested my head against the glass as we tore over the city, the car rocking around the corners. The pipe that ran between the tracks breathed in loud gasping sighs of steam and heat as we ripped along. Below us the city dropped away as we went over the terraces. The farther we got from the Bellingrow, the newer the buildings. Everything smelled like fire and energy, up here in the ambitious orbits of Veridon.

My mind was numb. A storm of concern gathered around my temples, but I couldn't get through it yet. The Corps would be looking for me, asking questions about Prescott and the angel. Whoever sent the Summer Girl too, whoever had burned a killer's pattern into her head and remade her body into a weapon out of myth. The gun must also lead somewhere, must have someone behind it. There were a lot of troubles rising out of the *Glory*'s wreckage.

The storm was still tearing up the sky when the pneu, let me off at the Torchlight extension. I walked the Bridge District, bought some kettle soup and ate it as I went. I felt thin, like the night's trouble had calved me over and over, leaving splinters of me behind with each step. My remnants drifted up into the Torchlight.

While I walked I fished the ID card out of my pocket. Wellons peered up at me, clean shaven, young. It was hard to match that with the overripe face I had seen up on the Heights. No matter. Someone must know who he was, and how he got into the Tomb's summer estate. I put the card away and thought about it. Calvin, maybe? Would he be up yet?

Calvin's place was an off-base barracks, really, an apartment block that the Corps hired to keep all the senior staff that it couldn't stuff inside the walls of the fort. The building was old clapboard, thin planks peeling away from their nails, stains and pitch leaking down their warped sides. Nothing's too good for the Corps.

Staying close to people like Calvin was why I kept my room on the Torch'. My contacts in the Corps were really all I had. That and a good name, but they could only get you so far. There was a guy out front, a guard, but he knew me. We smirked at each other, as I went inside. Calvin wasn't up, at least not before I started pounding on his door. He opened it eventually, wearing his dress coat and little else.

"You look like shit," he mumbled.

"You look like an ensign who's been fucking sheep all night. Let me in, Cal."

We went way back. Academy together. Expelled, for completely different reasons, together. I think Cal blamed me at some karmic level for his own fall from the ranks of Pilot. He had settled into a desk job, and I had settled into a life of crime. We both had our moments of envy, but we got along well for all that.

"Fair enough," he said, and let me in. His room was a mess, but inspections outside the walls of the fort were infrequent. I sat on most of a chair while he spun up a tiny frictionlamp and scrounged up a largely empty bottle of rum.

"What's eating Jacob Burn, at this hour? Unless this is a social call?" he asked, tipping the bottle my way. I shook my head.

"What are you into these days, Cal?"

"Debt," he said with a smile. "And loose women. Less often than I'd like."

"I mean professionally. Last we talked about work, you were overseeing requisitions for the downfalls campaign."

"So, not a social call at all," he said. He looked a little glum. "You never come around anymore, just to chat."

"It's because I no longer love you, Calvin. I'm in a very satisfying relationship with a signpost. Now, will you focus for a second and listen. What are you doing these days?"

"Why do you want to know?" he asked.

"There's someone I need to find. A marine by the name of Wellons. Need to know his last assignment, maybe where he is."

"Not a lot to go on. But," he stood up, finished the bottle and tossed it on his bed, then started looking for some pants. "I know where to look. What do you know about him?"

I produced the ID card. He peered at it, frowned, then distractedly put on his pants with one hand while holding the card up to his face with the other.

"This should say, shouldn't it? How'd you get his ID if you're looking for him? What'd he do, lose it?"

"Left it behind," I said. "At a girl's house. And now the father wants a word, you understand."

"Oh, well then, I don't think I could help you, Jacob. Got to protect my brothers from the angry fathers of the world."

"Just put on your pants, Cal. You can help me find him?"

"If he's on assignment, sure. I'm in the Registers now. Signing checks, balancing books."

"You know a guy named Prescott?" I asked.

"He's a twat."

"Well." I looked uncomfortably around the room. "He couldn't have been that bad."

"Says you. Now come on."

We went out his hall and down the road a bit. The Registers office was a diminutive brick building with uneven walls and tiny windows. Everyone seemed surprised to see Calvin so early. We went back to his tiny office and huddled around the desk while he flipped through ledgers and frowned nervously at balance sheets. Eventually, he pulled out a sheaf of loose assignment rosters and began shuffling through them.

"You know, Jacob, I think it's very odd that you're doing this sort of thing. Was she a friend of yours?"

"Who?"

"The girl. Wellons's little honey."

"Oh. No. I mean, her father and my father. Anyway. It's just a job."

"So you're getting paid for this? Well. I don't feel so bad, then."

"About what?"

He shrugged, rolled his eyes around the room. "Anyway. I just didn't think you were the type to hunt down lost lovers and such. I always thought you were doing, you know. More interesting stuff."

I sighed. "I have bills, too."

"Hm. Well, if you ever want a job with the Registers…"

"I'll let you know."

He chuckled, then plucked a sheet out and lay it on the desk. It was an oil stained parchment, a copy of the original document.

"I suppose this is it, then. Tell your father's friend hard luck."

"What?"

"He's dead." He ran his finger across a line on the sheet. Wellons's name, ID number, rank. Deceased, two years ago. I looked over the rest of the sheet.

"These people all died at once?" I asked.

"Yeah. Special assignment, whole team lost. Let's see… nothing about where or how. Just dead."

There were fifteen names on the list. Marcus was one of them.

"This guy, Marcus Pitts," I said, gesturing at the paper. "He wasn't a military guy."

"You knew him, too?"

"Yeah. I don't think he was in the service."

Calvin shrugged, looked over the paper. "Well, he died in the service."

"And there's nothing about what these guys were doing?"

"Nope. Special assignment. Probably running drugs or something morally negligible like that."

"Can I get a copy of this?" I asked.

"Absolutely not." Calvin took a pen and clean paper out of his desk, set it next to the deceased notice, and pushed them both towards me. "It is against regulations for any official document of this service to fall into the hands of civilians. Especially criminals like you, Jacob Burn."

"Thanks."

"Of course."

I started copying names, starting at the bottom, to see if there was anyone else in this special detachment that I recognized. I noticed the death notice was authenticated by good old Angela Tomb. None of the other names struck a bell. They were all sergeants, even Marcus. I stopped at the last name on the list. Coordinating officer. Captain Malcom Sloane.

The foyer to my building was quiet. The entryway was draped in layers of threadbare carpets, each one thinner and older and moldier than the one beneath. The paint on the walls cracked. Weather up on the Torch' was hard on architecture. It was hard on everything. The building creaked in the wind that would blow up the crags and howled into the too-close sky. Hard to sleep in this wind. People in my building came to bed drunk, or so tired that hell itself wouldn't keep them up.

Mostly zepdock folks lived here, managers or protocol officers who could afford the luxury of sleeping near work. This place was about as cheap as this district got, unless you were wearing the gray and had a barracks to flop.

The Torchlight had started as a tiny fort on the spit of rock just downriver of the city proper, a sentry post to watch the river. Time and market forces, along with the sudden dominance of the zepliner in the course of Veridon's ascendance, had made this real estate valuable. The Torch' had been absorbed into the city, connected by the wide avenue of the Bridge District. Space was at a premium, and expensive. This whole building was strapped precariously to the sheer cliffs of the Torchlight. The walls creaked in the wind, but the views were spectacular.

I stayed here for business. My money was in the docks, in the people I knew from my time in the Academy, people who hadn't washed out, people who were now officers and gentlemen of the line. For every Commodore who hated me, every instructor who wouldn't care if I washed up dead on the Reine, there were three old friends. That was my money; old friends and the tolerance that came with a

Founder's name and a father on the Council. Even a father I hadn't spoken to in five years.

Hadn't been enough to keep me safe last night, I thought as I eased into the foyer and checked my box. The carpet here smelled like river water had soaked it into mold. It smelled especially rank this morning, or maybe that was me. I walked up the creaky old staircase to my room on the third floor, near the end. I bolted it once I was inside, stripped and lay on the bed. That smell was definitely me. I wanted to sleep, but here wasn't safe. I probably shouldn't have even come here, now that I stopped to think. I'd just been running away from whatever had taken the Summer Girl, away from the Tomb Estate on the Heights and its complications. Whatever was going on up there, I was out of my league. All the way down the mountain I had thought about it, about the gun and the photo and that... thing. The Girl. I didn't know which one I had killed, the girl or the thing she had become. What the difference was, for that matter. And what any of it had to do with the *Glory of Day* and the artifact-cog. The Cog that I had left...

In Emily's apartment. I sat up sharply, remembered where I should have gone first. I stood up and started to pull on clothes. I must have slept, because I didn't hear the man outside my door until he was picking the lock.

I froze, one leg in my pants, the other in mid-air. My balls socketed themselves and I dropped my belt and quietly crept to my jacket and the gun. I got it out just as the door was opening.

It was Pedr, one of Valentine's runners. He was a short man, and thin, with a head that was a little too big and cheekbones that were so thin and sharp they looked artificial, like he had a trick skull that was coiled to spring through his pale skin. He saw me and dropped his lock pick.

"Oh. Oh, fuck," he said.

"Oh fuck indeed." I stood there glowering at him, not bothering to cover my nakedness or the pistol in my hand. He averted his eyes and tried to shuffle out. I pulled him into the room and shut the door. "What's happening, Pedr?"

"I just, I thought." He sat on the bed and clammed up. He twined his fingers in his lap, twisting the ends of his dirty cuffs over and over. I set the revolver on my tiny desk and resumed getting dressed.

"You thought." I finished with my pants and pulled out the most nondescript shirt I had. I watched him while I buttoned up. "What did you think, Pedr?"

"Nothing. Just that you'd be up at the Manor, still. Rain and all."

"Thought you'd roll my pad while I was on the boss's business?"

He winced, looked at me sidewise. Nodded.

"Okay. So, really," I sat next to him on the bed while I fixed my socks and pulled on my boots. "That's your story? Honestly? You were going to rob your boss's weapon of choice."

He looked down at his feet, twisted his cuffs. He might have nodded. "Sure."

"You're a little shit, Pedr, but you're not stupid." I stood up, took the gun and leaned casually against the hearth. "Who was it?"

He sat and squirmed and looked like he wasn't going to answer. I leaned forward and popped him across the jaw, just enough to knock him off the bed. Big head like his, it didn't take much force to put him off balance. He whimpered then scooted back up.

"Someone told you to break into my room, Pedr. If I search you, if I can hold my breath long enough, I'm going to find some money. A clean, shiny roll of crown that you haven't had a chance to filth up yet. Right? If that happens, if you don't talk and I have to search you, and I find that money, well. I'm going to get loud. I'm going to wake the neighbors up, breaking things over your goddamn head, until you do talk. Right?"

"That's not what I want, man."

"That's not what any of us want. My neighbors included. So let's sit here, and let's talk."

He snorted, rubbed his face and neck, then dug into his coat and threw a roll of coins onto the bed. A lot of coins.

"Keep it," he said. "I didn't know the guy."

I smiled and pushed the coins around on my bed with the barrel of the pistol. "Sure you didn't. But you saw him. That's where we're going to start."

Pedr shrugged. "Big guy. He was... he looked like something official." He glanced up at me. "Looked like money."

"Your money guy, was he in some kind of uniform?"

"No. No, but he looked like he could have filled a suit, you know. Like he'd be comfortable in uniform." His eyes found mine. "Kinda like you."

"Like me. And did he..." I stopped. There were footsteps on the stairs. They stopped outside my door. I whispered. "You expecting backup?"

Pedr's eyes were wide. He shook his head and squirmed up over the bed, standing up with his back against the far wall.

"Stay quiet." I stood by the door, behind it. Whoever was in the hall had stopped moving. I could hear him breathing. He had heard us talking, no question. He turned and started down the stairs, fast. When he was gone I turned back to Pedr.

"I'm about to throw you out there, man. With whoever that was. Sure there's nothing else you want to tell me?"

He blanched, but shook his head.

"Okay, well. Go get the hell out. And if you ever take money from someone who isn't the boss, to break into my place or follow me or anything. Well." I walked over and patted him on the shoulder. "I'm not going to do a damn thing. But I'm going to tell Valentine that he's got rats in the walls, and we'll just see what he does."

"Sure," he said. "Sure thing, Jake."

"Sure thing. Now go."

He left fast, scooping up the money from my bed as he went. I listened to him clatter down the stairs. I hadn't gotten all the answers I wanted, but there was only so much he'd know. People like Pedr make a living out of not knowing, not seeing; just take the money, do the job, forget about it. I understood. I finished dressing, tucked the *Glory* revolver into my shoulder harness and went out.

THEY FOUND ME on the Pauper's Bridge, two of them. There was a third, up ahead, who tagged me when I tried to run. They were Valentine's boys, people I knew. They didn't act too familiar.

Coming out of my building, I looked up at a clear morning sky. The storm had finally passed, and the zepdocks were busy. Had one of the ships gliding above me carried word from the Heights, or was it still storming at the higher elevations? Couldn't tell from here. I was still thinking about that when I made my tail, shortly after I joined the traffic on the Pauper's. Big guy in an old suit, too formal for morning traffic, but the suit was too ratty to mark him as money. An affectation. I hated strong boys who played dress up. I made the second guy five steps later, loitering not ten feet behind the first. Playing too close. Wanted to be seen, maybe. He was in the same get up, black vest suit that was going gray at the cuffs, too many watch chains and monocle clasps.

The Orrey boys. Following me, acting like they didn't see me ten feet away, when I had dinner with them the day before my little trip downfalls. Imagine that.

Thing is, the boys had chosen their spot well. Pauper's is just a big bridge, despite all the shops and cartstands along the way. No alleys to duck down, no sideroads to loop through. One way in, one way out, and a fifty foot drop into the Ebd river below. The whole place groaned underfoot; a tangle of chains and wooden arches kept the place up. It wasn't safe, but it wasn't going to fall down today. There were crowds, but the boys weren't trying to stay hidden at all, so there was no way I was going to get enough people between us to lose them.

I took the only out I had. I ran. I put my elbows into the crowd and crawled my way through. The boys stayed on me, not hurrying up. They spread out, in case I tried to double back, but they didn't try to keep up. Still didn't look at me, either. It was like they didn't care if they lost me once I got to the end of the bridge.

I looked forward, forgetting the boys. If they didn't care what happened once I got off the bridge, it could only mean that I wasn't getting off the bridge. I saw the trap, a guy in front, waiting. Not someone I knew. He wasn't as big, but his coat fell unnaturally over his shoulders. I drifted right and he drifted with me, like he was a kite on a string. He was going a little slower than me, getting closer with each step. I slowed down hard, nearly stopping. The guy behind me stumbled into my back, fell on his ass. Whatever the guy had been carrying, a bag or basket of fruit, scattered and rolled in oblong patterns down the cobbles. He was swearing as he stood, but the tail to my front was having similar problems. An old lady had dropped a jar of coffee and was yelling at the tough's unturned back. I shot forward and to the side, my fingers brushing the pistol in my coat as I passed him. I risked a look over. Under his coat there was a lot of metal and the tiny whirling dance of gears and flywheels. He looked up at me, unconcerned, his eyes dead stone pits. I pushed hard on the crowd and broke into a lull in the traffic, an open courtyard between rivers of pedestrians. I dashed across, squeezed between a sausage vendor and a closed stall and got off the bridge.

Fourth guy. He put a hand on my chest, the palm wide, his other arm hidden behind him. He looked me right in the eye and smiled.

"Burn. Where you headed?" He said. It was Cacher. Friend of Emily. Good friend.

"I don't know, Cacher." I looked back to see the Orrey boys and the metal guy amble up. "Where am I headed?"

It wasn't one of the quayside warehouses, so that was okay. Whatever was going on, it wasn't that bad. The third guy kept really close, his eyes dead. Other than Valentine, this guy was the most metal I'd ever seen. His face was a steel plate, the eyes pitted ball bearings that looked like river stones. However he saw, it wasn't the way I did. Just his jaw and teeth were original issue. When his coat flipped aside there was more, a plain of tiny gears spinning through their cycles. Most of it was probably just for show, but I made a note to never gut-punch this guy. Probably lose my knuckles in the grind. He kept those dead eyes on me.

The others were real casual, like we were buddies out for a walk. Hell, we were buddies, of a sort. I didn't always like to be around Cacher when Emily was in the room, but we all got along well enough.

"Boss could have just arranged a meeting," I said. "My appointment book is open."

"I figure he just did, Burn," Cacher said. He grinned. His teeth were lined in black gunk, drippings from the cassiopia he had tucked into his cheek. "An urgent meeting, I figure."

"Fair enough. Still." I shrugged. They had taken my gun, chuckled as they read the inscription on the service piece. "Coulda been more direct about it. You make me feel like I did something."

"Well," Cacher sighed. "Well, we'll see. We'll let the boss talk that out for you."

"Sure."

I was still on edge from last night, tired and wired and itchy to find Emily and that damned Cog. That could be it, though. Em could have gotten the Cog to Valentine, and maybe Valentine wanted to talk about it. Maybe. Not sure why that warranted an armed escort, though.

They led me to a quiet street on the River Road, the wooden sidewalk under our feet echoing hollowly. We stopped at a house, literally just stopped. Cacher and the other boys leaned against the yard post and lost interest in me. The street crowd was lean, just businessmen who didn't have to keep a clock, going off to work on their own time. The house was nice, a neat little breadbox place with clean paint and windows that looked into a tidy sitting room. It could have been situated on the country road to Toth, rather than crowded up against a dozen rowhouses, blocks from the river Reine. I saw someone move, just a flicker behind the curtains and then the room was empty again. I looked around at Cacher.

"I'm supposed to go in?"

He ignored me. I went in. The inside of the house was just as neat and clean as the outside. The wooden floors hardly creaked, the heirloom furniture was polished, and the upholstery was so sharp and uniform that it looked uncomfortable. I poked my head into the sitting room. It was empty, but I could see out the window, see Cacher and his crew still standing around.

Back in the hallway there was still no sign of Valentine. There were two more rooms off the hallway, and a staircase. A final door at the far end of the hall, not twenty feet away, probably led to an alley entrance. I could see from here that the bolt was off, and the door unlocked. I was walking down the hall before I realized it, deciding to run before even thinking about it. The first room I passed, to my right, was a kitchen. No lights, and no Valentine. I thought I heard something upstairs, the barest whisper of movement as I passed the stairs. There was a door at the top of the stairs, a bright light shining around the cracks where the door didn't sit properly in the jamb.

The final room was an office. Hardwood on all sides, and bookcases, heavy golden spines peering out from behind glass doors. The room smelled of hot metal and must. There was a desk and a chair. Valentine was sitting at the desk, his hands folded, the unnatural bulk of his shoulders slumped forward. He was looking down at the desk, facing the door. He didn't move as I went past.

I had my hand on the doorknob leading out, waiting, listening to see if Valentine would try to stop me. There was no noise, only the slight metallic creak of Valentine's machines and my groaning heart. Whoever was upstairs shuffled, something dragging across wood, like a boarding hook on a ship's hull. I backed up and went into the office.

"Hello, Jacob," Valentine said. He didn't move, his eyes still calmly on the desk in front of him. I came into the room and found a chair, leaning against the near bookcase.

"Valentine." The room was hot, all the windows shut up and covered, the morning light only getting through in thin streamers of dust. I settled into the chair and looked the puzzle-box man over.

People approach cog-modification two ways. The guy outside, with the eyes like dead stones, they go for the machine look. He's a pure, straight killing factory, an algorithm of danger and intimidation. Guys like that don't hide it, they leave the metal plates showing. But Valentine? No, Valentine isn't like that guy. That guy's machine. Valentine is art.

It's mostly his face. Valentine's head is carefully carved darkwood, polished bright, no metal showing at all. His face is a minimalist sculpture; darkwood lips, cheekbones, the impression of a chin and nose and eyebrows suspended over an emptiness of shadow and the bare twitchings of gears. The individual pieces are animated, moving silently on hidden tracks, clacking softly against one another when he smiles or talks or scowls. He was scowling, looking at me, waiting.

"Busy day you're having," he said. His voice was a trick of metal, the kind of voice a harp might have.

"Yeah. I mean..." I wondered how much he knew. "Yeah."

"Me too. Having a busy day." He sat up a little and spread his hands across the desk, like a blind man feeling up his environment. I always felt like his hands were a little too big, almost awkwardly proportioned compared to the rest of his body. They seemed clumsy. "I wonder if our days are similar at all. If maybe we're having the same... complications."

"Could be."

He nodded absently. "Could be. Where's Emily, Jacob?"

"Emily. I don't know. Shouldn't you be asking Cacher that kind of thing?"

"I think Cacher would like to ask you that himself." Valentine gazed over my shoulder, staring at the wall. The machines of his face went a little slack. "I think him asking you would be a lot less pleasant." He refocused on me, leaned forward. "For you. So. Where's Emily?"

"I said I don't know. Haven't seen her since that job."

"I have a lot of wheels spinning, Jacob. Which job?"

"The Tomb thing, and the deal with Prescott. You sent me up the Heights to take care of it."

"I sent you up the Heights. And the deal with Prescott." He nodded. "I tasked Emily with making the deal with Prescott, and I take it she contracted you."

"Correct."

"And you arranged to make the deal," he paused, his eyes on his hand. "Up at the Heights?"

"Emily said that was part of it, that Prescott would only make the deal there." Of course, I knew that wasn't entirely true, at least according to Prescott. But I told the story I knew. "And while I was there she had me do the Tomb thing, too."

"The Tomb thing." He folded his hands. "She had you on another contract, for another outfit?"

"No, I..." and then realized that I didn't know. She had said the Prescott deal was from Valentine, but she hadn't been specific with the Tomb part of the deal. "She implied the deal was from you. That the Tombs had been making overtures and that you wanted to lean on them a little. She gave me something to give Angela Tomb, figured I could make the meeting because of my history."

"What was it that she gave you?"

"A music box. Some old hymn."

He was quiet for a while, just staring at me. His face ticked slightly, clenching and unclenching, the darkwood tapping. I squirmed in my seat, trying to look calm but probably not doing much of a job of it. There was an uncomfortable line forming in my head, running from the Cog to the inexplicable events on the Heights and intersecting with Emily. I was worried for her.

"Is she missing?" I asked. "Is she okay?"

His face evened up, like he had been absent and was now re-summoned to his body. "We don't know. She missed an appointment with Cacher yesterday, and another last night. No one has seen her. There's been a lot of trouble, Jacob."

"We should be looking for her."

"We are. But like I said, a lot of trouble. Council's been tumbling a lot of my operations. Kicking in a lot of doors. It's unpleasant."

"You have a mole in the outfit," I said.

"I know. That's what I'm getting at."

"It's Pedr. He broke into my place this morning. Told me he'd been hired by a guy, someone who looked official. It's Pedr you should be talking to, not me."

"Pedr is a known quantity. He's been a fink for the Council for years. I only let Pedr see the things I want the Council to see. He's been a very useful tool, Jacob."

I could hear muffled clawing upstairs, like heavy cloth being torn. I glanced up. Valentine followed my gaze.

"The Henri-Bearings. Owners of the house. By the time they get free or someone misses them, we should be well on our way. Unless the Badge is already on their way, Jacob. Say, if someone who came here was being followed. Or escorted."

"Oh. Oh, you don't think it's me?" I leaned back in my chair, very careful to keep my hands on my knees. "You can't think it's me."

"Tomb has been talking to me, but no one knows that. Not Emily, not Pedr. But you know it."

"Emily told me. She said..."

"You have family on the Council, Jacob. You went to the Academy."

"Which is why I'm good for you. That's the very reason you hired me in the first place: the people I know, the places I can go without causing a stir. Valentine, seriously, you can't think it's me."

Again, he was quiet, unmoving. Upstairs someone shifted, slid heavily across the floor.

"I don't. It's an interesting angle, but I don't think it's the right one. See, these Council goons who are tumbling my operations, they're looking for some people. Specifically, they're looking for you. And they're looking for Emily."

"That's not good. Maybe I should duck down for a while, find a deep hole and bury. You have a place I could do that, Valentine?"

He shook his head. "I can't have it, Jacob. I can't have the Council tearing down the industry I've built. It's a fragile thing, depends on trust as much as it depends on gold. People need to feel safe with me, Jacob. I can't offer that with officers of the Badge kicking in my doors, can I?"

"You can't... you aren't going to turn me in, are you?"

He smiled. It looked like a theater mask, a wild grin playing to the back seats. "I'm not. That's also bad for business. But look, I can't have you around. I can't help you. And I can't help Emily. Whatever's going on, you need to fix it." He stood up and walked to the door. "Stay away from my outfit until things are cleaned up. It's been good working with you. Cacher will leave your piece out back, behind the house."

He walked out of the room, just like that.

"What am I supposed to do?"

He paused in the hallway. I could see his broad back, facing away from me.

"Survive. It's what people do, Jacob. Or they don't, and then it doesn't really matter."

And then he left.

Chapter Five
Beetles of Memory and Blood

I CLEARED OUT of the house shortly after Valentine made his own exit. Cacher and his boys had abandoned their posts at the front, probably to escort Valentine back to some other safehouse until the Badge pressure eased. Rather than follow Valentine and maybe catch the eye of some curious passer-by, I took the back door.

The pains in my chest were getting worse. This happened sometimes, some bit of the damaged machinery worked loose or missed a cycle and I was left with a heartache that pounded through my bones like thunder. It usually happened after a bit of traumatic repair to my meat, but worked itself out in a couple days. Just a very inconvenient time to have my secret machine grinding into my ribcage like a drill bit trying to work its way to fresh air. I kept a hand to my chest as I clambered down the porch stairs and into the close, wood-rot smell of the back alley. I could feel the thrum against my palm.

I took my time on the stairs, thinking about what had just happened. Valentine's cashing me in, I thought. He's had his use for me, and now I'm too much trouble. Maybe later, if the pressure eases and I can be of use to him again, maybe he'll let me back in his little gang. Well. Fuck him.

I stepped off the porch and Cacher came from under the loose fencing of the staircase and tried to put a leather-wrapped baton into my skull. I caught sight of him just out of the corner of my eye, had time to curse myself for not expecting it and get a hand blindly into his swinging forearm. The baton skated off my shoulder, just glancing my head as it arced down. I stumbled, grabbing most of his collar and pulling his coat awkwardly over his shoulder and head. He struggled to pull free and get a good swing, but I kicked a heel into his knee and then we were both on the ground, swinging and grunting and rolling around in the puddles and muck.

It ended when I got my arm across his throat, fist on shoulder and elbow punching down. He looked up at me with such angry eyes, mad eyes, that I almost stumbled back at their fury. Instead I waited until his grip loosened on my arm, then I straddled him and punched him twice, fast, across the cheek. I got up and kicked the baton into a gutter, then frisked him. My service revolver was in his coat pocket.

"What've you gotten her doing, Burn?" He was on his side, and the words were wet and distant. I rolled him onto his back, made sure he knew I had the revolver.

"Nothing, Cach. Certainly nothing worse than what you had her doing."

He sneered, his mouth an angry smear of black teeth and red gums. "Just cuz she made you pay like..."

I leaned down and casually put the brass inlaid butt of the service revolver into his temple, backhand, then dragged him under the stairs and left him.

EMILY LIVED IN Highmarche, pretty much the center of town. Half of Veridon above you, half of it spread out below you in broad, flat terraces. It was a place of neat houses with peaked roofs and lace drapes over windows that looked out onto clean streets laid out in squares and broad avenues. None of the narrow claustrophobia of the old city, or the decrepit apathy of the harbor districts. I had to walk for a while to get there, and by the time I navigated the market traffic and the press of carts moving from the harbors, an unnatural early spring heat had settled over the city like a fog. The stone glittered underfoot with warmth and the smooth shine of heavy wear.

I was sweating. I kept my coat on, my hand on the revolver in my pocket. When I took it away to wipe sweat from my brow, my fingers stank of hot metal and cordite. The misaligned gears of my heart had taken up a stabbing beat, lurch-wince, lurch-wince. I tasted oil in the back of my throat, thick like blood.

I hitched up to a doorway about a block shy of Emily's place. Leaning against the railpost, I could see most of the street in front of her address. It was a quiet brickfront home, split and split again to house a number of young couples anxious for a good address but thin in the pocket. The crowd in the street moved steadily, no one lurking or doubling back to patrol. If Valentine had someone posted here, they were doing a fine job of it.

I walked down past her place, around the corner, spent a minute in a bakery then went back. No one seemed to notice me as I walked by the door; no one looked familiar or suspicious. I went around to the back and palmed the dropstone Emily and I had used to arrange meetings. There was a key inside. I put the 'stone back in its notch, went around front and let myself into the building. The same key opened her door. Once I was inside I locked up and then jammed a chair under the door.

The key in my hand was new metal and smelled of oil, as if it had been freshly pressed. It didn't look familiar, but I had never seen Emily handle a lot of keys. The 'stone downstairs usually held a coded message, with times and places. I pocketed the key and looked around.

Emily was neat, almost mechanically precise in her tidiness. The apartment reflected that precision. The desk where she and I had sat the day before was clean and empty, the chairs set at an angle. Maybe even the angle I had left it at when I stood up. Valentine said that Emily missed a meeting with Cacher, and I remembered her mentioning that he was on his way over. That's a tight window of opportunity. Would Valentine have leaned on me harder if he'd known how tight?

I opened each of the drawers in turn, emptied them completely and checked for hidden compartments before I moved on. It took about ten minutes, and at the end of it I didn't know anything new. There was no Cog. There were no secret instructions from shadowy agencies about my meeting on the Heights, or anything to indicate that Emily was anything more than the whore and fixer I had known for five years now. I put everything away and looked around the rest of the apartment.

There wasn't much to see. Her clothes were all neatly arranged in the bedroom dresser, her bed was made. The room smelled like her, like summerwisp blooming in spring. I didn't spend a lot of time in the bedroom, and the kitchen nook was just a drawer of cutlery and a coolbox that was empty. There were no signs of struggle or forced entry, but the gun she kept in the closet by the front door was missing, as were the ledgers she had been working on when I left. Those had been for Cacher, I remembered, which meant he had been here. Probably let himself in, couldn't find Emily so he took what he had come for and left. Did he take the Cog, too, or had Emily taken it with her? For that matter, where did she go, and why?

I sat on the divan that looked out over the street, laid the service revolver in my lap, and turned the situation over in my head. Lot of ways to come at this one.

The least likely, least worrying possibility was that Emily was just on some business.

Not missing, just laying low while she attended to... whatever. Either one of her Haven Hill clients or some deal that required her personal attention. And maybe she took the Cog with her, intending to drop it with Valentine or whoever, as part of her errand. But if that's what was happening, Valentine would be able to track her down. For that matter, it seemed awfully early for Valentine to be concerned about Emily's whereabouts. People in this business disappeared, they went to ground fairly easily. Being able to stay out of trouble is what made fixers like Emily valuable.

And the gun? It was her home defense piece, a cruel foot and a half of metal, just the critical bits of a shotgun with the rest cut away. She had a traveling piece, always left the shotgun in the closet in case someone jumped her as she came into the apartment.

That left the more worrying option. Emily, surprised somehow in the apartment, caught off guard. Taken without mess or struggle. Taken, and the Cog with her. Not a lot of people could pull that on Em. Maybe there had been a fight, and the creep cleaned up before he left. I looked around the room; everything was obsessively aligned, clean, perfect. It would take time to get a room back into this state, and there wouldn't have been a lot of that, between my departure and when Cacher had arrived. It didn't make sense.

I was standing up when I heard them on the stairs. I snapped out of my revere and immediately understood why I hadn't seen anyone stalking the house from the street. They were across the way, two Badges in gray overcoats peering calmly through a rented window. Fucking stupid and lazy; my head just wasn't in this staying alive thing. Now that the move was on, their boys hammering up the foyer stairs, they had given up hiding behind the curtains and were leaning out into the street, sighting the long rifles that the Council rarely issued and that you never saw in the city limits. I rolled away from the window just as the glass splattered into bright shards and the far wall crumpled into plaster.

I took four squatting steps to the door before I remembered the feet on the stairs and threw myself back into Emily's room. The front door began to flex under officer's boots, flakes of plaster dusting down from the jambs like snow. I fired twice into the door and then winced as a shot from across the street splintered the bedroom window sill and sprayed the room with splintered glass. I leaned over and, bracing with both my feet, flipped the mattress over and against the window. Better that they fire blind. The pounding on the front door started again. I belly-crawled over to the fireplace and scooped up the iron poker. Another bullet came through the window, dust and feathers puffing out of the mattress, wood splintering from the bed frame. I wedged myself into a corner of the bedroom and started hacking at the plaster ceiling. Emily lived on the second floor of a two-story building. When I got to the plank slating I climbed on a chair and put my fist through, depending on the laced bone conduit of my Pilot's interface to hold me together. There was a lot of blood, the skin flapping back from my knuckles, but I got through. I pulled myself up into the darkness as they cleared the front door.

The attic was dark, and it was hot. There was only a little light, coming in from the gable vents. I had plaster dust in my eyes and mouth, and my hands were bleeding all over my gun. The floor of the attic was just beam framework over slating, so I balanced carefully toward the vents. A spattering of fire came up through the floor, the Badgemen getting damn desperate. I was pretty sure they wouldn't follow me up, all of them too precious to be the first one to stick his head up into the darkness.

I kicked the vent out and shimmied up onto the roof. It was all of two heartbeats before the goons across the street shot at me. Hard to miss with a rifle like that, but they did. I rolled down the opposite decline of the roof, hooked my leg over and crawled, slowly, too slowly, down the drainage pipe and into the street. People had cleared out, all the gunshots and kicked out architecture had scattered folks. The Badge came out of the building, just about the time I was putting my boots on the ground.

I didn't bother aiming, just shot, cycled, shot, bullets nicking off the brick wall of Emily's building. I was on my heels, backpedaling so fast that I was falling. The Badges dropped to the ground or ducked behind doors and barrels. I only counted four of them, but there were more inside.

I finally came down on my back, rolling around the corner of the building and coming up on my knees. I realized that my last couple shots had been dry, the cylinder empty. Kneeling, I dumped the hot shells into my lap and started to quick load, keeping one eye on the building front. The Badges started to peek out. I had a brief memory, kneeling like this in the empty room of the Tomb Estate, fumbling bullets into this gun as that thing came down the hall. I thought I could hear the dry rasp of wings on wallpaper, blinked and realized I was frozen, a bullet pinched in my fingers, the

Badge slowly creeping across the street towards me.

I snapped the cylinder closed and fired hurriedly. Luck put the bullet into one of the Badgemen, into the meat of his arm. He fell and the others crouched and started firing. I scrambled out and ran down the street. I wasn't sure how many shots I'd loaded. Not a full cylinder, surely, and one fewer now. I looked for a place to pull off and finish the load.

I darted around a corner and dragged to a stop. There was an iron carriage, the shutters riveted shut, parked across the avenue. It was cold, the chill washing off it in sheets, breathtaking in the day's freakish heat. I had never seen such a thing. I was cold just standing here. There were Badges all around it, leaning against walls or talking quietly among themselves. They were dressed in winter gear, heavy gloves on their hands. Their skin was pale and their faces were puffy, like they hadn't been sleeping well. They looked up.

I shot the closest one, stepped forward and put my shoulder into his chest as he staggered, knocking him into one of his boys. The rest started to draw, but I kept my gun low and shooting. I fired three times before I heard that horrible dry snap of an empty chamber. The Badges were down, either bleeding or behind cover. There had been other shots, I slowly realized, and my chest and leg were hot. I looked down, saw that I was on one knee, saw red, red blood running down my shirt.

I stood up, staggered, stumbled past the carriage. Someone was yelling and I turned. The street was incredibly close, a tunnel of buildings and a burning sky pressed down. The Badges were hidden behind the iron box of the carriage. I waved my pistol at them, shuffling backward. My chest was tearing itself apart.

Another carriage rolled up, pulling between me and the iron box. Its engine clattered like shuffling plates as it idled. I put my hand on the side. There was a lace of blood between my fingers, and I winced as the door opened. It was Emily, and she was waving that wicked little shotgun at the Badges.

"You're making a lot of noise, Jacob."

"Yeah," I mumbled. My voice sounded flat in my head. "We're having a little party, me and the Badge." I coughed and pain lanced through my lungs. "You joining us?"

"No, no, I think we'll be going now. Get in."

"Not sure I should. Where you been, Em?"

She grimaced. "Get in or get fucked, Burn."

"I gotta choose? Any way we could arrange both?"

Emily cuffed me and jerked my collar. I rolled into the carriage and lay down. Emily closed the door and, with one last look down the street at the iron carriage and its lurking guard, drove away.

I WOKE UP with most of my ribs broken and some guy's bloody hands fiddling with the damage. He was a tall guy, thin, his skin paper smooth and his face long and narrow. He was formally dressed, the cuffs of his sleeves neatly folded back and pinned in place. His arms were all bone, like the meat had been sucked away. I didn't know him, so I tried to sit up. The pain knocked me down before I'd gotten very far into it. It felt like my lungs were stapled to the table. I moaned and rolled my head to one side. Emily was there, her hands folded in her lap. She smiled a little.

"Who's the guy?" I asked. My voice sounded ragged, and the pain in my chest bundled up again.

"Wilson. He's a friend of mine, Jacob."

"Wilson," I grunted. "Wilson. You were part of that group of blockade runners, during the Waterday riots. That Wilson?"

"Different guy," he said.

I started to pull myself up. "All respect, Emily. I don't get cut by someone I don't..."

"Stop being stubborn," she said, pushing me down. I told myself I was struggling, but honestly I just collapsed. "You're in pretty awful shape."

"You're in dead shape, son." Wilson smiled and shrugged. It was a complicated shrug, like he had a collection of shoulders under his white smock. He turned away and I saw a hunch that covered both shoulders and traveled down his back. Anansi then, trying to fit in with the regular folks. The anansi were a spider-like people who had populated the cliffs around Veridon for years before humans had found their way to the delta. They resisted when we moved in. There weren't many left, and most of those were in positions of virtual slavery to various academic and governmental organizations. Anansi had an uncanny knack for technology, for all that they lived in caves and ate their meat raw.

"I've seen worse," he said, "but not in people who were talking." He turned back to me, holding something that looked like a prehensile corkscrew. I saw the other signs of his type, the tiny sharp teeth, the hooked talon fingernails. He smiled. "You should hold still."

I did. The next bit hurt a lot, and I probably passed out for the bloodier parts. Next clear thought I had was hunger, and I was sitting up in some kind of stiff chair. Wilson was looking at me curiously, like he wasn't sure what I was. I nodded to him.

"Thanks for taking care of me. Kind." I found it hard to talk, like I was short of breath from running. Wilson smiled that tiny teeth smile again.

"It's the sort of kindness money can buy, Mr. Burn. Money and curiosity. You really should be dead."

"PilotEngine." I waved at my chest. "Keeps the meat going so the zep doesn't flip out in case the Pilot gets hurt in bad weather or war. In some ways, a Pilot is the only important person on a ship."

"No," he said, shaking his head. He was wearing city clothes now, a tight vest and dress shirt. The hunch was more pronounced. It shifted while he talked. "You're no Pilot, Jacob Burn."

"Fuck you, okay. I know my history, I know what happened. I remember. I don't need people telling me."

"Excuse me." Wilson folded his arms. "Let me step in. I don't know anything about you. Okay? Maybe you're some kind of crime world celebrity or something, but I don't fucking know. I find your reaction amusingly self-important, but you need to just listen to me. You're not a Pilot."

I stared at him. I didn't know what to say.

"Not a Pilot. But, the Academy?"

"Oh, you might have trained to be a Pilot. But that," he pointed one long, sharp finger at my chest. "That has nothing to do with piloting. Not in the immediate sense, at least. How much do you know about biotics?"

"Biotics. Like the Artificers Guild?" Like the Summer Girl, I thought.

"Right. Specifically, in how it relates to cogwork. Their relationship."

"It doesn't. I mean, they're separate sciences," I said.

"Separate sciences that do similar things." He walked slowly around the room, and for the first time I became solidly aware of the space I was in. It looked like an operating theater, the surrounding tiers of seats dusty and abandoned, disappearing up into the unlit heights of the room. The ground level operating room had been strewn with the stuff of a house: a desk, two chairs, random narrow tables that held all manner of devices, even a bed shoved up against the circular wall. The tiled floor was grimy with mildew, and a few thin rugs had been set down around the perimeter. Wilson stopped by one of the tables and picked up a tiny jar. He began to unscrew the stopper. "Not so separate, once. The Academy, as you say, trains Pilots. But once it served a more civilian purpose. Do you know what this is?"

He held the jar out in front of me. It smelled, a sharp stink of decay and dry vomit. I wrinkled my nose and glanced inside. There was a blanket of crushed leaf, and a shiny beetle rooting around inside. Wilson plucked it out with two sharp fingers.

"Engram beetle," I said.

"Yes. An engram beetle." He held it in his palm and presented it to me. The beetle's back was smooth. It hadn't been imprinted yet. "One of the few remaining practices from the old Academy. Left over from a time when the institute was committed to learning, to exploring the world around us. But now all that's left is the Artificer's Guild, and their little entertainments."

"I wouldn't call them little. The engrams are pretty incredible."

"Nothing compared to what they could be. What they were before you were born, before the Church... nevermind. Bitterness clouds my argument." Wilson held up his hand. The beetle was crawling around his knuckles, eventually climbed its way to the top of his finger, clinging to the talon. "Biotics is the study of the living form. What it can do, and what it can be. The patterns found inside, and how those patterns can be used to change the form."

"Sounds like the Church."

"The Church is interested in the pattern without. The Algorithm of the Unseen, as their Wrights are fond of saying. They try to divine a pattern from the cogwork they dredge up from the river, the scraps that come downstream, and they seek to impose that pattern on the world." He flourished the beetle, waving it at my face in slow circles. "But there is already a pattern. Here," holding up the beetle, and then waving at me, then at himself, "And here, and here."

"Still sounds like the Church to me," I grumbled. "Is this going somewhere?"

"It is," he said and smiled. "Your engine, supposedly designed to allow you to impose your will on the mighty zepliner, is something else. All cogwork derives from the patterns of the Church, and yet this is something different. Something I have never seen, and I have seen a great many things. It is a pattern." His smile was uncomfortably bright. He presented the beetle, "That I wish to understand."

"The Academy installed it. Ask them."

"They are not here. Beetling is nothing to be afraid of, Jacob Burn."

I looked around the room, desperately. My chest hurt like hell, and Wilson's eyes were exceptionally bright, his teeth exceptionally sharp. "Where's Emily?"

"She's not here either. Take the beetle. I only want to imprint the pattern of your heart, to see what has been done to you."

"I told you, it's a PilotEngine, the Academy installed it."

"They may have, but I assure you." He leaned into me, close. His breath smelled like old linen stored too long. "That is no Pilot's Engine. If it were, you would be dead. The Engine can do many things, and yes, it is designed to provide the Pilot with a great deal of resiliency. But nothing the Church can produce would have saved your life today. So." He took my chin in his hand and forced my jaw open. He placed the beetle delicately on my teeth. I struggled, I put my hand on his wrist but in my weakened state his muscles were like iron bands. The beetle scurried forward, clicked against my back teeth as I gagged to keep it away, and then it was down, it was forcing its way down my throat until all I could feel was a dry scuttling in my lungs and heart.

I fell back against the table, the light leaving my eyes, the darkened ceiling of the theater swelling down to fill my head and I was gone.

Chapter Six
The Daintiest Whore

EMILY WAS LEANING across me, her breasts smashed against my ribs. I tried to make a joke and coughed instead. It sounded like a rusty winch, that cough. She sat up suddenly and put her palm in the middle of my chest.

"You look horrible," she said.

"Feel it." My throat was sandy-dry. I put a hand to my mouth and felt sticky blood on my lips. "Nice friends you got."

Emily shrugged. "Wilson does his things, and he does them well. You should feel lucky that he owes me. His services are expensive."

"My debt." I tried to sit up, but the pain in my chest was too much. "Where is he?"

"Out. Some things he needed. He wanted to wait until I was back. Didn't want to leave you unattended."

"And you? Where were you, while your expensive friend was stuffing bugs down my throat?"

"Some errands." She leaned away from me and looked around the theater. The room looked brighter, but that might have just been my tired eyes. "Strange things going on, and I have interests to protect."

I coughed. My throat was a little better, but not well. Felt like I was breathing glass. "You want to errand me up some water?"

Emily stood up and got me a glass, poured from a tap in the grimy wall. She sat next to me on the bed while I drank. The water was warm and cloudy. It tasted like blood. That might have just been me.

"Better?" Emily asked. She was standing by the bed with her hands on her hips.

"Some." I tried to sit up again, and it went better. My chest felt like a stack of very precariously balanced plates, cracked and tottering. I put a hand on Emily's shoulder. Her skin was cold. "What the hell's wrong with me?"

"Wilson said something about the bug not reading right. And you're mending fast, like nothing he's seen." She carefully shrugged off my hand, took the empty glass and set it on one of the work benches that circled the room. "The healing is taking up a lot of you, all at once. Here it is."

She came back to the bed, holding a stoppered bottle. She presented it to me, turning it so the bug inside clinked against the glass. "Make any sense to you?"

I peered in at the bug. The beetle was dead, its legs curled up like burnt eyelashes, its back shiny and black. The pattern scrawled across its shell was complicated and unfamiliar.

"What do I know about engrams?" I peered at the pattern on its back. When you took foetal metal for an implant, the docs had you memorize a pattern for the living steel to imprint upon. That pattern should somehow be reflected on the beetle. It had been a while for me, but the bizarre scraping in my hand looked like nothing I'd seen before. It hurt to look at. "Mean anything to you?"

"Mm," Emily said, her lips pursed. "Means you're one complicated son of a bitch. Wilson thinks maybe the beetle was bad, or the massive damage in your body threw it off. He insists you couldn't make anything with a pattern like that."

"Well." I slid the beetle back into the bottle from my cupped hand, put the stopper in and set it by the bed. "That's a mystery for another mind. How'd your errands go?"

"Poorly. Lots of Badge out there. Most folks are just staying low. You've made a hell of a mess out there, Jacob Burn."

"I have. Did you get in touch with Cacher?"

"No," Emily said quickly. "I was... his business and mine don't cross, right now."

"Business." I grimaced. "He seemed pretty worried about you, last I saw him."

"Well. Maybe with good reason. Hanging out with you seems to be a world of trouble."

She was leaning against the bed, her arms crossed, just a crack of a smile leaking across her face. I smiled and put a hand against her elbow. She didn't move it.

"Hanging out with me has always been trouble. Why should now be any different?"

She smiled a little more, but didn't move her arms. She turned away and walked to one of the tables nearby.

"I got you some new clothes. Took the sizing from the ones you ruined. I hope the cut's not too modern."

"I'm sure they're fine. Emily, what happened in your apartment? What did you do with the Cog?"

She paused, rearranged the clothes on the table, folding and refolding the pants and vest.

"What's the story with that Cog, Jacob? What's the real story?"

"Like I said. Marcus gave it to me, but I think there's a lot going on with it." I didn't want to tell her more than that, yet. I didn't know what she had to do with all this. Didn't know I could trust her.

"A lot going on with it." She nodded and turned to me, leaning against the table, her hands behind her back. "That's one way of putting it. There were some men, after you left. They must have been watching the place."

"What men? How were they dressed?"

"Nondescriptly. Perfectly... unremarkable. It scared the hell out of me. They were asking about you, what my business was with you."

"What'd you say?"

"That I didn't know you. Never heard of you, or anyone fitting your description. They didn't pretend to believe me."

"Did they ask about the Cog?"

She turned back to the clothes. I could see that she had hidden the shotgun among them, and was now refolding the clothes and checking for grease. She set the shotgun aside. "They asked about any strange devices. If you'd tried to sell me anything, or seemed anxious to move any strange property."

"How the fuck did they know?"

She shrugged and hefted the shotgun, then turned back to me. "Point is, they knew."

"Who were they?"

"I told you, there was nothing remarkable about them."

"Who do you think they were?" I asked. I realized I was leaning forward, gripping the bed. My chest wasn't hurting anymore.

"They were Council. Had to be. One of them was really creepy."

"Sloane."

"You know the guy?" she asked.

"We've met. And I've seen his name around." I flopped back onto the bed. I wanted to have a little talk with Mr. Sloane, one of these days.

"So where's the Cog?" I asked.

"I hid it. As soon as they left I took it and went out the dumb waiter. It's safe."

"There's another way out of that place? You could have told me, Em. I had to do some damage to your property getting out."

She smiled. "Girl's got to have some secrets, Jacob Burn."

"Your secret almost got me killed."

Again, she shrugged. She put the shotgun into a travel bag, along with some food and a knife she produced from her skirts.

"You got out, and then I came and rescued you, and took you to my very competent and expensive friend. So we're even."

"I'm going to leave that ledger open, Emily."

"So what about you? Did the meeting with Prescott go okay?"

"Did it go... my god. No, Emily, it did not." I was standing and didn't remember doing it. "Everything about it went exactly not okay. I don't even know where to begin."

"Did you make the deal?"

"Yes."

"So that went okay."

"Except Prescott insisted that the meeting place was a requirement on our side. That Valentine or Cacher or you had required we meet at the party. Was that your requirement, Emily?"

"No, of course not. I just handed you the job." She finished with the bag and folded it closed. "The details came from Valentine."

"From Valentine, or from Cacher?"

"Well... Cacher. But he said—"

"Nevermind. Someone set up that meeting, and not for the cassiopia. Strange things happened, Em. Where's my coat?" I stumbled across the room, the bedclothes clutched around my chest. Emily raised a hand and put it against my arm.

"Oh, no. You're recovering fast, but you're not going anywhere."

"Not yet at least, but I don't like staying still. Now where's... here." The coat was thrown across one of the tables, blood still spotting the chest and arms. I started to rummage through it. The revolver was still in the pocket. I took it out and turned.

Emily had that shotgun of hers out, braced against her hip, the dark little barrel staring at my belly. I held up my hands and let the pistol dangle from a finger.

"Jumpy?" I asked.

"You're acting strange and pulling guns. I have every reason to be jumpy."

"Just look at the pistol, Em."

She grimaced and lowered the gun. "Sorry, Jacob. Strange days."

"Strangest." I reversed the grip and handed it to her.

"It's seen some use, but it's pretty clean," she said as she turned it over in her hands. "What am I looking at?"

"Provenance."

She peered at the inscription along the barrel. "*Glory of Day*? Did Marcus give you this, too?"

I shook my head. "Nope. But someone did, up on the Heights. And if that were the strangest thing that happened, I'd thank the hidden cogs and become a holy Wright."

She snorted and handed me the pistol. "The monk's life doesn't suit you, Jacob. It'd be such a waste."

I realized I'd lost hold of the blanket, and that most of my chest and leg was exposed. I flushed, and Wilson barreled into the room.

"You're up," he said. He turned to Emily. "What's he doing up?"

"Making a point," I said, taking the pistol from Emily's hand and covering myself with the sheet. "Where have you been?"

"Been? I've been down the street, trying to find a way in without getting caught. The whole iron-damned Badge is outside. Some kind of big metal carriage trundling around." He rushed to his table and began throwing things into a belted pouch. "You should get your things together."

"The Badge?" Emily asked. "I saw that patrols were up, but that's no reason to go rushing out. Jacob's still recovering and—"

"Jacob looks plenty recovered to me. Though really, Miss Emily, you should leave the medical examinations to the professionals." Wilson smirked, then looped the satchel over his chest. Emily tinged crimson then stalked to her bag by the bed. The wiry anansi looked at me and smiled. "Get your things together, son. Badge man is coming."

"You said a carriage? Iron?"

"Yeah," Wilson said. "We can chat about it later."

"How close did you get? Was it cold?"

Wilson paused and turned to me. "Could be. Thinking about it, yeah. There was frost on the iron, and the closest Badgemen wore heavy gloves. What about it?"

"I saw the same carriage, outside your apartment, Em." I turned to her. "I think that's how they're finding us."

"Some new trick?" she asked. I shrugged. Wilson stared thoughtfully up into the rafters.

"Well, it could be—"

"Figure it out later," Emily snapped. She tossed me my new clothes and pushed Wilson back to his work bench. "Mystery later, kids."

I caught the clothes and, doing my best to forget the lovely lady in the room, pulled them on. I shrugged into my jacket, slipped the revolver into the inside holster strap and turned. The others were waiting.

"Out the front?" I asked. "Or is there a back door?"

"There are many doors, but by now all of them will be watched. I barely got in." Wilson looked uncomfortable, then shrugged in complicated ways. "Forgive me, but there's only one way to do this."

He stepped forward, his back lurching as he moved. He seemed to writhe in place, his shirt bunching and crawling around his shoulders. Eventually the shirt tore free and the rest of him, the spider part of him, came out. Rising like wings gutted of their feathers, eight thin legs fanned out from Wilson's back. The legs were hard carapace, the color of bone, and about as thick as a naked arm bone as well. They clicked as he spread them, the hard talons at their tip scraping against the tile wall. Wilson sighed contentedly, stretching and flexing the legs.

"Hate tying them up," he whispered. "Hate binding them down. But what's to do, in people town, hm? What's to do?"

"Well, enough reminiscing," I said. "We getting out of here or what?"

Wilson looked at me sharply, his placid face suddenly hard and wild. I was reminded that the anansi were not all tame and kind. Wildness still surged in their blood. He grinned with his rows of pointed teeth. "Of course, of course. My apologies." He made it sound like a curse, then sprang up onto the wall and scuttled out of sight, into the darkness high above.

"Well," Emily said, craning her neck to look up. "That's good for him. What are we supposed to do?"

"Oh, that's nothing, Em," I said. "We'll just fly. Sprout wings and fly."

She snorted, but her hands were still white on the gun.

"Wilson," I yelled. "You got a ladder up there or something? A way up?"

There was silence, then the cycled whining of metal. The sound was coming from the door Wilson had entered moments earlier. Emily and I looked at each other, then took cover behind the bed.

The whining stopped, but seconds later came the *thud-thud* of boots in the hall. The door kicked in, and the iron masks of Badge in full storm gear peeked around the corner. We didn't move.

"This is it," the lead guy said. He didn't sound too sure, more like a question than anything. He poked his shortrifle in then crept into the room. Others followed. He wasn't ten feet away when Emily started shooting.

She had the shotgun low, braced on her shoulder as she lay under the bed. The shot went out through the metal framework of the bed, cutting a bright red line through the Badgemen. A couple fell, their knees pulpy red, screaming. Their mates fired back, grabbed the downed officers and dragged them out. The door closed again.

"What the hell was that?" I asked.

"It worked, right? They're gone."

"They're going to come back, lady. They're going to come back with more people." I stood up and slid one of the tables so it blocked the short hallway to the door. "They're not going to take any chances with sneaking in or clearing the building. They're going to burn us out."

"I think not," Wilson said from high above. "They have enough people out here. They seem intent on taking us alive."

A heavy rope fell in the center of the room, its end trailing up into the darkness. I grabbed my bag.

"Get up," I said to Emily. "They'll take a few minutes before they try again."

"After you," she said. "I won't have you looking up as I go."

"Godmercy. The daintiest whore in Veridon. I half think—"

She really stepped into the blow. She put the heel of her palm into my jaw, twisting my teeth into my tongue and spinning my head. I sat down on the floor.

"Watch the fucking door," she spat, then hiked up the rope with her satchel across her back. I waited until she was good and clear of the floor before I followed. My mouth was leaking blood.

On the roof, Wilson seemed to have resumed his civilized demeanor. He still had his legs out, and his eyes were wild and free, but when he talked it was with a reasonable voice. He was perched at the top of a steeple, his legs pinched down on the windvane, his hands clutching a long rifle. The rope came out from a skylight that ringed the steeple, the panes blackened with pitch. The whole roof slanted precariously to the street. I held on to the rope and hunkered down.

This collection of buildings was on a narrow terrace between broader districts. All the stone had settled like tired soldiers at the end of a century of marching. The narrow, crooked streets were full of Badge. Wilson's building fronted a tiny square, part of the old academic district, from before the Algorithm's dominance. The walls were all close together, the streets shadowed by stone and mossy eaves. They weren't built for the large automated carriages that dominated traffic in modern Veridon. The Badge had all the routes blocked. I could see two whole fists of the gray-coated officers standing in bunches or knocking on doors in the district. The sky above was slate, a low cloud cover that threatened rain.

"What the hell are we supposed to do? Fly?" Emily whispered.

"We'll go by roof, until they see us. If the zeps get involved, we'll just have to bite the bullet and find a way out by street." Wilson checked the load on his rifle then scampered down the roof. We followed, but carefully.

Wilson led us to what looked like a warehouse. His building was part of an academic complex, the whole block seemingly abandoned. Getting to the warehouse was a trick, but it looked like Wilson had practiced this route before. He scuttled down the roof then pounced across the alley and rolled behind a chimney. Emily and I waited at the gutter, looking at each other nervously, until the thin man reappeared with a board. It wasn't wide enough to make for a comfortable crossing, but we made it. He was pulling the board back when he stopped, his face pale.

"The beetle." He turned to us. "You have it?"

"I don't," I said. "Emily? Where'd you put that little bottle?"

"Back on the table. You can always make another."

"I need to go back," Wilson said, scraping the board back into place. His spider legs were twitching spastically, their hard talons clicking against the brick of the warehouse walls. "I don't know what that pattern means, but I don't want to hand it to the Badge."

"We'll wait," I said.

"No, you won't. Go down the roof here. You'll have trouble crossing to any other buildings without my help. There's roof access from that little shack, a stairwell that leads into the building. From there—"

"We'll wait," I said. I crouched behind the tiny brick wall that ringed the roof and nodded to the domed building we had just abandoned. "Go get your bug."

Wilson looked between us, then nodded and hurtled across the gap. His human limbs didn't even touch the shingles as he scuttled up to the peak of the roof and disappeared into the skylight.

I glanced over at Emily. She had her head down, the shotgun peeking over the roof's edge at the street below. She wouldn't look at me.

"Where'd you say you found this guy?"

"An old friend. He fixed things for me, back when I was a kid."

"He's a little creepy," I said.

"Hm," she said. She turned her shoulder to me. I kept my eyes down on the square. The Badge seemed to be organizing. The word was spreading. They'd found the building, and reinforcements were on the way. I looked over at Emily again. Her back was stiff.

"Look, I'm sorry. You know I don't mean shit like that."

"What?" she asked.

"The whore thing. I didn't mean it like that."

"How did you mean it?" she asked. "The whore thing?"

"Just... I don't know. I didn't mean it in a bad way."

"Sure."

I pocketed my revolver, spun the cylinder then drew it again. Spun the cylinder and shifted on my heels. Emily still wasn't looking at me.

"Anyway. I'm sorry."

"Sure," she said. It was quiet for a little while.

"Your creepy friend is taking his time," I said. "You sure you left the bottle on the table?"

"I said so, right? I put it right back where—"

The building across from us exploded in gunfire. The blacked-out skylights were limned in red. Wilson burst from the open window, his back to us, the long rifle dipping into the building. He opened up a long line of fire. The Badge in the streets below looked up. I cracked a shot at them, enough to keep their heads down.

Wilson got to us in a flash. His face was black and thin lines of blood traced the path of shattered glass across his cheeks.

"I couldn't find it. They came through the door with a storm engine. Didn't think I would make it out." He shot a look down at the street. The Badge was swarming. "We won't be taking the stairs. Follow me."

Behind us the dome of skylights wrinkled and a terrible roar tore up from the roof. Glass shattered in a long cascade, and a thin rope of wind twisted up from the building. Lightning flashed down its length, then the whole entity collapsed into dust. There was a lot of yelling in the streets.

"They're not fucking around," Emily said next to me. I shook my head and turned to Wilson. He was already gone, scuttling to the next building over, hopping to the roof with practiced ease.

"I don't suppose any of us are, anymore. Whatever's going on, Em, it's big. And it's dragging us along with it."

She grimaced, and then the two of us crossed to the next roof. Wilson was waiting. We spent an hour hiding, running, looking for someplace in the city where we'd be safe from whatever forces pursued us. We didn't talk much. It was grim work.

WE FOUND A hole and planted. Veridon is full of holes, burrows in the steep slopes or nooks under the built up terraces of the modern city. This one was a warehouse that had lost its floor to a cistern that had collapsed, one of the ancient rivers that ran under the city shaking off its domestic borders and cutting into the architecture.

We set up on the ledges around the lake. Stairs led down into the water, and under the old first floor there was a cave of brick and mud, just a sliver of space that couldn't be seen from the street. It was cool down there. The bricks were mossy and slick, and the air smelled like dead fish.

I lay my coat out on the brick and tried to relax. Wilson was setting up in the corner, and Emily was crouched at the water's edge, staring down into the cold.

"Don't get too comfortable, Wilson," I said. He was hanging his tool belt on the wall, holding it there with some kind of viscous gunk. "We're not sticking around."

"Was that some crude swipe at humor?" he asked.

"I don't know. Was it funny?"

"Not particularly." He kept his back to me. His shoulders were twitching.

"Well then. I guess not."

"We're going to need food," Emily said. "And we can't be hiding in empty buildings forever." She craned her neck to look at us over her shoulder. "We need a plan."

"We need to know what we're dealing with, first," I said, struggling up. "There's a lot more going on than is apparent."

"Every Badgeman in Veridon is hunting us, Valentine has banned you from the organization... there's more than that?"

"Yes," I said.

"The gods are trying to kill us or something?" Emily asked.

"Something like that."

Wilson snorted, but he didn't say anything. I folded my coat open and fished out the list I had gotten from Calvin.

"The guy you talked to, after I left. A little shorter than me, neatly dressed. Could have been military at some point. Bald. Leather gloves?"

"Yes," she said. "It's the gloves I remember the most. And his hands were hard. Very strong."

"That's Mr. Malcolm Sloane." I took the paper and spread it out on the ground, smoothing it down. "Right here at the top."

Wilson and Emily gathered close, stooping to look at the list.

"What is this?" Emily asked. "Angela Tomb is on this list. Where did you get this?"

"A friend. It's a list of deceased, all from a single military unit. Their date and cause of death was censured, by order of the Council. Angela's name is here because she authorized it. Sloane was Coordinating Officer."

"Then he's not the guy who came by Emily's place, is he?" Wilson looked at me. "I mean, if he's been declared dead."

"Two things," I said. "Coordinating Officer is not a field rank. It's administrative. These other names could be the deployed unit. Sloane was the guy they'd report to when they got back to the city. Secondly, recognize anyone else on the list?"

"Marcus?" Emily said. "I didn't know he was military."

"Neither did I. A man of surprises, our Marcus."

"This guy, too," Wilson said. "Gerrus. I know he wasn't military. A very clever thief, but never military."

"So maybe this isn't a military list after all?" Emily asked. "Maybe it's something else. A list of criminals?"

"I've seen the original. This is military, trust me." I took the ID card out of my coat and set it next to the list, by Wellons's name.

"You collect military records now, Jacob?" Emily asked.

"This I got off a body, up on the Heights. It was in the quarters of the Artificers, surrounded by dead Guildsmen."

"A marine. You're saying a marine killed a bunch of Artificers? Or someone killed them, and this guy tried to defend them, got himself popped?" Wilson grimaced. "Seems unlikely."

"No. Our friend Wellons was long dead. At least a couple weeks."

Emily and Wilson stared at me dully for a few breaths. Finally Emily nodded as though she understood.

"Huh," she said.

"So." Wilson murmured. He sat back on his heels. "So, we've got a list of people, with deceased dates two years old. Only we know two of them didn't die two years ago. But both of those people are dead now. This is good." He smiled. "This is meaty."

"There's more." They both turned to look at me. "I think I know who Marcus was running from."

"When he crashed the *Glory*?" Emily asked.

"Yeah. The guy I told you about, the one who jumped. I saw him again, up on the Heights."

Emily got dead still. "You could have mentioned that."

"Been busy getting shot. At least I think it was him. And he changed, he became some kind of... an angel."

"Angel," Emily said.

"Yeah. Wings of steel and cog, talons like knives. Angel."

Wilson was staring at me. They both were. Didn't blame them. Angels were part of the mythology of Veridon. The Church of the Algorithm claimed that the wreckage they strained from the river Reine was sent to them by angels of steel and wire. They claimed to have been visited by one specific angel, a girl named Camilla. She was sick, and they were able to help her. In exchange, she gifted them with the secrets of the river. No one believed it, not even me, and I had seen an angel. I had killed an angel.

"This is... unusual," Wilson finally said. He was fiddling with his tool belt, worrying it between his thin fingers like a prayer chain. "What did he want?"

"The Cog. Everyone wants the Cog. I saw him with the Artificers, and again later after I did the deal with Prescott. Later that night, I thought to go talk to him, went to see the Artificers. There was Wellons's body, dead Guildsmen, the Summer Girl missing. He killed Prescott, probably thought I'd given the Cog to him, then came after me. Nearly killed me."

"You're a hard man to kill," Wilson said.

"We've covered that. And you're right, I am. I put him down. Her, it turned out."

"Her?"

"There was a performance that night. The Summer Girl. It was her, the angel was her. When she died, the bugs fell away, the angel dissolved. There was just her."

"That's awful," Emily said. "Gods, you killed that girl?"

"No. I killed that monster," I hunched over the list, gathered up my coat. "I didn't know."

"What is this Cog?" Wilson asked. I sat up and looked at him.

"Not sure. I picked it up off a dead friend. Marcus here," I said, pointing to the list. "Things have been weird ever since."

"I have that problem sometimes," Wilson said. "Dead friends leave strange gifts. This friend of yours, he brought you this Cog?"

"It ended up in my hands." I stood up. The ruined ceiling was close. "I gave it to Emily to look after. See if she could find anything out about it."

Wilson looked to Emily. "You could have brought it to me."

"Things got strange," she said, not turning around. "I had to ditch it fast. Some people showed up at my place, then Jacob got shot. It got complicated."

"So." Wilson said. "Angels and Councilmen. This must be one hell of a Cog." He turned to Emily. "Where is it?"

"Tomb has it. I gave it to the Family Tomb."

I nodded and loosened the revolver in my holster. The hammer was smooth and warm under my thumb.

"Complicated," I said.

Chapter Seven
Trustlocks, Tombs and Eyes of Pale Flesh

Emily explained. Part of the deal Tomb had going with Valentine involved safe houses. Tomb was one of the most successful of the old families, one of the few to maintain both power and money. They had interests all over Veridon. Valentine was borrowing some of those interests, to hide people and things he needed put quietly away when there was trouble. Emily was aware of the deal, and took advantage. The Cog was buried in one of Tomb's houses, safe as it could be.

Right where we couldn't get to it. Right where we'd have to be crazy to break in.

"How do you know about that?" I asked.

"What, The hiding places? I arranged the deal."

"Not according to Valentine. He told me it was true, that he had been talking to the Tombs, but no one knew it. Not even you."

Emily flinched and sat down. "Let's chalk it up to self interest."

"How?" I asked.

"I've been snooping around Valentine, months now. There's a lot of money going into that operation that's just disappearing." She gave me a sick look. "I'm just trying to get a piece. Looking out for myself, I guess."

"And you found out about his secret deals with one of the Founding Families?" Wilson asked. "That's some deep secret you dug up."

"It wasn't easy. The Tombs were overconfident. One of their couriers..." she looked embarrassed and shot me a hot look. "He likes me. So. I found out."

"Well. You could have mentioned that earlier."

"You don't react well, when I bring up that side of my life."

I shrugged. Wilson chuckled. "So what now?" he asked.

"You put it there," I said. Emily was facing away from us again, a little pale. "You can get it back. Right?"

"I was about to say. That's what I was trying to do, while you were laid up at Wilson's." She shifted in her seat. "It's gone."

"Gone? What, like someone came through and cleared the place out? Stole it?"

"No, just it. Just the Cog. Everything else was the same, near as I could tell."

"You tell anyone else you put it there?"

"No."

"So someone magically guessed that it was there, broke in, and took just that."

Emily squirmed. "They didn't break in. There are signs, trustlocks that have to be maintained. Someone in on the deal had to take it. No one else knows the patterns."

"The deal? The one between Valentine and Tomb, you mean?"

"Yeah, that deal." Emily turned to look at me. She looked sorry. "So someone on the inside. Valentine's people, or Tomb's. No one else knows."

I sat back. Trustlocks were tricky. It took a combination to open them, a combination based on the configuration of the lock. And when you closed it again, it never went back in the same way. Had to be set. The whole deal was based on one use-codes and algorithms. You could pick them, but you couldn't put them back without the codes, least not in a way that the next guy opening it wouldn't notice. Tamper-proof. They got used a lot, by people who didn't trust each other.

"So one of Valentine's. Or one of Tomb's." I rubbed my eyes. "Valentine doesn't want any part of this. So let's say it's one of Tomb's. Let's say the Lady Tomb has this thing, now."

Wilson sighed. He had taken up a spot in the corner of our little room, sitting on his hands and watching us argue. "What does that mean to us?" he asked.

"If we're serious about figuring out what's going on here, it means we have to go get it," I said. I took my revolver out and laid it on the coat, then started to disassemble and clean it.

"Yeah. So what? We break into the Manor Tomb and steal it?"

"Probably not," Emily said. "That's probably too much of a task, even for the great Jacob Burn."

"Yeah, yeah." I kept focused on the pieces of the revolver. A simple puzzle, a task I knew. "Probably asking too much that she has it on display somewhere. Probably going to take talking to her."

"You want me to handle that?" Emily asked.

"You've had contact with her?"

"No, I just..." she stuttered to a stop. "No."

"No, you haven't. I have. This is my job. This is just the sort of job Valentine hires me for." I sighed and sat quietly for a minute as I finished up with the revolver. When it was together again I put it into my shoulder holster, then stood up. "Stay here. I'll be back, soon enough."

"Like hell," Wilson said. I paused at the door to the basement and turned. He was standing.

"You don't trust me?" I asked.

"Better. I don't even know you. You're asking us to stay here, to stay put, while you go running around the city. The Badge is looking for you, Jacob, and they're looking for us too. They catch you, it isn't going to be long before they get us."

"Look, I do this kind of job all the time. It's what Valentine pays me for. Look smart, talk to the pretty people, maybe threaten some milksop then get out." I turned back to the door. "All the damn time."

"It's not like that this time, Jacob." Wilson walked over to me, wedged himself between me and the door, and crossed his arms. "This isn't some drug deal, okay? I'm going with you."

"A bug," I turned to Emily and waved my hand. "Em, maybe, but I'm not taking a bug." I stopped talking when I felt the steel against my cheek. I turned, slowly.

"We don't use that word," Wilson said. "Civilized people like us don't use that word."

"Right. Sorry," I muttered. He lowered the knife. "I just don't think Tomb is going to be too friendly to me showing up with an anansi. That's all."

"It's okay," he said, sheathing the knife. "You'll tell them that we're friends." He looped his arm through mine and pulled me toward the door. "Good friends."

"Be careful, kids," Emily said. I think she was chuckling.

"Yes, dear," I said.

I clambered out of the flooded basement, swirling my coat on over my shoulders. Dusk was settling down on the streets of Veridon. The frictionlamps were humming.

"And while we're out, we can look for some engram beetles, for your pattern," Wilson said with a sharp smile and a tug on my arm.

I thought of the sharp legs clawing their way down my throat, the blood and chitin flaking off my lips when I woke up. I grimaced.

"Sure," I said. "We'll look."

✿

It worked like this. The Families on the Council, both the Founders and the new breed that's buying them out, they have their own servants. Drivers, butlers, handmaidens, stablers... the whole domestic scene. They have their own little brute squads, too. House Guard. Housies, we called them. They, you know, guard the house.

Tomb's House Guard was nowhere to be seen. The Manor Tomb sits in the older part of town, just on the edge of what could be called respectable real estate. It was high up in the city. It started out posh, but the years had built up and the wealth had migrated. Now the smoke from the Dunje-side factories formed a putrid strata that clung to the streets and scraped against the walls up here. Rich as the Tombs were, they couldn't afford to move their address. Grandpa was inside, and grandpa was immobile. And when grandpa went, the whole family went, the writ of name already mortgaged off to one of those new families. So. The manor stayed.

The Manor Tomb was an impressive place, all stone and wrought iron, the brows of the mansion scowling at the street below. The wall that surrounded the grounds was stone, and the gate was well maintained and usually guarded. Not today. Today, the gatehouse was empty. Perfect opportunity, right, except for the street around the manor. The street was full of officers of the Badge. They looked like they were preparing for a war, agitated, the men clutching their weapons as they faced away from the manor, like they expected Veridon to rise up and invade the place. Lots of Badge, with equipment and officers and marching orders. It didn't look right.

It was going to be tough to get an audience with the Lady under those circumstances. Of course, the alternative was to squat in that flooded basement while Wilson stuffed bugs down my throat. I figured to give it the old Burn try, at least.

Wilson and I circled around the Manor, crossing streets until we were out of sight of the wall and then working our way back to the postern. There was Badge back here, too, but they were playing sneaky; hiding in shops, gathering behind the boarded up windows of warehouses. We picked our way closer to the postern, trying to not catch the eye of the Badge. Wilson walked with his head down, his hunched shoulders twitching under his coat.

The grounds of the Manor Tomb were old. The wall was original to the founding, from when the Veridon Delta was still a dangerous place, and didn't contain that much space. In the generations that had since passed, the

Tombs had filled the interior of the wall with buildings and gardens and the like. That left no room for stables or garages for the family carriage. These things were outside the postern now, spilling out into the district.

I ducked into the stables, Wilson close behind me, and hunched my way to the gate. The Badge outside hadn't stopped us, so that was half the fight. I looked down at my grimy shirt. I couldn't look too good, I thought, probably not good enough to bluff my way into the estate. Best to be direct.

There were two guards by the postern, looking nervously between me and Wilson. They were armed with shortrifles and had been eyeing us since we came around the corner. I smiled at them and bobbed my head.

"Morning, boys. Here to see the Lady Tomb."

"Lady's not taking visitors today," the OverGuard said. He had his back flat against the iron bars of the gate. Over his shoulder I could see a dozen more Housies, peeking around corners and kneeling behind barrels. He looked briefly at me, and then pointedly at Wilson. Wilson smiled, his mouth full of tiny, sharp teeth. It would have been better if he didn't smile.

"Something up? Awful lot of steel in the street this morning," I said.

"Badge is agitating. Say they've got reports of a riot in the area. They're offering security."

"Generous of them," I said. "So you said Lady's not taking guests today?"

"Not today. Considering the situation."

"Maybe tell her, anyway. Someone who knows something about the little problem she had up on the Heights."

"That some kind of code?" he asked.

"Nah. But she'll let us in."

He grimaced, then nodded to someone behind the gate. A page ran up, got the message from the guard, and ran off again. We all stood around smiling nervously and peering out into the street while we waited. When the page came back there was another guard with him.

"He's in," the page said, out of breath. He poked his finger at Wilson. "That one stays outside."

"Well, that's too bad." I turned to Wilson. "You'll just have to stay here and..."

Wilson, still smiling, leaned close to me.

"If you leave me here I will climb the walls and find you," he hissed. "I will kill every man, child and widow's dog that gets in my way. And when I find my way to your bitch-Councilor's side, I will wrap her in gum and vomit fly eggs down her throat."

When he was done he leaned away from me again, slowly, keeping his eyes on mine but smiling all the while. I turned to the guards.

"It's best if he comes with me."

"Lady said—"

"Angela will understand. Honestly, everyone will be a lot better off if he comes with me."

They inched back a little. The messenger shrugged, and the watch captain nodded.

"It's on your head if he causes any trouble," the captain said to me.

"Sure, sure."

The other guard unlocked the gate and let me in, then locked it again from the inside. The guys outside showed no sign of having keys.

"They leaving you out in the cold?" I asked the OverGuard. He shrugged, then put his back to the gate and stared out into the stables.

"Come on," the new guard said. He was a lot cleaner, his uniform fit too well. He probably didn't like being near the gates at all. I nodded and followed him into the manor. Once we were away from the gate I shot Wilson a look. He shrugged and stopped smiling.

"You aren't leaving me behind in this, Jacob."

"I see that. But there's no need to threaten."

"Threat is a language you seem to understand." He shot his cuffs and rearranged the knives hidden in his coat. "But there's no reason we can't work together in this."

"If you say."

There were a lot more Housies inside, more than I expected. Maybe that riot story was true. They hadn't even bothered to disarm me when I came through, either. I fingered the revolver at my belt and looked around. The house was quiet.

She met us in the dining room. The long table was clear, the phalanx of chairs tipped against it. The only other furniture was an empty china cabinet.

Angela was standing by the window, looking out over one of the pocket gardens that spotted the grounds. She wore a riding jacket and pants in deep maroon. The guard left us and closed the door. I motioned Wilson to one side, a step behind me. Maybe if Angela thought he was some sort of servant she would ignore him.

"Angela," I said.

"I thought it might be you." She had her arms crossed, and didn't turn. "When Harold said it was someone with news from the Heights. I thought it must be you."

"I was hoping we could talk about that," I said. I crossed to the table. "There are a lot of strange things going on. Maybe we can, I don't know, clarify some things."

She nodded, almost absentmindedly.

"You were able to get through the Badge?" she asked.

"Yeah. Came around the back."

"No officers that way?"

"Some. They're hiding, but they're there."

She nodded again, then scratched at her cheek and looked at me. She paused when she saw Wilson, raised her eyebrows and looked at me questioningly.

"A friend," I said.

"Well. Friends are good," she said. She sighed, and it sounded like she was enormously tired, like a child about to fall asleep after a long summer day. It reminded me of the younger Angela, the girl I'd known. It was hard to see, in these clothes, in this place. Hard to remember we'd been children together.

"What about the Heights?" she asked. She motioned to the empty table, then walked over and tipped a chair onto its legs. She sat. "What did you want to talk about?"

I took a chair across from her, keeping my hands on the table. Wilson went to the window and pretended to ignore us. "I've had a pretty active couple of days, Angela."

She smiled. "I'm sure. But I thought you were used to that. The stories I've heard, you lead a pretty active life."

"Stories." I shrugged. "It's been more interesting than usual. A lot of the things that I know about how this city works," I spread my hands, palms up. "Haven't been working. The Badge has been very... persistent."

"That's unusual? The Badge enforcing the law?"

"One of Valentine's men was rolling my room when I got back from your little party. Insisted it wasn't at the boss's behest, and later that day the old clockwork told me he couldn't get involved. Didn't want me in his gang until this was all straightened out."

"Until what was all straightened out?" She leaned forward, touched the table with her elbows. She seemed to be hovering, just off the wood.

"There are some names I want to ask you about, Angela. Some people I've met, if briefly. Tell me if they're familiar to you."

She was very still, watching me. She didn't say anything. I took the paper I had gotten from Calvin out of my pocket and lay it on the table between us. She took it, unfolded it, looked at it for a solid minute without speaking. Then she folded it back up and set it on the table again. She sighed.

"Where did you find that?" she asked.

"Friends. Part of my interesting life. Now, I know some of those people. I killed at least one of them, and I've seen the body of another. And a third I met at your party. Who are these people, Angela?"

"Wellons," she said. "Is he the one you killed?"

"No. But I saw him, sure enough. In your house. Sloane, too. But it's Marcus I killed, on the *Glory of Day*. And he gave me something."

"A dirty conscience?"

I smiled. "You know what he gave me, Angela."

She wouldn't meet my eyes. She stood and crossed to the china cabinet, ran a finger down across the wood inlay.

"Let's say that I do," she finally relented. "What does it have to do with what happened up on the Heights?"

"You saw that thing, Angela. Everyone there did. What are they paying those officers to keep quiet? An Angel, ransacking the Manor Tomb? That can't be good for your reputation."

"They're all good boys, Jacob. Good citizens. They know what to keep quiet."

"But someone will talk. They'll get drunk, and they'll talk. And what are they going to say? They saw an Angel. The myths are real. There's an Angel in Veridon, Angela."

"What are you doing here, Jacob? There are people trying to pin you for the death of those Guildsmen, you know. And the Summer Girl. And Register Prescott."

"You know I didn't kill them."

"I know you didn't kill all of them," she said quietly. She turned to me. Her eyes were worried. "What's the Angel doing, Jacob. What did it say to you?"

"It was after something, Angela. Something it thought I had. And so was Pedr, and so is the Badge. Something they all think I have. And I'm hoping you can help me with that, Angela, because we both know I don't have it."

"Say we do, whatever it is." She turned again, refused to look at me. "What's that matter to me?"

"You know I don't have it. You're on the Council. Council holds the reins of the Badge. Call them off."

She leaned against the cabinet and crossed her arms thoughtfully.

"The Council is a complicated place. Maybe the seats pushing the Badge around right now don't have the whole picture."

"You're saying you don't have a handle on the army outside your door?"

"It's an interesting question," she said. She crossed over to the window, looked out over the grounds. You could see the rooftops of the surrounding district, poking out over the wall like distant mountaintops made of shingle and soot. "What they think they know and what they actually know. An interesting question. But let's crack to the marrow here, Jacob."

She went back to the cabinet and slid one of the drawers open. There was a lot of business, sliding things around, fussing with fabrics; then she came over and placed the Cog on the table. It whirled like a hurricane, the inner wheels buzzing in near silent period.

"You have it," I said. I knew she probably did. "So why are they still chasing me."

"Because this is just a part, Jacob." Her voice was fragile. I looked up. She held a pistol, a small, ornate piece, its barrel drawing a line to my eye. "Now, slowly, let's have that piece up on the table. Very. Slowly. And your friend shouldn't move. For his own sake."

I complied. Wilson had stiffened at the window, looking sternly at the two of us. Soon as my pistol was on the table, half a dozen Housies came into the room. Harold was there, looking at me with a disapproving eye. He smiled at me tightly. The old guy had a new scar across his face, and it pinched his cheek when he smiled.

"Not what I was expecting," I said. "Not exactly."

"Like you said, Jacob. Strange days." She leaned her head to Harold. "Let's get this all out of sight. We'll have to wait until the Badge gets out of the way before we can act."

"There is the postern gate, ma'am," he said. "The carriage could be—"

"They're out there," I said.

"Yes, Jacob was good enough to come in that way. They're hiding around the—"

"No," I said. I nodded to the pocket garden out the window. "They're out there."

Everyone turned. A half dozen Badge were scrambling over the hedge wall, shortrifles in hand. They spotted us and raised their weapons. A bullet splintered the window, then there was a fusillade of return fire. The glass fell like a waterfall. I threw myself to the floor.

"Harold! Hold the room!" Angela shrieked. "Jacob, you will come with me. There are depths they wouldn't dare breach."

The door behind us cracked with gunfire, wood splintering under incoming fire from the hallway. The Badge had gained the house, it seemed.

"M'Lady, perhaps now is the time for negotiation," Harold said. Angela spat angrily, wrenched the man's pistol from his hand and fired out the window.

"Like that, you sot!" She crushed the weapon back into his hands and then looked at me. "Come on."

Angela swooped by the table, picked up the Cog and then, ignoring the increasingly frantic skirmish around her, levered open a concealed door in the wood panel wall. She disappeared. Shooting a glance at Harold, who was paying desperate attention to the reloading and aiming of his weapon, I slid my revolver off the table and into a pocket. I lost track of Wilson, turned just in time to see him go into the corridor. No one stopped me, so I followed them through the secret door, hoping Wilson didn't do something rash before I caught up to them.

The corridor was a small space, wooden walls that quickly gave way to unfinished stone. I put a hand on Wilson's shoulder as soon as I could. He had the knives out, but gave me a nervous look then let me go ahead. Angela was only a little ways ahead, hurrying through the semi-darkness. We passed various listening holes as we went, placed to spy on the house in secret. There was fighting throughout the manor. I smelled smoke once, but it passed, and I didn't say anything. Angela must surely have noticed.

"I didn't want it to be like this, I swear. By the Celestes, I swear," Angela whispered. "Not my intent at all. You've armed yourself again, I assume."

I took the revolver from my coat and cocked the hammer in response. She nodded without looking around.

"Good. May need it. You trust your friend, there? Is he good with those stickers?"

"Good enough, ma'am. As soon as I figure out who to poke."

She laughed, not a trace of nervousness or fear in her voice. "I never expected them to make such a vulgar play."

"Who?" I asked.

She paused at a branch in the passage, considering our path. One way led down, the other up. She looked nervously down, then behind us, over my shoulder. I could hear feet, far behind.

"Can't risk that," she said. "Some things can't be put into play."

We went up.

"Who's doing this, Angela? You said someone in the Council was pushing the Badge around. Who is it?" I imagined these things happening at the Manor Burn, my family hiding in the walls, my father arming the manservants and bolting the doors. "This is practically war."

"It does seem a bit much," Angela said. We were moving quickly up a tight spiral staircase. We passed through another hidden door and were again in the common hallways of the house. The floors here were dusty, but there were windows and sunlight. The fighting below had quieted, but there were still Badge outside. "I may press a formal complaint in the Chamber."

She led us to another stairway, another spiral that went up, this one hung in tapestries. We were running now. There was no question of making a stand. We were just trying to find a place to hide. We ended up on a balcony, a tiny cupola that overlooked the estate grounds. Badge were crawling over the grounds, tramping through gardens and kicking in doors. Angela motioned us down behind the railing. Wilson peeked his head over, as though measuring distances and heights.

"If we're quiet, and lucky, we'll escape notice. This is a unilateral action, Jacob, what the Badge is doing. Someone is acting without orders, or with secret orders. I don't know who, exactly. But it's only a matter of time before the actual authority reasserts itself, and they pull back. We've just got to—"

A bullet whizzed off the stone rail by Angela's head. On another cupola, lower, an officer stood with a rifle. He was pointing at us and yelling to the courtyard below. There were already feet on the stairs behind us, hammering closer.

"I don't think quiet's going to be enough, Angela. We're going to need to secure the door and—"

A loud shot, and fire filled my chest. I looked down to see my shirt blackened with powder. The blood started, hot across my ribs.

Angela turned her pistol to Wilson, holding it steadily at his head. "I'm sorry, Jacob. I can't let them have it all. If not us, if not the Founders; well, then no one."

"Yeah," I choked. I could feel the bullet, grinding against the machine of my PilotEngine. Or whatever it was, whatever secret thing lived in my chest. She probably expected to kill me with that shot. It's what I expected. "Yeah, sorry."

I slapped the pistol aside and punched her. She fell in a heap, the Cog falling and rolling to my boot. I picked it up. Darkness was filling my head, an icy void that reached up from my chest to my eyes. I stumbled. Wilson put a hand under my arm. He was clearly torn between holding me up and slitting Angela's throat.

Blood and the cycle of my heart pounded through my skull. I put one hand on the railing and pulled myself up. In the courtyard below, the little gray officers of the Badge had slowed down. The one with the rifle was still in his cupola, still looking at me. He was shouting, but the noise came through as a soft roar. I remembered the feet on the stairs and lurched to close the door. The lock was simple, but it took my clumsy hands long heartbeats to secure it. I leaned against the old wood. The Cog had slipped from my hand. I bent down to get it again and when I stood a shadow was passing over me.

The Angel. Twenty, thirty feet from the balcony, flying in lazy circles. Wilson was staring at him, his long face slack with shock. I raised my pistol and fired. The bullet went into him, drawing a contemptuous scowl. I fired again, again, the heat going out of my hand, my arm turning into river clay. He watched me, waiting. The hammer fell on an empty chamber. I leaned against the railing and looked down. Long way down. Wilson was standing between us, both knives out. I put a tired knee on the railing and started to lift myself over.

The door behind me opened, the lock popping with barely a fight. Badgemen, their shortrifles glossy black in the sun. They looked at Angela, blood leaking from her lips, then at me. I made ready to jump. Wilson was a clever climber, right? He'd make sure I got down safely. Right?

The Angel hit me, hard, screaming. Bullets ripped past me as the Badgemen fired in blind panic. Hot lines traced across my chest, then I rolled to my feet. Wilson was dragging at my sleeve, blood across his face, one knife sheathed and the other dripping metal blood. The Badge had fallen on the Angel. He stood and shrugged them off in bloody majesty. Wilson and I jumped for the door and stumbled down the stairs in a dizzying array of thin arms and fainting legs. He followed, awkwardly, his wings tearing at the tight walls.

I followed our path back, found the secret door Angela had brought us through. My head was hammering with the grinding tear of my heart. Blood was leaking from my chest, mixed with the oily gunk of my secondary blood. I started coughing and couldn't stop. Wilson put an arm around me, carried me down. I stumbled to the floor of the secret passage and vomited while Wilson paced nervously around me. He was talking, but I couldn't hear what he was saying. Eventually I stood up and continued on. I smelled more smoke, but that might have been me. My mouth tasted like ash. Wilson kept looking at me nervously, moving ahead of me down the corridor, then coming back to make sure I was still moving. Twice we passed dead bodies,

Badgemen who had been cut by Wilson's knife. I no longer heard the angel behind us.

Wilson stopped us at the corridor where Angela had paused. He propped me against the wall and bent to my chest, poking and frowning. Actual smoke was coming up out of the metal of my heart, leaking in oily plumes out of my mouth.

"You're looking bad, son."

"Yeah. Feel it."

"We can't go much further. That dining room is clogged with Housies. Looks like that Harold guy got his balls together."

"About time." I held up the Cog and pushed it against Wilson's chest. "Get out, bug. Figure out what this is, what they want with it."

He took the Cog, looked down at it. His eyes looked like a child's eyes, so full of awe and wonder. Finally, Wilson shook his head and slid the Cog back into my pocket.

"Not yet." He nodded down the stairs. "What's that way?"

"The old guy," I said.

"Seems like a hell of a place to keep your senior citizens."

"He's a hell of a senior citizen." I was feeling a little more stable. The smoke had cut back. I didn't like that. I don't remember smoking before. I spat and stood up.

"Come on. Maybe there's another way back here."

"There's not," Wilson said. He took my arm and pulled me towards the stairs. "This is the only way."

"Well, then. We go this way."

We took the downward stairs. I could hear the angel behind us, distantly, smashing vases and tearing furniture. He was looking for the entrance to the secret passage. Wilson pulled faster, and we hurried down.

The stairs here were ancient, maybe older than the house itself. They were rock, but smoothly joined as solid stone, as if they had been grown in this form. The air was quiet and wet. The sounds of fighting passed, and I slowed down. Wilson stayed at my side. My legs were heavy lead, and my lungs felt as though they were full of broken glass. I kept one hand, revolver and all, over the hole in my chest, and the other clutched tightly around the Cog. Angela shot me, I thought. She shot me.

We came to a door. It was old and heavy, the hinges gummy with rust. I fell against it while Wilson ran his hands over the surface, looking for an opening mechanism. It was warm, and as I lay against it, the iron seemed to beat like an ancient heart. I was just summoning the strength to stand and try to give Wilson a hand when the door opened. I fell inside, and the door shut behind me. Wilson rushed to support me. He got in just before the heavy iron slammed shut with a tortured grind.

The room was like a bowl, terraced circles leading down to a pit at the center, a stage of dark, polished wood. On each level there was crowded refuse, like a scrap heap, machines that hissed and gurgled and twitched in the bare light. Stairs led down through this mess. There were frictionlamps at regular intervals. They spun up as we came into the room, covering everything in soft, warm light. There was a lot of brass, and a lot of deep, brown leather. The air smelled like a furnace that was about to blow. There was something at the bottom of the pit, something on the stage. It was swollen and alive, like an abscess of the architecture ready to burst. Light shone off metal and coils quivered. Something was breathing with the cold metal regularity of an engine and valve.

I walked down the stairs on stiff legs. The pain in my chest was a searing flare. I'm going to die down here, I thought. I approached the thing on the stage. Wilson hung back, his attention caught by the collected detritus of the pit. He looked at me nervously.

"I don't think we should be here, Jacob," he hissed. "I think this is the kind of place the Tombs would kill you for seeing."

"Tried once, already." I paused at the edge of the stage, my hand on my heart. "What's the harm?"

"There's always harm," Wilson said. He crept up behind me. "What is it?"

It was a face, iron, huge. It reclined on the ruined wood of the stage, eyes closed, fat cheeks and lips relaxed. It looked like a giant, sleeping. My hand was on the chin. Cables spilled out from all sides, twitching with power and hydraulic currents. I stepped back.

The eyes opened, slowly. Behind the lids were eyes of glass, windows into a tank of green liquid. A body floated there, bloated and ancient, the flesh pale, cables making a ruin of the flesh.

"Patron Tomb," I said.

Chapter Eight
A Fallow Harvest

"You are the Burn child." The voice came out of a box, near my feet. Each word sounded like the final exhalation of an old man, dying of wasted lungs.

"Yes," I said.

"Yes." The Patron had signed over his family's Writ of Name generations ago, to be enacted on his death. He lived on, here, always dying but never gone. "Angela speaks of you. Who is your companion?"

"This is Wilson, a friend."

"He is anansi," Tomb groaned.

"Yes," Wilson said. He sounded nervous.

"Wilson, of the anansi. We have met before."

"I think you're mistaken," Wilson said.

Tomb was quiet for a minute, the body in his eyes drifting slowly around the cold liquid of his chamber.

"Of course I am. Pardon an old man." His machinery rumbled. "Burn, you are close to Angela? A friend?"

"She and I were friends, when we were younger."

"And now?" The mausoleum's voice was slow, each word weighted with time and patience.

"I couldn't say. Times have been strange."

"Times have always been strange, child Burn. Time in Veridon is a graceless thing, lurching through the city, leaving ruin and promise equal in its wake. And even its promises are ruinous."

"Yes, well." I held down a cough, cringed at the bright crimson pain that arced through my ribs. "This is the sort of strange where she shot me. It's hard to get past that, childhood friends or not."

The Tomb was silent for a moment. "When next you are offered the opportunity to die, child Burn, I would consider it more closely."

"You threaten well," I said, shifting away from the Patron, "for a body in a tank."

"I don't make threats." He was silent for many long, metallic breaths. "It was advice, from someone who has gone on ahead."

I waited in the silence, in the dark heart of the strange theater, listening to this living Tomb breath and remember.

"What's going on, upstairs?" I asked. I had heard stories of how the Patron lived throughout the house, like a pilot on his ship.

"You said yourself, child." The body behind the eyes seemed to shift. "Strange times."

When he didn't go on, I prompted. "Is it the Church? Are they moving against the Council, trying to leverage the Families apart so they can take over?"

He made a harsh noise, something that might have been laughter.

"The Church will never upset the balance. They are the balance. They are the power! No. This is the business of dead men. Their choices come back to tempt us."

"If not the Church, then who? Someone in the Council?"

Another long silence. Sounds of fighting drifted down through pipes and duct ways, distant and tiny in this crowded room.

"I remember your grandfather," he said. "Or his father. It's hard to keep track. We built this lovely city, out here on the edge of the world. Built it on the bones of old gods, among mysteries and wonders." The voicebox rumbled. "I wasn't a Tomb then, either. Walking, that's the name I was born with."

"Yes, Patron. I know the histories. But what's happening to your city now?" Would the old man know anything about his Family's plans, or was his time spent in addled nostalgia?

"Now?" The face seemed to settle, as though it was drifting into sleep. "There is a great deal of desperation, Alexander. The girl has gotten involved in more than she can handle. You shouldn't have asked it of her."

"What?" I asked. I exchanged a quick look with Wilson. He shrugged. Tomb had forgotten which Burn I was. He mistook me for my father. "What shouldn't I have asked of your Angela?"

"Do you keep things even from yourself? A bad habit, Alexander. This plan of yours has become too much."

"I believed she could do it." How to uncover the plan without tipping off the source. "But she has failed me, hasn't she?"

"Your son, he's the failure. He's the damn weak link, Burn. You trusted him with too much. Don't blame my Family for your wastrel's dim headedness."

"Listen, you fat shit! Jacob's business is his own. He doesn't want to be involved in your goddamn power games. Leave him out of it."

The Tomb tensed, then seemed to settle, again with that sound that passed for laughter.

"Perhaps he thinks himself more clever than the old man. Perhaps he thinks himself too clever by far." A long sigh. "Don't play those games with your elders, Jacob Burn. It's beneath you."

"What did my father ask of you, of your family? I'm tired of being jerked around, Patron Tomb. I've given enough to this city." I snarled and poked my finger at his metal chin. "Tell me what's going on."

"You threaten the dead, child. With what? Disrespect? Violence?" The body shifted behind the green eyes, the puffy face floating near the glass. "Do not think to threaten us."

"There is more in the world than you, old man." I tapped my foot against the metal tubes that fed his body. "What good is the Patron if his Family is gone? What will you be if the Family Tomb is no longer respected in Veridon?"

Long silence, metal breath. "He shouldn't have asked it of her," he said, crossly, the anger coming through the voicebox as a sharp hiss. "She didn't grasp the whole picture. I advised against it."

"What, exactly, did you advise against, Patron?"

"Why are you here, Jacob Burn? What brings you into my house, to disturb my rest? Alexander didn't send you. Ask yourself why, Jacob. And why, if he hasn't let you in on the secret, why should I?"

"I didn't come to see you, old man." The pain flared in my chest again. I was feeling better, I realized. I was feeling almost normal again. "I'm here on my own business."

"But not Family business. No, you don't stand for the Family Burn, do you? Are you here as a representative of your new family? What is that wind-up thug's name. Valentine?"

"I am acting on my own, Patron. I stand for myself."

"Noble words. But what you mean is that you've been abandoned. Again. Valentine has foresworn your service, forbidden his people from working with you. Isn't that right?" He seemed to leer up from his watery bed. "That must be a feeling you're getting used to, eh? Being cut out, like a sickness."

"I am not alone. Friends stand with me. You don't know the whole game, old man." He was distracting me, diverting my attention from the central point. "What is my father's role in this? What is your Family's role? If I'm meant to be a part of it, as you imply, then how can I be of any help if no one will tell me what's going on?"

"You are here for the artifact, yes? The one taken from the Church, in secret. Passed on by a criminal. I believe they buried him in the backyard, all those years ago."

I ran a finger down the Cog. However it had gotten here, it hadn't been years ago. The Patron was talking about something else. What could it be?

"Perhaps. What is it? It has something to do with all this trouble?"

"Something. What do you want with it?"

"I'm going to solve this thing, old man. Whatever my father intended, I'm going to put an end to this."

"Mm. It isn't the sort of trouble that can be solved, child. Merely avoided, and survived."

"Is that why you're down here? Hiding from the trouble?"

"My Family's future depends on my survival. You wouldn't understand."

I laughed. "Did you fear death so much, that you trapped your Family into preserving you? Is that why you signed that terrible contract, blackmailing your Family with their place on the Council?"

"Is this life! This fallow harvest, Jacob, is this living!" Heat rose from the Tomb, and the cables hummed. "You have no idea, sir, what this is. We make sacrifices, Jacob, for family. For the city. Your father, he understands. He knows what it is to sacrifice for family."

"My father? Noble Alexander! Tell me, Patron, if he understands the value of sacrifice, of family, what is it, sir, that he valued so much that he sacrificed his own family, his own blood, his goddamn son!"

Tomb was quiet. Eventually, "You wouldn't understand."

"Now that," I said, leaning in toward the massive face. "That I believe."

"It is here."

"What?"

"Your artifact. Third shelf, against the wall. An ivory box. They made it into something holy, those churchmen. I don't know where the key is hidden."

I stood up. Wilson was already up the pit, rummaging in the area Tomb had indicated. "Why tell me? If it has been hidden all this time. What would Angela say?"

"Angela has gone a great deal farther than I think is prudent. And I am tired. Now, go."

He settled down, the face shifting ever so slightly into slack inattention. I bounded up the stairs. When I looked back the face was still open, the glossy green eyes staring up at the darkness with their pupils of bloated flesh.

Wilson brought me the box. We squatted in the walkway. It was a long, narrow container, the flat planes thin sheets of ivory set in tarnished silver fittings. It was a simple matter to crack open with my knife. The artifact clattered out. I squatted above it, looking for damage. It was quiet in the hallways.

The artifact was a cylinder of steel with grooves. Something twitched inside me, like a stolen memory burning through my head. Without thinking I ran my hand down the artifact, triggered some hidden catch, then balanced it on one end. The cylinder blossomed, like a flower.

There was wire, a fly wheel, and a tightly packed central axis of stacked metal segments. It spun up. Plates folded out from the central core, supported and guided by the wires, which stiffened as they expanded. The plates spun in wider circles, shifting, sliding by each other until they blurred into a single brilliant image. Viewed from above it made a picture, like a cinescope.

It was a map. Most of it looked like nothing to me, just lines and rivers and a coastline, far in the top left corner. And then I saw Veridon, or where Veridon should have been, near one edge of the map, in the arms of the Ebd and the Dunje. From there I found the Reine, the Breaking Wall, the Cusp Sea, the Tavis Minor and Major, the Salt Sweeps. It was different than the map I knew, the one I learned at the Academy, but some of the landmarks were similar enough. I followed the Reine where it left the Cusp, far beyond the borders of the Academy's maps.

There was a city, massive, if the scale was to be believed. It was at the center of the map, sprawled on both sides of the Reine hundreds of miles downriver from the Cusp. So far beyond the ken of the Academy's far ranging Expeditioner's Corp I could only stare in amazement. I felt like there was someone over my shoulder, a presence both ancient and young, a presence that stank of fear and isolation. I looked at that city and the phantom in me spoke with my voice.

"Home," we said.

"WELL NOW," WILSON muttered. "Well, well. Now isn't that interesting." He hooked an arm under my shoulder and dragged me to my feet. I realized I had been lying down. He propped me against a shelf, littered with the parts of a shattered clock.

"We need to get out of here," I said. My throat felt like it was lined in barbed wire.

"Be a hell of a time," Wilson said. "Lots of folks out there. And I don't think Angela's going to like us walking out with that thing."

"Yeah." I tested my legs, found I could stand. "Well, maybe there's another way out of here."

Patron Tomb shuffled, his eyelids cracking just slightly. "There is."

"You can get us out?" Wilson asked.

"No. But I can show you the way." He paused, his eyelids flaring wider in surprise. "There is something upstairs, a presence. It has found the hallway."

"What?" I asked.

"Something... brilliant. What is this thing?" Tomb's voice was low, in awe.

"The angel," Wilson whispered. "We need to get the hell out."

"Yes, you do. My gods, you do. He's at the door."

The door at the top of the stairs clanged. Dust settled from the roof in wide sheets. The clanging continued, steady, metronomic.

"This is going to be interesting," Tomb said. "I should thank you, Burn. It's a good day you've brought me."

"It will try to kill you," I said.

"Perhaps. Here," machines cycled, and a narrow door opened in the wall opposite the main entrance. "That leads to a covered canal near the Bellingrow. It's quite a trek, I'm told. In case they ever need to get me out."

"You would never fit through that door."

"Desperation and technology can do amazing things," he said. "Now, hurry. He's persistent."

We rushed out the door. I paused to look back. The old man's bloated eyes were settled on the other door, watching the angel break his slow way in, like the tide battering a rocky coast. The door closed behind us.

I DON'T REMEMBER much after that. The darkness faded into gray, tunnels of brick and dirt that stretched for an eternity and when I came to I was lying on a hard stone floor, Wilson looking down at me.

"You're trying to show me wrong, son," Wilson said quietly. His face was bent very close to mine, so I could smell his breath. It smelled like ground up flies and specimen jars. "Trying to die, aren't you?"

"Far from it." My voice was a whisper. "Just other folks, testing the theory."

"Well. More luck than science, this time." He picked up a tin cup and rattled it around. There was a deformed slug at the bottom, shiny with blood. "Frail gun she shot you with. More ornament than weapon, I suspect."

"She who?" It was Emily talking, somewhere. I couldn't see where exactly, but it sounded like she was standing near my head, looking down. Behind me a little. I twisted and saw her face, grimacing down at me.

"Tomb. Little Lady Tomb."

"Bullshit," she said.

"Fine, Em. Whatever. It was the Blessed Celeste. But she looked a hell of a lot like the Lady Tomb."

"It was her alright," Wilson said. He grinned tightly up at Emily. "Pretty as you please, nice to meet you, and here's a bullet for your time."

"What dumbass thing did you do to get her to shoot you, Jacob? Did you break into her house? Steal some silverware?"

I tried to answer, but it came out as a dry rattling cough. Wilson put his hand on my chest until it settled down. When I could talk again, even I had trouble hearing me. Emily bent down close. She smelled like sweat and dry flowers.

"Badge broke into her house. Stormed the place. We were running, got cornered." I paused to spit, but came up empty. My tongue felt like a strap of leather. "She said some shit about not letting them get a hold of me. Then she put a bullet in my chest."

"Hm," Emily said. She stood up and walked out of my field of vision. Wilson watched her go, then looked back at me. His eyes were carefully neutral.

"How'd you get out," she asked.

I started to answer, but Wilson shushed me.

"We lost her and found a back door. Things were very..." he paused, nodding to himself. "Very confusing. For everyone, I think."

"Lost her? You didn't kill her, did you?"

I shook my head. "Angel's back," I said.

Emily raised her eyebrows. "That's sudden. Thought you said you'd killed it?"

"I killed something. But it was the same guy."

"I've been meaning to ask you about that," Wilson said, washing off his hands in a puddle of rain water. "I have some thoughts."

"Are they warm, happy thoughts?" I asked. "Thoughts that are likely to reassure me as to our own safety?"

"Not completely," he said. "But they may shed some light on what we're dealing with here."

"Then keep them to yourself." I stretched out on the floor and laced my fingers behind my neck. "I'm limiting myself to good news for a little while."

"Let's hear it, Wilson," Emily said, shooting me a cross look.

"Ever since you talked about killing the Summer Girl, I've been churning away at what could have happened there. What happened, exactly, to bring about that specific transformation."

"I hit her with a hammer," I said.

"Not... gods, you're horrible. Not that transformation. The one where this little girl turns into a murdering angel."

"Ah. Continue."

"Well, the way that the Summer Girl works, the way all engram singers work, is the maker beetles. That and the queen fetus. The Artificers burn a pattern into the queen, the queen takes up residence in the singer's internal machinery, and then the beetles burrow their way—"

"What?" Emily almost shrieked. "They burrow into her body?"

"You've never seen an engram singer?" I asked.

"No, you filthy noble pig. I grew up watching normal people sing normal songs, that they had memorized or made up or something."

"Oh, right. I keep forgetting I was born so much better than you."

"Listen, you little fucking—"

"Okay!" Wilson interjected. "Okay. So the beetles burrow in," he turned to Emily, "through her machine. There are little tunnels that run through her body. Most of the transformation is facilitated by the machine, but it's the beetles that do it. The machine is kind of like... like a hive, I suppose. Okay?"

"It's still weird."

"The point is, there's a pattern, held by the queen. Sound familiar?"

"Cogwork," I said. I suppose I had always known the two practices were similar, I had just never thought about how they were almost identical. "The Wrights have you memorize a pattern, they inject the foetal metal, and the metal makes itself into whatever the pattern dictates."

"More or less," Wilson said. "The pattern is also inscribed onto a coin and put in with the foetus. But without the pattern, the foetal metal is nothing. Just hot metal."

"Where do the patterns come from?" Emily asked.

"The Church," I answered. "And where do they get them? Who knows. But it's the foundation of their religion."

"So the Artificers and the Church, they both make their technology the same way?"

"Let's make no mistakes, Emily." Wilson sat up straight. "The Wrights only have what they've found. Their holy vessels come down the river, and the Wrights catch them and scrounge out any mysteries they can manage. They're very good at it, and very good at applying what they find, but it's not creation, really. More like scavenging."

"And the Artificers?" I asked. I'd never met anyone willing to talk about the Artificers and their technology. Ever since their Guild had been unofficially disbanded and their role in the city gutted so many years ago, their methods were not a matter of public discourse. If they hadn't been allowed to continue the minor entertainments like the Summer Girl, most folks wouldn't even know the Guild had ever existed.

"The Artificers? Oh, well. They do things differently. Let's leave it at that," Wilson said. "The point is, there's a pattern involved. Every piece of cogwork, from the zepliners to the simplest abacist, has at its heart a holy pattern of the Wrights. Including your PilotEngine, Jacob."

"Yeah, well. Maybe they fucked mine up."

"Maybe. That's why I keep trying to get a good read off you, with the beetles. Trying to see the pattern of your heart."

"Anyway. The Angel?"

"Yes, the Angel. You're sure it was the same one?"

"Sure as hell," I said.

"But you killed that one, or one very much like it, yes? On the Heights?"

"Right."

"And that one, the one you killed on the Heights, the one we saw at the Manor Tomb just today, it's the same one you saw on the *Glory*."

"He jumped off, just before we crashed."

Wilson stood up and, hunching over, began to pace the room. "Jumped off. Just before you crashed. And Jacob, you found this other fellow, this marine, in the Artificer's rooms?"

"Wellons. Yeah, but he'd been dead for a while."

"Do you think the Summer Girl was on the *Glory*?" he asked.

"No, of course not."

"Of course not. Do you think Wellons was?"

"I didn't..." I stopped. "You're saying the Angel was Wellons?"

"At one point. And then, for whatever reason, it left Wellons and became the Summer Girl."

"What? How?" Emily asked.

"I don't have an answer for how." Wilson stopped pacing and pulled the Cog from his pocket. "But I have an idea about why."

He set the Cog on the ground near my feet, then crouched over his bag and produced a glass jar that jingled as he moved it. He unscrewed the lid and rummaged through the contents, then set what looked like a coin on the ground next to the Cog.

"What do you see?" he asked.

I sat up. Emily and I leaned closer to the two objects. The Cog I knew. The coin was a flat metal disk, dull, with lines etched into its surface and cog-teeth along a quarter of its perimeter. It looked old.

"Algorithm," I said, pointing to the coin. "That's one of the Church's pattern-coins."

"For cog, yes. This is what serves as the groundwork for all cogwork. Put one of these in your mouth, inject the foetus, and something grows in you." He nudged the coin around, examining the pattern. "In this case, a musical instrument that replaces your lungs. Or something. I forget. The point is, it's the blueprint for cogwork. What else?"

I looked more closely at the coin, then the Cog. "I don't—"

"Pattern," Emily said.

Wilson pointed at her. "Pattern. Yes." He held up the Cog. "This is a very big, very complicated pattern coin."

"My gods," Emily said. "For what?"

Wilson shrugged. "I don't know. But we could find out."

"I'd rather not," I said. "So, Marcus and Wellons and whoever else was on that list stole this from the city, and now that angel is chasing them?"

"City?" Emily asked. "Which city."

"I didn't tell her," Wilson said. "Yet."

"We found a map, at the Tomb place. It shows a city, huge, way downriver."

"Like another Veridon?"

"Nothing like Veridon. Veridon's a damn outhouse compared to his place. I don't know what it is."

"Okay. One thing at a time." Wilson pointed to me and shook his head. "I don't think so, by the way. I don't think they made it all the way to that city. But I think that's where they were going. They just ran into some trouble."

"The Angel?"

"The Angel. Maybe he was a scout, maybe he lived well outside the city. If they'd gotten all the way there, I don't think we'd be having this conversation. I think there'd be a whole swarm of those things turning Veridon to mulch."

"Shit," I said. I meant it, too. Veridon had been tough on me, but it was home. People here I cared about. Streets and buildings I'd known my whole life. "So, what? They found an outlying building, stole the Cog, and then the angel caught them and chased them."

"Better than that. Or much, much worse. Depends on your point of view. I think they found that angel, killed him, and stole the body. Or at least part of the body."

"Why would they do that?" Emily asked.

"Question for Marcus. Or Wellons. Maybe that Sloane guy you met. But I think they've done it before."

"Stolen body parts from angels?" Emily asked.

"Where does the cogwork come from, Emily? Where do they get their patterns? They aren't making them up, that's for sure." Wilson was pacing again, agitated. He stabbed his finger out at us. "That's for damn sure. They're getting it from somewhere else. What's to say that this isn't the source?"

"We should ask the Church," I joked. "I'm sure they'll be very forthcoming on that."

"Not the Church," Wilson said. "But the people on your list. Angela Tomb. That Sloane guy. They'll know."

"Yeah, well. But Angela doesn't seem much like talking. And Sloane? I'll ask him, if I find him. But what makes you say they stole a part of the body?"

"Because now we have it. And they want it back. And so does the original owner."

"The Cog?"

"Yeah. I think this is nothing less than that angel's pattern. I think it's his damn heart."

"So what happened with Wellons?" I asked. We had decided that whatever the Cog was, we had to keep it out of the hands of the Council. For now at least. I wanted to know more about what we were doing, what we were handing over.

"For whatever reason, the angel seems to need a host. I'm going to assume that has something to do with this," Wilson said, holding up the Cog. "And so far he's only infected people who have been heavily cogged. You said Wellons was an assault trooper, right?"

"According to his uniform, yeah. And those guys are metalled up to the balls."

"Lovely terminology. And the Summer Girl, we know, had the beetle hive implanted. None of the other Artificers would have had any modifications, so she was the only choice."

"Infect? Like he's some kind of disease?" I asked.

"More like a parasite," Wilson answered. His eyes had a far away look, and his voice was drifting into university professor territory. What had he done with his time, before his days as a black-market doctor? "Takes over the body and the mind, remakes it. If the angels really are the source of Veridon's cogwork, then who knows how advanced they are. What they're capable of."

"That's creepy," I said. "But isn't that Church theology? That the early Wrights were able to heal the dying Camilla, and in return she gifted them with the first cogwork?"

Wilson shrugged. "Seems a convenient story, but maybe. Maybe."

"So it infected Wellons," I said. "Then followed Marcus back to the city. For whatever reason it had to leave him, then took over the Summer Girl. So what happened when I killed her?"

"You tell me. What happened?"

"She... fell apart, I guess. It looked like the maker beetles, leaving her body, splashing down into the rain."

Wilson nodded. "And it might have been something very similar. Maybe the cog-heart serves as his pattern, holds him together. And he needs the host body just for the pattern in their implanted cogwork. Something to hold him together. Disrupt that, and the thing falls apart."

"And then what? How does it find a new host?"

"Goes dormant? Reforms somehow, and latches on to someone new? This is all just theory, Jacob."

"But we saw it again, so we know it happened. Somehow the thing reformed."

"A new host," Emily said. "Who was at the party?"

"Pilots," I said. "Lots of Pilots."

"There you go." Wilson spread his hands and grimaced. "If cogwork is necessary for infection, Pilots are pretty close to the perfect candidate. If one of your Corpsmen wandered down into the gardens, maybe looking for you, they could have stumbled into the angel's scattered corpse and gotten infected without knowing what happened."

I looked down at my palms. "How did I not get infected?"

"Who knows? Maybe when you disrupted the body it needs some time to spin up again. Let's just say you got lucky, and you'll be more careful in the future."

Emily had been quiet, standing a little ways away from us. I turned to her.

"So what are we going to do now?" I asked her. When she didn't say anything, didn't even seem to hear me, Wilson stepped in.

"Badge is after you, that thing in the sky is after you." He shrugged. "Sounds like maybe the Family Tomb is after you, too. We're going to need a better place to hide."

"What's wrong with here?" Emily asked. She seemed distracted.

"Not deep enough. Too close to the Families, to the centers of the Badge's power. Too many crowds. People here don't love the Badge, but if they're serious about finding you, well. Someone will talk. Enough money and enough threats, people will talk."

"So where do we go?" I asked. I stood and stretched my back. My thighs felt like lead, and my chest was stiff. "I can't go far, or fast."

"I have some ideas. We'll wait until tonight, until you're a little better."

"I feel pretty good right now. I just don't want to push it. And with that thing in the air…"

"I think the Tomb set you up," Emily said. Wilson and I stopped and turned to her.

"What do you mean?" I asked.

"I think she set you up. That bit about the Badge interrupting, I don't think that was part of the plan, but I think she set you up."

I walked carefully over to the wall and sat down with my back against it. "What makes you say that, Em? What do you know about this?"

"Nothing. I mean, nothing solid. But the Cog missing like that? It hadn't been there long, like they were waiting for it to show up. And they had to know you'd come for it."

"Maybe. But that's hardly evidence."

"And on the Heights too, I think."

I tensed up. I'd been wondering about the Heights, what Emily knew about that job, really.

"That job wasn't from Valentine, Jacob."

"Okay," I said, carefully.

"I wanted to make sure you'd take the job. I knew you wouldn't turn down work from the old clockwork."

"That was risky. If he found out, if I said anything to him about it. A real chance you took there, Em."

"The drugs, with Prescott, that was his. But the music box wasn't."

"That got Prescott killed, you know."

"Yeah. I know."

I flexed my hands, loosened my shoulders. "So. Who did the job come from, then?"

"I don't know. A guy, he looked… I don't know. Noble."

"Like he was a Family guy. Someone's important son?"

"Right. He gave me the box and told me it needed to go to Tomb. At the party. He said you needed to do the job."

"You were really looking out for me there, Em." I kept my voice as even as I could. "Really watching my back."

"Sorry. I'm sorry. You're pretty good at handling yourself. I figured it was some Council thing. Some… political statement."

"Yeah," I said. "So. Angela Tomb gets me up on the Heights, then tries again at the Manor." I remembered the troop of soldiers outside my door up on the Heights. I hadn't given that much thought, what with all the bloodletting and falling out of windows. What had they been doing there? They couldn't have found Prescott or the Artificers, then rushed to arrest me on basic assumption. "So what does that mean?"

"I don't know." Emily shrugged. "Honestly. I could be wrong about the whole thing."

"Well. We'll see. Anything else, Emily? Anything I should know?"

She shook her head, kind of sadly. "Nothing else."

"Where does that leave us? Angela Tomb wants me alive, then she shoots me." I leaned over and took the Cog from Wilson and held it in my palm. "And lots of people want this. How many groups are we talking about? Tomb. Whoever's pushing the Badge around from inside the Council. Whoever paid Pedr to break into my room. Someone sent that gun up to the Heights, that wasn't Angela. Sloane, we know he visited Emily after I left the Cog with her. And his name's on that list, along with Angela, Marcus, and Wellons." I looked up. "Lotta folks interested in us."

"What do we do?" Wilson asked.

"I don't know. Hide some more. Dig up some information about this thing. Why everyone wants it. Figure out who we're up against, and why." I slipped the Cog into my coat pocket and stood up. "But first, we hide."

Chapter Nine
The Church is an Engine

We moved at night, down the Prior Grosse and into the Long March wards. I was careful of the sky, dashing between buildings and staying to the narrow alleyways. We followed the terraces down towards the Reine, where the streets covered generations of pipework and history. We went down to the cisterns.

Walking through the old avenues reminded me of home. We were uncomfortably close to the Burn family grounds. Tomb was near the top of Veridon, but great old Burn made his lands farther from the thick walls of the old city. I saw the eternal lights of Tower Burn looming in crimson stained glory over the other buildings on its terrace. I hurried on.

Emily drew up beside me. She had her hands in her pockets. Wilson was a shadow behind us.

"Jacob, I'm sorry. I didn't mean for it to go like this."

I kept my eyes forward. "Sure. You had your reasons for doing things."

"No, I mean it." She plucked at the sleeve of my coat, an irritated gesture. "Don't get all noble on me. It was a gamble, but I figured you were up to it. I figured that if the Tombs were involved, well." She shrugged. "That's just the sort of job you were born for, isn't it?"

"Born and raised. But next time you gamble with my skin, lady, maybe let me know."

"You might have turned down the job."

"I might have. But I might have gone in better prepared. When did it occur to you that Tomb might be trying to get a hold of me, Em? When those men came looking for me, in your office? When the Badge chased me out of your apartment?" I turned to look at her. Her face was pale, like winterglass. "Was it when you sent me into the Manor Tomb, to fetch that Cog?"

"No!" she hissed. She turned her shoulders to me. Her face was pale, sure, but it was anger. She slammed her finger into my ribs. "Damn it, no. I wouldn't sell you out like that. If I thought it, before then, if I thought it was a trap… who else has been with you since the start, Jacob Burn? Since you fell from your fancy house? Valentine? Cacher? Old Man Burn? No, cogs-dammit, it's me. If you ever, ever once, accuse me of selling out on you I'll gut you and hang your noble god damn head on my wall. Emily Haskin doesn't sell out her people."

We had stopped walking. Wilson disappeared, probably scrabbling up some wall to get away.

"Okay, Em. Forget it. Forget I said anything."

She balled her fist and lay her knuckles lightly against my jaw line, then let her nails brush my cheek.

"Forgotten."

She marched down the road, disappearing between two buildings while I stood, my hands still in my pockets, the lightning burn of her touch traced across my face. Wilson was back. He patted me on the shoulder as he went by.

"This is good, the two of you. It's good."

"Shut up."

He laughed, a sound like an ungreased winch, breaking.

"Just shut up."

Veridon was a city of terraces, streets and avenues that crossed canals, canals that became aqueducts and then tunnels and pipes. There were locks that raised and lowered the domesticated rivers of the city. Waterfalls spilled into plazas, fed pools that drained into cisterns which in turn burst out at lower terraces to rush in torrents along bricked canals through the streets. River and tunnel, the flow and the fall, but everywhere there was water, rushing and collecting, in deep stagnant pools or wild torrents, driven by gravity or muscled along by ancient pumps that seemed to pre-date the city on their shoulders.

The city had settled in layers over this veinwork of water, leveling out and spreading further toward the shore. Parts of Veridon extended far into the river Reine, held up by piers and pillars that kept the lower wards from sinking into the water. A brisk trade was done there, on the river beneath the city, tar-blackened boats with shuttered lamps creeping in to secret docks beneath nondescript buildings. I rode those boats, in the messy, early days of my exile. Before Emily, and Valentine.

The truly secret places of the city, though, were higher up. Between the streets and the stones were hundreds of miles of cisterns, piped canals, aqueducts that had been strapped down with bridge after building until there was no daylight to reach their grimy currents.

We hid ourselves in the guts of the city. It took hours to find the right place, somewhere that had been abandoned by the service crews and criminals alike. We ended up on a stone pier that stretched into a cistern, the water deep and still, the walls smooth stone that echoed with our voices. It made us feel less alone. It was hard to believe that the city had ever been this low, or the river this high. We collapsed on the pier, wrapped ourselves in jackets, and slept like the dead. When I woke up the tip of my nose was frigid, and my back was stiff. Acceptable, for a man who should have died twice in as many weeks. Three times, if you count the *Glory*.

Wilson had already left. I spun up the frictionlamp to find his coat in a rumpled heap, the rest of his belongings carefully stashed in notches along the wall. Emily was asleep nearby, breathing quietly. I crept over to Wilson's things and searched them carefully. There were bottles and envelopes of dust, a glass rod that was warm to the touch and seemed to vibrate against my fingernail, other mysterious things that could have been tiny machines or just rare insects, killed and dried.

His shortrifle was there, loaded. He had taken that wicked knife.

"He went out, about an hour ago. Said he needed something. Instruments or whatnot," Emily said. She had turned to face me, her eyes puffy with sleep. "Said he'd be back in a few hours."

"Maybe he'll bring us some dinner. Though I'm not sure I look forward to discovering the joys of anansi appetite." I returned Wilson's things to their proper place.

"Oh, he's not a monster, you know."

"If you say. But if he brings me a sandwich of fly wings, you know who I'm going to blame."

She snorted and sat up. "You're a ridiculous man."

"If you say." I rumpled Wilson's jacket, to make it look as it had when I first touched it, then stood up and stretched. "Emily, how well do you know him?"

"Wilson? Well enough. Feeling suspicious?"

I shrugged. "The Badge showed up, right on his heels. And maybe he let them know I was going to visit the Manor Tomb, for the Cog."

"You said yourself, they saw you go in. You walked right past them, up to the gate. You announced yourself, Jacob." She rubbed sleep from her face and stretched, luxuriously. "No, Jacob. I think that whoever is pushing the Badge around figured out Tomb had the Cog. You just forced their hand, showing up like that."

"You're probably right." I sat on the pier, my feet over the water. "Still. You trust him?"

"I do. Not every rock hides a snake, Jacob."

"Just the rock that kills you, picking it up."

She snorted again and stood, adjusting her riding skirt. How she kept up with us in that thing was a mystery to me. She sat next to me and sighed.

"What now, Jacob Burn?"

"Lots of stuff I want to know. Why Angela shot me. Who sent me that gun up on the Heights. What this..." I had a panicked moment, a stab of suspicion as I patted my pockets, searched frantically, found the Cog with a sigh and held it in my hand. "What this thing has to do with it all. I mean, if you're right and Tomb set me up, well. She had the Cog. What does she need me for?" I fiddled with the Cog absently, running my finger down its edge. The metal hummed at my touch, sending smooth fire into my bones. It felt nice. My chest seemed to almost vibrate with calm.

"Tomb. Sloane. Marcus. Wellons." I took the slip of paper out of my pocket. "Not a very likely bunch of companions. And I don't know anyone else on this list."

"Can I see?" Emily asked. I gave her the paper. She flattened it out and then traced her finger down the list of names. "Is this an exact copy?"

"No. I just took down the relevant details."

"So, 'Hire: 4', there was no other indication what that might mean?"

I looked over at the paper. Emily had her finger over the second to last line, just above where Tomb was listed as the Council Approval.

"No idea. I think it might have been spelled out, rather than the number."

"Because the rest of these names, with the exception of Wellons, are all common criminals."

"Right. So?"

"I don't know Sloane. Never heard of him before this mess. And I know everyone in the crime market. Is Angela the kind of girl who hangs out with criminals?"

"Gods, no. Not her particular social circle."

"I didn't think so. So someone else made the contacts."

"Makes sense," I said.

"Jacob. Four."

I looked at her, and it hit me. I was a fucking idiot.

"I'm a fucking idiot," I said. Matthew Four was an old friend of the Families, and probably the first criminal I'd ever met. He provided Veridon's rich with whatever gray market items they needed, without disturbing the social fabric of their expensive parties. If Angela needed to hire a bunch of roughs, of course she'd go to Matthew. "Godsdamn it, Em."

"I'll forgive you. But he seems like someone worth talking to."

"Yeah, yeah. And he might know who gave you that music box, too."

"I thought we decided it was Tomb's doing. Getting you up there, trapping you."

"Oh, she had her part in it. Sure. But other forces intervened. The angel, for one, in the form of the Summer Girl. And the gun. Someone sent that to me, either as a warning or a threat."

"Do you think it was the actual pistol, the one from the *Glory*?"

"I don't know that it matters. Someone was telling me that they know what happened up there, that night, they know what I did to Marcus. I didn't tell anyone."

"You told me," she said.

"Is that what happened, Em? Did you mail me a secret package, then send your angelic minion to kill me before I figured it out?" I grinned a little grin.

She laughed and leaned back, resting on her elbows, kicking her boots out over the water. She arched her back and smiled.

"Yes, darling, you have me. I'm the secret angel minion killer. I've been in the business of killing my friends with secret angel minions since I was a wee child. My father, you see, was heavily involved in the sale and maintenance of secret angel minions."

I smiled and twisted to look at her. My arm brushed the warm strength of her belly. Her eyes flashed.

"You're a ridiculous woman," I said.

"Perhaps."

We sat there for a moment, quietly. The water beneath us was very still, the stone cold.

"So," Emily said. "What now."

"I'm going to talk to Matthew. See if I can find out where the package came from. What happened to that girl."

She flashed her dark eyes down to my hands, the holster on my belt, then settled on my face.

"And me?"

"You? I think you should stay here. Watch this." I set the Cog on the pier between us. "Wilson will be back."

"Sooner or later." She pulled her hair from its knot, let it fall as sunshine cascaded across her face and down her neck. Her body was stretched, the muscles taut beneath the soft comfort of her dress. She smiled at my distraction.

"I think I'm going to take a bath," she said quietly. "I'm in desperate need."

I stood awkwardly and busied myself with my belt, fitting the holster more comfortably.

"I'll, uh. Be back," I said. She laughed, a delightful lilt that glanced down my spine and stuck in my bones. "Watch the Cog."

"Attentively," she called to my retreating back.

Behind me I could hear fabric falling, water splashing. I closed my eyes and hurried out.

I GOT EMILY'S laughter out of my head by walking. I stitched my way across the city, crossing bridges and riding carriages, climbing the gentle avenues that led up to higher terraces or descended to the city's lower districts closer to the river, traveling randomly to lose the image of her stepping into the water, her dress falling away, hair loose as the water rose up her legs, the warm hum of the frictionlamp the only light on her skin.

I sighed and signaled for the busser to pull over. I was where I needed to be, where the guy I wanted to talk to was most likely to be found. I got out of the carriage, paid, and lost myself in the crowd. Plenty of crowd, even this time of night, here in the Three Bells. In other parts of the city, this many people on the street was usually the preamble to a riot. Three Bells, though, this is just what happened at night. Drinking, carousing, art. I used to be comfortable in this crowd.

The crowd slowed around the BlackIron Theater. The show was getting ready to start, and folks were trying to sneak in before the gate closed. I edged my way around the logjam until I was standing by the reserved gate. Reserve ticketholders arrived when they wanted to, sat where they wanted to. Trick was, reserve tickets couldn't be bought. Something you had to be born into. I went up to the gate.

"Evening, sir," said the well pressed guard behind the iron bars. He looked over my clothes with little respect. "This gate is for reserved seats. Main entrance is that way."

"I'm familiar with the arrangement. I'll be claiming the Burn seats this evening."

"Ah. I don't know that I'm acquainted with your claim, sir."

"My claim? Should I bleed out a little nobility for you? Or are you unfamiliar with the Family Burn? We have a tower, don't we, right over that goddamn hill. Would you like a tour of the grounds, perhaps, a short walk through the Deep Furnace? Would that suffice? Sir?"

The man had gone pleasantly white. "Ah, no, no. What I mean, sir, is that the Family Burn is here frequently. Just the other night. And, ah, I am... I know them all, sir."

I tilted my chin, hooked my thumb in the loop on my holster in the traditional dueling stance of the Families, and stared him down.

"I am Jacob Hastings Burn, first son of Alexander, formerly of the Highship Fastidious."

His face fell. He looked me over again, trying to decide if he could turn me down based on my history, my unsure place in the complicated world of obligation and honor that ruled among the Families.

"No weapons in the theater, sir?" It was a desperate try.

"Bullshit. Every father's son in there has his iron. Don't think to lock me out on that."

He looked down, fiddled with the baubles on his cuffs, worried the corners of a program that he had picked up.

"So what's the show, friend?" I asked.

"*The Ascension of Camilla.*"

"Swell." I stuck my hand out for the program. "Let's see it."

He looked at the program in his hand, deflated, and handed it to me through the bars. With a clatter he slid the gate open and showed me inside.

"This way, sir."

"I know the way." I shouldered him aside and disappeared into the velvet darkness of the theater. The BlackIron was a remarkably complicated building. A complicated entertainment, really, but it served to show off the city's extravagant innovation. It was a majestically conceited engine.

The main hall was cool and dark when I slipped inside. The show had started, and the terraced rows of booths were bathed in the reflected light of the stage. It was just enough light to find my way. I spent a lot of time here in the fragile days of my youth, but it had been a while. I stood by the entrance while my eyes adjusted, scanning the rows of booths. Matthew Four put in an appearance at the BlackIron almost every night. He was in the business of being available to the Families. Probably the first criminal I had ever met.

Tonight's story was of young and imperfect Camilla, and her being raised by the Church of the Algorithm. It was one of the thinner propagandas, but the trappings were remarkable. Unlike the more primitive theaters, the stage of the BlackIron was at an angle, slightly steeper than the terraced seats of the audience. There were dozens of trapdoors and metal tracks, whipping cables of wire and rope gathered up by pulleys, all of it painted black to give the impression of a blank slate, the empty table of storytelling.

Into this emptiness came the contraptions of the Theater. Moved along the tracks or across the pulley-lines, the actors of the BlackIron told the story of little Camilla, following her from childhood, portraying the struggles of her family, the conditions of their poverty at the hands of an uncaring king, a distant court. I had seen the play a hundred times. It was an old favorite of the city, a familiar tale repeated until it was ritual. Much like *The Summer Girl*, come to think of it. I shuddered, only half watching the production.

They told the story well, precisely, hitting every cue, reciting every line. But of course, their perfection was the conceit, for these were not the actors of just any theater. This was the BlackIron, renowned and remembered, the pride of Veridon. These actors were artwork, engines of cogwork and performance, assembled especially for each show, half-made and remade every night.

As I stood in the dim hall, Camilla herself was taking the stage. The preamble was over, and the ascension was beginning. I had seen it dozens of times, but it always held my attention. The director here was a clever man, personally rebuilding the performance-engines each night, bringing out some new reaction from the cogwork, so that every show was slightly different, slightly more... perfect.

Camilla appeared from the central trapdoor, high up on the stage's palette. She unfolded, unbound by the rules of biology, shuffling open to her full size, exaggerated to aid the viewing of the audience. No bad seats at the BlackIron. The girl's voice was gentle, quiet, but utterly clear. She sang about her family, gone over the falls, swept away by flood. Her voice wavered as she went on, describing her sickness, the rot of her lungs, the weakness of her heart. My heart is falling, winding down. My heart is empty, falling down. I whispered along.

Another voice, offstage, joined her. The churchman, the Wright. His brown robes and oil-grimed hands whirred into view along a track. Their voices joined, the song continued on, rising until the hall shook with her sickness, with his solution. The complicated trick that was the center of the spectacle began, her arms first folding out, unbecoming, the Wright adding, replacing, creating. Making her something more, something complicated.

I lowered my eyes. It was a metaphor, for the city. Whatever we were, whatever power we held, the Church was behind it. Their god was the secret machine, and their worship was the cogwork that ran the rest of the city. They didn't let us forget, not the Families, not the people. The Church was the engine, and we were the gear.

I looked up and saw my man. He was at a booth by himself, off to one side of the upper rows. Available yet discreet. I went up and sat at his booth. He looked startled, both before and after he recognized me. He was an older man, his hair perfectly coifed and his face deep with powder and age. His skin looked like old parchment.

"Mr. Burn," Matthew said. "Not someone I expected to see out and about."

"Why's that, Mr. Four?"

"Things I've heard, conversations that have been going around."

"Conversations?"

He nodded, then slowly brought his hands up from under the table and lay them flat on the linen.

"You're the subject of a lot of conversations."

"Are you going to tell me what kind of conversations, Matthew?"

He shrugged. I rolled a coin across the table. He snatched it up, gave me a disapproving look for being so overt, then settled his attention on the stage. I waited, my eyes going between Matthew and the performance.

"How long have I known you, Jacob?" he asked, eventually.

"I don't know. A while." On stage the ascension was continuing. Camilla had extended into something ridiculous, her ribs a broad and white cage that held the machinery of ascension. The Wright was below her, carefully snipping off her legs with garden shears.

"A while." Matthew nodded. "Quite a while. The better part of your life, I suspect. And in those years, I have seen some things."

He drank from the nearly empty glass of wine by his hand. The play had gotten very loud, the Ascension Song crashing down from the stage. Camilla's heart levered onto the stage, shattering into cogs and wheels that magically arranged themselves into patterns. The ruins of the girl grew.

"Some of these things, I never expected to see." Matthew said, almost too quietly to be heard above the music. I leaned close to him.

"Tell me, Four. Did you ever expect to see this?" I took out the paper, lay it out flat and slid it in front of him. He squinted down at it.

"If I go for my glasses, are you going to shoot me, Mr. Burn?"

"I'll save you the tension. That's a list of names, Matthew. People who are supposed to be dead, people hired by the Council to do a job." I took the paper back. "Your name is on this list."

"Hardly shocking, Jacob." He settled back into the plush leather of his seat and looked at me. "We both know the services I provide to the Families, as well as the Council."

"This specific list is causing me a lot of trouble. I'd like to talk to these people, but like I said, most of them are dead."

"Are you saying I'm about to be dead?" he asked, smirking.

"That's not my call. I have no beef with you, if that's what you mean. I just want to know what these folks were hired to do. And you seem to be the man to have hired them."

"Well, in matters such as these, Jacob, the confidentiality of the client is of utmost importance. I couldn't possibly—"

"You know a guy named Sloane? Malcolm Sloane? He's on this list."

"Ah. Oh, well. In that case, I'm positive I shouldn't discuss this matter. Please, Jacob, don't make me tell you no."

"I guess I'm not asking, Four. These people... Marcus Pitts, Wellons, Sloane... they did something, went to find something, and they've kicked up a whole world of trouble. The kind of trouble you wouldn't believe. It's not just my own skin we're talking about here. Lotta people could die, this doesn't get settled."

He looked at me coolly, his hands still flat against the table, his face emotionless.

"And now I know you're threatening me, Jacob. But because we're old friends, because we go way back, I'll tell you this. I've never met Mr. Sloane. But I know the deal you're talking about."

"Couple years ago?" I asked. He nodded.

"Angela Tomb enlisted my services. She needed a group of people who wouldn't be missed, men who could handle themselves in a fight. Preferably men with some out of doors experience."

"Did she say why?"

"I'm smart enough to not ask. But that Sloane fellow, he was the one I was supposed to send them to. I was to keep the Tomb name out of it."

I chewed my lip and looked around the theater. No one was paying us any mind.

"You're causing me a lot of trouble, being here," Four said. He hadn't taken his eyes off me, hadn't moved his hands.

"Why? People tell you not to talk to me or something?"

He nodded slowly. "Valentine, for one. I suspect you know why. I'm risking my standing with the old clockwork, talking to you like this. People are talking about you, Jacob Burn."

"What are they saying?"

"That you killed a bunch of people up on the Heights. A bunch more at the Manor Tomb, the other day. The Council is cutting itself up, trying to get to you."

"Yeah, well. I'm the kind of guy people want to talk to. You should feel privileged." I slid my hand under the table, loosened the pistol in my holster, then tried to look real casual. "Anything else? Any idea, for example, why Angela Tomb would want to kill me?"

"Kill you? Gods, no. If anything, she wants to keep you alive."

"She has a funny way of expressing that. And how do you know what she wants, anyway?"

He swallowed, glanced around. "Because I'm an old friend of the Families, you understand. When she asked me to hire those people, she made a point of saying that you weren't to be involved. And I should avoid hiring people you might know."

"Well," I said. "Well. That's funny. I don't like it. But I've got reason to think she's changed her mind about keeping me safe. Reason and a bullet they had to dig out of my chest."

"She shot you?" he purred. "Dramatic."

"Do you know where I can find this Sloane guy?" I asked.

"I could probably scare something up," he said. He was much calmer now than when we first started talking. He drank a bit of his wine, then dabbed his lips with a napkin. "What do you know about him?"

"Not much. Met him at that party up on the Heights. And he talked to Emily, once."

"Up on the Heights? He was there?" Four folded his napkin and lay it on his lap, then leaned closer to me. "Does Angela know that?"

"Why wouldn't she? I assume they're working together in this."

"Mm. You should pay better attention to the matters of the Council, Jacob. It's your family's business, after all. The forces that align with Sloane are, distinctly, no longer friendly with the Family Tomb."

"Did he have something to do with the Badge kicking in her front door?"

"Sounds his style. If I were to postulate, Mr. Burn, I would say that it is this matter, this list, that drove them apart."

I looked back up to the stage. The ruins of the girl had become a tableau of the city of Veridon. Gears and levers fluttered into buildings. Camilla's face appeared briefly in the streets, the canals, the skyline... only to disappear like a ghost. I shivered. If Sloane and Angela weren't working together, it just meant more groups aligned against me. There might be some way to play them off one another, but for now it just meant more trouble for me.

"Jacob," he said quietly.

"Four, I need to know who stands with Sloane, and who stands with Tomb. And what they want with me, for that matter." I turned to him. There was a pistol flat on the table, his hand folded around the grip.

"You had to know, son." He sounded legitimately sorry. "And I've heard all about your remarkable stamina." He wiggled the gun. "Bane."

Bane was one of the things that got the original Guild of Artificers disbanded and its Elders hung in the public square. A living bullet that took itself apart inside you, then ate its way out in a thousand pieces, in a thousand directions.

"That shit's illegal."

"We're all illegal, Jacob. And I thought you might be coming by. Now," he folded his napkin with one hand and nodded to the nearest exit. "I have an arrangement with the guard. If you'd be so kind. And leave your piece on the table."

I laid my pistol among the ruins of his dinner and stood. He slipped my gun into his coat and followed me out. As we walked, he stayed far enough behind to keep me from taking him by surprise, but close enough that he was sure to hit with his first shot. No one looked at us as we left. He'd done this before.

"So, all that stuff you told me before, you make all that up?" I asked.

"Of course not, my boy. More of an investment. I suspect the people we're going to see will have some questions for you. You'll serve as a fine messenger. Let them know what I know, what I've managed to connect. Maybe I can sell them something."

"I'll just lie. They won't hear what you want them to hear."

Four chuckled. "The way they ask questions? No, you will tell them what you know. Everything you know."

We went outside. The guard even held the door for us, smiling, then locked up behind us. There was a carriage in the alley, its engine already alive. We got in. The driver's compartment was separate from the passenger's seating. I sat across from Matthew. He drew the curtains and we rumbled off, the driver going faster than was wise on Veridon's narrow roads.

"So," I asked. "Who's buying me?"

"Patience, Jacob. You'll have plenty of time for questions once you're delivered."

"Sounds like they'll be asking the questions, and I'll be in no shape to ask my own."

"Oh, no, no. You misunderstand. They're not going to beat the answers out of you. Nothing so primitive, my boy."

I sat with my hands in my lap.

"They're not going to hurt me? Did they tell you this, or is it just a lie you need to believe, to salve whatever conscience still survives in that powdered skull of yours?"

He grimaced and poked the pistol in my direction.

"You won't be hurt. Not your body at least. They've been very clear about that."

"They've been clear. Because when they told you to take me, they also told you to bring me in unharmed."

"Well..." he flexed his fingers around the trigger of his pistol. He was holding the grip white-knuckle tight.

"Which means you won't be shooting me with a load of Bane. Will you?"

He raised the pistol. "Is that a risk you're willing to—"

I was. I lunged, ducking down. By the time he realized his error, finished calculating the risk of displeasing his masters versus the imminent threat of my attack, it was too late.

I had my hand on his shoulder. The shot went wide. The metal wall of the carriage sizzled. I punched the old man twice, then hissed as a blade went into my shoulder. I batted the pistol out of his hand and looked down to see the other wrapped around the hilt of a knife that was digging around for my lung.

"I'm sorry, Jacob," he said through gritted teeth. "Things change. We have to move with the tide."

I broke his wrist, broke his arm and then plucked the knife out of my shoulder and put it into his throat. His powdered face flushed, then drained of color and he went limp. The driver was yelling. I banged on the wall of the carriage and we slid to a halt. By the time I got out, the driver had ditched and was disappearing around the corner of the nearest darkened alleyway.

The side of the carriage was brittle from the Bane. Not much good against inorganic material, certainly not as dangerous as it was to flesh. I picked up the pistol and checked the cylinder. The rest of the load was normal shot. It rarely took more than one. I fished my gun out of Matthew's pocket, then leaned over the carriage wheel and threw up. I left Matthew his pistol, crossed his jigsaw puzzle arms over his chest and closed his blank eyes.

I ran. It wasn't more than a block before the blood stopped leaking out of my shoulder, and in another block the wound didn't hurt at all. I tried the arm out, twisting it back and forth. I was fine. Wilson was right. Whatever artifact had been installed in my chest was mending me, and it was doing a better job of it. I felt less real every day.

The ease with which I'd killed Matthew was still settling in. I'd known the old man since before I went into the Academy. He had betrayed me, fair enough, but to throw him away like that... it didn't matter. I could feel the desperation nagging at my heels. I didn't like being desperate. I was done being desperate.

I stumbled into our hidden cistern and started gathering my things. Wilson was back, busy in his corner under a frictionlamp, Emily peering over his shoulder.

"Any luck?" Emily asked. Her voice betrayed none of our earlier awkwardness.

"Kind of. Had to kill an old friend. But I found out some interesting stuff."

"That your method now? Beating secrets out of old friends?"

"Hardly. He forced my hand."

"Who?"

"Matthew Four. He pulled a gun on me. Bane."

"Shit," Emily said. Wilson looked up.

"He wasn't bluffing?" Wilson asked.

"Nope. He only had the one round, but it was the true thing."

"Shit," Emily said again, just to be clear. "Valentine's not going to like that. Four was a resource."

"I'm getting tired of other people's resources, Em. Right now I'm taking care of myself." I finished packing my things. "But like I said. Learned some good stuff."

"What, exactly?" she asked. Wilson had turned back to his work.

I told them about Sloane and Tomb, and about the split that seemed to be forming in the Council. If the Founding Families were aligning against the new Councilors, the industrialists and the commercial mavericks who had been buying out the Council seats for the last twenty years, then things were going to get difficult. If that split centered around Marcus's mission downfalls, and this Cog, then the complications were just going to get worse and worse.

"One thing's for sure. If there's a fight brewing in the Council, there aren't going to be any neutral parties. In the city, or in the Council."

"You think it's that serious?" Emily asked.

"Maybe not yet," I said. "But soon. Council trouble always spills out on the streets."

"That's how it was with the Guild," Wilson said. "Disagreement among families, and a new ally in the Church of the Algorithm. They took a vote, and by the time the ballots were tallied there were Badgemen kicking in doors all over the city." He nodded absently, not looking up. "It can get bad fast, Emily."

"So what are you going to do?"

I straightened my jacket, did the best I could with my hair. Living under the streets was doing nothing for my reputation as a rogue noble.

"Time to talk to the Family, dear." I sighed. "Time to make a little call home."

Emily appeared thoughtful, as though there was something else she wanted to add but couldn't decide if she should. I filed that.

"Stay safe," she said, eventually. "And be careful who you believe."

"Yeah," I said. "I will."

"I was hoping to beetle you again," Wilson said, turning to face me. He had a small vial in hand. Something brown and shiny scuttled up its length.

"Gee, sorry to miss that," I said. I checked the load in my revolver one more time and headed back up to the streets.

Chapter Ten
Water Like Air

When the Manor Burn was planted, generations ago and gone, this part of the Veridon delta was nothing but mossy stones and waterfalls to carry away the heat. Steam used to billow up in halos around our house. Now we piped it away, piped it and harnessed it and sold it by the pound of pressure. The ancient, deep furnace that was our family's ticket into the circle of Founders still burned, would always burn. Its heat blistered the rock under my feet. Most of the family's early money had gone into making the Manor livable in the presence of such incandescent fury. The high tower of the vent stacks glittered against the sky, spilling out flakes of burning ash and coiling sparks. My mouth filled with the scent of burning air and charred stone. Good to be home. Hard to forget a taste like that.

They let me in my own house. That was unexpected. I was nervous, walking into the dusty marble foyer. They had done a bad job of fixing the banister I'd busted up, the day I walked out. The day everything changed.

"Master Burn is in the library, gathering his morning thoughts and taking breakfast. He will attend you shortly."

"Thanks, Billy." I surrendered my coat, but not my holster. Billy disapproved, but that was okay. Billy usually disapproved in my presence. He disappeared.

The tower looked much the same. Older. Emptier. It reminded me of a store struggling to make the lease. Sell what it had in stock, not able to replenish its wares. Starving itself off, dying, but still alive. Hoping for some desperate gamble to pay off, to turn the corner. Failing in slow motion.

"Boy," Alexander Burn said as he walked in. He was wiping his hands on a well soiled napkin, bacon grease on the carefully trimmed curls of his mustache. His hair was falsely black. Still fat, too, but at what cost. "Haven't seen you on the grounds in a while. Here to beg for your allowance, perhaps?"

"Doesn't look like you could provide it, even if I asked." I looked around the room. "Nice of Billy to answer the door, let me disturb your meal. You hoping I'll offer a loan?"

"Careful. You're little more than a guest here, Jacob."

I put my hands in my pockets and did a turn around the room. He watched me walk, chewing the last of his breakfast.

"Are you going to tell me why you're here?" he asked. "Or is this just an opportunity to show off that remarkably gaudy pistol and rub your father's face in your new lifestyle?"

I smiled and turned to him. "Going to make me stand in the foyer all day? Father?"

He grimaced, finished wiping his fingers with an obsessive twist and tossed the napkin onto an empty coat rack.

"Fine. In here. Williamson, a coffee. Jacob?"

"Of course."

"Two, Williamson," he said, then left the room.

"Thanks, Billy," I said over my shoulder, then followed the elder Burns into the ballroom.

The place was done up. Sconces hung with holly and beads, the walls draped in bright fabric. A massive automaton was suspended from the ceiling, the sort of thing that would tell a slow, syncopated story when it was in full swing. Everything was thick with dust, even the bowls of wax fruit and most of the floor space. I remembered something about the family hosting a Beggars Day ball last year. Maybe they were hoping to reuse the ornaments next year. Or they couldn't afford the workers to take it all down.

It had just been starting, when I left. My childhood was awash in trivial wealth. Nothing about those days of summer estates and lavish meals had hinted at this end. Though, thinking back, perhaps the signs had been there; the first desperate thrashings of a dying house.

There were chairs, mismatched, pulled into a tight circle by the grand window. A newspaper rack sat off to one side, and a cart with the cooling remains of breakfast. So this was the library now. I wondered what that other room looked like, the walls of dark wood and leather spines. Did father eat here so he wouldn't have to face those empty shelves?

Alexander indicated a chair, then sat down. I took a different seat and propped my feet against the cart. In a few minutes, time spent invested in scowling and small talk, Billy brought coffee. It was good stuff.

"So, what's this about?" father asked, firmly clanging his spoon around the cup as he stirred in his sugar.

"Tell me about the Council," I said.

"Finally taking an interest in your nameright? That's nice, but it's a little late. I'll be passing the seat on to your brother, once he gets out of the navy."

"Gerrald won't take it. He's married to the river, and that trollop from the outer banks. But that's not what I mean. Tell me about the Council right now. The problems you people are having."

"Problems like what?" he asked. Alexander folded his hands in his lap and looked uninterested in a carefully cultivated and well practiced manner.

"Let's not play games, father. There's something going on, in the Council. Either you've been sleeping through the sessions, or you've picked a side. I need to know what you can tell me about it."

He grimaced and plucked a newspaper from the rack. Rather than look it over, he folded it into a tight square, and then unfolded it. Once it was open, he started over.

"Look, Jacob, son. This is all very intricate stuff. Yes, there's some tension in the Chamber Massif. People are balancing obligations, weighing allegiances. Trying to get a little advantage. But that's the way it always is. There's nothing new about this squabble."

"Angela Tomb shot me." I pointed at his chest, then mimed a pistol shot. "Close to me as we are right now."

Alexander looked at me dully. "I'm sure you're mistaken, Jacob. I'm sure Councilor Tomb—"

"People keep saying that to me. I'm the one who got shot, father. I'm the one the bullet went into. Are you saying I mistook the bullet?"

"The bullet, no, but her intent, Jacob. Surely she didn't mean to kill you. Perhaps the gun went off by accident? Knowing you, you probably gave her plenty of reason to hold a gun on you."

I slammed my palm down on the wooden arm of the chair. The slap resounded through the room. Billy rushed in, a broom in hand. We ignored him.

"If not us, if not the Founders! Well, then no one! Bang! What does that mean, Dad? What about that did I mistake?"

"Sir, if I may—" Billy began.

"Later. And my coffee's cold." Alexander leaned closer to me, poking his finger at my face. "We need to be very clear here, Jacob. The Tomb is a close ally of this house, and a good friend of the Family. We don't go around shooting one another, and to say anything less is plain absurd." He swatted the breakfast cart with the folded newspaper and stood up. "Now, unless you're going to say something sensible, I must bid you good day."

"Do you know Malcolm Sloane?" I asked. My father was already on his way to the foyer, to see me out. He stopped.

"What did you say?"

"Malcolm Sloane. Is that name familiar to you?"

Alexander crumpled the paper in his hand, then returned to his chair and sat down heavily.

"Sloane. Yes. How do you know that name?"

"We met, at Tomb's party on the Heights. Who is he?"

"He's… a friend to the Council. To some of the Council."

"Is he a friend to you?"

Alexander winced and looked out the window. "We have worked together, but no. I would not call a man like that my friend."

"What does he do?" I asked.

Father kept his eyes out the window, leaning forward, his hands clasped between his knees. His eyes were watery, I thought, like an old man's rheumy eyes.

"Difficult things," he said. "Things Councilors can't do. Not directly." He turned to me. "I ask again, how do you know that name?"

"Like I said. We met at Tomb's party. It was casual."

"There are no casual meetings with Malcolm Sloane. In the same way that there are no casual meetings with bullets, or back alley knives. Sloane is a weapon, Jacob, an animal. He's a damn summoned monster for the Council. Whatever business you have with him, abandon it."

I laughed. "Gladly. But I seem to have his attention. I'm in some trouble, and he keeps popping up, everywhere I look for a way out."

"So here we go, at last. You're in some trouble, and you need the old man to get you out. Upfront, Jacob, you could have told me that."

"I can get my way out, sir. All I need from you is information, and a little good will."

He stood over me, not a tall man, but an angry man. "Both are in short supply, boy. What do you need?"

"I need to know what Sloane has to do with the current trouble. Because, for gods' sakes, it seems to involve me."

"It doesn't," father said firmly. "It's nothing to do with you."

"Angela thinks differently. As does Sloane. Now out with it. What's splitting the Council, and how bad is it."

Alexander ground his teeth, staring at me with his dark eyes. The newspaper was still in his hand, crushed and smudged. He walked firmly to the window and stared out at the weedy remains of our formal garden. The room was quiet. Billy came, poured fresh coffee and then left. Father's cup had stopped steaming before he spoke again.

"Stay here," he said without turning around.

"Excuse me?"

"Stay here. Until it blows over. I can't keep you in your rooms, but you could be comfortable. Safe. Gods know they would never look here."

I stood up and went to the breakfast cart. The sausage was cut-rate, but the eggs had been cooked properly. Too bad they were cold. I made myself a plate. Father wouldn't look at me.

"That your plan, dad? Keep me safe and hidden away. Maybe use me to bargain with whatever rogue element in the Council is hunting me down. Maybe, if you're lucky, get the artifact in the bargain."

"Artifact?" he asked, half-turned towards me.

"Coy, old man. Yes, the artifact, the one you and Angela sent Marcus and his boys downriver to collect. The one that came in on the *Glory of Day*, right up until the whole ship burned up. That must have been a bitch, huh? All those plans, and the damn zep flames out at your doorstep."

He turned to face me, his mouth set in a distasteful grimace. He looked like he'd drunk bad milk, lumps and all.

"You seem to know more than you're letting on, boy. Trying to trick your old man?"

"Seems fair." I ate a mouthful of eggs while I watched him pace the circle of chairs. "You weren't going to tell me anything useful, not willingly. First you act like there's no problem in the Council, then you offer to shelter me? So who do you stand with, pop? Sloane or Angela?"

"Would it matter?"

I shrugged. "Sloane hasn't shot me, yet."

"You'll be lucky if, when he finds you, all he does is shoot you. He's an unpleasant man."

"Sure. So who are you with, Alexander? Who has your loyalty?"

He set his shoulders and leaned against the chair opposite me. He was still angry, but the anger was trimmed in shades of cold pride and desperation.

"The Family Burn. Always, Jacob, always my first loyalty is to the Family. As yours should be."

"I lost track of loyalty about the same time you threw me out on my ass, Alexander. So tell me what this is about, or tell me to get out. I don't care which way it goes."

He let out a long, slow sigh, then sat down and drank from his cup of cold coffee. He stared at me with his wet eyes while I ate. When I set the plate aside he laced his fingers together and set them in his lap.

"Angela Tomb came to me, a couple years ago. Probably three years now. She was talking to someone inside the Church. Maybe someone who had access to the Church, but whose purposes lay in direct opposition to the Algorithm. This person had an artifact that they wished to sell."

"Those guys are a pretty devoted lot, father. I have trouble believing that a Wright would be negotiating with the Council to sell a bit of his God."

"We had trouble believing it, too. And the deal itself was complicated. Many proxies, many dead drops. A deal of many hands. But the deal was made." He stopped and took a drink of coffee, grimacing as he swallowed. He set the cup aside. "But the deal came up in open session. At first it was just us, just the

Founders. What's left of them. But the others found out. The industrialists. They were... very interested. And they held enough sway in the Chamber to force their way into the deal." He reached for the cup, paused, then wiped his brow. "That's how Sloane got involved."

"He was the representative for the Young Seats, then?" I asked.

"Yes. He put a couple of his own men on the team. Some marines—"

"Wellons?"

"I don't remember the names." He squinted at me. "How do you know them?"

"After the fact. I found Wellons's body, shortly before I met the Angel for the first time."

"Ah. Angela mentioned that. Anyway. We had a map to something... something marvelous, Jacob. And we sent a group of people after it."

"And they never came back." I said.

"Until a couple weeks ago, correct. By then, the Young Seats had split from us. They were already organizing another party to head down. When Marcus made contact with us via messenger, both sides started maneuvering. He must have been in BonnerWell at the time." BonnerWell was the furthest of the messenger stations, barely a scratch of dirt on our maps. "He was coming in. And he had trouble."

"I'll say. So you brought him in?"

"On the contrary. We told him to stay put. We'd send someone. Whatever was following him, we didn't want it in the city. So, Marcus stopped talking to us. Maybe he started talking to the Young Seats. Maybe he stopped talking at all. We don't really know. And then," he shrugged, "he just showed up. Sent a message from Havreach. Nothing but the name of his ship."

"*Glory of Day*."

Father nodded. "We had teams on the shore, waiting. I can't properly express my shock at how things went. We were going to quarantine the ship until we had Marcus and his artifact in hand."

"Looks like he found a way around that."

"Probably not how he planned it. Anyway. We wrote it off, figured he had died in the explosion, and the artifact destroyed. And now we're learning that we were wrong."

I nodded my head, and doubted. Alexander told the story like Angela had come to him with the artifact, but Patron Tomb had been pretty clear that my father had initiated whatever plan was being undertaken. I'm sure there was some truth in what my father was telling me. I just didn't know which parts were honest, and which were careful lies.

"And all this business in the meantime. Angela shooting me, the Badge chasing me out of Emily's apartment, and then Wilson's place. That's just you guys trying to recover the artifact?"

"I can't speak for the actions of the Badge, Jacob. Or for Angela, for that matter. But yes, we're just trying to get that artifact."

"You couldn't ask?" I smiled.

"You would have answered?"

I shook my head. He was right, of course. I wouldn't have listened, wouldn't have trusted. Didn't trust him now.

"So what is it, this artifact?" I asked.

"You tell me. We haven't seen it." He stood up and went back to the window. Angela has seen it, I thought. For that matter, Angela has held it in her hands. I put another check in the careful lies column. Or maybe the Tombs weren't being as forthright with their allies as old Alexander thought. "But it's something to do with the Church's power. Something that will shake them off our backs."

"By our backs, you mean the city? Or the Council?"

"The Families." He put his hands in his pockets and sighed. "They have too much favor with the Young Seats. They have too much power. They've helped, of course. Without the Church there would be no zepliners, no cogwork. We'd still be dealing with the Artificers Guild. But they need to be put in their place. Restrained."

"Good luck with that. Suppressing religion always goes well." I stood up and wiped my hands on a spare napkin. "Thanks for the answers. And the breakfast." I started to leave.

"Just like that? You're going to walk in here, demand answers, and then walk out?"

"Looks like it," I said.

"And give me nothing in return. You know I can't let you do that, Jacob."

"You know you can't stop me, either. I don't have the Cog with me. I'm not going to tell you where it is. You can't call the Badge, because they'll take it to Sloane and the Young Seats. Are you going to stop me? Is Billy?"

He folded his arms and looked at me. He was tired, I could tell. I shrugged and walked out.

NO MATTER HOW I felt about my father, about his lies and his betrayals, I had the feeling he had mostly been straight with me back there. Nearly the truth was the best kind of lie. And the bit of the story that had me most interested wasn't the stuff about Angela and the Young Seats and Sloane. That was all development, complication. What interested me was the seed of it. Someone in the Church, he had said. Someone with access to the Church of the Algorithm.

The holy men of the Church of the Algorithm, the Wrights dedicated to the machine's maintenance and liturgy, were devoted to their clockwork deity. They didn't break ranks, and no one left the service intact. I had seen the hobbled Wrights in the street, their peaceful faces, the smooth machine of their skull pumps. I shook my head. They went in to the service knowing that there was no out. The Algorithm was jealous of its revelation. For there to be someone inside who was willing to sell bits of that revelation to the Council; it was unthinkable. There were no former Wrights. Well. There was one, and he had gotten out in a very unconventional way. He had died, drowned, and ended up among the Fehn. I swung by the cistern first, to pick up the map. I thought it would interest him.

He drank water like I breathed. He kept a glass in his spongy hand, and every time he stopped talking he lifted it to his blistered lips and drank. His voice gurgled.

"These are unusual questions, Jacob."

"You wouldn't believe." We were near the river Reine, two doors down from a publicly accessible basement pier on Water Street. One of the few contact points with the Fehn. People came here to visit lost relatives or trade with the people of the river. What they needed with money, I was never sure. Then again, they sometimes demanded more exotic pay for the treasures they dredged. "But what do you know about it?"

He gestured to the pistol I had laying on the table, the one from the *Glory*.

"You think it's the real thing?"

"I think someone's trying to scare me, or warn me. And the people who would want to do that?" I leaned back in my chair and looked the dead guy square in his milky eyes. "Those kind of people would take the time and effort to get the genuine article."

He nodded, then picked up the pistol in both hands, touching it only with his fingertips.

"We were contracted, of course. You know that. The Council hired us to recover the wreckage, for their memorial. This would have been part of that."

"And all that material, all the wreckage, it went to the Council."

He nodded. "The bodies as well. We kept our percentage."

"Some of the victims have joined the Fehn?" I asked. It would help to be able to talk to some of them. Maybe talk to Marcus. "Was there a guy named Marcus among them?"

"Marcus, Marcus. The name is familiar, but he was not among our tithe. Those we took have not hatched yet, if you mean to interrogate them."

"Maybe. But if Marcus isn't among them, there's no point. So you think this pistol is the real thing, maybe taken from the wreckage for the memorial?"

"Unless someone paid one of us to steal it. Unlikely."

"But could that happen? Enough money or shiny beads or whatever you people trade in, someone could ask for a specific thing?" I leaned forward. "Get one of you to fetch it?"

"Fetch." He curled his lip. "Fetch. Yes, I suppose. If it were important."

"How would I find out? If this had been… retrieved. And who paid to have it done?"

"The way you talk about these people, it seems they would pay a great deal to have it done. And a great deal more to keep that transaction from public eyes."

I sniffed, then regretted it. He smelled like stagnant water and the sickness of swamps.

"How do I find out?"

He waved his hand, spreading the fingers like a fan. "Is that all this is about? This gun? Really, Jacob, you're usually so much more interesting than this."

"It's important, Morgan. I can pay."

"No, Jacob. You can't. Just because we live in the river doesn't mean we don't hear things. And you've been making a lot of noise. The Council, Valentine, some of the Founding Families." He drank a long and slow glass of water, savoring my discomfort as much as the slosh. "I was looking forward to this discussion, Jacob. I thought you might come to me for something interesting. This?" He tapped the revolver, then shook his head.

"There's more than this involved, Wright. Your old buddies, they're in on it, too."

He paused, just as he was reaching for the pitcher to refill his glass. Just a second's hesitation, then he completed the action. When he set the pitcher down, he stared at me with cold eyes.

"The concerns of the Church are much deeper than this. You can't claim to have caught the attention of the Algorithm, Jacob. Unless there's much more to this than I've heard."

"Do the Church concerns include angels, Wright Morgan?" I picked up the pistol. "There's something in the city. Hunting."

"How dramatic," he said glibly, but he had the glass halfway to his lips, and showed no sign of moving it.

"A friend of mine, an anansi familiar with the Artificer's Guild, says it looks like a cross between the cogwork of the Church and the Artificer's biotics. It's killing people, and it's looking for something. Looking for me, too."

"Well." He set his glass down, then rubbed the slack skin around his eyes. "Your friend is a heretic, comparing the holy pattern of the Algorithm to those Artificers and their damn beetles." Drink. "But he has a lot correct, as well. The pattern, as manifest in the seed-coin, is the body of God. Longing for the pattern in us. Together, we are becoming something more complex. More beautiful."

"Minus the theology."

"Cog needs blood, and it needs our mind." When he talked I could barely see the writhing pool of flat, black worms that replaced his organs, squirming at the back of his throat. "That is the layman's version."

"So this Angel?" I asked.

He crossed his arms and stared just above my shoulder. Several long drinks later, he refilled the glass from his pitcher and then steepled his fingers.

"That interests me," he said.

He was quiet for several moments, not even drinking. When he spoke, his voice was still, like a deep pool.

"I had heard, of course. The events at the Manor Tomb have been spinning the rumor mill. To think, another of the Brilliant would visit us, all this time later."

"Another?"

"Camilla. Jacob, you know your books." He was reproachful, disappointed. "Her gifts raised the city up. I wonder what this visit portends."

"Camilla's a story, Morgan. A parable." I took a drink of water, to fit in.

"A story? A story." His voice rose gradually, like the tide. "Scripture, Jacob. Truth. True enough to end worship of those ghosts."

The Church liked to bring up the usurpation of the spiritual reign of the Celestes whenever possible. Especially in the company of the Founding Families, who held the ethereal creatures holy for the longest time, held out against the encroachment of the Algorithm. My childhood home had been littered with the Icons of the Celestes, hidden away whenever Churchmen were to visit.

"Not even your own Master Wrights acknowledge that story anymore. Camilla is an origin myth, a convenient vehicle to describe the Church's ascendancy, and its mastery of the Cog. A child of the Angels, really? No one believes that's real anymore."

"The child?" he asked, a grin leaking across his face. "Or the Angels?"

I grimaced. "Two weeks ago, no one believed in Angels."

"Of course not." Morgan sniffed, a strange sound in a river-logged head. "Such an enlightened age for Veridon. Clearly absurd to think she was the child of Angels. Right?" Drink, a messy slurp that drained his glass and sucked air. "Because then there would be such a thing as Angels. Which brings us, Jacob, back to your question. What was it, again? What did you want to ask me?"

Morgan's bond to the Algorithm may have dissolved when his boat capsized and his life washed away so many years ago, but it was clear they still had his loyalty. Strange, but it was probably that fierce devotion that kept him so animate. So many of the Fehn simply faded into the dark current of the Reine, bumping against the piers and scaring children.

Still, he had me. Deny as I may, the problem at hand was an Angel. Mythic or not, propaganda or not, I had seen it twice and killed it once. It was real.

"Yes, okay," I said, shifting in my seat. "Okay. But it wasn't just at the Manor. I saw it before, a couple days ago. Up on the Heights."

"The Heights?" he asked. "The Tombs again? What have they done to attract its attention?"

"That's what I'm looking into. Though, to be honest, he seemed pretty interested in me. In something I have."

"I am an old man, Jacob, and dead. Stop playing around with me. What do you have, and what do you know?" He leaned forward. "I can't help you out if you're not honest with me."

"Two things. One was given to me, one I took. A friend of mine, guy I hadn't seen in a few years. He died, on the *Glory of Day*. Seemed pretty desperate to get away from someone, desperate enough to crash a Hesperus class zepliner."

"Sabotage? I thought it was an accident. Faulty PilotEngine, just like..." he stumbled to a halt, awkwardly aware of how close he was to old wounds. He refilled his glass to cover the silence. "Who was your friend?"

"Marcus, the guy I wanted to talk to," I said, letting him off the hook. "He was coming home from a long trip. Gave me a Cog." I held out my hands to show the size. "Like nothing I've ever seen."

"Oh," he said, and leaned back. "I see. And do you... do you have any idea where your friend might have been coming from?"

"Sure." I slipped the map-artifact out of my coat and put it on the table. Wright Morgan looked stunned, tried to cover with a long drink of water. His bloated hand was shaking. I spun up the map. He nearly dropped the water in his rush to cover the mechanism.

"No need." His voice was quiet. "So you have it?"

"I do."

Morgan was troubled. He wouldn't look at me, and his hands kept moving from the table to his face, pausing to tug at his slowly drying robes.

"So, so. Hell of a thing to bring to me, a man like me. And he gave it to you."

"He was dying. He asked me to bring it to Veridon."

"And Tomb? What did they have to do with this?"

"The map comes from their house. They sent him down the falls. I don't know what they hoped to find."

"They had no idea. All these years, nothing." He picked up the map, held it gingerly in his hands. "All these years, and then Tomb gets it. She gave it to them."

"She?"

He stared wistfully at the map, then set it on the table.

"Do you keep up with your services, Jacob? Does the Family Burn still honor the House of the Algorithm?"

"It's been years. But my father still goes." I didn't bother mentioning the Icon of the Celestes he kept in his pocket every time he crossed into the Church's corridors.

"You should return. Find a seat near the Tapestry of Hidden Ambition. There is a pillar there, the Pillar of Deep Intentions. North center of the room. Near the old Burn pews, if I remember."

He stood. Water sloshed from his chair onto the grated floor. He touched the map one more time.

"I've been here too long," he said. His face was looking a bit soft, like a leather balloon half-filled. "Best to you, Jacob Burn. And good luck with your legends."

I watched him turn and go. He left a rapidly drying trail of water, sloshing out from his river-logged feet.

Chapter Eleven
The Chamber of the Heart

THE CHURCH OF the Algorithm is the heart of Veridon. It sits on the south bank of the Ebd river, a gnarled fist grasping the current in fingered bridges, the water flowing over its open palm. Most of the Church is above the river, but the water is harnessed by flow channels, and unknown depths of the holy building exist under the river-turbines and boiler rooms that belch and hiss in the middle of the water.

From the outside, the Church looked like a cancer of architecture. It grew, walls expanding, roofs adding domes and towers that grew together until they became walls. The whole structure bristled with chimneys leaking oily smoke, smoke that pooled in the courtyards that surround the Church. Everything around its bulk was smudged black. The ground rumbled with the hidden engines of their god. I could feel it in my heels as we walked up.

Emily and I stood outside the penitent's gate, watching the line of beggars huddled in the flank of the Church. These were men and women who couldn't afford the upkeep on their cogwork, people with clockwork lungs and oiled hearts who could no longer pay for the licensed coggers in the city. They came to the Church, the source, the holy men of cog. They paid in blood and time, lent their bodies to the Church's curious Wrights. They came out changed, or not at all.

My father had suggested that I come here, when the Academy's doctors failed, when the best money my father was willing to spend couldn't find a cure. He had meant it as a threat. I took it as surrender, and left.

"They creep me out," Emily said. She stood close to me, her hands inside the wide shawl we had purchased that morning. She had a gun in there, to my dismay.

"Not their fault. Rotten people, with rotten hearts." We went across the stone courtyard to one of the strangled gardens, passing through to the next little courtyard. "What should creep you out is inside."

"I've heard it was beautiful. Or at least impressive."

"Those are very different things." I ducked my head as we approached the Church's hulking flank. "You'll see."

Like so many things in Veridon, the presence of the Algorithm was a privilege you had to earn. Beggars stayed outside. Citizens approached the murals, the finished mysteries of the pattern. To reach the heart, the ever changing center of the Church, you had to be a Councilor, the blood of Veridon. Today, we were citizens.

The pillar that dead Wright Morgan had described to me was near the heart, in the privileged audience of the machinery. I wanted to get there, but things were too dangerous at the moment. I didn't know what role the Church was playing in all this. If they were part of the shadowy pursuit that I seem to have attracted, I didn't want to walk into their parlor and present my credentials. That hadn't gone too well with the Tombs, and I thought I knew what to expect of Angela. The Church I didn't understand.

The doors were plain. The Wright standing to one side didn't pay us any mind, bobbing his brown robed head at the clink of our coin. He didn't even ask us which door, just cycled the Citizen's Gate.

The heavy wood clattered behind us. The corridor was dark and smelled of coal smoke and overclocked engines. The only light was from the altar manifolds around the corner. It took a minute for my eyes to adjust. Emily was tugging on my sleeve. She had the gun out, close to her body. The air around us was heavy, the walls slithering with barely perceived clockwork, deep vents puffing and groaning in the darkness.

"Let's get this over with." She glanced back at the door behind us. "It's like being eaten by the city."

"You would have been a terrible Pilot," I said.

"Like you would know."

The closer we got to the mural room and its s, the clearer we could see the walls around us. Everything shuddered with the constant grinding of the engines. The very blackness seemed part of it, vibrating at an incredible pitch. The air in my lungs felt like hydraulic fluid, crashing, surging, driving me forward.

The Citizen's Room was little more than display. It was a long, thin hall that ran through the width of the building like an axle through a wheel. The walls were alive, cogs instead of bricks, shafts instead of pillars, sunk into the floor or powering intricate murals on the ceiling.

That was all show. The true mysteries were clustered at the altars. Waves of cogwork bulged out into the hallway, like some great sea beast that burst from the wall and beached itself on the stone floor. These were the most active parts of the room, highly articulated, nearly sentient in their complexity.

"Is that a face?" Emily asked, motioning to the nearest altar. I had a brief flash of Patron Tomb, possessed beneath the Church and communing with the Algorithm, but then the vision passed.

"More than that." I pointed over. The altar was a long tongue of cogwork lolling out from the wall, pistons and gears convulsing in tight waves. The tip of the protuberance ended in the shoulders and a head, a metal man who struggled against the floor. With each convulsion he was swallowed a little, drawn into the tongue like an egg being swallowed by some enormous snake. He gasped and clawed his way forward, scrambling against the stone until the next convulsion; drawn back in, and the struggle continued.

"That's foul," Emily said. "People worship these things?"

"They worship the pattern behind them." I left the cog to its eternal struggle and went on to the next altar. "These things are salvaged from the river, Em. Pieces and bits, dredged up from the depths, sometimes arriving in whole parts. So the Wrights say. The fact that they fit together at all is pretty amazing."

"The fact that the Wrights spend years piecing them together, now that's amazing."

"Obsession is a powerful thing." I stopped at the next display. It seemed dead, a complicated mouth of pistons that glowed with some inner fire. Waves of heat rolled off it.

"So where's this pillar?"

"Different room. We're going to have to sneak through." The hallway was fairly empty at this hour. Most supplicants paid their awe after work. "For now, just look suitably devout. And put the gun away."

"This can't be coincidence," she said.

"Hm? The gun, Em." I turned to look at her. She was across the hall, the pistol dangling from her thin hand. "Hide it."

She grimaced at me, then folded the shawl around the revolver and tucked the bundle under her arm. She motioned me closer. I went to look.

"What is it?" I asked.

"This." She pointed at one of the altars, a smaller display that looked like a puzzlebox. Sections of it slid and shuffled, disappearing into the box and re-emerging elsewhere. There was some iconography on the tiles, so that it looked like an animated story, but I couldn't find any rhythm.

"What?" I asked. "It just looks obscure to me."

"Here, right here." She had her hand close to the box, as though waiting to pluck up one of the tiles. "No, it's gone now. Hang on." Her hand drifted. "There!"

A box shifted out of the central structure of the altar, sliding along the top. It was a music box, the fragile fingers of its comb dancing along a cylinder as it went. Seconds later it was gone, but the music lurked through the hallway.

"It was that song," I said.

"The music box, that I gave you to take to Angela Tomb." Emily turned to me, played with her lip nervously. "It's the same song."

"And where did you get it?"

"Some guy. He hired me to hire you. I thought it was a Family thing, but it could have been the Tombs, trying to get you up on the Heights—"

"Or it could have been someone from the Church," I finished for her. "Same as the two who visited your office. And maybe the people who hired Pedr to toss my place, too."

"Are we sure we want to be here?"

"Oh, I'm sure I don't, actually. But Morgan said—"

"He's a Wright. Or was," Emily said. "You sure you can trust him?"

I sighed and looked nervously back at the altar. The music box made another pass, the same song, faster this time. Emily gripped the bundled mass of the pistol tighter, working her hand under the cloth to touch the grip.

"Can I help you, citizen?"

We whirled like children stealing candy. There was a Wright standing there, the guy from the door. He had his hands folded beneficently at his waist.

"It's all... it's just." I gasped, trying to work up the kind of dull awe the guy expected. "It's amazing."

"Oh, I understand. The pattern is such a thing to behold. Do you often make the trip to the Algorithm?"

"Frequently," Emily said. "I mean, every chance we get. In the city. Tell me, uh, Wright. We've heard that there are deeper chambers. Where the pattern is more... more raw."

"Purer miracles," I quickly added, tapping into my childhood to summon the correct wording. "The raw stuff of the pattern."

The Wright raised his eyebrows at me, but shook his head. "The inner chambers are reserved for the glorious, my children. The Elders of the Church and the Founders of the city. Now, unless you've found a way onto the Council, I don't think I can take you there."

"I do," Emily said. She had the pistol in hand. "We're very serious about our enlightenment."

I swore under my breath. Wrights like to talk about their little miracles. I felt sure we could have talked our way in. Emily's eyes were wild.

"Now, child," the Wright said, raising his hands and backing away. "There's no need for violence."

"Look, holy man. I seek the godsdamn pattern. Show it."

He paled, glanced at me. I nodded. We got our way.

THE CHURCH OF God, the Church of the Algorithm. The church of pistons and gears, angles of driving pulleys, escapements clicking, cogs cycling in holy period; a temple of clock and oil. The chamber of my youth.

We stood in the central sanctuary. The room was a geode of machinery, walls of cogs spinning, meshing, divine murals of clockwork that moved across the walls, generations of timed gears scrounged from the river and reassembled. The Wrights searched for the holy Algorithm, the hidden pattern, the divine tumble of tooth and groove that would reveal itself only to the purest, the most humble. Ages of Wrights had worked this building-engine, fitting axles and aligning screws. Always working. Devotion was measured in oily hands and callused fingers.

The room was loud and close. It had been large once, a grand hall dedicated to the study of the hidden mysteries buried under the city. Time had taken that away, layers of cogwork accreting on the walls, clenching tighter and tighter until the ceiling was close and the air was closer. The floor shook with the clashing pistons, the grinding gears.

I steadied Emily. I remembered that I had been overwhelmed myself when I first came here as a child. My father had prepared me, in his way.

"You've no right to be here!" The Wright yelled. His voice was a quiet roar among the machines. "This is a holy place."

"It is," I said. "We're only here to show our devotion."

"Then put the gun away," he said, nodding to Emily. "And let me call my brothers."

"No." I shook my head. "We won't need your brothers. Not today. But, my dear," I placed a hand on Emily's shoulder. "Maybe the gun is unnecessary."

"What?" she asked, her neck still craned towards the ceiling. I leaned close to her, let my cheek brush hers.

"The gun."

She stashed it sulkily, then returned to the cogwork.

"She sees the glory of it, son." The Wright looked pale, but stern. "Not you. Where's your awe in the presence of God?"

"I'm unable to contain it, Wright. It fled. Now. The Pillar of Deep Intentions," I said, reciting what Morgan had told me. "Near the Tapestry of Hidden Ambition. I have a deep... fervor... to see it."

The Wright paled even more. "That is... there is no such miracle in the house of the Algorithm."

"There is. I believe, brother." I grasped him by the shoulders and looked deeply into his eyes. "It was revealed to me. Prophecy, call it. Now where's the pillar?"

"It is not... not for people. Not for the unholy. The pillar is a very peculiar gift of God."

"Yes, it is. That's why I must see it. You must show me. Surely you wouldn't deny a pilgrim?"

He set his lips, looked down and shook his head. Emily hit him.

"Fair enough," I said. "Morgan gave me an idea. Just hoped to do the easy thing."

"We can't stick around," Emily said, looking down at the fallen Wright. He had crumpled at her touch, and was curled up around his chest. "Make it quick."

I ignored her. Memory served, and I found the old family pews. Without sermons and choirs, services of the Algorithm were less structured than the older ceremonies of the Celestes. Ironic, if you thought about it. The pews were scattered around the room, facing different directions, arranged in different ways.

I ran my hand over the soft wood of our pews, sat and closed my eyes. That was familiar. My heart seemed to sync up with the room, rumbling in my bones. When I opened my eyes, I saw the pillar, off to my left and across a haphazard aisle.

"Emily!" I yelled, and crossed to the pillar.

"This is it?" she asked. I nodded.

Up close I saw that it wasn't really a pillar. More like two closely fit camshafts, sheathed together and turning very quickly, so that it looked like a single column. There were carvings on the pillar's face. The rapid cycle of the shafts animated them, so the patterns danced and crawled up the cylinder. It looked like water flowing, like rivers twisting and slipping through the steel. The air was hot, rushing up from the floor where the shafts disappeared into the stone.

"I know you!" I turned. It was the Wright, his mouth bloodied, holding himself up on my family pew. “Burn, the child. Your father sent you!”

“Not for a long while,” I said.

“He did, I know. The brothers will know.”

“What can you tell me about this pillar?” I asked. He clammed up, then sat on my pew. I looked up the length of the pillar. There was something familiar, near the top.

“I need to get up there,” I said. Emily nodded and looked around for some way to make the climb. The whirling pillar wasn’t something you just shimmied up.

“The pews,” she said.

“Oh. Dad’ll hate that.” I smiled and crossed the aisle, dragging the Wright from his seat.

We tipped the pew up on end. It took both of us. We leaned the heavy wood against a nearby mural. The gears chattered against the wood, then seized up. Something deep in the wall broke, and gears plinked across the stone floor.

“That’ll get some attention,” Emily said. The old guy was gone anyway, snuck off while we struggled with the pew.

“I’ll be fast.”

I scrambled to the top of the pillar, my hands slick against the polished wood. At the top I bent as close to the pillar as I dared, the speed of their cycle a hot breath on my face.

"You aren't going to believe this," I yelled down.

There was a cog, meshed between the shafts, driving the pillar. It had many teeth, many gears, concentric circles that slipped together and flowed like quicksilver.

"It's the Cog. The fucking artifact," I yelled. Though it wasn't. Similar, just as complicated, just as beautiful. I realized that its cycle was matched in every mural. The room meshed with it. "It's running the whole place."

"Can you get it out?"

The door banged open. There were Wrights carrying ornate hatchets and hammers. I slipped, the pew slipped. It banged onto the central pillar and shattered. I fell, landed among the stacks of cogs that hadn't yet been distributed to the Algorithm, cracking my head on the stone floor and scattering the gears. I lay there, the world buzzing around me. People were shouting. There was a boom, yelling; I heard Emily's voice. I rolled onto my side and fought through the haze.

Emily was standing in the narrow aisle, pistol in her right hand, hammer in her left. There was blood on her face and oil on her dress. She glanced at me, concern etched across her eyes. She was shouting. I nodded. She fired at someone unseen, shook the hammer in the air, and disappeared for a second. When she came back there was blood on the hammer, and more on her. She looked at me again. Everything was so loud.

The bullet entered at her shoulder. Just above the meat of her breast, blood puffing up, misting across her face. The hammer slipped from her hand. She gestured weakly with the pistol. Her lips were slack, and she fell.

I rolled to my feet, revolver out. There was a crowd of Wrights, carefully approaching Emily's body. There were others, on the floor. One had his face caved in, blood and mucus running across shattered teeth. They looked at me. They hesitated.

I shot the first two, bullets into their chests, a slug for each lung. Walking past Emily, I emptied my chamber, dropped the pistol and scooped up her hammer. I didn't even see the next three, just put the heavy, dead metal through them, crushing them, moving on. A bullet skipped past me. Found the guy, cowering behind a boiler, fumbling with the lever on an antique hunting rifle. Spent some time on him. When I turned around the room was empty, just bodies and smoke. The gear walls were slick with blood, the filth passing from cog to cog, tooth to tooth, each cycle spreading it farther and deeper into the pattern.

I cradled Emily against my chest. She was light, like a bundle of twigs. There was a lot of blood. I picked her up and headed for the door. Just before I got there it irised closed. I heard hammers, and iron. A lot of yelling in the hallway beyond. The door wouldn't open.

I turned back to the chamber. So many cogs, walls and walls of gears flashing and spinning in a cacophonous roar. There had to be another way out. I set Emily gently on the floor next to the toppled pew and looked around.

Every natural door in the place was sealed shut, clogged with accretions of cogwork. Some of it spun quickly, some creaked lazily, but all of it moved, and none of it allowed passage. In places the original walls had been removed, tunnels burrowed out by camshafts and long boiler pipes that clawed into the foundations of the Church. There were gaps around the pipes that went deep into darkness, but there was no way I could crawl through there, much less carry Emily out.

I went to check on her. She looked okay, I told myself. She was going to be okay. I stuffed her chest with some clean rags and told myself it was going to be okay.

Outside the door the hammering had stopped. Were they getting the Badge, or did the Church have its own security measures?

What sort of horrors did they keep in the cellar of this place? Childhood stories bumped around my head. I went back to searching.

If Wilson had been here, we might have been able to climb up to the dizzy heights of the chamber. There were more gaps there, and I could see natural light filtering in from the cathedral's original stained glass windows. I began to regret leaving him in the cistern to guard the Cog. I looked over at Emily's still form, breathing slowly. I began to regret bringing her, too.

What I found was hardly the best solution, but it was the only way out. Near the Pillar of Deep Intentions there was a cluster of pipes that led down. The pipes were cold, leading in from somewhere deeper in the Church before heading under the floor. Where they disappeared, there was a long axle, a camshaft that spun slowly around. With each revolution I could see far down, to a stone floor at the bottom. There was light there, and ladder rungs were built into the shaft-way. Maintenance access, probably. I just needed to stop the cams.

I moved Emily closer to the tunnel, then dragged the family pew over. From the direction of the door I could hear machines and heavy footsteps. I was sweating, gods, I was sweating a river. I leaned the pew on its end, the weight almost too much to bear, but I had to do it. Emily started to bleed again. I walked the precariously balanced pew to the lip of the shaft-way. One chance, I suppose. When the shaft cleared the cam, I pushed the pew forward and dropped it straight down into the duct.

It fell about three feet before the cam came back, crushing the wood. The remainder of the pew splintered and fell. The cams ate it up, shattering and scattering bits of wood and leather all over the room. I fell over Emily. Splinters stung my back. There was a lurch, then quiet. I looked up.

The remnants of the pew were lodged in the camshaft's workings. The whole mechanism moaned under the strain. Nearby cogs pinged and fell out of cycle, teeth grinding against their drive shafts. The shaft-way was clear, but not for long. I wasn't sure I could make it down all the way. I looked at Emily, at the door, down the shaft. No choice.

I hefted Emily over one shoulder, ignoring her moans and the blood on her chest. I took the rungs three at a time, more falling than climbing. It reminded me of the obstacle courses at the Academy, only much more difficult, with higher stakes. My shoulders were popping in protest.

Some of the pew slipped, and the cams started again. I flinched against the wall, but the cam roared at me, the wide metal face of the thing oily and flat, a hammer to the face, a tidal wave of force and energy. It stopped, inches short of me. I looked up and saw a Wright, looking down.

"Come on up, son," he yelled. "We can work this out."

Something loomed behind him. It was a rough parody of a man, ten feet tall with arms of latticed steel and wire. Its clenched fists like barrels.

I let go and dropped. I hit first, cradling Emily. Pain went through my legs and back as I rolled, keeping her off the stone. I was bleeding now. As I hit, the axle lurched, the pew finally shattered, and the camshaft whirred into life. The Wright looked down at me, the cams blurring as they sped up. He shook his head and disappeared.

I stood, picked up Emily, and tried to run down the corridor. The world was roaring in my head. Emily opened her eyes, briefly, and stared at me.

"It's okay, it's okay," I hissed. "Everything's okay."

She coughed blood, then closed her eyes and shivered. I ran faster, faster, blind into the dark tunnels beneath the Church of the Algorithm.

Chapter Twelve
Pieces of the Girl

THE TUNNELS BELOW the Church weren't meant for escape routes, and they weren't built to accommodate carrying an unconscious person. They were tiny, clogged with machinery and oil-slick. I was lost, I was tired, and Emily was dying. The Wrights kept getting closer, their frictionlamps stuttering in the period of whirling cog walls, their voices drowned in hammering machines. I almost gave up.

Eventually I dropped into an open space, a room that was built like a trench, the ground narrow and the ceiling wide. The walls slanted away from me. Here at the end the ceiling was close, but twenty feet on, the trench opened up. I couldn't see its height in the darkness, but the air was damp and my footsteps echoed as I went forward. The walls were cut stone, or something very similar. Dull gray veins ran through the rock. We were deep beneath the Church. How were these tunnels kept so dry? Anything this far below the city should be drowned in the rivers.

I ventured down the trenchway. When the low ceiling ended, the darkness stretched above me. It was an unsettled darkness. Something moved far above me. It looked like storm clouds seen at night, indistinct shreds of cloud ripping across a muffled moon. There was a sound like a river of smooth stones tumbling in the distance. I struggled forward under that barely seen, buried sky, carrying Emily close to my chest.

There was a door at the end of the path. It was a simple door, wood, the brass handle smudged with use. The sound of that river of stones came from somewhere beyond it.

The room behind the door was a funnel. Its wide mouth was high above me, the lower tip about twenty feet below. Pipes entered the room on all sides, wide and narrow, iron and brass. I realized that the barely glimpsed movement in the ceiling behind me was a single enormous conduit, glass bound in steel, that carried murky quicksilver. Shapes moved within the confines, twitching and lurching in the current.

All the pipes, regardless of their origin or size, led down to the tip of the funnel. They branched and narrowed until they reached an intricate caged sphere. The room was hot and loud, a cacophony echoing off the sloped walls and distant ceiling. The pipes sweated a black liquid, thinner than oil but darker.

A set of stairs led down. They were lovingly worked, shiny wood that would not have been out of place in the loftiest manor. Though the rest of the room stank of oil and engines, there wasn't a drop of grime on these stairs. The banisters were tightly carved in the holy symbols of the Algorithm. Ancient, but beautifully maintained.

I stumbled down the stairs. When I got to the floor, I registered a terrible cold in my feet. The floor glittered with frost, the freezeline melting quickly along the wall about three inches up. The frost crackled under my feet like tiny shards of glass. I was careful as I walked. Emily was getting heavier.

There was one pipe that was not a pipe, I realized as I got closer to the cage. A single brilliant column twisted up into the ceiling from the center of the intricate sphere. It hummed, and as I approached I saw that it was the Pillar of Deep Intentions from the Church, far above. It spun rapidly. I shuddered to think how long that axle must be, that led from here to that mystical cog on the surface.

I shuffled closer, to see where the pillar led, and looking for a place to set Emily. The shaft plunged into the center of the spherical cage. There was something inside. Closer, and I saw that the sphere was little more than a hollow cage, bars supporting pipework, much smaller tubes continuing in. Leading to a girl.

She was held in place by a complexity of iron fittings, wires and pipes and axles that sprouted from her fingers or hooked to her bones. Again, closer and I saw that she was no girl, but a machine in the form of a girl. Much of her was missing. Her arms were stripped to the bone, the occasional fleck of porcelain skin pinned in place like an unfinished mosaic. Her fingers were long and thin, the tendons nothing more than wire and pulley. One hand was missing. She had no legs. Her torso was little more than framework, the bones matte pewter, her ribs spread or snipped away to reveal the engines of her inner workings. Her heart was a void, the spine glistening through. The column that traveled from such a height down to this chamber narrowed as it approached her, then evolved into a whirring spindle that meshed with her spine. The sound and speed was a high pitched ticking that hovered at the edge of hearing.

Her shoulders were slumped but largely intact. The skin there was pale white and smooth, very like the shoulders of any normal girl. Where it ended over her ravaged chest, the edges flaked like mica. It looked as though the flakes squirmed, blind inchworms looking for the next blade of grass.

Absolute peace and resignation rode her face. Again, some of that was missing. Her jaw was a sketch of metal bone, her lips hanging over empty air, her teeth gone. Cheekbones that looked like polished marble framed perfect eyes, eyes that could have been chiseled from sapphires. The skin of her face was a jigsaw of porcelain and bone. Her hair was a flat wedge. Behind her were spread two broad vein-works, like trees that had been pinned in place, then burned away.

"Wings," I whispered. She stirred.

Camilla. The martyr child, daughter of Angels, broken mythology.

She looked up at me.

"I have been waiting," she said, and her voice was like sweet crystal wind. "So long, I've been waiting."

"For me?" I asked. The air around her cage was so cold my bones ached. My breath rolled out in frosty tendrils.

"For anyone." She straightened briefly, fixing me with her cut glass eyes. "And you? Have you traveled great distances to find me?"

"I came a ways to get here, but not all of it of my own volition."

She nodded, a sad fragment of a gesture drifting from her shoulders. "That's the way of these things. Your friend is broken."

"Yeah," I said. "I'm not sure... not sure she's going to make it."

"People die," the girl said, flatly.

"Yeah," I said. I looked down at Emily's still face, the soft lines of her lips, so pale and so quiet. "Sometimes."

There was a wooden chair nearby, its legs splintered by the cold. I set Emily carefully down and turned back to the girl.

"Would you have this one stay?" she asked. "Or is her passing acceptable to you?"

"Acceptable? No, not really."

The girl twitched, the wisps of her wings rising and falling. "There is a pipe. That one. Take it in your hand."

"What?" I asked. She indicated a pipe near my head, maybe an inch thick. I wrapped my fingers around it. The metal was briefly cold, then seemed to melt in my hand. Slick gray liquid began to leak out from around my grip. The drops sizzled when they hit the floor.

"She is dying," the girl said. "You should hurry."

"What is it?"

"The tithe of my servants. It keeps me here, living, available. Put it against the wound."

The pipe came free in my hand, slippery and flexible as rubber. A gout of metal splashed across the floor. The scattered pool resolved into tiny snowflake-sized cogs, clattering over the frost like spilled coins. I pulled the loose bandages off Emily's chest and pushed the pipe against the bullet hole.

"What will this—"

Emily gasped; her eyes open wide and full of fear. She breathed in, struggling, her hands clawing against the old wood of the chair. She looked at me and I flinched back. She tried to scream and burbled instead. Viscous gray liquid bubbled out of her throat and ran like syrup over her teeth and down her chin. Frantically, I pulled at the pipe but it wouldn't budge. It felt hooked to her ribs. When it tore free a thin line of sandy metal streamed out and then stopped, resting against her chest. Emily spasmed and fell to the floor.

"What the fuck did you do?" I shouted.

"Unkilled her, child. She'll be fine."

I pulled Emily up off the ground. Her skin and clothes stuck to the icy floor. The liquid that boiled out of her mouth had hardened into a scab of clockwork pieces that tore free and clattered to the ground. She was stiff, but I set her on the chair and shook her. She was breathing, but unconscious. Her teeth were lined in pewter and blood.

"What's wrong with her?" I whirled on the cage and wished I had my sad little pistol. "What the fuck's wrong with her!"

"The foetus is setting." She sighed and slumped against the bars of her cage. "So excitable, people. This one is not going to die today. Is that acceptable?"

"I... I suppose." I looked back at Emily. She was breathing. "Better than I could do for her."

The girl was quiet. I stepped closer to her.

"Are you..." I started. I didn't know how to talk to a myth. "How did you come to be here?"

"Has the world forgotten me, then? Different days. I was a miracle once. A goddess, tightly held."

"So you're Camilla. You're really her."

"A man gave me that name, once. The only man I trusted, honestly." She shifted in her bonds, the flexible piping grinding together like stones. "I had another name. I think that part of me must have been taken." She looked down, her eyes unfocused, like a child trying to recall her sums. "Yes, it must have been taken away. I don't forget things."

I sat back on my heels. My mind was whirling, a slippery storm brewing between Emily's injuries and the shock of meeting the closest thing Veridon had to actual divinity.

"You have the codex within, yes? I can taste it, on your blood."

"What do you mean, codex?"

"Your engine. You are one of those children, the bleeders. The ones who fly, in their awkward way. They bring them to me, sometimes, when they are to die. So that the spirit in their blood does not go to waste." She stretched closer, the frailty of her ribs straining against their bonds. Her eyes were warm and light. "Is that why you are here, Pilot child? Are you about to die, to feed me?"

"That wasn't my plan, no."

"Ah." She settled back. "Well, then. Did you come that I might save the girl?"

"That wasn't my plan either. But I thank you for that."

"Of course."

"That was foetal metal. Pure," I said. I nudged the handful of fresh cogs with my toe. "It could have killed her."

"Perhaps." She shrugged, and the wisps of her ravaged wings twitched. "I didn't think it likely."

"Well. I'd have liked to know her life was in danger."

"Her life is in danger," she said. "Yours as well."

"What?"

"Being here, talking to me. The Wrights will want you both dead."

"Well, yeah. That doesn't surprise me. Why are they keeping you here?"

She wasn't looking at me anymore. Her eyes were focused at a distance greater than that allowed by the room. When she didn't answer I tried a more direct question.

"At the top of this pillar, high in the Church above." I nodded to the whirring spindle that emerged from her back, jointed to give her some range of movement. "There is a peculiar Cog. What is it?"

She looked at me as though she had only just noticed I was there. Something was moving behind her eyes; comprehension, or horror. She kept her voice even.

"What business is it of yours? What have you come here to do?"

"Like I said. I'm here by accident. I came through... I came from up above." As horrific as her situation seemed to be, she had called the Wrights her servants. And they were keeping her alive. I didn't want to anger her with their deaths, until I knew her position in all this.

"No one is here by accident. There are always patterns to this life, codex. Whether we see them or not depends on our eyes. And my eyes tell me things that make your presence very non-accidental."

I backed away from the cage, laying my hand on my belt. The holster was empty, of course. "What things?"

She leaned closer to me, until the fragments of her porcelain-perfect face were inches from the steaming bars of the coolant cage. There was hunger in her voice.

"It has been a long while, here in this place. I have a wide eye, but it is weak, like peering through fog. These people, these *Wrights* crawl through my bones, they siphon off my blood and feed it back to me, they scry the dissected bits of my soul and look for some star-damned mystery in the spatter of my gore. What do I see, you ask! What do I sense! I taste the blood of the Wrights, near my heart. I hear the scurrying of the Elder's servants across my skin, as yet unaware of your location. Unaware because I have not told them, unaware because I will it to be so." She shuddered with a long, terrible sigh. "So, child. Let us begin again. I sense something about you, and you are asking very difficult questions. Why are you here? What do you know about that peculiar Cog, as you say?"

I saw no reason to not believe her. If she said she could warn the Wrights, I wanted to avoid that.

"I have seen another, here in the city."

"Another?" She sat up, leaning closer to me with unnatural energy. "There is another heart in the city."

"I have held it in my hands. I know where it is."

"And its owner?" she asked. Her eyes were scared and hopeful, all at once. "What of the owner?"

"He is in the city as well. Killing people; chasing me."

Her face fluttered between shock and rage.

"It is an ugly thing you have done, Pilot. You people... you take everything we give you and make such a mockery of it."

"What are you talking about?"

"This!" she yelled, twitching in her cage, "This place, the heart! Gods, that you would follow the path laid out and at its end return to me with such a foul offering." She tensed, her fingers curled into claws, her hair slowly rising until it swirled and snapped in whipcord tension. "You are a people of filth and discord. This place should be wiped clean. Gods, that I had the power."

I paused. It was the first time I'd heard a deity swearing in the name of other gods.

"Let's try this again, lady. I think I know what that Cog is, the heart you keep talking about. And I'm not the one who fetched it. I'm just the unlucky fuck who ended up with it, and all the damn trouble that follows. I'm just trying to get out of this thing without getting killed."

She looked at me incredulously, then set her mouth in a grim line. "You asked about the pillar, and the Cog at its tip."

"I did."

"And you have held a similar Cog in your hand. Yet you do not know what it is, for certain." She settled back, closed her eyes. "A messenger, then. Sent only to deliver a message. But is it a threat, or a misbegotten offering." She seemed to be musing to herself. Her eyes open, full of calculation. "Who sent you to me?"

"No one. I'm here on my own." I considered for a second if I was being manipulated, if events had been planned to get me down here, in this chamber. Things were unfolding faster than I could think about them. "This thing fell into my hands, under difficult circumstances. And, frankly, circumstances have done nothing but gotten more difficult every damn day since."

"Fell into your hands?" She stared at me in disbelief. "Like stars fall out of the sky! This is a place of madness. What is it you want to know? I will tell you. The cog on the pillar, high above, the one whose cycle runs this seething cancer on your city? That is my heart. Plucked from my chest and put on display, that these fumbling idiots may learn a truth that was not meant for them. It is my heart, the heart of cursed Veridon."

"Your heart?" I asked. "But you're still alive."

"It is a careful balance. What they can take, how far they can reduce me without losing me entirely. They've managed so far."

"It hurts?"

"Something like pain, yes. Something more intimate than pain." She leaned away from me, her rage flickering as she thought back. "Some parts of me die, when they take them. Some live, either in their chapels or implanted in surrogates. Their echoes crowd the city, like lost children drowning." She shuddered. "The sound of it is too much, sometimes."

"Why are they doing this?"

She laughed, a clattering sound like an engine flying apart. I was amazed she was able to talk at all, lacking as she did a true mouth and lungs.

"They fed the city on the secrets of my bones. The cogwork, the zepliners, your PilotEngine... all derived from the hidden patterns of my body. Pale reflections of the master pattern, of course, but—"

"That's impossible. The Church has been passing out the benefits of the Algorithm for generations. Over a hundred years."

"One hundred twenty-six," she sighed. "They have been very thorough in their ministrations."

I would have sat down, but I was worried about sticking to the frost cold floor. I put a hand on Emily's chair and looked down at her. She wasn't going to believe me, when I told her who we had met. I wish she was awake for this. I didn't trust myself to ask the right questions.

"And the other Cog, the one that I was given?"

"We can't live without some connection to our heart." She looked down, crestfallen. "I'm afraid that, by sending them the map, I may have killed one of my brothers. It was not what I intended."

"The map?" I asked. "You gave them a map?"

"The Council, yes. I don't know if they realized who they were negotiating with. I have agents, here in the Church, and in the river, among the Fehn. I hoped they would catch the attention of one of my people, perhaps summon a rescue party."

"Oh," I said, "I think that may have happened. I think one of your people might be wandering the city right now."

She straightened up.

"Bring him here, Pilot. Or tell him how to get here. Do it quickly, before they capture him. I would not consign another to my fate, and feed Veridon a new pattern."

"He keeps trying to kill me, and take that Cog. Everyone seems to want those two things. Me, and that Cog."

"You flatter yourself. The Cog is all that matters."

"Yeah, well," I shrugged. "You said that an Angel can't live without their heart?"

"Angel. Such childish mythology. Yes, the... Cog, it gives us our pattern. Without it we're just the metal." She nodded at the pipe feeding foetal metal into her system. "We can't hold together."

"Then I think your friend's already screwed. He's fallen apart at least once, I saw it. I did it. He just melted into little cogs and left someone else's body behind."

"One of your friends, probably? A Pilot or some such?"

"An engram singer, but you have the idea. Someone who's been cogged."

"He's seeking patterns, trying to recover his heart before he dissolves completely." She brushed her cheek with one fragmented hand. "Not much time. You must take that Cog to him, and then bring him here."

"And if I do?"

"What do you mean?"

"What will happen to this building, this Church?" I crossed my arms. "What will happen to the city?"

"Does that concern you? You didn't seem too concerned about the well-being of the Church when you broke in."

I shrugged. "This is my city. The Church and its devices are the core of Veridon's power. I don't have to like that, but it's plain truth."

"You don't look like someone who shares in that power, despite your enhancements. You look like a thief." She leaned close to the bars. "You even smell like a..." her voice faltered. "Thief. You said my brother still pursues you, even without his heart. How long has it been?"

"I don't know. Weeks. Maybe months."

Her sad face cracked into a grin. "You have seen both Cogs, yes. Mine, and the one stolen from my brother. How would you say they compare?"

"The one upstairs, your heart. It looks different. Simpler."

"No offense taken." She smiled like a broken bottle. "I was a messenger. Like you; sent by other hands. We had been sending material down the river for eons; long after the sleep cycles started, we continued. It was realized that, recently, the missives were not getting through. I was sent to find out why."

"And the other heart?" I asked.

"It is the heart of a destroyer. It has great potential."

"Big trouble, I take it."

"Trouble that you can still avoid. Go back to whoever sent you and beg them. Beg with your life, Pilot. Tell them to bring me that Cog, and I will leave. And I will take my brother with me."

"You would just go?"

She shrugged. "In my way, in my time. But yes, I would go."

"And you were a messenger?" I asked.

"Yes, sent to find the gap in the system. The failure in the river."

"Sent? By whom?" I found it strange to be hearing about the true origin of the Church's vessels. That their religion was based on misplaced baggage seemed appropriate.

"Ancient machines. Deep places. Your churchmen, these Wrights, they were taking the vessels from the river and making things with them. That cursed Algorithm of theirs."

"And you told them to stop?"

"They wouldn't," Her face fell. "I underestimated their... fervor, I suppose."

"When you didn't return to the deep engines, no one wondered where you were?"

"We move in very long cycles," She sighed. "And most of us are off the line. It will be a while before I am missed."

"So you sent a message, somehow, to the Council. Directed them downriver in the hope they would kick over a wasp tower and your friends would track them back upriver and rescue you." I leaned closer to her. The air around her smelled like burnt oil. "You meant to destroy the city."

She looked up, her eyes following the lines of the cage, the webwork of pipes and the pillar growing out of her spine, then looked down at the dissected ruin of her body.

"Can you blame me?"

"Yes. Not in principle, I suppose, but in practice. This is where I live, see, and where I'll probably die. But I'd rather it not happen like that." I paced around the cage, looking over her limp form suspended from the pipes. "No matter what these people have done to you, that doesn't mean the whole city deserves to die. Hardly any of them know you exist. I certainly didn't."

"And if they did? Do you really think they would clamor for my release? Give up their cogwork and their airships, the power those things bring to the city? Would you?"

"Give up my cogwork? In a damn second. It's been nothing but trouble." I laughed. "Ruined my whole life."

"So. You have it in your power to do that, right now. Help me. Release me."

"I've got my own trouble, ma'am. I just want out from under this thing. I don't want to add your little crusade of destruction to my list. Your psycho friend can find you on his own, or he can fall apart and die in a gutter. Not my problem."

"Ah, but you don't need him. His loss is tragic, of course." Her eyes were manic. "But I am weak only because my heart is so far away."

"So you're saying I could bring you the other Cog and you'd just be able to walk away."

She nodded, her hands tingling with nervous energy. "With that heart, an Avenger's heart, and all this metal. I could walk out."

"They would try to stop you."

"Yes." Her eyes glittered like knife points. "They would try."

"And you would kill them. And then? You would wreak your vengeance on Veridon. Am I right?"

"No, no, of course. Well. You could be there to steady my hand. Guide me. Certainly there are elements of this city that need purging, yes?"

"You would kill the people I asked, root out the institutions I demand." I nodded my head. "And if you get overexcited, if you started to rampage."

"You could stop me," her voice was smooth, her hands together in prayer. "Guide me."

"I could try." I smiled grimly. "You see my point. If this heart is as powerful as you say, I'd be a fool to give it to you. I understand the need for vengeance, believe me I do, but you've been through too much to be trusted." I turned to go.

"It's not a question of helping me! It is not a matter of saving your city! You will help, and your city will fall. What is not decided is whether you will live to tell about it." She rose to her full height, her every fractured limb and organ twitching in rage.

"Yeah, crazy bitches don't get weapons of the apocalypse," I said. "Sorry about that."

"Your own vengeance then." The cold coming off the cage was titanic. It froze the sweat

I didn't realize was on my forehead. I turned back to her. "I can show you how to use that Cog to save yourself. Save those you love!"

"My problems are big, and my grudges are deep. But I've never felt the need to destroy a city. I handle myself, thanks."

"I know you. I scented it, earlier, but I wasn't sure. Burn, isn't it?"

I stopped. "How do you know that name?"

"Jacob Burn, son of Alexander. A boy of such talent and promise."

"How do you know my name!" I screamed.

"How's the Air Corps, Jacob?"

I rushed the cage, yelling. "Tell me how you know my name! Tell me!"

"Or has the Air Corps not worked out, hm? Because of your PilotEngine, perhaps?" She smiled, a pretty little girl smile. "It doesn't work, does it?"

"You seem to know already, bitch."

"I do. Because your Engine is not your own. It is mine, Jacob. You are one of my children, crying in the night."

Blood rushed through my head. I was numb, tired, instantly drained. "No. It's a PilotEngine, installed by the Academy. An accident, and now it's taken on a life of its own, but it's just that. Just an Engine."

"Your father was most anxious to please the Church. The Family's influence slipping in the Council, his power dwindling, his riches falling away. The Church needed someone, someone they could trust. Take my son, he said. He'll never—"

"Quiet!" I kicked the cage with the heel of my boot, shattering the thin covering of frost. It drifted down in fat white flakes that dusted the floor. She was laughing. "Quiet! My father was outraged, heartbroken! He blamed me, the Academy, my mother... everyone but himself and the Church. You don't know what the fuck you're talking about!"

"Take my son," her voice was mocking. "Give it to him, instead of the PilotEngine. He'll never know. I'll make sure of it."

Rage tore me up; my hand was trembling and white. "He wouldn't. Not his son. Not me."

"Tell me, Jacob, how the city deserves to live. Tell me they don't deserve a taste of that rage. The Council, the Church... your Family. They all knew. How has the city treated you, Jacob? Well?"

I stared at her. Long ago I accepted the disgrace of my family as inevitable. Only recently had I come to terms with my exile. To learn that it was intentional, that my father had sold my future to curry favor with the Church he claimed to despise... it was too much. It was too much.

"Forget your Family. Avenge yourself on Veridon, Jacob. This place has used you, as it used me. It doesn't care about you. Take the heart and let it change you. Let it make you into the vengeance this wretched city deserves."

I looked at her, broken and fractured in her cage. I saw myself in the same place, a tool of the Church, my life carved away to serve the city, to feed it, to let it use me and abandon me. Emily stirred.

"I'm not going to do that," I said. "I'm not going to become that thing."

"You will, perhaps. You never know."

I grimaced. The air had suddenly gotten hot. Emily's eyes fluttered open. She stared in clear shock at Camilla.

"They are coming," the girl said. I whirled to her, then to the door. I could hear footsteps.

"We have to get out," I said. I lifted Emily. She was heavier, much heavier. She tried to talk, but her voice seemed gone.

"Behind you," Camilla said. "I have friends. They will guide you."

I turned. A plate in the floor slid away. Black water slapped against the metal, slopped over onto the frosty floor. Two hands slid out of the darkness, pale white and bloated. A man pulled himself into the room.

"Camilla," he said, sadly.

"Wright Morgan." Her voice was empty.

He nodded, then took my hand and led me to the water.

"I can get you to the river, Jacob. No further. I can't get involved."

"What are you doing here?" I asked.

"Old crimes, friend." He looked at me glumly, and smiled. "Old sins. Come on."

We went into the water. The current was thick under my feet. The river took me in a hand of a thousand tiny, flat worms and bore me away. I moved as though in a dream. I don't know what I breathed in that time, but when I reached the surface my lungs were heavy with water, and my mouth tasted like swamp sickness. It was the Fehn, the wet mind that wriggled through the mud of the Reine. The flat black worms of the Fehn, helping us through the river's depth.

The water broke over my head, and I began to thrash. There was a weak light around me, and the air smelled like close, rotten wood and stale sewage. As I watched, Emily rose up from the water, borne aloft a cloud of mucous black sludge that dissipated as I took her in my arms. I began to swim wildly, losing the battle to Emily's new weight and the river.

My hand slapped against wood and I looked around. We were under the city, under

Water Street, on the part of the Reine that flowed beneath the streets and houses of the Watering District. There was a dock under my arm, its frictionlamp barely lit.

I pulled myself up with a rope that was trailing off the pier, then bent down and hauled Emily onto the planks. I did what I could, I did what I remembered from the Academy. She vomited a long, clear stream of water, then lay there, breathing. She opened her eyes, saw me, then closed them again.

I sat there, huddled over her, shivering and watching her breathe.

Chapter Thirteen
Different Friends, Dangerous Friends

THE DOCK WAS attached to one of the houses on Watering Street by a set of narrow wooden stairs. When I stopped shaking, I forced the door, then carried Emily upstairs. It was a nice house.

I lay Emily on a couch in the drawing room, then found bandages and a ready-pack poultice in a pantry by the kitchen. I cut away her shirt and dressed the wound as well as I could. There was a thin hole, front and back. It was plugged with matte gray pewter, the flashing flaking off onto her skin. The bullet had gone through. Her survival was a matter of blood loss and the abuse of our trip out of the Church. I wasn't sure what effect

Camilla's foetal metal had on the wound, but it seemed to have stabilized her. I covered her in a flannel blanket I found in the great bedroom on the main level. There were no sounds in the house, other than my frantic rushing around and the occasional tight sigh from Emily. Once she was settled, I searched the place to make sure we were alone.

There was a child's room on the second floor, shelves of wooden toys, dusty. The linen closet smelled like mildew. The bed in the master was made, but there was none of the detritus associated with daily life. The picture frames that lined the hallway were empty, and I found scraps of old photos in the ashes of the den fireplace. I felt confident we wouldn't be disturbed. I went back to check on Emily.

She was pale and cold, but still breathing. Shallow. I slipped my hand behind her neck, adjusted the pillow. She mumbled, but didn't wake up. I checked the curtains, the doors, all the windows. Emily again, still breathing, still pale as death.

The wine stocks were kept in a dry storage off the kitchen. I got a bottle and a corkscrew, along with a dusty glass that I washed out in the tepid water of the sink. Walking back to the drawing room, I stopped by the door to the private dock below. I had cracked the frame. I tilted the door open and listened. I heard water, the messy slap of waves on wood planking, creaking rope. It smelled like a drowned dog. I closed the door as best I could and shoved a bookcase up against it.

The wine was good. A '14 Sauvignon, vintner from the Brumblebacks across the Ebd. An expensive pour, and I was drinking it out of a greasy water glass in an empty house. Wax from the cork flaked into the glass when I poured, but I didn't mind. I pulled up a stool and sat by Emily, drinking and watching her and waiting. I didn't know what I was waiting for.

Her breathing seemed to even out. Her lips were slightly parted, a little teeth and tongue showing between. I wiped the last of the metal dribble away with a rag soaked in the sauvignon. She sighed, and her eyes fluttered open.

"Hey," she whispered. "Good wine."

"Nothing but the best." I put the bottle down and brushed her hair from her eyes. "How are you feeling?"

She cleared her throat and nodded to the bottle. I went to the kitchen and got a shallow bowl. She drank carefully while I held the wine to her lips.

"Were you trying to drown me?" Her voice was dry, and she dropped half the words, but I understood. "I'm just asking, because I feel that may have been part of your plan."

"You feel that way, huh?" I grinned.

"Purely an observation, Jacob."

"Right. So you're feeling better."

"I feel like I was shot, held underwater and then dragged through sewage."

"You forgot the wine," I said, sloshing the bottle.

"Right. All that, plus wine. Amends made."

"It is a very good wine."

She struggled to sit up, but gave up and settled into the couch again. She licked her lips and closed her eyes.

"What was that?" she asked.

"Yeah. I don't know how to explain it." I looked over at her and drank a little wine. "What do you remember?"

"A girl, tied up and half gone. Like some kind of experiment."

I nodded. She was breathing slowly, her heart rate slowing down. I thought she was almost asleep when she stirred.

"So what was it?"

"Some kind of legend," I said. "Forget it. It was a dream. We'll talk about it later."

"Later. Okay." Several long, slow breaths. "Where's Wilson?"

"I haven't gone for him, yet. I didn't want to move you, or leave you here. I dressed the wound. We'll get to him, when you're well enough to move." I put down the bottle and leaned closer. There was fresh blood on her shirt. "I think you're bleeding again."

"Okay," she said.

I adjusted the bandage, carefully folding her shirt over her breasts. The wound was gummy, a little red seeping at the edges. The plug of metal had worked loose. I plucked at it, and saw cogwork churning underneath. I grimaced, then tightened the cloth, added more gauze, returned the shirt.

"That should hold. No polo for a few days, okay? Em?"

Her lips were parted, her breath deep and even. I crept back to the kitchen and cobbled together a meal of stale bread and traveler's stock in a can. I set up at the writer's desk in the drawing room, a muted candle by my side so I could see her as night fell outside.

Her face was a warm moon, floating in the night. I watched her while I ate, and listened to the city outside.

I MET EMILY before. Before everything, before the shit happened. I met Emily while I was still at the Academy. I just didn't know her yet.

We were in the habit, the boys of Twelfth Cadre and I, of getting well-deep drunk on Friday nights after field exercises. It was our only free night. Technically, the sainted elect of the Pilot's Cadres had every night off. We were the nobility, after all. But practically, between the daily drills, classwork and recovery from the layers of surgery, we didn't have even minutes to commit to leisure most nights. An accident of scheduling gave us Fridays. Most of those nights were a drunken blur, time spent unwinding. I didn't even remember most of them. I remember this night, though.

I was recovering from the final round of the Engine surgeries. They staggered our recovery times, so that most of us made all the classes. It was the responsibility of the healthy to help the invalid, so they didn't lose class time. I spent the week in my barrack, trying to decipher Hammett's notes. Scribbles. But I passed all the tests, the examinations. I was cleared to fly. Tomorrow. I remember. It was my last night as a Pilot.

We went to the Faulty Tooth, our usual place. I felt good. A week in bed on a diet of cereal and water meant I got drunk easy and hard. The night started well for me. Plenty of girls, and they all liked the uniform. Common girls, girls whose fathers I didn't know. My kind of girls.

Emily was working. I didn't know. I suppose it would have mattered to me, at the time. It would have bothered me in different ways than it does now.

She stood by the bar; we had a booth. Girls circulated, laughing, holding hands. Drinking things we bought them. She was gorgeous and stood apart. She talked to various men, and seemed familiar with the barkeep. I hadn't seen her before.

When the time came, when I felt it was right, I went to the bar. Pretended to be impatient for the wench to make her rounds back to us. I stood beside her and placed my order, then stretched and, as casually as a butcher laying out the prize pig, struck the best pose I knew. She smiled, but not the way I intended.

"Nice pants," she said.

"Thank... uh. They're just part of the uniform." I flicked the cuff clasps. "Pilot Cadre."

"Mm." She drank some wine. "Well, they're kind to you. Big night?"

"Oh, you know." I rolled my hand to the boys, who were staring at us while they pretended to ignore us. "Just getting out."

"Living the big life, huh." She wasn't quite dismissive. I didn't think. I couldn't tell if she was making fun of me or just had a very peculiar way of showing interest. "They let you prizes go anywhere?"

"Hey, we go to the sky. The sky goes everywhere."

She laughed and covered it with a drink of wine. I thought it was a good line. I looked back at the boys. Their attention was absolute.

"Look," she said. "You're a nice kid. And the Corps will be good to you. Stay with it.'

"It's not a slag job, you know." I gathered up the drinks I'd ordered. "Tough work. Keeping the skies safe for citizens like you." I went back to the boys. They were unbearable.

I drank the rest of the night quickly. When she left I made some excuses and followed.

It almost felt staged. I was so fucking angry. There was a light mist, gray streamers drifting across the cobbles, the street rain slick and blurry behind the beer in my blood. She was well ahead of me when I came out. She went around a corner and I followed quickly, fists in my pocket. I wasn't going to hurt her. I just wanted to talk, to make her see. She needed to see that I was someone worth paying attention to. She would see.

The night tightened into a narrow, drunken tunnel. Someone slipped out of an alley, near where she had just disappeared. He was closer to her, and faster. Seconds after he slipped around the corner there was a scream. I ran.

I wasn't fast enough to save him. Which wasn't what I was expecting.

She stood in front of him, her dress ruffled, her hands around a long thin blade. He was against the wall. Some of him was on the pavement, leaking into the drain. She dropped him and looked over at me.

She was breathing heavily, her careful hair coming out of its tress. I looked down at the blood on her fingers. She tossed the blade onto the steaming body, then wiped her hands on his coat. She took a bag from his pocket and hid it in her dress.

"Were you... did he try to..." I stammered drunkenly.

"Either way, are you going to turn me in, Pilot?" She lowered her head, staring at me like a predator. I took a step back. "We don't all need heroes, friend."

I didn't know what to say. She left me there, to explain the pilfered body to the Badge that was just about to come around the corner.

THERE MIGHT BE a fever. I kept checking, but it was hard to tell. Her face was still very pale, but she breathed evenly. I prepared a small meal, best I could do in this weird house. She ate some and then fell asleep almost immediately. I tried to make her comfortable, but it was hard to tell if I was doing any good.

While she was out I changed the bandage. I was probably doing that too often, but I didn't know what else to do. I folded her shirt carefully, kept it as decent as possible. The tiny hole in her chest was still bleeding, soaking into the gauze in a startlingly brilliant crimson. I didn't know if that was normal, or if I should be concerned. I didn't know what Camilla's newborn machine was doing inside her, how it was remaking her. I couldn't see any visible changes on the outside. There were usually changes.

I needed to go get Wilson. Medicine wasn't something I did. Generally, I did the thing that necessitated medicine. The precursor. Wilson would know what to do, even if there was nothing to be done.

I soaked a rag in cold water and put it on her forehead. That didn't look right, so I folded it and put it behind her neck. She squirmed and started coughing. The rag went back into the sink.

Wilson would know. I crouched by the front window and peered carefully out into the street. Not much traffic. Night was ending, the first hammered silver light crowding into the overcast. If I was going to do it, I needed to get at it, before morning brought the crowds back to the street. Just an hour, and not even that. I looked back at her. So pale. I checked for fever again. Coughs tore through her chest, upset her carefully draped shirt. I put it back, then got another bottle of wine from the pantry. Morning filled the room slowly, lining her face in pewter light.

Wilson would know. But Wilson would have to wait.

It was two years. I had enough on my mind during that time to forget Emily. But when I saw her, standing across the bar and smiling… it came back.

Different bar, different district. Different friends. And the pistol I had strapped to my leg wasn't part of some uniform, nothing ceremonial or exquisite about it. Things had changed for Jacob Burn. But she was still there, still brilliant. I stood up, to go talk to her.

"Wouldn't," Matthus said, his hand lightly on my elbow. He glanced at me, then at Emily. "Cacher's girl, one of Valentine's people. I wouldn't."

The rest of the table looked. One of them said. "Yeah, I know her. Whore. No harm in it, Jacob."

"She's not working tonight. Doesn't pick up men in bars." Matthus snorted into his beer. "Her clientele make appointments. Not the like of you, son."

"Then what's she doing here?" I asked. "Alone. If Cacher cares for her so much."

"Girl can't get a drink?"

"This isn't a safe district, Math. Bad people about." The table had a chuckle at that. Bad people. I had a sudden flash of her standing over her attacker, the memory rolling through me, the blood on that blade, the look in her eye.

"It's your funeral, mate." Matthus said, then wrote me off. Kind of friends I had.

I went to her, my table snickering and being generally bad people. Old noble Jacob, talking to the ladies. Forgotten who he was, or more accurately, who he was no longer. A good laugh, for the crew.

She seemed amused to see me coming. One look, then her eyes were on the bar in front of her, the slightest smile on her face.

"Buy a girl a drink?" I asked. She looked at me, no hint of that smile evident.

"Girls have money too, you know."

I shrugged. She turned to the barkeep. "Castle Crest on the rocks, compliments of the gentleman in the dull gray coat." I winced. Crest was expensive stuff. My dad drank Crest, after a good vote in the Council. We sat in silence while the 'keep poured into his cleanest glass, the ice cracking under the slow amber liquid. She drank it quickly.

"Satisfied?" she asked.

I clattered my empty glass at the barkeep and he refilled it, with less care and flourish. More foam than brew. We stood there in silence again. She started to turn away.

"You could at least talk to me," I hissed, so the crew couldn't hear me. "That's the least you could do for my coin. Don't make the fool of me like that."

She turned back. Her eyes were cold as stone.

"I hadn't realized this was a transaction. Is that what your mates told you? That I have a slot," she spat. "You can put coins in it?"

"I... godsdamn it. No, that's not what I meant." I flushed and busied myself drinking my warm beer. I spilled a little and had to wipe it on my sleeve. "It's not at all what I meant."

"Then what, exactly, did you mean?"

I stared off behind the bar. The bottles back there were dusty. A painting hung above, a copy of a copy of a masterpiece I had seen hanging in the artist's studio when I was a child.

"You don't remember me, do you?" I asked without looking at her. Out of the corner of my eye I saw her toying with her glass. She signaled the barkeep, waved off another pour of the Crest and pointed to something a little less elegant.

"I do, actually." She looked at me, a brief flash of eyes, a smile. Her voice was quiet. "I wouldn't, honestly, not if you hadn't had such a spectacularly bad day the following."

I grunted and drank. The people who remembered me usually remembered me for that day. Those who forgot me, too.

"I've often wondered, you know. What happened to that boy I met? The one who fell from the sky."

I turned to her, remembering the ridiculous pose that I'd struck on the night. I looked down at myself, the drab clothes, the stained sleeve. The only thing about my appearance that was in order was the pistol, oiled and black.

"Looks like he kept falling," she said.

I turned away, signaled for another beer.

"I've kept myself," I said. "Troubles, but I've kept myself together. I don't need sympathy."

"That's good. Sympathy's not something I do well. We've all had bad times. Just because your childhood was one of privilege and potential, that doesn't make your days any tougher than mine."

"If you say."

"Two ways to go, Jacob." She drank her cheap bourbon slowly, wincing as she ran it around her mouth. "People who have trouble like yours can go two ways. They can get all morose and indignant, and crumble under the weight of their own tragedy. Or," she whispered as she turned to face the bar. "They can adjust. Get stronger. Help themselves. Stand up for themselves. They become one of those two people. Strong or dead."

"Which one of those people takes advice from whores in bars?" I asked.

She smiled, thin and tight. Her hands were twisted around her glass.

"Let's say I don't pound you for that, Jacob. Just this once. Those your friends?" she asked, nodding to my table.

I looked over. A rough bunch, all cheap coats and pilfered finery that was mismatched and smudged. I remembered that Marcus was there. He was looking at me kind of nervously. At the time it didn't register. People were nervous around me, around my pewter eyes.

"That's them."

"Do you have any other friends?" she asked. I shook my head. "Really? From the Academy, the Council? All those years growing up, you didn't make one friend."

"They don't talk to me anymore."

"Dressed like that, it's no surprise. And you don't seek them out, do you?" She put her back to the bar and leaned on her elbows, looking out over the smoky vista of the room.

"It's safer down here, isn't it? Folks like this, they don't expect much of their friends. It's hard to disappoint them."

"You don't know what the hell you're saying, lady."

She laughed. "I think I do. What drove you down here? Honestly. What puts a boy like you in a place like this? And don't tell me cursed fate or your father." She took a drink and winced. "People make choices. People stand up to them."

"Pretty smart for a whore."

"You keep saying that. You think it's clever. I'm getting tired of it," Drink, wince. "Not because it hurts for you to know my true nature. Not because you've shamed me. I'm getting tired of how clumsy it is. I really thought more of you. Thought you'd be better at this."

I was quiet. I didn't like the rocks she was flipping over, the scabs she was poking. It had taken me a while to get here, to drag myself up from the shit my life had become. I wouldn't say I was happy, but I was content.

"What're you getting at?"

"You think your old friends would talk to you again? If we got you cleaned up. Maybe buy you a pair of those smart pants that suit you so well. Could you mingle in those circles again?"

I looked at her harshly. She was smiling. She turned her face at me and winked.

"There are some people I know, Jacob. Friends. They'd like to have a friend in those circles."

"I'm not that friend." I shook my head, indicated the filthy bar. "If you haven't noticed, I don't walk in those circles anymore."

"By choice," she said. I started to protest, but she put a hand on my wrist. Fire rushed through me. "I know. You'll say you were forced out. Shunned. But that's just you, letting yourself collapse."

"It's not that easy," I said.

"Nothing is. But I think, if we give you some money, a place to stay, a chance to clean up, that you'd be surprised how many of your old friends would come calling."

"I don't think so. Not the people I knew."

"Well. You're no longer the friend they knew, either. You're something else. Something dangerous. And people in those circles, they like to have dangerous friends."

"Maybe."

"Believe me. I know." She flashed a devious smile, almost angry. "The beautiful people like to have dangerous fucking friends."

I looked back at my table, and the drunks and the criminals I'd spent the last two years around.

"What would I do?"

"Favors," she said. "That's how this whole thing works. Favors and friends."

I nodded. Emily smiled, then hooked her arm around my elbow.

"Pay up, then let's go see someone. A good friend. A particularly dangerous friend."

"Who?"

"A man by the name of Valentine."

My bones went cold, but I nodded and she led me out.

I WOKE UP, startled, then stood. My chair clattered back, banging against the desk before spinning to the hardwood floor. Emily was looking at me, her eyes half-open.

"Dreaming?" she asked. Her voice was dry and harsh. I went to get some water, awkwardly aware of my rapidly softening erection. I ran my hands under the cold water from the tap, then brought Emily her glass.

"Yeah," I said. "I think so."

Emily pulled herself into a sitting position, wincing once then not putting any pressure on her injured arm. She drank some water.

"Anything good? Your dream?"

I shook my head, took the empty glass and set it on the desk.

"Are you feeling hungry?" I asked.

"Maybe." She rubbed her eyes with one hand, then looked around the room. "Are we safe here?"

"No. Not completely. The owners could come back, or a neighbor could get curious and report us. But that hasn't happened yet." I went into the kitchen, wrapped some cold cured bacon into a roll and went back into the dining room. She was staring out the window. "Eat this."

She took the sandwich and dutifully consumed it one mechanical bite at a time. When she was done I gave her more water, cut with what was left of the wine.

"Thanks," she said, wiping her hands on the priceless virgin calfskin divan. "I owe you."

"Probably not," I said. "Just friends doing favors."

She smiled.

"Is this how you think of this, Jacob? That I'm just a friend, doing you a favor, helping out with this problem of yours?"

I shrugged and turned away, busying myself with the plate and empty water glass. She gathered the blanket up under her breasts and leaned back, staring at the ceiling.

"Well," she said, quietly, "I'm still grateful."

I took the dishes back to the kitchen and put them into the sink. When I came back she was still staring at the ceiling.

"How are you feeling?" I asked.

"Still shot. But better. What about you?"

I hadn't thought about it. My ribs ached, and I realized there was a crushing pressure around my head. "I'm fine. Have you heard, Wilson says I can't be killed."

I ran my hand over her forehead. Her skin was cool and slightly moist. Her hair fell across her face, so I pushed it aside with one finger. She looked up at me with those watery brown eyes that hinted at red and gold.

"Jacob. Uh." She bit her lip and looked over my shoulder. "I'm really sorry."

"For getting shot?" I sat on the couch. "Yeah, I'm pretty sore at you for that. Inconsiderate."

"No, no." She put her hand on my chest, rubbed my collar between finger and thumb. "This whole thing. It's such a complicated situation, and I'm sorry you're having to go through it. I almost feel like, if I hadn't sent you to the Heights, none of this would have happened."

"Nah. That thing would have just come for me in the city. Maybe come for you, too. It's not your fault."

"Maybe. Still, I feel bad. And the last few years, Jacob. I know it's been difficult for you."

"What? Being thrown out of my wealthy family, living as a bandit? Nothing to it. And I've met some interesting people, at least."

She laughed, then winced and deflated.

"Take it easy, Em. You're not—"

"No, that's not what I meant. I mean, I know it's been difficult for you. With me, and Cacher."

"Oh." I straightened up. "Well, I mean. Yeah."

"Yeah. It's just a tough thing, Jacob. Cacher's an important guy, and I need him. Him and Valentine, both."

"I know." I started to stand up. "Maybe you should try to get some more sleep. I can go get Wilson, probably."

She pulled me back down.

"Listen to me. Okay? For one second, brush off your wounded pride and your goddamn pathos and just listen. It's been tough for me, too. What I do isn't glamorous, or even pleasant. But it's what I have to do, and you know it. And without Cacher, it would have been a whole lot harder. I couldn't risk that, losing that protection. No matter how I felt."

I sat looking at her for a minute. She seemed genuinely sorry. Though that might have just been the blood loss talking.

"Well, I mean." I scratched my hand. "You could have given me discount, at least."

Emily moaned.

"You're such an asshole, sometimes. Such a damn asshole."

She grabbed my collar with her one good arm and pulled me down. Our lips met, teeth clicking, and then I was buried in warmth and softness. She tasted like… nothing I knew. She tasted perfect.

When I sat up she was crying, and there was fresh blood on her shirt.

"Maybe next time don't lean on me like that."

"Oh, shit, Em, I'm sorry. Damn it." I stood up quickly and got more bandages and a clean alcohol swab. When I came back into the room she was leaning up on her good arm. "Lie back and let me—"

"Shut up," she hissed. I stopped. There was a clatter on the front sidewalk, like someone spilling coins.

We stayed perfectly still, staring at the door. The sound came again, closer. I dropped the bandages and went for my gun. It was still gone.

"Can you walk?" I whispered.

"Maybe." She was already sitting up, her legs tossed sluggishly over the edge of the couch, feet on the ground. She leaned forward and rested her head in her hands. "Maybe."

I gave her my arm. Together we got her upright and began to shuffle to the hallway.

"We'll hide downstairs, on the dock," I said. "I'll swim. There are other docks nearby, have to be. One of them must have a boat."

"And if they come downstairs?" she asked, her teeth grinding. Her eyes were squeezed shut tight.

"Then I'll perform a heroic rescue. That might be better, actually. I've always favored the idea of heroism."

"Looking forward to that," she said, little laughs escaping around the pain.

The front door burst open. There was a machine. It was a twisted array of pipes, crudely bolted together and animated by a set of arms and legs of rough artifice. It stumbled into the room. A valve clapped open and emitted a low moan. Its voice sounded like a pipe organ channeling a hurricane.

"Jacob godsdamned Burn, don't you let them keep me like this. For mercy's sake, you kill me, you fucking horrible bastard. You fucking kill me again."

Emily slumped against me, gaping. I nearly dropped her. I knew that voice, twisted as it was through metal.

"Marcus?"

"Oh, hell." Emily buried her face in my shoulder.

"Marcus, indeed. Good boy, Marcus," Sloane said as he walked through the door. He reached down and banged a lever on the thing's back. The machine that spoke with Marcus' voice clattered to the floor.

"Now. Stand still." He pointed a pistol at us. Dozens of Badgemen flowed in behind him. "We need to have a chat, Jacob Burn."

Chapter Fourteen
Things That Always Hurt

It was a short fight; it wasn't a fight at all. I stepped forward to meet them and Emily collapsed from my arm. In turning to her, I turned away from them. They were on me in half a breath. They trussed me tight in leather belts and steel. I lay on the couch. Emily was still on the floor.

"Don't leave her there, you bastards," I gasped through bloody lips.

"She'll be attended. In good time," Sloane said. He lay his pistol on the desk, then removed his thin leather gloves and tossed them next to it. I saw that the revolver was brass inlaid, just like the one I had, from the *Glory*. "Anyone else in the house? Tell us, or we'll kill them when we find them."

"No one," I said. He nodded, then signaled five men to search, and another five to secure the door. They rushed off, as though anxious to be out of his presence.

Leaning against the desk, he stared at me with casual indifference. When the men came back and shook their heads, he sent them out into the street. Once we were alone he turned his attention to Emily.

"You're concerned for her. She's breathing still, if that's your interest." He craned his neck. "And she appears to be bleeding." He turned back to me, his eyebrows up. His tone was conversational. "She's been shot? Or stabbed? Good stuff. Ah, here we are." He bent closer to her and raised his voice. "Good morning, dear."

Emily moaned and stirred. I twisted to see her, but couldn't get my head around too well. Sloane pushed me back with one foot.

"Yes, good morning, lovely. Feeling well? You'd be Emily, I suppose? Gone off the treaty a bit, haven't we, my dear?"

She levered herself up, panting in pain. He nodded to her.

"Up, up, up. Onto the couch, quickly now." He picked up the pistol, delicately, as though it would leave a foul stench on his hand if he gripped it too firmly. He waved it indistinctly in Emily's direction. "No laying about on Mr. Sloane's time, is there?"

"Where did you get that?" I asked, hoping to distract him from tormenting the girl. It was definitely a service revolver of the Air Corps.

"You like it? I thought you might be interested." He held it so I could see the crest. *Glory of Day*. "Tell me, where do you think I got it?"

"From the Fehn. From the river."

"Good. Dots are beginning to connect. And where do you think you got your pistol?"

I squirmed on the sofa and tried to sit up. He watched me disinterestedly, then smacked me lightly across the face with the pistol.

"Where. Do you think. You got your pistol?"

"You know." I spat.

"Of course I know, Jacob. Because you got it from me. I wrapped it in that box and had it delivered to you at the Manor Tomb. Mysteriously. Mystery is such an effective tool in the paranoid mind, Mr. Burn." He leaned happily against the desk and folded his arms, the pistol tucked under his elbow. "Speaking of which. Where is your pistol?"

"I left it at the Church. Dropped it."

"Dropped it. At the Church. Really." He looked over my shoulder at the wall. "I wonder what they're going to make of that. Interesting."

"What was the point, Sloane?"

"You didn't give me a lot of time, Mr. Burn. I only found out you were going to be at that party that morning. Had to do something to keep you out of Angela's hands, didn't I? I figured getting you a little paranoid would do the trick."

"So it was a setup?" I looked at Emily. "They got me up there to capture me. What about the Angel?"

"Yes! What about the Angel. I was hoping you could tell me, Jacob. What do you know about him?"

I laid out a long, tired sigh. "This is how you ask questions? I'm not telling you anything, man. Not anything."

He smiled at me, a grim, empty smile.

"No, I suppose you're not. Not at all." He turned to Emily again. "On the couch, woman. I am patient, but not in that way."

"Fuck off," Emily spat from the floor. Sloane raised the pistol and cocked it.

"You get one warning. It's a pity you use it on such a trivial thing." He fired into the couch, inches above her head. I yelled and struggled forward. He kicked me in the face, without looking.

Grimacing, Emily dragged herself forward. He held the pistol on her, a little half smile wrinkling his face, until she collapsed next to me on the sofa. Her skin was cold and pale, and sweat beaded her face.

"Enough? This is a good start, but we really don't have much time. Not the usual leisurely chat, for us. I'm going to start by assuming that you don't have it with you?"

"What?" I asked.

He reached forward and cracked my face with his pistol. With my arms bound I fell to the ground, smearing blood on the carpet.

"I don't want to sit through this again." Arms on my shoulders, he grunted as he lifted and then dropped me onto the couch. Emily was gaping at him. When I looked up he was leaning against the desk, as though he had never moved.

"Jacob…" she whispered. "Fucking… Jacob…"

"That wasn't my question. I don't blame the boy, of course. From what I've heard you're a talented girl. But let's keep to the subject. Is it with you?"

"You mean the Cog?"

"I do."

"Never heard of it," I spat, blood dribbling down my chin.

His face didn't change, but he hunched forward. Emily pressed herself back into the couch. Didn't make any sense to me. I was the one getting punched, no need for her to flinch like that. Only the spook didn't punch me, not yet. He set down the gun, then pulled on the thin leather gloves. His hand on my knee was heavy, like lead.

"Jacob. There are things you should know. Secrets. I know this whole thing has been very difficult for you." He turned his head to look at Emily, then back to me. "Your family, as well. Hard on all of us. I'm not here to make things more difficult. It may get difficult, in the short term, I'll admit that, but what happens is really up to you. Okay?"

"You're a psychotic fuck, Sloane. Don't play with me."

"I'm sorry. It's just my nature." He squeezed my knee like an old grandfather. "But really, I'd like to help. Is there anything I can answer for you? Any questions you might have that might make this whole thing go easier?"

"Say you have me, and you get the Cog. What are you going to do about our winged friend?"

"The Angel?" He smirked. "Things are being lined up for him. Don't worry. And now, I suppose, it's my turn."

He pulled his gloves tighter, then leaned close and ran a finger across my face. His face was screwed up in concentration.

"They did quite a job on you, Jacob Burn. I can feel it, burning out of you. The bruise is already fading. There is a fracture, as well. Here." He stabbed an iron finger at my cheek. Pain shuddered through my face. The bones ground. I did what I could to not scream, but it was a near thing. "Yes, but not for long. Healing already."

"What do you know about that?" I gasped as he dropped me back on to the couch. He wrinkled his brow.

"Yes, see. Curiosity. Questions." He pulled a chair over and sat down, his hands folded casually in his lap. "And then answers. All very simple. So. What do I know about your little talent."

"Don't listen, Jacob," Emily whispered, angry. "He's just a thug. He's just making shit up to get you talking."

"Does it matter? I'll tell you what I know, and you can believe it or you won't. Doesn't matter." He leaned close to me. "Your heart, Jacob, is a favor done for some very powerful people. A debt that will be repaid, you understand."

"Let me guess. You're here to collect."

Again, that smile. That dead, damn smile.

"It's not your debt, Jacob. Now. My turn. The Cog isn't here?"

"Fuck off."

"I will take vulgarity as a demure negative. But you have it?"

"Fuck. You."

"Hm. Look, Jacob. We both know that I can keep breaking you, and you can keep unbreaking. And as much as that idea interests me, well." He tossed his hands up. "Time. It's all down to the damn time. It's just not in our favor."

"Jacob..." Emily said. Her voice was laced with terror.

"But it's just your body, right? There are ways around that." He stood up, peeling off the gloves, throwing them on the table. Walking over to the jumble that was apparently Marcus, he rubbed his hands together. "Dear Marcus, for example. I could not... speak to his body, in my usual way. You made sure of that, yes?"

Hauling up the roughly dressed pipes and crude bolts as though they were foil, Sloane held the machine in front of us and flipped it on.

"Marcus?" he asked.

The pipes moaned. The legs struggled to find purchase, like a drunk on ice. Finally, the device stood on its own.

"But we found a way, didn't we, Marcus?"

"Jacob? He's here, isn't he?" the pipes groaned. "Right here. I found him, like you said. Like the deal."

"Deal is such a broad term, Marcus." Sloane rattled the machine. "You found him, like we demanded."

"That's just a trick, Sloane." I squirmed until I was sitting up. "There's nothing of Marcus there."

"Oh, but there is. Bits of him. The bits that can still be hurt." Sloane ran a hand gingerly across the manifold, then slapped the lever off. Again, Marcus fell. The noise of the collapse was heavy.

"Like the soul machines in your lovely zepliners. You remember those, Jacob." He twirled his fingers, like a butterfly in flight. "The spirit in the pipes, away from the body, in the machine. And if the body goes, well, the pipes are still there. And the soul."

I thought of the captain on the *Glory of Day*, his metal voice on the *Glory*.

"Marcus was dead," I said.

"Yes. Hugely helpful, you killing him. Something about souls, Jacob, and the people who kill them. Like two magnets, brought together." He patted the collapsed shell of Marcus. "It's slow, but inevitable."

"This is how you kept finding us?" Emily asked. "At the lab, and now here?"

Sloane shrugged.

"My point, Jacob, is that I don't need to hurt your body. And I don't need to wait until you die to hurt your soul. It's easier that way, but that's... simply not on the table."

"I'm terrified. Really. You should tie some more straps on me, because I might shake apart with the trembling, Sloane."

"Brave man," he said, grinning. "And funny. A god damn waste, kicking you out of the Council. Still," he picked the leather bag up from the floor and set it on the desk. "You've served your purpose well."

"Whatever you do, Sloane, leave her out of it. She doesn't know anything."

"Probably true." The brass clasps snapped open, the buckle shrugging free to clang against the desk. "Wouldn't that be interesting? Finding out what you know, girl. Finding all your secrets."

Emily paled and shrank into the sofa. I wrestled with the straps across my chest. The leather was biting into my arms, but I thought that, with time, I'd be able to get free.

"Another time." Sloane opened the bag and drew out a long tangle of hoses, bound in tarnished brass clasps and piped fittings. There was some central core to the machine, a complication of pumps and coiled springs. He set this on the table. It scarred the shiny veneer of the wood.

"Do you want to know about this? What it is, what it does?" Sloane held one of the rubber hoses across his thin palms like a holy relic. "Will that make it easier for you?" He looked down at me, his eyes flat, dark pits in his face.

Cold sweat broke out across my hands and face, something I couldn't avoid. My toughest face wasn't good enough for this.

"It helps me, sometimes. Knowing what's going to happen. I form it in my head, smooth it out. See it." Holding the hose in one hand, he cupped my chin, then ran a dry finger across my cheek. "In your situation, though. I understand, not wanting to know."

He took the hose and looped it loosely around my head, gathered it up and looped it again, the coils building up beneath my chin. Each time he gathered, the hose snuggled up against my throat. It tightened. My head filled with the sound of my hammering blood. I tried to struggle, to flop free, but my body wouldn't respond. I felt paralyzed, caught in the strange formality of the ritual.

"Emily, dear. Your eyes." He planted his palm flat against my forehead and grimaced. "I would close your pretty eyes."

With a jerk he tightened the hose. Emily screamed and threw herself off the couch. He brushed her aside, kicking her as she fell. My whole head squeezed shut, my tongue lolling up out of my mouth, my eyes wide and hot. I struggled to breathe, to scream, but my body felt farther and farther away. Through the hammering blood, I heard his voice.

"This is the worst part, Jacob. The worst." He held the hose easily in one hand, his knuckles tight against my throat, holding me up. With his other hand he loosened his collar and showed me the old scars, the shiny skin of his neck. "I know. I understand. After this, my boy, there is nothing but darkness. The worst is almost over."

He was right. The darkness came, and silence. The last thing I heard was the machine on the desk starting up, and the pulse moving through the hose, my neck, my blood, into my heart and dreams.

I WOKE UP to a taste, and nothing more. It was like tarnished brass filling my mouth, only I had no sense of mouth or tongue. Just a taste, hanging in emptiness.

There was nothing of my body, no feeling of pain, no sense of place or orientation. I could see nothing. Not blackness, as though I had closed my eyes or stood in a perfectly sealed room, but absolutely nothing. The idea of sight was distant, something remembered but unfamiliar.

"There, Jacob, you see? This isn't as bad, is it? Not at first, anyway." The voice of Sloane arrived without direction or weight. Just words I knew I was hearing, somewhere.

"Now, before we begin, there's something I need to show you, Jacob. Pay very close attention to this. Are you ready?"

What followed was nothing like pain. Pain has limits, it has durations and intensities. It leaves scars and teaches lessons. What followed was suffering, pure and simple. It was loneliness and loss, the obsessions of spurned love and the emptiness of lifetimes spent in isolation. It was being alone forever, again and again. It stopped, leaving nothing but the taste of brass.

"There. Do you understand now, Jacob? Emily seems quite concerned. You put on quite a show. Let her know you're okay, son. Just say yes, Jacob. Tell her you're alright."

Speaking without a voice is strange. I fixed it, like some talent I didn't know I had.

"Ye—"

He hit it again. Five more times before he asked another question. I learned to scream too.

"Do you understand now?" he asked.

"Yes," I said weakly. Could Emily really hear me, or was my body lying nerveless on the couch?

"Very good. We will start simply. Who on the Council is funding you, and what dealing have they had with the Church?"

"I..." I wasn't sure what to say. "No one is funding me."

It started slower, just a background tearing of emotion, an undercurrent of wasted life and depression.

"Someone must be standing with you. Emily is here. Should I evacuate her, see who she's willing to name?"

"There's no one, Sloane. Everyone seems to be trying to kill me or capture me. I'm running from everyone."

The tearing continued for a while, pulsing through me like a thorned rope, then it receded.

"We'll let that stand for now. How did you get in touch with Marcus?"

"Again, I didn't. I was downfalls on other business. I saw him on the return trip."

"You just happened to be aboard that specific ship, on that specific day."

"Yes."

Suffering, for a while.

"We know Marcus was in conversation with the city. He told someone his plans, which ship he'd be taking, and when. That he was being pursued. They promised him safety, pledged it, once he got to the city."

"He didn't make it."

"No. Because you were sent to gather him up. And things got out of hand."

"I wasn't even supposed to be on that flight, Sloane. I got delayed on my job. It was just chance."

The next jolt lasted longer, if eternity can last longer. I had a brief, shocking feeling of my body, drifting farther away from my floating consciousness.

"Stay with me here, Jacob. I don't believe you. This can go on for a long time. It can go on forever. All I need is your body, remember. You don't need to be in it."

"Go to hell," I whispered.

"Of course. But first, I need to understand. You say that you just happened to be on the *Glory*. Of the thousands of people in the city, the hundreds of thugs who could have been on Valentine's business, by pure chance, it just happened to be you that he sent."

"Pure chance," I repeated.

"Wrong." Jolt. "Wrong, Jacob." Shattering jolt, my soul falling apart, my body leaving. "I don't believe in chance. Not in these matters." Jolt, less memory and more severing of my body. I was leaving, I could tell, leaving the world for an eternity of brass and suffering. "You will tell me, Jacob, and you will..."

The pain ended. The taste left my mouth, and time passed in darkness. I have no idea how long it was. When I woke up the street outside was bright, sunlight pouring in around the shutters of the front window. Sloane was sitting at the desk, thumbing through a sheaf of papers.

"Ah, good." He looked up at me, nodded. "Sorry about the delay, Mr. Burn. There has been, well. A development. An interruption to our little discussion. Sorry."

"Don't mention it." I spat and looked around. Emily was gone.

"Yes, your friend has been moved."

"Where is she?"

"Elsewhere. Not here. That's all I think you need to know. You'll be moving soon as well."

I struggled to sit up. He hit me again, and the jagged line of pain in my cheek put me on my ass. As I fell, a loop of belt fell off my shoulder. My arms loosened. I curled up on the couch to cover it.

He stood up and came over, peering at me curiously. "What happened to her, by the way? That surgery for her wound, it was very... intuitive. Primitive, but still elegantly done. You didn't do that, obviously."

"Fuck off."

"This again. You should try harder to offend me, Jacob. It would at least make our conversations more interesting."

I pulled myself up, best I could. The belts loosened just a little more. It was going to be okay, I thought. It's going to work out.

"You aren't worth the effort, Sloane."

"Ah, well. You tried at least." He pulled up my chin to look at my eyes. "Yes, I suppose that's the most I can expect of a child like—"

I swung my arm up and grabbed his wrist. His bones felt like stone.

"Ah, yes," he said anxiously. "Yes, yes, yes."

I punched my elbow at his waist, but he pulled back. I stood. He took my arm in both hands and threw me against the wall. It was a well-built house, and I crumpled to the floor.

"This is much better, I suppose. At a different level. Still. Invigorating."

I struggled out of the bonds, letting them slip over my legs. I wasn't quite free when he got to me. His fists were steel, and precise. I yelped.

"Okay. I can't let this go much longer." He was barely breathing heavily. "Perhaps another few rounds, and then—"

I kicked both heels into his knee. He went down, his face carefully disappointed. I rolled over him and crawled towards the desk. He came at me from behind, cracking my head with both fists. My nose jammed into the floor. I breathed in blood.

"Gods... fuck." Sloane struggled up, leaning against the desk chair. "You're making this difficult, Jacob."

"Fuck off," I hissed, then slapped the desk over. The papers scattered, but the pistol rolled next to my hand. I took it up in both hands and fired two quick shots through the room. Sloane stopped talking and jumped. I rolled behind the couch.

"This isn't going to go well for you, Jacob. We have the girl. If you don't come out, right damn now, we're going to ruin her."

I stood and crossed the room. He stood.

"Good call, Jacob. Hand over the pistol."

I knuckled the revolver and punched him with the chamber tight in my palm. His lip split, and he went down.

"Where is she?"

"Elsewhere, Jacob." He smiled through bloody teeth. "Elsewhere."

"I don't give warnings, Sloane. Where is she?"

He shrugged. The Badge broke in the door. The wood splintered, and I stepped back. Sloane punched me on the inner thigh and I staggered all the way to the couch. Sloane ducked out. I fired another shot, catching him in the shoulder. He lurched into the street, yelling. The Badge looked back at their boss, just long enough for me to put holes in them.

I went to the door. The cold iron carriage was there, the one I had seen earlier at Emily's apartment. Marcus's carriage, I realized. I looked back at his crumpled form. The Badge was forming up outside. There had to be a back door.

As I left the room, I paused by Marcus' metal form. I thought of the timeless suffering, the taste of brass and the tearing of my soul. There was a valve, sealed shut. I got a length of pipe out of the kitchen and tore it off. He rushed out like an exhausted wave on the beach, his spirit washing through the room in horror and relief. When he was gone, I took another shot out the open door, scattering the Badge, then went upstairs. There was a back balcony off the child's room. I jumped to the next roof and ran.

I KNEW IT was wrong before I got there. The sounds, the light. None of it was right. I almost turned back before I got there. I stood at the last corner, my hands and face resting on the cold stone for ten minutes. I kept hoping to hear something; Wilson complaining to himself, or working on some experiment. Anything.

The cistern was torn up. This is what had happened, what had interrupted Sloane's questioning. They didn't need me to tell them where the Cog was. They had it. They came in here and got it. They had come in with guns, explosives. Stone fell from the ceiling, choking the water. Whatever secret outflow had swallowed the spring was blocked, and the cistern was rising. Dark water was pooling up over the rocky pier, flooding the floor of our hideaway.

Wilson's things floated in a half foot of water, tubes and shattered jars swirling in the new currents. Specimens, leaves and dead bugs clumped together like tiny islands. His delicate netting was torn and burned, hanging in charred tatters from the bullet-eaten walls. There was blood, smears, spatters, thin whirls in the water, drifting among Wilson's abandoned wreckage.

No bodies. Shell casings, one of Wilson's cruel knives, broken and bright in the water. Emily's shotgun was in a far corner, near the sunken tip of the pier. I waded out there, scooped it up and stared down into the deep water beyond.

I stood there a long time, waiting for something to come out of that water, or for me to sink down into it. Nothing happened. I slung the soggy belt of the gun over my shoulder and went out. I had some questions for dear old dad.

Chapter Fifteen
Gods Without Churches

"Billy," I said.

"Master Burn is not—"

I punched him pretty hard. Harder than I meant, but better that than too light. He went down, his lip burst like a balloon. I stepped inside and closed the door.

The foyer was empty, no sound but the half dozen clocks dad kept on display, each one a little out of step with all the others. I dragged Billy into the coat check, tied him as best I could with an old scarf that was lying in the corner, and locked the door.

Cradling the shotgun in my hands, I started to search the rest of the house. I didn't have any shells, but my father was a rational man.

Even the threat of the gun would keep him in line.

I didn't find him, or anyone else for that matter. Mother lived with the kids, my sister and her officer gallant, upriver in their exciting new life as expatriates. My brothers were in the navy. The Academy wouldn't take any more chances on the Burns. Father Burn lived here pretty much alone, him and Billy, a couple servants and the rare itinerant mistress. Most of the house was closed up. It looked like father was living mostly in the ballroom, sleeping in one of the private sitting rooms that clustered around the dance floor. How bad had things gotten?

I went back to the foyer and opened the coat check. Billy was in the corner, free of the scarf, using it to mop blood off his face. He stared at me with narrow eyes.

"What was it you were saying, Billy, before I interrupted?"

"You're a psychopath, Jacob," he hissed. "Alexander was right, putting you out."

"I'm getting to that. Maybe you're right, but maybe you don't know what the fuck you're talking about. Now," I cradled the shotgun in my arms. "What were you saying?"

He looked down at his feet. His shoes were badly scarred, but well polished.

"You're going to kill me."

"Where is he, Billy?"

"No. You're going to kill him, too. You can..." he sobbed, a noble little kink in his voice. "You can do what you want with me, but I'm not going to let you kill him."

"I can just wait, Billy. I can sit here and lock the door and wait for him to come home. And I know he's coming home eventually. My old man, there's nowhere for him to go. Just tell me, Billy. I'm not going to hurt him, but there're some things he and I need to talk out."

"You expect me to believe that? Look," he wadded up the bloody scarf, held out his crimson hands. "Look at me. Look at what you've done. You're a violent, horrible, ugly man. You're just a godsdamn thug, Jacob. Just a violent, angry, broken man."

I stared at him. He was crying, but only in his eyes. The rest of him was stick straight and furious.

"Tell me where he is. You have my word, Billy. And I'm sorry about your face."

He was trembling, the scarf knotted up between his fingers, fresh blood on his lip. His shirt was ruined, and I couldn't imagine he had that many shirts, not working in this house.

"Williamson," I said. "Where's my father?"

"The Singer," he whispered, tears anew in his eyes. "He's at the Singer. Praying."

I nodded, then set Emily's gun in the corner of the tiny room and went to the kitchen. I came back with wet towels and a bottle of dad's better whiskey. The shotgun had been moved, bloody fingerprints on it. He probably picked it up, just long enough to see it wasn't loaded. I'd never seen Billy use a gun, and I didn't expect that to change today. I cleaned his face, made sure he drank three expensive fingers of the whiskey. He felt guilty about that, I could see, drinking the master's bottle.

"You won't hurt him?" he asked.

"And give him a way out? No." I picked up the shotgun. "Thanks, Billy. Williamson. Get some ice on that lip."

"Billy's fine," he said. He followed me out, locking the door behind me.

The Dome of the Singer sits on the edge of the river Ebd, on the far south side of Veridon. It's seen better days, and most of those days were a decade ago. We kept one of our old gods here, one of the Celestes the original settlers found waiting for them in silent vigilance, hovering over the delta that would eventually become Veridon. That was from before the Church of the Algorithm, and their techno-spiritual dominance.

There are five Celestes, or were the last time I checked. Used to be six, but the Watchman flickered and disappeared, twenty years ago. I barely remember that; my mother crying in a closet, my father drawing heavy curtains across the dining room window and burning secret, heavy candles that smelled like hot sand. My parents followed the old ways, at least in private.

The door to the Dome was open, so I went in. The walls were thick, three feet of stone shot through with iron braces to hold it all together. The other Celestes had ceremonial houses, just places for worship and ritual. The Dome of the Singer was, at first, a practical matter. She sang, loudly. Or she used to. When I stepped into the cool dark interior of the Dome, all I heard were feet scuffing on stones and the low moan of breezes circulating through the drafty heights. She was silent, and I felt a chill.

The main level of the Dome was a single open room. The floor was loosely fit stone, time-eroded and haphazardly level. The walls were hung in the remnants of holy tapestries, framed in sconces that held cold torches. There was little light, at first just the illumination from the open door at my back.

I walked inside. In time my eyes adjusted. There was other light, a bluish glow that descended from the second floor. A broad central staircase of wrought iron twisted up at the center of the room. It circled a patch of empty dirt like a screw ascending a pillar of air. The ceiling was thirty feet up, with a matching opening, about twenty feet wide, through which the staircase rose. The glow came down through that hole.

Pausing at the bare patch in the floor, I looked up. I could see the shadowy smear of the Celeste eclipsing the smooth white ceiling of the Dome. She hung in empty space. I looked down at the bare dirt. One thing we'd learned about the Celestes; you couldn't build under them. They exerted some kind of eroding force straight down. Any structure below them would wear away into this gritty gray sand in a matter of weeks. The flagstones near the sand's perimeter were starting to show age, the corners crumbling like stale cheese under my feet.

The staircase ran around the perimeter of this circular patch of god-eroded dirt, slowly ascending until it reached the second floor. The inner handrail was raw, pitted rust. I put a foot on the first step and listened to the metal complain.

When I first entered, I remembered, I heard footsteps. They were still now. This level was empty, so whoever was here had to be upstairs. My father, hopefully. I sighed and started up. The staircase groaned and popped the whole way. Halfway up I swung the empty shotgun into my hands. It felt good, even though it was a threat I couldn't follow through on.

The higher I got, the brighter the Singer seemed. I kept my head bent and my shoulders turned, to keep her out of my direct field of vision. I needed to be able to see clearly. I was making enough noise that whoever was waiting up top would surely know I was coming.

The staircase held up, and I made the second floor, crouching as I cleared the floor level. At first glance, the room was empty.

There were prayer shrines against the curved outer wall of this level, six of them, one for each of the other Celestes, including the boarded up shrine of the dead Watchman. They were arranged so that the supplicants would face the appropriate dome elsewhere in the city. Two of these shrines were on my side, dark wood for the Warrior, iron and glass for the Mourning Bride. The Watchman's shuttered shrine was there too, smeared in the wax drippings of the mourning candles. I turned to squint past the luminous form of the Singer.

She hovered in the air at the center of the opening in the floor, surrounded by an iron railing. Her skin was pale against her bulbous, crimson robes. Her clothes were dark red and shiny, retaining form almost like a chitinous shell. Her eyes were closed. Her lips and the tips of her fingers were blood red and smooth. Light poured off her skin like mist on the river in winter. I had forgotten how beautiful she was, hidden away in this drafty stone building. How had we forgotten this, how had the city gone on to other gods?

"Put the gun down, son."

He was just behind the Celeste, on the other side of the platform. Alexander was formally dressed, very sharp, a long black coat inlaid in crimson. He had one hand in the pocket of his coat, and with the other he pointed a revolver at me.

"I'd rather keep it," I said.

He shrugged and flicked the pistol to his left. I came around the railing and walked toward him, the shotgun casually cradled in my arm.

"Here alone?" I asked.

"Yeah. You? All your friends waiting outside?"

"I'm alone."

We both nodded thoughtfully. I looked up at the Singer and leaned against the rail.

"She's quiet," I said.

"Has been," Alexander said, barely taking his eyes off me. "Three years now. Went from full volume to nothing in an hour."

"You were here?"

He nodded. "We all were, all the Families."

"But you still come?"

"Some of us." He looked away, glanced at the shrine of the Noble, then back to me. "I still come, at least."

"There's a story for you. Dead goddess, still worshipped by the dying Families of Veridon." I smirked.

He scowled at me and poked the revolver towards me.

"Get rid of the shotgun."

"It's not loaded," I said.

"So why carry it?"

"Same reason you come here, I guess." I smiled bitterly. He didn't like that, but he dipped the revolver down.

"So why are you here?" he asked.

"Looking for you, I guess. Had a word with Billy. He says hi. I was at the Church of the Algorithm, earlier." I turned to him. "Do you still carry an Icon of the Singer in your pocket when you go there?"

He grimaced, ran a hand over the smooth pocket of his formal coat. "That's not a chance I take anymore. Times are too difficult. Too little trust, these days."

"Yeah, I can bet. When did you stop?"

"Oh, I don't know. Shortly after you left, I suppose."

"Were you carrying an Icon when you sold me to the Church, dad?"

He froze, absolutely still.

"That's not—"

"You sold me out, pop. Sold out everything I cared about." I took a step forward, prompting the return of the pistol. "People died, Alexander. Friends of mine died. And for what? What did you get from those grease-fingered Wrights?"

"Jacob, listen. I'm sorry you got involved in this, but—"

I stabbed my finger at him, yelling. "You set me up. You knew why everyone was chasing me. You knew that this thing in my chest had something to do with the Cog. And you let me walk out of your house, easy as pie. What the hell?"

The lines on his face were very deep, and his skin was gray. He looked tired.

"Jacob, it's... I'm sorry. It's very complicated."

"Which part, dad? What's so complicated? That you sold me to the Church? That you used me, my life, to curry favor with the Wrights? Is that it? That you abandoned me, treated me like it was all my fault, my failure, that led to my expulsion from the Academy? Is that what's so godsdamn complicated?"

I got too close, the old man stepped forward and swung the butt of his revolver in a short upper cut that landed on my chin. I fell back on my heels, then kept going until my head hit the floor. He stood over me, the pistol in my face, his shoulders shaking in rage.

"Don't try! Do not try to come to me with righteousness, Jacob Burn. I never meant to exile you from the family. You did that. You came home, boiling inside. Nothing could get to you, no one in the family. It killed your mother, drove her out of the house, out of the damn city! My wife left me, Jacob, because you drove her out. It almost killed me. I know you blame me, and maybe you should. But no one kicked you out of my house."

I lay there, looking up at him. Eventually he calmed down and let me stand up. He stood by the railing, looking peacefully at the Singer.

"So, what?" I asked, wiping blood off my mouth. "You thought to sell my body to the Church, then coddle me in the Manor until I was ready to hatch?"

He didn't move. We were quiet for a while. I was about to ask again when he spoke.

"I wasn't sure. It was a chance, and I took it. I'm sorry it came out this way."

"Well. Me too," I said after a moment's silence. I picked up the shotgun and brushed off my pants. My jaw was throbbing, but after the events of the day I barely noticed.

"So what is this thing, in my chest?"

"Do you know what the Cog is? What it can do?"

I nodded. "It's a pattern. It's what keeps that Angel together. That's why he's trying to get it back, before he loses control."

"Oh. It's more than that." He gripped the railing, squeezed it and let out a long sigh. "Look, this is going to be hard to believe, but the legend, the one about the girl? Camilla? That's true."

"Yeah. We've met."

"You've... met." He looked at me tiredly. "Yes, I suppose that's the sort of impossible thing that would happen to a man like you. So you know. The zepliners, the cogwork... all of it is just derived knowledge. Technology that we've sifted from her dissected heart."

"She has some thoughts on that. You know the map came from her, right?"

"I had my suspicions. And my concerns, about her motives in doing so. But," he glanced around the room, at the various shrines. "But people in the Council wanted to move forward. Too great an opportunity."

"Of course," I said.

"So, yes. The thing in your heart. It's kind of a reader, I suppose. A translator. It's very good at implying and imposing the holy patterns of the Algorithm."

"You sound like a Wright. The Church let something like this out of their care?"

"It required a living body. The Wrights won't take modification of any kind. They could have put it in anyone, but they needed someone they could trust."

"And they chose you?" I asked. "Last supplicant of the Celestes?"

"Trust might not be the best word. They needed someone they could control."

"Ah. Desperation begets control. Of course."

He sighed. "Of course."

"Kind of irresponsible. Hiding this artifact in me and then letting me run off to the gutters."

"We had our eyes, close to you."

"Who? Valentine? I can't imagine him working for you."

He shook his head, still not looking at me.

"Who then?" I stepped close to him, one hand on the railing. The pale light of the Singer made my father look frozen in place, in time. He almost looked noble. "Who were you paying to be my friend?"

He grimaced and looked at me, his eyes sad and hollow.

"Emily."

I gripped the railing and the shotgun. The trigger creaked under my grip.

"Bullshit. Emily's a friend, a..." my voice stumbled "...we're close."

"Yes. That was the job description."

I punched him, weakly, my fist glancing off the sagging fat of his jaw. He hardly moved, just leaned away from me, then batted my arm down.

"You're a fucking liar, Alexander Burn! It's not possible, Emily would never, she couldn't. She could never do that to me. You're just a damn liar."

"Yes, I am. The Church required it. There was always a chance you'd go off on your own, stray from the desired path. We set it up, before, to make sure you would take to her."

I slumped against the railing. Her shotgun clattered to the floor.

"I'm sorry, son. It had to be like this."

"No. It didn't. Nothing does." I braced myself, trying to find a place in my mind to fit Emily the spy, the traitor. "Who knew?"

"The Council. Elements in the Church."

"Tomb?"

"Angela was her handler. That's how we knew the Cog was in the city, finally, once we lost contact with Marcus."

I put both hands on the railing and looked down. The sand below was smooth and blank. "What am I supposed to do," I asked, more to myself.

"What can you do? You have the Cog, and your heart." He turned from me, looking at the Singer. "You can do pretty much anything you want."

"I don't have the Cog," I said numbly.

"What? How could you... who has it?"

"Sloane. I think. He tracked it down, stole it. I think he killed a friend of mine."

"Jacob, you can't mean that. We can't let them have control of that thing. If it gets back to the Angel—"

"Why would it be any safer from the Angel with me? I haven't done a great job of protecting the things I care about, recently."

"They've... for fuck's sake, Jacob. Sloane and his people are negotiating with the Angel. They're offering him some kind of sacrifice."

"A deal? But what can he offer them?"

"They'll think of something," he said bitterly, then hunched over the railing and closed his eyes.

"If she's your agent, do you know where Emily is now? Sloane took her, said he had special plans for her."

He nodded, slowly. "We know."

"What? What are they going to do with her?"

"Jacob," he said carefully, "The Angel can't hold together, not without that Cog. And they aren't going to offer him that. But a body, specially modified for the purpose—"

"Emily! They're going to give Emily to the Angel? But, can she survive that? Why would they pick her?"

"Something happened to her, I think. Our sources indicate that there was some kind of surgery, before Sloane got a hold of her. Makes her an ideal candidate."

"Camilla. Gods, I'll bet she knew. I'll bet that little bitch thought to use her to get out. Godsfuck."

"Whatever it was, they have her."

"Where is she?" I asked again. I turned toward him and staggered forward. "You know. I can tell, you know."

He rolled his eyes to the ceiling and sighed. He was measuring me, weighing his options, my possible reaction.

"I can't tell you, Jacob," he said, finally, sadly.

"I'll find out. You know I will."

"Not from me."

"Then in spite of you."

He nodded slowly, but didn't move. "Forget her, Jacob. Don't go rushing in..."

"To get her. To get captured," I snarled at him and poked the air in front of his face. "That's what you're afraid of, isn't it?"

He flinched, then flexed his fingers around the pistol grip. "Perhaps."

"Which is why you told me. That's why you flipped your card. If I knew she didn't love me, that the last five years have been staged and she was your little spy, you thought... you thought I would abandon her."

He didn't look at me.

"I don't want you to waste yourself on her." He spoke quietly, as he spoke to me when I was a child. "They have her, yes. They're using her as a lure. Think about it, Jacob. They'll get you, and then they'll have everything."

I watched him, stared at him, his pale, noble face watching the motionless Singer.

"We don't understand each other, father. If that's what you thought, that I'd abandon her."

"You can't save her."

"So what? I can try." I turned angrily from him and snatched up the shotgun. "I can fucking try."

His shoulders sagged, and he closed his eyes.

"Actually, Jacob, your father understands you quite well."

I turned. Angela Tomb stepped out of the shrine of the Noble, along with three of her Housies. Wood clattered. Guards emerged from all the shrines, shortrifles in hand.

"He wanted a chance to dissuade you," she said. Her voice was cold and numb. "He had it."

"It was a lie, then? About Emily?" I asked as I twisted my hands on the empty shotgun.

"It was not," Alexander said without opening his eyes. "I'm sorry."

"We're all sorry, Jacob," Angela said. "But we really can't let them get you."

"You've said that before, Ange. You're going to shoot me again?"

"Someone here will, if needs must." She grimaced. "We're all packing Bane this time, Jacob. Don't make it happen."

"You can stop them," I said. "You can go to them and stop them."

"We can't," father said. "We're sorry. There's too much at stake."

"Let us handle this our own way, Jacob. Let us negotiate. If they have the Cog, and we have you... terms came be made."

"Not good enough," I said. "You're going to let this happen, Alexander?"

He shook his head. "I'm sorry."

"Maybe," I said. I backed up until the railing was against my legs, the quiet goddess at my back. I raised my empty gun.

Chapter Sixteen
Her Eyes Were Open

"I GAVE YOU your chance, Alexander," Angela said. She had one hand on her hip, the other flourishing a heavy caliber dueling pistol. "We can't have it both ways. Give it up, Jacob."

"I can't, Angela." I twisted the shotgun in my hands, like a wet rag. "I just can't do that."

"We're your family, son," Alexander said, though his spirit wasn't really in it. "Who else are you going to trust? They have the Cog. We really can't let them have you as well."

"But you won't be content with just me. Will you? You'll want the Cog as well, and what sort of terms will you come to with

Sloane to get it? The Cog is powerful, but nothing like it could be if you had my heart to go along with it."

"One item at a time. We can enter negotiations with Mr. Sloane later on." Angela smirked, then flicked her pistol to the guards. "Now. Put down the shotgun."

"Where's Emily?" I asked. "Where's Sloane holding her?"

"Why does it matter?"

"I'm going to save her. You fucks won't take care of your girl, I'm going to."

"Always the brave lad," Angela said. "Always the hero. You'll never get her. They have her locked up tight, up on the Torch'."

"Why up there?"

"Council's got part of the base sectioned off, has for years," Alexander said. "Experiments, trying to break free of the Church's grip. The surgery they're giving her, it's very specialized. Building cogwork without a church-sanctioned pattern. Very difficult stuff. And the equipment they'll need to do that, it's up there."

"You have to let me go. You have to let me help her."

"No, we don't," Angela said. "Now put down the shotgun and come with us."

"You heard the lad!" A voice called up from below us. I turned and looked down.

Wilson. He was standing in the middle of the gritty sand below. His skin looked like it had been scrubbed with charcoal, and he was wearing a knee-length black duster that was singed at the edges. He looked blasted. His hands were in his pockets, and his spider arms were bunched up around his shoulders like restless wings.

Angela and a couple of the Housies joined me at the railing.

"A friend of yours?" she asked.

"Maybe. Getting hard to tell, these days."

"Ah, yes. Still mourning the affections of our little spy-whore. Tell him to come up here, or you're both dead."

"Wilson..." I yelled.

"I heard the bitch." He took his hands out of his pockets and held them wide apart. Each held a small glass jar, squirming in the pale light. "I'll be right up."

He dropped the jars, then immediately leapt onto the iron corkscrew staircase. The jars broke with a muffled pop, and glittering hordes swarmed out onto the sand. Beetles.

"Put him down!" Angela screamed. The guards responded, without thinking.

They really were packing bane in those shortrifles. The shots crackled off the wrought iron, the staircase began flaking away like thin ice. Wilson bounded up, much too fast for their aim. One got close and the anansi yelped, but he kept coming. I turned and smacked the nearest guard in the head with the butt of the shotgun, then scooped up his weapon as I slung Emily's shotgun over my shoulder.

"Jacob!" Wilson yelled. I looked down, only to see him gesturing up. I looked up. At the Singer.

Her eyes were open, her arms raising slowly in benediction.

I threw myself back, just as the rest of the Housies were rushing forward to take me. I fell between them, sliding on my back. Angela was still looking down, firing wildly at Wilson.

My father was on one knee, hands folded calmly on his leg, facing the Singer. I covered my ears and curled up.

Her voice was catastrophic in the close roof of the Dome. My memories of her were quieter, a gentle murmuring that splashed through the building like a stream. This was a tornado, an avalanche of voice. It was three years of pent up divinity, forgotten by its servants and furious in its glory.

We fell, even my father. The building shook. I saw Angela tumble forward, screams drowned out by the Singer's master stroke. None of the Housies had caught on to what was about to happen, and lay prone, clutching at bloody ears. My father was flat on the floor, his face slack. He might have been asleep for all I could tell. Wilson crawled over the top rail, grimacing. He scuttled to me and pulled me up.

I tried to tell him where Emily was, and what they were going to do to her. My voice was silent against the Singer's roar.

We ran to the staircase. It was crumbling, the iron brittle as glass. The steps twisted under our feet, the handrail coming off in sharp flakes whenever we stumbled and reached for its false support. We fell the last ten feet as the whole latticework failed. I came down in the sand, grimy with bugs.

I landed next to Angela. Her mouth was open and bloody, half full of sand. Her arms and legs were awkward, and her chest was caved in. I stood up and ran. Out the door into the impossible quiet of the streets, the crowd gathering at the unexpected noise coming from the Dome; the gunshots, the newly ignited Singer pouring out the open door. I pushed past them into the street and ran, the world a mute humming in my ears. No sound but the impact of my feet, my heart, my lungs. The sun was incredibly bright, the buildings seemed to peel back and the sky was blue and quiet.

Wilson caught up with me and pulled me into an alley. I looked at him once, the grit on his burned face sticky with blood. I put a hand on his shoulder, then leaned over and retched onto the cobbles.

WE ENDED UP in the basement of a burned out house on the Canal Blanche. My hands were still shaking as I set down Emily's shotgun and collapsed against the mossy brick wall of the cellar. Wilson looked nervous.

"You look like hell, boy," he said. "What was that all about?"

"How did you get there?" I asked, ignoring his concern. "And what happened to the Cog?"

He grimaced, then squatted on his heels across from me. His many arms folded out, hanging in a rough circle around him like the spokes of a wheel.

"They came for us again. Quieter his time, more serious. Some of them were in the water, using some kind of breathing mask. There was no way out."

"There must have been," I said. I lay the Cog beside the shotgun, then struggled out of my coat. "You're here."

"They didn't care about me. They came for that trinket." He watched me carefully, relaxed but ready. "Showed up right after you left, actually. I put up a fight, but they had the numbers."

"So how'd you get out?"

"I ended up on the ceiling. After the collapse, I crawled up into some of the new cracks." He shifted awkwardly, his hand running nervously over his scalded pate. "They tried to burn me out."

"And the Cog? Where was it, while you were hiding away?"

"Long gone, Jacob. The ones in the water, they got it before I even knew they were there. They took it down through the channels, then blew it up behind them. That's what took the roof."

"I left it with you, Wilson." I lay my hands palm up on my knees. "I trusted you."

"We trusted each other, Jacob. Funny timing."

"What?"

"I said, funny timing. You left with Emily, and they came in on your heels." He flexed his extra arms nervously, his prime arms folded loosely in his lap, hand near the open fold of his scorched coat. I remembered that he had two knives, and I had only seen one broken in the cistern. "You see anything on your way out? Talk to anyone, maybe?"

"You have to be kidding," I said. "All that's happened, all that we've seen... you're accusing me of selling you and Emily out to the Badge?"

"You show up, take the girl, and rush right out again. Tell us some kind of story about hitting the Church of the Algorithm," he said evenly, the anger I expected paved under a layer of fatigue. "Badge walks in, and you're heading out the door."

"So you think I told them where the Cog was and cut my losses? That I made a deal?"

"Makes some sense. You had Emily with you, knew she wouldn't get hurt. Probably couldn't just hand the Cog over, cuz they'd put you down rather than pay you. Me, they weren't so careful about."

"Why in the hell would I do that, Wilson? Why would I sell you out?"

"Things are bad, Jacob. Complicated bad. Maybe you found yourself a way out, and knew I wouldn't take the deal. And you didn't want to give Emily a chance to turn it down, either."

"Seriously, fuck you."

He shrugged. "My loyalty is to her, Jacob. Not you. If you sold us out, I'll learn of it. If you let them hurt her—"

"Let them hurt her? Let them? Do you have any idea what she and I went through after we left you? As long as they didn't have the Cog, it didn't matter what they did to me. Soon as you let them get it—"

The knife was against my throat before I could move. It was plenty sharp.

"Say that again," Wilson said, quiet. "Tell me it was my fault one more fucking time."

I swallowed and tried to back into the wall. His hand followed me the whole way, steady as stone.

"Two ways we can go from here, Wilson. One of them gets Em killed. The other one, we talk this out, come up with a plan, and break her out."

"And kill the people who have her."

"Of course."

"You're assuming that I can't get her free myself, Jacob. That I need your help."

"You do. And I sure as hell can't do it without your help."

He stared at me for a while, his dark eyes reflected in the barbs and arcs of his blade. Finally he put it down.

"This is true. So tell me, Jacob Burn. Where have you been? And what shall we do about our girl?"

"You won't believe me. I don't believe me. But I learned that the thing in my chest is a very old artifact, hidden there with my father's blessing. And the Cog is the heart of a dead god."

"We already knew that," he said.

"Now we know it for sure. I've seen another one, in the Church of the Algorithm. And I've met the girl."

"Girl?"

"Camilla. Martyred goddess of Veridon."

I told him loosely where I'd been, what I'd seen. He looked at me without expression. When I was done he nodded once.

"These things are connected?" he asked. I nodded. "So, the Council found something and they're trying to keep it from the Church."

"Better. The Council is trying to keep it for themselves. There's a split, the old Families and the Young Seats. Like you said, things are bad complicated."

"And they've taken Emily—"

"To get to me. To lure me in. Also, they're planning on offering her to the Angel. They're making her the ideal host."

He nodded thoughtfully. "Your father?"

"Ambushed me twice, betrayed the Council to deal me to the Church, then tried to get me to surrender to the Tombs. You saw that part."

"Yes. I followed you from the Manor Burn. That servant, what's his name? William. He left right after you."

"Probably to warn my father. I had to move slow, avoid the patrols. That's how Tomb had those guards waiting for me." I crossed my arms and gave Wilson a curious look. "Why were you watching my house?"

"I had my suspicions. If you dealt us to the Council, it was only a matter of time before you showed up at home."

"Fair enough," I said.

"So. What do we do?"

I sighed and folded my hands.

"We need to decide who we trust. Tomb told me that Emily is with Sloane. It was the Badge that attacked you? You're sure?"

He nodded.

"So that makes sense. She said they had her on the Torchlight."

"The Torch'?"

I nodded. "In the base."

"That's a fortified compound. We'll never get in there."

"Oh, I imagine we'll get in. They want us to get in. It's getting out that has me worried."

"That's something that has us all worried, Jacob Burn," a voice said behind me, from the shadows of the shattered staircase. The voice was musical, pipes and pistons in a semblance of humanity.

Wilson didn't move. My hands were working the action on Emily's shotgun even as I remembered it was empty.

A dark bulk resolved into a man of cogs and metal. Valentine. He was not alone. Others stood behind him, keeping to the shadows, weapons in their hands. I counted at least three.

"How do people keep finding me?" I muttered. "What the hell are you doing here, boss?"

"You are cutting a wide wake through the city, Jacob. I have had eyes on all the major players for the last couple days. Ever since the incident at the Tomb Manor. When your path crossed your father's and the Lady Tomb, I decided it was time to step in. We have some things to discuss, I imagine."

He took an envelope out of his waistcoat and dropped it in my lap. It was addressed to Valentine, City of Veridon. The edges of the envelope were dirty and worn. I opened it and read the single sheet of paper inside.

-As we agreed: GLORY OF DAY. Have your best men on board.

-Signed, Marcus Pitts.

"Yeah," I said. "I imagine we do."

"I DO NOT think of it as dishonesty, Mr. Burn."

We were in a carriage, too many of us for the cabin. Wilson and I stank of ash and sewage and blood. The leather seat creaked as we tried to make enough room for all of us, and our guns and knives and mistrust.

"I do. It's nothing personal, Valentine. But all this, I have to call it dishonest."

"Good to know it's not personal," Cacher spat. He had been glaring at me ever since he stepped out from behind the boss back in the basement. He had a handful of dirty looks for Wilson, too. Some history there I didn't know.

"Quiet," Valentine said, gave Cacher the barest nod. "Jacob, you have to understand my position. I cannot stand up against the Council and the Church. It would be open war. My organization can not have that fight."

"You could have warned me."

"I wasn't sure I could. I wasn't sure you wouldn't tell Emily."

"You knew about her?"

He shrugged. "I knew something wasn't right. But I wasn't sure."

"Where is she, bastard?" Cacher asked, menacing me with his black, blunt shortrifle.

"Fuck off, Cach."

"Don't tell me to—"

"Fuck off, Cacher," Valentine said.

"What else did you know about?" I asked. "About the Cog, and the Council? How did you find out about all of this?"

"Ah. Straight from Marcus, actually." Valentine shrugged and tried to settle more comfortably into his bench. Cacher struggled further against the wall of the carriage. The other two thugs were up top, driving us somewhere. "I started getting messages from him two weeks before your spectacular accident. More and more desperate, the closer he got to Veridon."

"You knew what he had?"

"Not completely. He wanted help, he was scared. Of that Angel, in retrospect, though he never specified. It was killing the expedition, one at a time. He was scared he wouldn't make it to the city."

"Like she wanted," I whispered, thinking of Camilla's plan to lure vengeance into Veridon.

"Who?"

I shook my head. "So, he wanted your help. And he tried to buy it with the Cog?"

"Yes. With knowledge of what it was, where it came from." Valentine spread his wide, flat hands. "I couldn't do it, obviously. Too many variables, and no idea if I could trust him."

"So you sent me?"

"I knew when he was coming. Knew he was pursued. I wanted a man in place."

"Me?"

He nodded.

"I'm going to get back to this, boss, because I really feel that it's pretty important. You could have told me."

"I didn't know what to expect. I had no idea what you were going into. How could I warn you?"

"You could have told me to be prepared."

"Jacob, the day I have to tell you to be prepared for trouble, that's the day I will no longer trust you."

I leaned back in the chair, staring off into the distance. Veridon rumbled past us through the wire webbed protective glass of the carriage.

"So what now?" I asked.

"I've been on the sidelines long enough. Things are precarious enough, now." He futzed with the clasp on his cuff, unbuttoning it, adjusting the shirt sleeve and reattaching the cufflink. "I think it's time for me to help."

I laughed quietly, once. "You want to help? Now? All the time I spent hiding, unarmed, the Badge and Council and Church trying to kill me. You want to help now?"

He shrugged. "Too many factors, Jacob. But I'm here now. Don't turn down an ally. You could use a friend."

"Yeah," I said, thoughtfully. "Yeah, I could. Okay. You want to help me?" I pushed the empty shotgun into his lap. "Let's start by loading this gun."

Valentine smiled. "That's my Jacob. That's the way." He reached behind the seat and produced a box of shells and handed them to me. Just like Valentine, to have an extra box lying around.

I loaded the gun, one shell at a time. It held six shells, lined up down the barrel. A good gun. I couldn't help but think of the Angel, coming down the hall as I knelt in the Manor Tomb, fumbling with the cylinder. That's what it comes down to, sometimes. Clear action in the face of danger. Keeping your head when everyone else around you is freaking out. I loaded the gun smoothly, one shell, then the next, until the cylinder was full. I snapped the gun shut, then laid the barrel against Valentine's chest. Cacher raised his alley piece and snarled.

Wilson's talon tipped arms pounced forward, a sharp edge resting on Cacher's face, his neck, below his eye. He pushed just hard enough that Cacher had to strain backwards to keep his skin intact.

"You're going to put your gun down, son," Wilson said, his voice low with menace and anger. Cacher complied.

"This isn't necessary, Jacob," Valentine said. "You can just tell me to fuck off. I would understand. Probably what I would do in your shoes."

"You wouldn't be in my shoes, boss. You'd hire some sucker to get the shit kicked out of him. You stopped getting your hands dirty twenty years ago."

"On the contrary. I keep my hands quite dirty. Part of the job. But you're right, I wouldn't let myself get where you are. So." He kept his clockwork face neutral, wouldn't look at the gun. "What now?"

"I want to be clear about this. I appreciate what you've done for me. Took me in, watched out for me. Gave a fuck when no one else would. But I think this was one too far. I don't want you as an enemy, Valentine. But I think I'm done with having you as a friend."

"Not the best move, Jacob. It's a different world, without my protection. Where would you be right now, if I hadn't put you on that zep with Marcus? You wouldn't have known anything was up, and the Council could have plucked you off the street without a word of trouble. You'd be dead, and you wouldn't even know why."

"Maybe. Would've saved me a hell of a lot of trouble. No, boss, this is it. Pull it over."

He banged on the carriage roof and we pulled over. I kept my gun on Valentine as we got out. Wilson left Cacher with a healthy set of new scars. We backed into an alley, the two thugs on top watching us go. Valentine smiled and waved.

"Good luck, Jacob. And stay out of my sight for a little while."

"I'll probably be dead, boss. But I'll keep it in mind."

We slipped away. A second later the carriage started up. When it was gone we ran, keeping buildings between us and the sky. Dark clouds were rolling in, and dusk settled with the sound of distant thunder rolling down the Reine, echoing off the city's high walls.

Someone had been in my room. No real surprise. They had torn through the rest of the city looking for me, I suppose someone along the way might have stopped in to my rented quarters up here on the Torch', to see if I'd left anything important behind. Their mistake. I didn't own anything important. That was the key to my life. Mobility, emotional and physical.

The bed had been taken down and cut open, scattering little curls of excelsior across the wood floor. All my drawers had been opened, the cabinets pulled apart. I didn't keep a lot of things, but everything I kept was in a pile on the floor.

"You need a woman in your life," Wilson said. "People shouldn't live like this."

"Shut up, bug," I said. I kicked a path through the room, then locked the door. The only light was the lightning flicker coming in through the massive river-side window that took up one wall.

"You shouldn't call me that. Bug. I thought better of you than that."

"It's been a shitty day. I can be unexpectedly cruel, on days like this."

"Well," Wilson collapsed onto the shredded bed, puffing up a cloud of wood shavings. "Let's try to focus that cruelty. We have need of it."

"This isn't about revenge. For me at least. If it was just revenge I'd have burned out long ago."

"So, what? You're going in because you love the girl?"

"Let's not be stupid, Wilson." I closed all the drawers, opened the curtains wide. The rain was really coming down. Hell of a storm. "I'm doing this because it's what I should do. It's what I'd want done, if I were in there."

"So loving the girl has nothing to do with it."

I sighed. I wasn't going to tell him about Emily, about her job with the Families. It wasn't worth the argument.

"Fuck off, bug," I said quietly.

He laughed a genuine laugh, the kind of laugh I didn't expect from him. He lay on my bed with his spider arms splayed out, his hands laced behind his head, staring up at the ceiling.

"So what are we doing, Jacob Burn? You got us up on the Torch' well enough. How much harder is it going to be to get in the Academy?"

"Very much harder." I tossed a revolver and a box of shells I had picked up down on the bed, along with the box of shells Valentine had given me for Emily's shotgun. I wanted something to eat. I started rummaging through the detritus of my house, to see if I'd left anything, anything that hadn't spoiled. "The facility that my dad was talking about, I think I know where that might be."

"From your days in the Academy?"

"The very days. Places we weren't allowed to go, hallways that always had guards and locked doors. I didn't think much about it at the time."

"How do we know your father is telling us the truth?"

"How do you mean?"

"Well. He's betrayed you how many times in the last two weeks?"

"Twice. Once to Angela. And I'm counting the original betrayal, with the PilotEngine. I think that one will always count, no matter how long ago it was." I found some crackers. They were stale.

"Right, so, how do we know he isn't going for three? He told you about Emily, about where she was. How do we know he isn't dealing you to the other faction in the Council?"

"Oh, I'm sure he is. I'm sure he and Angela gave me that information on the off chance I slipped away. I've proven so elusive, you know." I sat down on the bed and crunched my way through a messy stack of crackers. "I'm a dangerous man, Wilson."

"And they're going to contact the rest of the Council, to let them know you're coming?"

I shook my head. "I don't think that's necessary. They knew we'd figure it out, eventually. Knew we'd figure out where she was. They're waiting."

"So this is a trap?"

"Oh, gods yes."

"Then what the hell are we doing?"

"What they expect. Right up to the moment we do exactly what they don't expect," I said.

"Which is?"

"Well," I rubbed my eyes and looked down at Wilson. He looked terrible, in his burned clothes and charred skin. "I was hoping you had an idea."

"Oh, no. I got you out of the Dome. That was my daring rescue. This is your show, Jacob, my boy."

"Yeah. Well." I stood up and crossed to the window. "It's going to have to be a hell of a thing."

I watched a zepliner dashing in for the docks high above us. Lightning flashed along its sides, glimmering against the pale skin of the anti-ballast. The crew was on the main deck, hauling line and securing cargo. It looked like they were crashing, though I knew better. The docks were just above us, behind the stone walls of the Torch'.

"I know how it'll happen," I said.

"They'll fill us with lead and burn our bodies on the signal fire?" Wilson asked.

"You're a good guy to have around, Wilson. A real damn pick-me-up."

He chuckled. "You have a plan."

"No, no. But I have an idea."

"Good enough." He sat up and munched forlornly at a cracker I had dropped. He grimaced, set the cracker down, and looked around the room. "I'm getting tired of waiting."

"Yeah, me too." I packed up the revolver, threw Emily's shotgun over my shoulder and shoved my way through the pile of junk to my front door. "Let's get this over with."

"You gonna tell me how we're going to do this?"

"You wouldn't believe me," I said. "I don't believe me."

Chapter Seventeen
A Circle of Hammered Brass

Getting in was easy. I'd been visiting the Academy since I was a starry-eyed kid, spent the best five years of my life in its walls. The Academy and the base were one structure, sealed in stone walls and guard patrols. I had snuck out a hundred times, and snuck back in, with a bottle or a girl.

The streets were empty, but I didn't know if Sloane and his friends had cleared the residents in anticipation of our approach, or if it was just the weather. Either way, it was creepy. Space had always been tight on the Torch'. The only way I knew this place was crowded, herds of people squeezing through the tunnel-like streets, the narrow walkways that leapt across the many cracks and crevices in the hard stone foundation of the Torchlight. It was never empty, never quiet.

The rain made it worse. The lead skies had opened up, and it felt like the river Dunje was pouring between the buildings. The cobbles were several inches deep with cold water. Even though I walked down the middle of the street, the buildings to either side were hazy and gray.

"You cold?" Wilson asked.

"Nah. Just never seen this place like this."

"Yeah." Wilson stretched his arms, walked nervously nearly against the wall, trying to get a little protection from the storm's assault. "I don't get up here much."

"You? Scared of heights or something?"

"Scared of Pilots, actually," he smiled at me apologetically. "Pilots and the Corps."

I didn't ask. The Corps had done plenty in its time, during the various wars and skirmishes that kept Veridon in power. Resentment was natural.

"So how are we getting in?"

"I haven't really decided yet."

"I thought you had an idea," Wilson said. "A clever trick."

"I do. A brilliant trick," I said. I bunched my coat up around my neck, then grudgingly moved over closer to the wall opposite Wilson. "But that's for getting out."

We walked in silence for a while. I had the box of shells Valentine had given me tucked against my belly. I hoped the powder wouldn't spoil in this deluge. I wasn't real sure I'd get to use any of this kit, with Sloane's crew expecting me. But if I needed it, I'd rather it work.

"So, uh. How are we getting in?"

"You figure it out. I don't care. We go up to the door and knock. They're waiting for us, Wilson. We're not going to be able to sneak in."

"So what the hell are we doing up here, Jake? I'm not in this to walk in and get shot. Hey," he grabbed the back of my jacket and spun me around. "I'm not going to be happy just shooting a couple Badges, Jacob. I intend to get through this alive."

I stared at him a while. Did they have eyes on us, right now? Made sense. If they cleared the streets, if the shops were empty and the cadets tucked into their barracks, if they went to that much trouble, why not guards on the approaches? That's what I'd do. So, yeah, they're probably watching us right now.

"You think too much of me, Wilson. I'm not that noble." I pulled my jacket free and started back up the street. "We'll get through."

I didn't hear him for a dozen steps, then he sloshed through the gutter to catch up.

"I need more than optimism," he hissed, his face really close to my ear. "I need to know what you're planning."

"You think they're watching us, Wilson? You think they have people watching out for us?"

He stopped again, falling behind. When he came back he was lurking, one of the Badge's stolen shortrifles in hand.

"Cuz I think they're watching us," I said, when he was behind me again. "So that's why I haven't told you."

We were getting close to the base. Its bulk loomed up against the sky, eclipsing the storm for a second. Wind whipped around the stone walls. There were lights inside, bright eyes in the night. There were a couple of guard houses and a bridge that zig-zagged from the main path, each bend passing through a tower's watchful gate.

I hopped up onto the railing of the first bridge. It was iron and stone, and the rain had made it slick. Wilson followed nervously. I swung my leg over the edge, then tucked the ammunition into various pockets of my coat. I got the shotgun over one shoulder then turned to Wilson.

"Follow close."

I inched farther out onto the bridge's structure, keeping three points secure all the way out. The supports blossomed out into the open air, running to the towers and the other two bridges beyond.

"This is the plan? We're going to climb in?"

"They're watching every door, Wilson," I grunted, then crawled a little bit further. "Every window. Just stay close."

He had no trouble keeping up, obviously. He kept a couple protective spider arms hovering behind my back, another over my head. Halfway across the wind picked up, and the storm hit us. We were out of the Academy's lee, and I cursed and hunched close to the bridge. The iron was slick. Below us the Dunje was a foggy smear, the tiny lights of barges winking up at us like reflected stars. I paused to secure myself.

"Jacob, I'm not sure—" Wilson said, then I fell.

My lead foot skittered off the metal and I stepped into open air. Wilson's arms wrapped around me, too quickly, and I overbalanced and slammed against the structure of the bridge. My hands fell off their holds. I slapped at the bars, missed, slapped and ended up on Wilson. He swore in the tearing, shrieking language of the anansi. The wind pulled at us. I was kicking at the bridge, trying to find purchase. Wilson's arm came free, then his foot. I sagged against his body, completely away from the bridge now. Both his lapels in my fists, I dropped, he dropped, and the wind took us. Screaming, we cartwheeled out into sky, into the storm, and we were falling.

The rope caught about ten feet down. I thought it was going to tear me in half. I barely held on to Wilson and his clambering arms. The rope snapped taut, the movement of our fall arcing us back down under the bridge. I slapped at the dry understructure, felt it slip out from under my fingers. Wilson grabbed on and dragged me in. We climbed on to one of the supports, nestled against the stone and lay there, panting and breathing and staring at the rain.

"Think they were watching?" I asked.

"You fuck. You could have fucking told me."

"I wanted your reaction to be authentic." I held the rope up and pulled a section of it tight. "Cut me off this thing, will you?"

He squinted angrily at me, then worked his knife free of his belt and sliced through the rope.

"That's not even climbing rope," he said. "It's just a fucking rope."

"All I could get."

"We could have died."

"Yeah, well. If I kept track of all the times I could have died the last couple weeks, Wilson, I'd get bored."

He shook his head, then leaned back and rested against the stone.

"Is there some kind of secret entrance under here?" He craned his neck around to look at the craggy stone. "A hidden door that leads to the wine cellar or something?"

"Nah. We're going to have to climb."

"That's what I figured you'd say." He ran a wide, thin hand over the stone, picking at the cracks with his sharp little talons. "Could we at least look for a secret entrance, please?"

"There's no secret entrance, Wilson. Stop being such a whiner."

There were feet on the bridge above us, and soon rifles were poking down over the railing. Voices yelled all up and down the road. I pointed, then led Wilson around the edge of the tower's wall to the next bridge. Not long after we made the second bridge the guards were hooking up climbing harnesses and throwing down belay lines.

"They're going to find your rope," Wilson whispered.

"Then we better get moving," I said, and clambered off into the rain.

THE GUARDS WERE slow and careful, and the climbing harnesses were difficult to use in the rain. We were almost to the Academy before they found the rope. We were inside before they figured out what had happened.

We ended up in the wine cellar, as Wilson had hoped. There was a service winch with corresponding iron door. The lock had rusted away years ago. I wrenched it open then collapsed inside. Wilson crawled over to the near wall and started poking around behind the casks. Looking for his damn secret passage.

"Stop fucking around, Wilson."

"Just hoping. I was going to laugh if I found it."

"You're not going to find it," I said. I lay the shotgun and pistol out on the ground, then took off my coat and shook it off. Water sheeted out onto the floor. Once it was as dry as it was going to get, I put it back on and rearranged my arsenal. "Can we get on with this?"

We pulled the service door closed and secured it as well as could be expected. There was food by the door, I saw, and a dozen cigarette butts. There had been a guard here, probably pulled away to conduct the search up on the bridge. We had to get moving.

"They're going to be putting people on every door and window again," Wilson said, nodding to the guard's leavings. "We'd do well to get to the girl."

"Not yet. They'll see we were here. We left water everywhere, and the door's obviously been forced." I hurried up the narrow stairwell to the kitchens. Those clean white rooms were empty. "Once they figure that out, they're going to post guards around the girl. Probably already have."

"So let's get there. Hit 'em before they're ready."

"They're ready, Wilson. They've been waiting. We need to go somewhere they don't expect."

We left the kitchens and moved horizontally. The locked hallways where I expected to find Emily were on the south end of the base, near the center of the civilian part of the Torchlight District. We went north and up, gaining levels, going away from the buried, secret chambers of the Council's hidden experiments.

We heard guards patrolling in hallways beneath us, chasing the routes they expected us to take. I wondered how much they knew we knew, if they had planted the seed of the Council's laboratories in my father's ear, confident that he would pass that on to me? They had overplayed their hand, then. I knew I couldn't trust anyone, except maybe Wilson, though I trusted him more to act in Emily's interests than in mine or his own. I was comfortable with that.

Wilson and I busied ourselves with mischief. We set a fire in the barracks, tripped auto-alarms in the weapon guildhall. We avoided the zep docks. I had them in mind for our escape.

"Are we just having fun?" Wilson asked. We were destroying the escapements in all the frictionlamps we passed, ruining them in a sudden flash of illumination. It was slow work, and taking us no closer to Emily.

"We couldn't get to her before they closed their noose," I said. "We can't get to her now. Too many guards in too small an area. We could try, but that would just be shooting and heroism, and then we'd both be dead."

"I'm glad you've thought this all out."

"I have. Just listen. So we cause trouble. We fill their halls with smoke, we poke their eyes out." I shut my eyes and loosened the final bolt on the 'lamp I was working on. The room went sun-bright, then black. We shuffled to the next room. "Sloane only has so many men. He'll have to come for us."

"And then?"

"Then we go for Emily. Evacuating the cadets was a mistake. While they're searching the Academy, we take the girl."

"And if she dies in the meantime?"

"They won't kill her," I said. "Soon as she dies, they lose us."

"You're putting a lot of trust in that," Wilson said.

"They want me pretty badly, friend. They'll be careful."

He snorted, then continued with our campaign of trouble. It wasn't long before we ran in to our first patrol. Four Badgemen, poking carefully through a wardrobe hall like hunters in a haunted forest. Wilson bellied the first one with his knife, and I shot the rest. After they were dead I stood in the middle of the room and emptied each of their weapons wildly into the walls, to make the ambush look more frantic and horrifying than it had been. We cut away from our goal, and took the next two patrols that came to investigate, then put many chambers and halls between ourselves and the carnage. Not long after, the Academy was bristling with small patrols of very excitable Badgemen, talking loudly to one another and jumping at every sound.

"There, see," I whispered from my alcove above the grand fireplace in the feeding hall. "Pinch hard enough and the monster stirs. Should just be a matter of finding our girl."

We clambered down into the darkened hall. I had just reached the ground floor when a voxorator in the wall clapped open and started screaming. Emily.

"They're killing her," Wilson gasped. "They're done waiting, lad."

I coughed and wiped my mouth. They wouldn't dare, not until they had me. A lure with no bait is just string. The screams continued, clear and honest.

"Okay, we need... we need to get organized. We can go in together and—"

"Like hell, son. You said they're waiting." He unsheathed his knife and buckled another round into his shortrifle. "I'll make for the front gates, near where we got in. I'll make noise, like we're trying to get out. You get Emily, get her out."

"Make for the zepliner docks. That's where I'll be headed, once I have her. You'll never get out the front door."

"Probably," he said, then ran down the hall. I waited until I heard sporadic gunfire. I took the grand spiral to the main level, and started working my way quietly to the locked corridors of the basement.

THE HALLS WERE as I remembered them. Some childish part of my brain felt like a schoolboy again, in the halls between classes without permission. It was a ridiculous feeling. The roving patrols had thinned out, now that Wilson was making such a racket above me. My passage was undisturbed.

The locked hallways were still locked, but unguarded. I forced the door. The corridor beyond was dark and quiet. I slipped inside, secured the door behind me, then ventured out with my revolver in my hand.

When I was a cadet, my fellow students and I had spent a good deal of our recreational time discussing these locked spaces. The common mythology was that they were prisons, or held some entombed secret that the Academy could not suffer the light of day. We never saw anyone enter or leave these doors. If it was a laboratory, as my father insisted, then there must be other entrances, entrances that I did not know.

The walls here were stone, not unlike the rest of the Academy. Fewer wall sconces, too. How did the researchers do their work in such dreadful gloom? It wasn't long before I had to set down my revolver and assemble the tiny hand lamp I brought. Once it spun up, the lamp's soft amber light was the only illumination in the place.

The air smelled like crushed bugs. It was a familiar scent, but I couldn't place it. I descended a stairwell, then went through an oak door that opened smoothly on oiled hinges. Beyond the door was a room like a small dome. There were shelves all the way up most of the walls, irregularly spaced and heaped with piles of books, glass tubes, broken equipment and even stranger detritus. There were openings that looked like arched windows near the top of the dome; they seemed to lead to tunnels, or deep shelves, but I could see no good way up there.

The center of the room was clear and the floor was smooth and free of dust. Closer inspection of the walls revealed scattered handholds, too widely spaced and irregularly arranged to let me climb up the walls.

I set my lamp on a shelf and began to search through the junk. It didn't seem that Emily or Sloane were here. The piles on the shelves were interesting, probably arcane, but not what I was looking for. I took one quick pass through the dome, marveling at the odd handholds, the seemingly inaccessible upper shelves and tunnels.

They weren't here. But where, then? Wilson and I had been through most of the rest of the Academy, sowing distraction and drawing the guards off. I thought we were drawing them away from this place, but clearly not. We'd been everywhere, except...

The docks. The zepliner docks, at the very top of the Academy, where the old signal flame stood unlit and the airships came and went. Where Wilson had gone, to draw them away. He was headed right at them, right where they were waiting.

I hurried out the door. I thought I caught sight of something, a long pale face, wide eyes the same albino white as the skin, staring down at me from one of the tunnels. A second look revealed nothing, just books, a glass jar and cobwebs. The room was empty, and Wilson was in trouble. I ran up the stairs.

THE CAVERNOUS HANGARS of the docks take up the highest level of the Academy, great wooden structures that perch on the ancient stone of that place like an ersatz crown. They form a rough semi-circle around the launching derricks at their center. Rising above the derricks on a gentle dome of rock stands the structure that gives the district its name: The Torchlight.

In the early days of Veridon, a garrison lived on the rock to watch for mountain raiders as they crossed the plains to the east, or river pirates forging their way downriver from the principalities further upstream. They would burn the Torch to warn the soldiers below, so that everyone could make for the fortified parts of the city.

With the gift of flight, our sentry has grown lax. The original iron and stone building was replaced with a circle of hammered brass, a low wall whose lines were reminiscent of fire and smoke. The pyre is no longer kept dry and packed, and the honor guard no longer stands by with dry wicks and flints to sound the alarm. No armies approach Veridon, no raiders ply the Reine.

They were up there, a double handful of Badgemen, plus a couple other figures huddling away from the rain. I could only see them when the storm provided lightning. Sloane was there, and Wilson, tied up and bloody. There was something else, too, squatting where the Torch should be, filling the brass circle with a dark and complicated presence.

I snuck as close as I could. I kept to the hangars. Each building contained a single airship, lashed down for storm-running, the crews nowhere to be seen. The winds beat against the thin wooden walls, and the zeps lurched in their moorings.

The guards kept near Wilson, berating his crumpled form in the lee of the old Torch. Sloane circled, wary of the sky. Everyone kept looking up, then peering down the hill at the buildings where I was hidden. They were expecting something. The Angel, perhaps. And where was Emily?

Something yelped, and a spark jumped from the site of the Torch. The lurking darkness there was lit up, for a second, and I saw a brief, still image. A body, hung spread eagle, and a machine of brass and coiled wire. Emily. Their attention was to the center, to the Torch. I took a deep breath, counted the distance. I checked my revolver, and clutched Emily's shotgun in my off-hand. Sloane reappeared, yelling angrily at the men standing guard around Wilson. They jumped, then ran down the hill towards the barracks. Sloane watched them go, then turned back to the Torch. His back was to me.

I clambered forward, keeping low, keeping the declination of the hill in my favor. He was yelling towards the Torch again, strolling casually back to it. Now. Now or not at all. I stood and ran. The rain beat a tattoo across my face, and the storm roared around me. Not a noise from the Torch. Wilson saw me, nodded, then bowed his head.

I raised my pistol and ran.

I RAN AT him, my feet hammering the ground, the storm driving me forward. I was as quiet as I could be at a full sprint. Easy to get lost in this storm. Someone saw me. A cry went up, then shots. A bullet whizzed past me, ripping through the air; another snapped at my jacket. Sloane turned and yelled, then lurched towards the Torch. I raised my pistol and fired. Five shots, five bullets. They all missed.

I barreled into the man. I fell, and my revolver skittered away. The firing had stopped, everyone too afraid of hitting the boss. I rolled over him and put my fist into his throat. Sudden pain, and I realized he had a knife in my shoulder. I slapped it aside and punched him again.

A guard grabbed me around the shoulders. I threw him off, but Sloane slithered out from under me. I grabbed his leg, then the steel butt of a shortrifle cracked against my head. Next thing I knew I was face first against the rain-slick stone. Sloane stood up and faced me.

"You have no patience, Jacob," he said. "That is your failing. No patience and—"

I leapt at him. One of the guards yelled and tried to intercept me. Together we bowled into Sloane. The three of us started sliding down the hill, arms and legs banging against the stone, fingers bloody as we sought some purchase on the old rock. I ended up with my arms around the guard, my fingers around Sloane's throat. The Badgeman was trying to beat me around the head, but the leverage was bad. I squeezed closer to him, to keep him off balance. Sloane was kicking pathetically at me. We came to a stop among some coiled wires. Sloane's struggles were slowing down.

More Badgemen came to help. A crowd of arms descending on me, punching and grabbing, wrestling me off the dying Sloane. I dragged at his clothes, felt something tear away in my hand. They had me upright in a moment, and two of them were taking turns slamming their fists into my midsection. Sloane was on one knee, watching, a hand to his throat and the other steadying himself on the ground. I was yelling, but I don't know what I was getting at. Just a lot of yelling. Sloane stepped forward, weaved on his feet, then slapped me across the face. One of the Badgemen behind me dropped. Another yelped and spun away. Sloane looked startled.

Wilson stepped forward, the blade of his knife smeared in blood. The ropes that hung loosely around his chest were frayed, gnawed through. I picked up one of the shortrifles. Sloane was running.

"Good of you to show up," I gasped.

"Same," Wilson said. "I take it they weren't downstairs."

"No."

"Figured. You see anyone, down there?"

"No," I said. "I don't think I did. Sloane have the Cog?"

"Yeah. In a pouch around his neck."

I squinted at him, then picked up the fabric I'd torn off Sloane a minute earlier. The Cog slid out into my hand.

"Huh," Wilson said. "Good for us. Maybe we should try to run?"

"No. They've still got Emily." I gripped the Cog, watching the tiny wheels spin free against my palm. "Maybe we can make a trade. Or pretend to, at least."

"That sounds like it could get us killed," he said. We looked around. The guards had fled, though a cluster of them was organizing their courage down near the entrance to the Chapel of the Air, near the foot of the Torch. Sloane had disappeared into the hangars. "Let's clean up."

"What is that thing up there? The thing holding Emily?"

"Some kind of... machine. A brutal surgeon, Jacob. It's preparing her."

"Preparing her?" I clenched my teeth. "Preparing her for what?"

Wilson looked up at the sky. The Angel.

I started up the hill. Wilson put a hand on my shoulder. "Hold, son. Sloane's got the key. You're going to want to hunt him down, first."

"Is she okay?" I asked.

"You're going to want to hunt him down," he said, quietly.

I gave the Torchlight a look, squinted at the slowly lumbering darkness there, then turned my attention to the hangars. They shivered in the wind, their charges banging against the walls and straining at their moorings.

"Where'd he go?"

"Down there, somewhere." Wilson was on one knee, reloading a stolen shortrifle. I checked the chamber on the one I was carrying. It hadn't been discharged, not even once. Wilson stood up. We crept down the stone hill, into the lee of the nearest hangar.

Inside was one of the city's warships, *FCL Thunderous Dawn*. It filled the hangar, its battle sponsons grinding against the wooden walls of the long building. As we snuck along the perimeter of the hangar, I loosened each of the moorings that we came to.

"What the hell are you doing?"

"Thinking ahead," I said. "Just keep an eye out for Sloane."

We made it three quarters of the way around the building when the guards who had been cowering among the derricks put in an appearance. They kicked in the door and began rushing around the tight confines of the hangar. As soon as they saw the free moorings, they rushed the main carriage of the ship. The *Dawn* was larger than the *Glory* had been; there were dozens of ways into and out of the ship. The guards disappeared into the warship's armored interior, spun up the running lights and started yelling at each other as they searched. Wilson and I snuck out.

"How do you know Sloane didn't do that? Hide in the airship? He could be in there right now, talking to the guards."

"Could be. I think he went straight through that hangar, quick as he could." I crawled over to some barrels laid out between the hangars. "He's not really interested in running from us, Wilson. He doesn't get paid that way."

"So where is he?"

"Don't know. Waiting for us somewhere. We find a good place to hold up, he'll come find us. He can't afford to lose us."

"If that Angel shows up, do you have a plan?"

"I don't know. Kill it again?"

"You really think this shit out, don't you?"

"Yeah, yeah." I popped my head over the barrels, tried to get a good sight of the Torch. Too much bad weather, not enough light. There wasn't much cover between here and there, nothing but the night and the rain. "I'm not waiting around. Let's go get our girl."

We went up the hill slowly, squatting and peering into the night storm. There was light flickering around the Torch; not much, just enough to show forms and silhouettes in the darkness. We followed a trail of barrels and supplies that were strewn across the hill, cutting closer and closer to the Torch. When we got as near as we could, I gave Wilson a nod then we both jumped out and rushed the Torch.

Sloane stood next to a massive iron and brass machine, not usually native to the Torchlight. I imagined that it had been brought up from those basements. Probably why they cleared out the cadets. You didn't want something like this in the public eye.

Installing cogwork takes time. You inscribe the mnemonic engram in the patient's mind, usually through pattern memorization or hypnosis. Then you inject the foetal metal into the body. The metal latches on to the pattern in the engram, which directs how the cogwork forms in the body. Over time the foetus replaces the natural tissue of the patient with the prescribed cogwork enhancement. For me, it replaced my heart, parts of both of my lungs, enhanced and restructured my bones to serve as conduits and rebuilt my eyes. Even my blood is still flooded with foetal metal, anxious to rebuild any part of my body in accordance with the master pattern. It's how I heal so fast. Of course, my implants are different, something to do with hidden Camilla and whatever bit of her dissected form ended up in my chest. But that's how it generally works.

You can also hot-load the foetus. Give it some general pattern to follow and inject it into the patient without any sort of preparation. That's a much messier way to handle things, because you don't know how the foetus will interact with the body. Bones can break, skin can burst, but the foetus doesn't notice.

This is what happened with Emily. She had turned into a tumor of metal and wire. Blisters of metal traced her arms and shoulders. A thin brass cage covered her face, and a contraption of pipes and boilers had erupted from her chest and neck. That device was puffing smoke into the air, a black sooty discharge that smeared the near walls in grime. Her arms and legs were held spread, clamped in metallic shackles that were thick with cogs and pipes. Something was pumping into her blood from a hundred needles, intravenous lines bristling from her exposed shoulder and breast. Foetal metal, slate gray, dripped from the few needles that had pulled free. A belt of leather fit across her ribs and belly, laced shut with chain and a padlock.

Sloane stood next to her, grinning like a knife. He held a pistol to her temple. Above her a slow torsion pendulum twisted. She was dying, being made ready for the Angel's possession.

"You're showing a little spark, Jacob," Sloane said through gritted teeth. "A lot of trouble these last few days."

"Let her go, prick." My voice was incredibly tired. "You've got us here. Now let her go."

"Not yet. Hardly yet. Besides, I think she's getting used to it." He trailed the pistol down her cheek, touched it against her lips. "And I don't think she could survive, anyway. I think it's done too much damage. Would you like to find out?"

"I'm going to cut you, Sloane," Wilson said. "Cut you and cut you until your blood runs black."

"You're a brave bug, Mr. Wilson. I'm a little surprised you survived our visit in the sewers. Regardless, I'm glad you can be with us now. Our friend should be here any moment. The Cog please, Jacob."

"You don't need her anymore. You've got me," I said, and took the Cog out and held it up. "And I've got this."

"Ah, but that flying bastard's still around. And I don't think he'll let us go until we've come to some sort of... resolution."

"About what?" I asked.

"We've made a deal, him and me. The Cog for Camilla. A very noble bunch, these Brilliant. That's what the Church calls them, you know."

"You can't give him Camilla. You don't have her. And he can't live without the Cog."

"We can guide him, though. Give him your girl here, in her improved form, and he'll last for years. Long enough to get back to wherever he came from. And certainly long enough to retrieve precious Camilla. As soon as we tell him where she is."

"You're going to get him to destroy the Church for you."

Sloane smiled. "Excellent. And yes, then we're going to keep the Cog, and set up a new God. More of a factory, I think, than a Church. Very good trade to be made in miracles."

"Go to hell," Wilson said.

"Yes," He said. "Eventually. For now, though, kindly lay down your weapons or I kill the girl."

"If she dies, you'll have nothing to give the Angel."

"Perhaps. But I'm sure arrangements will be made." He cocked the gun and pressed it against Emily's temple. "Your weapons, please, and the Cog."

Sloane's eyes flashed. Wilson gawked at me, turning slightly, his knife dipping towards the ground. I let my shortrifle drop.

"Very good, Mr. Burn. A good choice. If you'll be so kind." He took a step forward.

I only had a lightning flash of his wings, the steel-gray lined in electric blue as he swept down from the skies. The Angel landed behind Sloane. Sloane's eyes rolled up in shock, then the Angel's blade-arms rose out of the man's chest. He scissored apart like a rag. The Angel looked at me. His blades folded away, and he held out his hand.

"The Cog is mine. Return it, and you will live."

Chapter Eighteen
Last Flight Down

I DROPPED THE Cog and swung my shotgun around. The Angel's eyes followed the Cog to the ground. I fired twice before he even remembered I was there. I put my foot on the Cog and fired again. The shot rippled across his body like pebbles striking a pond. Wilson yelped and threw himself forward, knife in hand.

Mistakes; I couldn't bend to pick up the Cog without letting down my guard. I couldn't keep firing with Wilson closely engaged. My shotgun was choked down, meaning the blast had put some shot into Emily's unconscious form. So many mistakes. Wilson's mistake was worse.

The Angel batted the anansi aside then advanced on me. I kicked the Cog behind me then fell back, firing as I went. The hammer eventually fell on an empty chamber. I dropped the gun and went for the shortrifle at my side. The Angel charged.

I raised the 'rifle across my body, deflecting the blow of his arms. His wings beat across my face, eclipsing the storm and blinding me. The feathers were knife sharp. They fanned across my arms leaving behind superficial cuts and thin streams of blood. I bashed his face with the butt of the 'rifle, kicked his knee out from under him, then lost my balance and tumbled down the hill. My head was resounding with the impact of stone against my skull. I crawled to my knees and peered up the hill.

He was searching the ground, looking for the Cog. I carefully checked the load on my shortrifle, sighted down the barrel and put a slug in his head. He put a hand on the ground to brace himself. A light dust of cogwork poured onto the ground, like sand from a cracked hourglass, hissing as it scattered down the rock. It clumped into the pools of water. He wavered there, staring down at the ground for a minute. Eventually, he resumed his search.

I stood and walked towards him evenly. Every third step I paused, sighted the 'rifle, and fired. His body groaned with each impact, the shot disappearing into the confused cogwork of his body. He was slowing down.

"This is too fucking easy," I said, then placed the barrel gently against the back of his head. He reached up and crushed the chamber. The shell exploded, peeling back the fingers of his hand and shattering the iron stock. He kept looking for the Cog.

"Jacob!" Wilson yelled from up near the Torch. I looked his way. He waved the Cog in the air. I ran to him.

"What the hell is he doing?" he asked.

"Looking for that. It's his heart, his pattern. He shouldn't even be able to hold himself together." The Angel's wings were beating slowly. "He doesn't give a rat's ass for us. Here," I took the Cog and looked over at Emily. "I'll keep his attention. You free her and get out of here."

"The Badge is swarming," he said. Down by the launch derricks a whole crowd of graycoats were milling about, staring up at us and the Angel. "We'll never get out that way."

"Just get Emily. Meet me down by the *Dawn*. I'll get us out."

Wilson went over to Sloane's body and started searching his clothes. I watched long enough to wonder at how little blood there was, and how Sloane's body had fallen in such symmetrical lines. I turned back and saw the Angel looking at me, at the Cog in my hand. I ran down the hill in the other direction, toward the open expanses of the Torch' and away from the hangars. He spread his wings and followed, the slow beat of those sharp feathers blustering him around in the wind.

There was a little wood on the downslope opposite the city. It was made up of iron-hard trees that grew out of the rocks, their roots pushing deep into ancient cracks, living on the barest soil. Their leaves were pale yellow, and their trunks were thin and springy. They whipped in the storm's fury like breakers on the shore. I threw myself among them just yards in front of the Angel. The trees knocked me down, and I tore the skin on my knees as I skidded down the hill, bashing into the tough bark of their trunks.

I came to a halt against the bole of the largest of these trees. Its roots spread across a large area, like a carpet of knuckles over the stone. I lay there, insensate, staring up at the beating rain.

"We had a deal, the man Sloane and I." His voice carried over the storm. I rolled over onto my stomach. The Angel wasn't in sight. "A proper host, and the location of the one he called Camilla. And then I was to kill you. Eventually, he would return the Cog to me."

"I don't like the sound of that," I yelled, then quickly moved away. I didn't think he'd be able to tell where I was just by my voice. The wind was howling, seeming to come from all directions. His answer seemed to come from the sky itself.

"He would never have given it to me. He knew what it was, where it came from. He would have betrayed me, before the exchange."

"Sounds right."

"You were about to give the heart to him, though."

I put the Cog into my pocket. I was out of weapons. I had seen him fight before, knew that I didn't have a chance. I just had to delay him. I just had to get away.

"Part of my plan," I yelled over the storm. "I wouldn't have let him keep it."

"Because you, too, know what it is."

"Yeah," I said.

"I wonder. Do you know the power it holds? I know what is in you, Burn. Part of her. I will need to take that, as well."

"You're shit at negotiating," I said.

"I am... not negotiating. But I am offering you a choice. You can live without the Cog. I can not. And you can live without the thing in you. I can show you, make you whole."

"Let's get back to the part where you can't live without the Cog! How do we go about making that happen more quickly?"

A low, rolling thunder filled the woods. He was laughing.

"You are an admirable man, Jacob Burn. Brave. But you have been used horribly by this city and its rulers. Do not let them trick you into dying in their place. Give me the Cog and be done with it."

I hunkered down behind the tree and stared at my hands. He was right, of course. I was here because of the Council, and the decisions they made. He was going to find me, hiding behind a tree, and when he did he was going to kill me. I took out the Cog and looked at it in the dim light of the woods. It flickered in my hands like solid lightning.

"Sloane, he promised me the girl. The one on the stick back there. Emily. He was going to make her a host for me, until the Cog could be secured."

"Can you shut up?" I yelled. "I'm tired of listening to you, and I'm tired of this gods-damn Cog!"

He stepped from around a tree and wrapped the fingers of his undamaged hand in my collar. His other hand was a ruin at his side. He was weakening, without the Cogheart. He wasn't reforming as he should.

"Then give it to me, as you know you should."

"What happens then? If I give it to you."

"The girl goes free, and we leave."

I sagged in his grip. My back was against the tree. I took the Cog out of my pocket and held it in both hands.

"Which girl?" I asked.

"The buried girl. The hidden girl. The girl this city has profaned."

"Camilla," I said. He nodded. "She won't let Veridon go unharmed."

He almost smiled. "Can you say the city deserves any less? I have been following you, Jacob Burn. I know what has happened to you, what has been done to you. By those you love, and those you counted as friends. And still you protect it. Give me the heart, and stand aside."

I held up the Cog. "Take it."

He set me down. As soon as his fingers were away from my throat, I slammed the Cog across his face. He faltered. His ruined hand came up and began its imperfect transformation into blade. I kicked at his feet. We fell, the knuckle roots of the tree digging into our backs. As he struggled to stand I came to my knees and put the Cog just below his eye, all of my weight behind it. His head snapped, cogs clattered away. He was coming apart. I pulled back to hit him again when his other hand, his good hand, tore into me.

I felt the blood across my leg and looked down. The pain was a second away, and I had a good look at the inside of my ribcage before the agony blinded me. His hand had become a thing of scythes and axles, spinning like a tornado. I collapsed, and the Cog skipped away behind me.

"My time is short," he said, rising slowly. His wings looked thin, and his chest was heaving. The rain that poured off his face fell to the ground black with oil and blood. "But I would do this one thing well. You have defied me at every turn, Jacob Burn." He slapped me awkwardly, and I fell onto my back. My secret engine was pumping hard to remake me, but I could feel it losing ground. "Every step of the way here, I have run across your people, your Veridians. Your soldiers and your thugs and your gods." I dragged myself backwards. He towered over me, unforming and reforming. He slapped me again, this time with his bladed hand. My cheek shredded.

"I am tired of your people. I am tired of this horrible city, perched on this rock, dredging up the trash of greater empires. You live on the junk of history, Jacob Burn, and history will wash you away. No one will remember your dreadful empire of filth and misery."

"I'm starting to take this personally," I gasped through blood and broken bone. I dragged myself backwards and found the Cog. He looked down at it, glimmering under my bloody hand. His eyes flashed furiously. He reached for it.

I rolled over onto my front, shielding the Cog from his view. I saw that I was on the edge of a cliff, one of the jagged walls that fell straight down into the Reine. It stretched out before me like a flat gray road that led straight down, far down. I dangled an arm over the cliff, jammed the Cog into the root bole of a scraggly tree clinging to the edge of the cliff. He put a hand on my shoulder and flipped me over.

"Give me the heart," he said. "And die as you should."

I put both feet into his chest and pushed. I slid off the cliff with a scrape then pitched down and back. The wind roared past me, the Reine rushed to take me in its wide, flat arms. A second later and the Angel's arms were around me, shaking me violently.

"Give me the heart or you die!"

"Fuck off," I said, but my voice was failing me. There was a lot of blood across my pants. I was battling to stay awake.

"Give it to me!"

"I don't have it!" I yelled, then held out my hands. "Do you see it? No. I don't have it."

He screamed in frustration and tried to drop me. I hooked my arms around his neck and squeezed. We floundered in the storm, corkscrewing down towards the water.

"This is how it's going to end, you bastard," I hissed into his ear as I rode him down towards the water. "You're going to fail, we're both going to die, and the bitch Camilla stays in the city. This is how it's going to happen."

He ignored me and beat his wings mightily. We crawled slowly up in the air. I clung to his back, tucked between his wings, and hammered his head with my bloody fists. My heart was burning with new energy. I could feel the hole in my side closing, the shreds of my cheek pinching shut.

"I can't fucking die, monster! You can't do it. You can't kill me, and you can't kill the city. I'll see to it."

"You are," he grunted as we reached the Cliffside, "tremendously annoying."

We climbed higher, high above the Torch'. He turned his head to me and stared into my eyes.

"Fly, Pilot. Fly, if you can."

He folded his wings and we fell. I clung to him. If I let go he would just spread his wings and fly away.

"You'll die, too!" I yelled.

"I will reform."

"Not without the heart! Not without a body to possess."

He considered this. Just before we hit, he flared his wings. I crashed into a tree, the ancient high tree I had hidden behind when first I ran into the woods. He peeled away, cartwheeling as he fell. I fell through the springy, fibrous branches of the tree. Things snapped inside me, but my fall was broken. The Angel fared less well.

When I came to the ground I lay there and spat blood. My left knee was ruined. Blood obscured my vision. The thing inside me was roaring, straining with the massive damage of my fall. I struggled to my hands and knees, and then, wavering, to my feet.

The Angel lay ten feet away, perfectly still. His limbs were indistinct pools of boiling cog-work. His wings were flat and immobile. He stared up at the rain.

I stumbled to the cliff's edge and, carefully, retrieved the Cog. Using a stick to steady myself, I limped back up the hill.

Getting up the hill was difficult. Once I was out of the woods the wind battered me, the rain blinded me. My limp was horrible, the bones grinding. I was in shock. The stone was slick under my feet. But I was free, I was clear. I held the Cog in my hands, looking down at it with a faint murmur of stunned disbelief going through my head. Something cracked behind me. Another. I turned. He was rising, coming out of the woods, cracking trees in half as he came.

I dropped my stick, almost fell over in shock. He was emerging from the treeline, half apart, his chest unfolding, his wings expanding. He was abandoning any semblance of humanity. His two wings became four, his head was little more than a howling mouth. I saw the human body he had possessed poking through, the half-rotted corpse of a young Pilot, his face horribly deformed, his arms flapping out of the shifting geography of the Angel's torso.

I held the Cog up like a talisman. He was yards away still. I felt my knee realign, the impossible health of my heart knitting bones. It used the last of my reserves. I could barely stand. I looked down at the Cog. It glittered in my hand.

What had Camilla said? Take the heart. Become the destruction of the city. Ruin the things you hate, save the things you love. I looked back up the hill. The Torch' was a blurry shadow behind me. I couldn't tell if Emily and Wilson were clear of the machine. I looked back to the Cog. How would I do it, how would it happen?

My body answered for me. My chest burst open bloodlessly, my ribs folding back. A flower of steel came out of my heart, spinning. It folded open, pulsing, yearning for the Cog in my hand. I stood there in the rain, shaking, staring down at the tortured mockery of my body. My hand quivered, the Angel's heart shivering between my fingers. Take the heart. Become the destruction of the city. Of all you love.

The Angel was rushing me, roaring. Become that, I thought, become him to destroy him.

I wouldn't. I would stand on my own and die on my own, but I would not become the dark angel Camilla dreamed of being. That was what the city was looking for, Sloane and his people trying to throw off the Church, the Church trying to keep the city in line with its secret, hidden girl. I wouldn't.

I willed my chest to close, and it did. The Angel was nearly on me. I turned and ran, my head down, my body screaming.

The Torch formed up in front of me. Wilson, damn him, was still there, tugging Emily off the contraption. She was naked, the needles and half-grown cogwork weighing her down. He saw me coming and straightened up, a question in his eyes. A second later he saw the Angel behind me and started pulling roughly at Emily's bonds. There was no time. No fucking time.

I fell as I reached the circle of brass around the Torch. I went down on my hands and skidded across the stone, my hands tearing. I could tell, even in that split second, that my heart was spent, forever spent. It hung in me dead. Whatever it had been, it would no longer repair me as it once had. I was happy with that, even as my skin came off my hands in sheets.

I ended up against Sloane's shredded body. Wilson was yelling, firing hopelessly at the monster at the Torch's ring. I fumbled to my knees. In searching for the key to the contraption, Wilson had emptied Sloane's pockets. His things were spread out before me: some photographs, his leather gloves, a thin knife, and a dueling pistol. I picked up the pistol.

The Angel reared back and leapt over the Torch. His body was deformed, held together by nothing but rage and the rotting corpse of that poor cadet. I held the pistol in both hands, took careful aim, and fired. The bullet sailed true, smacking in to the middle of the flying horror. I cycled the chamber. It wasn't necessary.

The Angel made a cracking sound, like thin ice breaking. He howled, howled with the wind and the rain. He fell against the wide arms of the torsion pendulum, squatting above Emily's limp body. His face was breaking apart. His scream reached the sky, his rage fleeing his body. The cracking sound became a crescendo of a thousand tiny bells, shattering in their first and last note. He burst like a pillar of salt, struck with a hammer's blow. Cogs rained down across the Torch, slithering over the stone and our bodies by the hundreds, the thousands. When he was gone, there was nothing but the rain and pools of snowflake cogs, clumping together on the stone.

I looked down at the pistol. Bane. Sloane had been packing Bane.

We got Emily off the contraption and, carrying her between us, started down towards the hangar. The machines that grew out of Emily's skin were greasy and ashen. They flaked off when we touched them, no more substantial than wet paper. I worried about what was beneath the skin. Something we'd have to figure out when we got back down to the city.

"What happened?" Wilson asked.

"I think I died. Or something. We'll figure it out later."

"You're bleeding a lot," he said. "Is that thing in your heart doing okay?"

"I don't think so. Seriously, we'll talk about it later."

"And your face. Man, that's some serious scarring."

"Are you telling me I'll never be beautiful again?"

He chuckled. "You were never beautiful in the first place. You were always ugly and violent and cruel. Now you simply look the part."

"I'm having the best time with you, Wilson," I grunted as we made our way down the hill. "We should do all this again."

"Anytime," he said.

We got closer to the hangars and stopped. There were lots of guards, clustered around the entrance to the Academy. They didn't seem too anxious to get close to us.

"We have a reputation," Wilson said. "How are we going to get out of here?"

"Over here," I said.

I led him to the nearest hangar and inside. The *Thunderous Dawn* was still half unmoored. I pried open the crew door and dragged Emily inside. We took her to the mess hall and lay her on a table.

"They're going to look in here eventually," Wilson said. "We can't hide here forever."

"We're not hiding. We're escaping."

"What do you mean?"

"This is an airship. We're going to fly out."

"But you can't pilot, remember? You're broken."

"And you're twisted. But I can fly a little. If memory serves, I was able to get my first ship nice and high in the air before we fell out of the sky."

"Jacob! This is a Flight of the City Line. It's a battleship. You can't just… fly it out of here."

"That's okay. I wasn't really intending to fly, exactly. Come on. Get her secured here then find someplace to buckle down. I'll be up top."

The *Dawn* was a newer design. It took me a little while to find the control room, and longer to get buckled in. There are usually OverMates and Ensigns to help with this stuff. I could have used Wilson's help, but I didn't want him getting nervous. Spoil my concentration. I lay down in the coffin, clipped in the few connections I could see, then lay back and let the automated integration process do its bit. Still a moment of sickness when the visuals irised into my eyes. My chest unfolded again, but the hungry flower was dormant. Everything fit, much to my surprise.

My heart hammered loud in my chest, then my body disappeared and my soul sucked off into the manifold. I filled the ship, dwelt in iron and the butane heat of the burners. I felt cramped in the close burrow of the hangar. There were people around, more than just the three of us. I was being boarded.

I groaned against the wooden walls of the hangar. My mooring lines strained and broke. The anti-ballast slithered against the ceiling, popping shingles off the slatboard roof. I angled toward the door, just cleared the archway. It was a close fit. I clacked open the voxorator.

"Wilson, we've got boarders." My voice tore from my throat in flat iron pipes. I forgot what it was like, talking straight from your soul into the vox.

"I'm on them. You're sure you can get this thing airborne?"

"Oh, sure. It's going to be great."

In truth, I already felt the queasiness of the decoupling. Last time I'd flown, last time I was ever supposed to fly, I had locked into the manifold and then lost control. Worse, it felt like some malignancy spread through the ship the longer I stayed hooked in. An ensign had pulled me out of the coffin, minutes later than he should have. No one else got out.

I didn't want that to happen this time. I'd just get us off the Torch', get us close to the city. Getting out of the manifold would be tricky, but once I was out hopefully the ship would just crash and we could get out. Hopefully.

I took us out of the hangar and off the Torch'. There was gunfire. I registered hits along the main deck, some that went into the anti-ballast. Adjusting for the loss in lift was easy. I'd forgotten how good I was at this. Without thinking about it, I was flying again, flying like I'd always wanted to, like I'd always dreamed. Since I was a kid.

The darkness filled me quickly. I knew what it was this time, the spirit of the girl Camilla living on in her dissected organs. She lashed out blindly through the manifold. I couldn't stay in here any longer. We were well on our way down, tipping over the Ebd and crossing into the city proper. Veridon spread out below us. Warning sirens were spinning up all across the city. I doused the burners, spun up the running lights to give people a chance to get out of our way, then started to decouple from the manifold. I went to the vox one last time.

"Wilson, status?"

"We're going down kinda hard!" he yelled. His voice was nervous. Imagine that, my anansi friend scared of falling out of the sky.

"That's okay. How are the boarders?"

"They're everywhere. I'm on the main deck right now. Should I get to a crash seat?"

"Oh, yeah, definitely. How's—"

The vox cut out. I decoupled. The sockets pulled from my eyes with a sickening wrench, and my heart slid shut. I sat up and tried to cough out the rusty taste in my mouth. The room was perfectly dark. The burners were guttering just beyond the bulkhead above. The air smelled like burning oil. The floor pitched at a horrible rate. I got up. There was something else in the air, something familiar. Summerwisp.

Emily was at the door, leaning against the frame. The engine sprouting from her chest had crumbled away. The blisters of metal along her arms seemed to have reasserted themselves though, and a ghostly halo sprouted from behind her head.

"Em, love, are you okay?" I asked. I was standing by the coffin. The ship was shuddering down, the pitch of the floor getting more and more precarious by the second.

"I'm fine, Jacob. You saved the Cog?" she asked. Her voice was weak. I had to strain to hear her.

"Yeah, I've got it." I pulled the Angel's heart out of my coat. There was a spattering of gunfire from one of the lower decks. I could hear the sirens from the city below, drifting thinly up through the ship. "Things are about to get difficult, Emily. We need to get you settled. Come on, come with me."

I reached out a hand to guide her out of the control, putting the Cog back in the inside pocket of my coat. I wanted to get us on the main gunnery deck, to one of the crash chambers. It'd be a good evac point, once we came down. Wilson could manage below decks.

"Difficult. Yes." She took a step forward. Light from the emergency lights danced off her halo. I saw that she had two small wings, one above each shoulder. They were each a foot long, delicate, ephemeral things of diaphanous beauty. Silver veins ran down her face, and her eyes were moon bright pools of empty light. She raised her hands. "I'm sorry, Jacob. She's the only body you left me."

The Angel leapt forward. Her hands tapered down to whisper thin blades of incandescent light. He took a swipe at me, missed and took a chunk out of the coffin. Elsewhere, an impact alarm started going off. We hit something, the airship twisting as it went through some tower or tenement and continued on. Emily came towards me, her hands on fire.

I did the smart thing and ran. There was an emergency exit to the control pod. I slapped the panic button and blew the door, then ran out onto the decking of the evac deck. The ship was pitched at such a radical angle that the cityscape seemed to spread out in front of me. We were rushing past at a tremendous rate. Our angle of descent almost perfectly matched the city's own downward elevation towards the Reine. As I ran down the evac deck towards a glide boat, we skipped off a warehouse roof, digging a wide, grinding trench in the shingles before we bounced back up into the air. I looked back. Emily was following me sluggishly.

When he fell apart, back up on the Torch', some bits of the Angel must have survived and infected Emily. Her new and vulgar implants were much less settled than my own. Perhaps that made her more susceptible. Perhaps they were designed to be particularly welcoming to the Angel's infection. Either way, something of him was in her. It couldn't be much. Her transformation was minimal. Enough to try to kill me, though.

I got around the evac deck and climbed down to the main gun deck. The cutter turrets were battened down and the shell cabinets were locked. Not that I needed a weapon that big. I hoped. I found a service box and clacked it open.

"Wilson! Where are you?"

"Occupied on forward observation." Grunting, and gunfire. I heard it twice, both through the vox and from the front of the ship. "You still in control?"

"No. Look, that thing has Emily. She's trying to kill me."

Silence.

"Wilson?"

"I heard you. Where?"

"Main gunnery. Get up here."

The vox clacked shut. Emily was down the stairs and walking towards me. I kicked open the service box and pulled out the revolver. Familiar gun, even if the inscription was different.

"Are you going to shoot her, Jacob?" she asked. "Your pretty girlfriend?"

I fired once, kicking splinters up out of the decking in front of her. She smiled, that smile I was so comfortable with, but not her smile anymore.

"I don't think so, Jacob. And it's a risk I'm willing to take."

She surged forward, arms out. I hesitated, the revolver in hand, the sight on her forehead. At the last second I flipped the pistol over and clubbed at her arms. The blades touched my skin and I yelped. Blisters formed across my forearm. I jumped back, but she kept coming.

"There, there, Jacob. It'll heal. Just give me the heart and we can all get back to life. You can have your girlfriend back."

But it wasn't healing. I was right. The thing in my chest had given up, faded out. My arm was on fire, and it was going to stay that way. I pulled the Cog out.

"This thing? This is what you want. How can I know you'll let her go?"

"I won't need her anymore. And really, Jacob. What choice do you have?" She held her bladed fingers against her cheek, resting the infinite sharpness on her skin. Blood broke out, running down her chin. "Tell me how beautiful she is, Jacob. How lovely she is."

I tossed the Cog onto the decking. It skittered then lay flat. I took a step back.

"Go ahead. Go on, take it. I want out, that's all. That's all I've ever wanted in this godsdamn deal."

"That's all any of us want, Jacob." She stepped forward, hovered in anticipation over the Cog. She knelt and touched it lightly on the edge, a shiver going up her arm. She picked it up, and her chest burst open, flowered, beckoned the heart.

"Sorry," I said, then kicked Emily full in the face. The Cog bounced and rolled down the deck. I ran to it. As I was running we hit a tower and the whole ship groaned and twisted. The deck bucked hard port, and I found myself running downhill after the rolling Cog. The pitch continued until I was falling, just falling, my feet barely skimming the deck. I lunged against the railing, my hand outstretched as the Cog winked and spun and glittered against the city spread out below. My hands slipped across it. It fell, then I was falling, falling and the city rose up to gather me in.

I jerked to a stop. My left hand was on the railing, holding my flailing body. My right hand was on the Cog. The deck corrected, and we were flying level again. I pulled myself back up, right into the Angel.

She punched me hard, blades sinking into my conduit-laced ribs. I coughed in shock and pain. The Cog dropped onto the deck. When she bent to pick it up, I rolled over the railing and onto her back. We grappled, blades sliding into and out of my body. I held back the pain, tried to not think about my lungs, the tightness in my throat, the loss of feeling in my leg. I cinched onto her, clamped her beneath my chest and pressed down. I pinned her arms. The Cog rolled off her onto the deck. Her flower chest snapped at me, hungry, angry. Her bright eyes flared in the darkness.

She battered herself against me. I tried to hold her, but I could feel her slipping free. Blood was flowing out of me, red blood. The metal in my system was expended, and my mind was going with it. I couldn't hold her here forever. I was going to slip, and she was going to stand up and kill me, and then take the heart. Free Camilla, and then the city would pay. Veridon should pay, I thought, but it won't. It won't be my fault. It won't.

"Wilson!" I yelled feebly. I was slipping. The air buzzed with static. I couldn't concentrate, couldn't feel my skin. My grip on her wrists was slipping. She was staring at me, the hate and rage arcing up into my skin. I was crying, I realized. I could hear gunfire far up front. Wilson wasn't coming. He wouldn't be here soon enough.

"I'm sorry," I said. "I'm sorry I couldn't do it."

"It's okay, Jacob. Just let go and it'll be okay."

"No," I said. "It won't."

I trailed my hand down her face, paused at her nose, her lips. The delicate line of her cheek. I lay my hand across her throat and squeezed. Her eyes widened, panicked, then she was thrashing like a snakefish. I bore down, kept my hips on her chest, my hand on her wrists. My fist on her throat. Her mouth opened, pleading, but I couldn't hear. Wouldn't. It took a long minute, my vision blurred with water and blood from my forehead.

At the last her eyes flicked off. The halo died, the wings crumbled into silver ash. Those brown eyes reappeared for just a second, immediately flooded with tears, then rolled back. I pulled my hand off immediately. She didn't move.

The *Thunderous Dawn* plowed into the Canal Blanche. The anti-ballast crumpled above us and fell, like the canopy of heaven closing on a life.

Sirens filled the city, and the skies danced with lightning. I took her in my arms and ran.

Epilogue
The Girl is Gone

I PLACED EMILY in the small boat. I built it myself, out of some barrels and part of a coffin. The coffin came from my father. Accepting the gift was the first step, I suppose.

She fit nicely. I had repaired the damage, covered the bruises and the last cuts the Angel had inflicted. Her eyes were closed. The scars from the metal blisters were under the loose white dress I had gotten from my sister's abandoned closet. It didn't fit that well, but it looked nice on her.

We were downstream, near the waterfall. Wilson wanted to be here. I told him I was doing it tomorrow. I rented a wagon and a mule. People pretended to not see me leave the city. They knew, without knowing.

The water was cold around my ankles, then my knees. I placed the Cog on the center of her chest, then crossed her arms over it. I stood there for a long time, knee deep, the water splashing peacefully against the side of the boat. I meant to say something, but I couldn't think of it. There was nothing to say, except things I should have said while she was still alive. Always the way.

I waded out deep. I wanted to get to one of the strong currents. She shouldn't run up against the shore. I wanted her trip to go well. I would dedicate a plaque, perhaps, in the city cemetery. But her body belonged out here, away from the city, away from the powers that had ended her. Maybe I would dedicate a plaque out there, on the frontiers downfalls. Maybe I would make a trip, to the far places, the places Marcus had gone, a trip that we two should have taken together. Maybe.

I got out there, far out. The water was past my shoulders. The mud under my feet was unsure. I fell, the river bottom falling away without warning. I flailed. The boat pushed out from me, my fingertips just barely guiding it in a straight line into the current. I went under and thought about staying there. I remembered Wright Morgan and the dark currents of the Fehn. Still, I stayed for a moment, felt the current pull me, watched the light fade and the chill creep in to my skin. Then my foot brushed a rock and I got above water. I gasped for breath, then fought my way back to the shore. The current pulled me, dragged me, held me back. The mud sucked at my feet. I fell, the water running over my head and I struggled on hands and knees closer to the shore. When next I stood the water was at my waist.

I realized I had almost died, there. Water spilled out of my lungs. I was shivering. I turned back to the river, to the thin white line of the waterfall as it tumbled away from Veridon.

The little boat was gone. Emily was gone.